Praise for THE CORONER
and the Coroner Jenny Cooper series

'Ed McBain semi-inaugurated the forensics genre, but Patricia Cornwell and Kathy Reichs parleyed his innovations into stratospheric sales. But the field has not become an exclusively female sorority – or an American domain. A highly talented male writer has offered a challenge . . . *The Coroner* by M. R. Hall was an instant hit'   *Independent*

'When *The Coroner* burst upon the crime fiction scene it made a considerable impact. It was clear that the author had created something new and exciting in the field. Not every male writer is able to create such richly faceted, convincing female characters as Jenny'   *Daily Express*

'A brilliant, original and gripping crime novel – I can't wait for M. R. Hall's next one!'   Sophie Hannah

'Hall shows with aplomb that a coroner is just as able to become a detective as the forensic pathologists of Patricia Cornwell and Kathy Reichs'   *Sunday Times*

'An outstandingly interesting first novel'   *Literary Review*

'This big, well-executed debut novel by screenwriter and producer M. R. Hall has meaty characters and a chewy plot in the Lynda La Plante style'   *Guardian*

'A fast-paced debut thriller'   *The Times*

'M. R. Hall . . . writes convincingly and compellingly of the difficulties facing anybody who dares to challenge a crushing and often corrupt system in an attempt to establish the truth'
                                 Daily Mail

'It's a terrific series, meticulously researched, sharply plotted and peopled with sympathetic characters, led by Cooper, who is always aware of the human consequences of failure'

Financial Times

'Excellent and compelling detective drama'   *Daily Mail*

'A substantial and satisfying novel which adroitly combines the personal and the political into an engrossing narrative that is ultimately about international paranoia'   *Daily Express*

'Intelligent and intricate, and grips from the beginning to end'

Woman & Home

'Breathlessly enjoyable'   *The Times*

The Coroner

M. R. Hall is a screenwriter, producer and former criminal barrister. Educated at Hereford Cathedral School and Worcester College, Oxford, he lives in Monmouthshire with his wife and two sons. Aside from writing, his main passion is the preservation and planting of woodland. In his spare moments, he is mostly to be found among trees.

THE CORONER is the first novel in M. R. Hall's CWA Gold Dagger shortlisted Coroner Jenny Cooper series.

m-r-hall.com
facebook.com/MRHallAuthor
@MRHall_books

M. R. HALL

The
Coroner

PAN BOOKS

First published 2009 by Macmillan

This edition published 2013 by Pan Books
an imprint of Pan Macmillan, a division of Macmillan Publishers Limited
Pan Macmillan, 20 New Wharf Road, London N1 9RR
Basingstoke and Oxford
Associated companies throughout the world
www.panmacmillan.com

ISBN 978-1-4472-4149-2

1 3 5 7 9 8 6 4 2

A CIP catalogue record for this book is available from
the British Library.

Typeset by SetSystems Ltd, Saffron Walden, Essex
Printed and bound by CPI Group (UK) Ltd, Croydon, CRO 4YY

Visit www.panmacmillan.com to read more about all our books
and to buy them. You will also find features, author interviews and
news of any author events, and you can sign up for e-newsletters
so that you're always first to hear about our new releases.

For P, T & W

PROLOGUE

THE FIRST DEAD BODY JENNY ever saw was her grand-father's. She had watched her grandmother, sobbing into a folded handkerchief, draw the lids down over his empty eyes and then, as her mother reached out to comfort her, sharply push the proffered hand away. It was a reaction she could never forget: accusatory, vicious and utterly instinctive. And even as an eleven-year-old child, she had sensed in this moment, and in the exchange of looks that followed, a bitter and shameful history that would rest and settle behind the older woman's features until, seven years later, she too shuddered unwillingly from her body in the same bed.

When, at the graveside, she stood behind her father as the coffin was lowered awkwardly into the ground, she was aware that the silence of the adults around her contained the poison of something so dreadful, so real, it gripped her throat and stopped up her tears.

It would be many years later, when she was well into troubled adulthood, that the sensations of these two scenes crystallized into an understanding: that in the presence of death, human beings are at their most vulnerable to truth, and that in the presence of truth, they are at their most vulnerable to death.

It was this insight, gained the night her ex-husband greeted her with divorce papers, which had stopped her driving off a

I

cliff or tumbling under an express train. Perhaps, just perhaps, she managed to convince herself, the morbid thoughts that had dogged her were no more than signposts on a dangerous and precipitous road which she might yet navigate to safety.

Six months on she was still a long way from her destination, but far closer than she had been that night, when only a flash of memory, given meaning by far too much wine, brought her back from the brink. To look at her now, no one would know that anything had ever been wrong. On this bright June morning, the first of her new career, she appeared to be in the prime of her life.

ONE

TEEN TERROR FOUND HANGED

Danny Wills, aged 14, was found hanging by a bed sheet from the bars of his bedroom window in Portshead Farm Secure Training Centre. The discovery was made by Mr Jan Smirski, a maintenance worker at the privately run facility, who had come to investigate a blocked toilet.

Mixed-race Wills had served only ten days of a four-month detention and training order imposed by Severn Vale Youth Court. Police were called to the scene but DI Alan Tate told reporters that he had no grounds to suspect foul play.

The son of 29-year-old Simone Wills, Danny was the oldest of six siblings, none of whom, according to close neighbours, share a father.

His criminal record comprised drugs, public order and violent offences. His imprisonment followed a conviction for the violent theft of a bottle of vodka from Ali's Off-Licence on the Broadlands Estate, Southmead. During the robbery, Wills threatened the proprietor, Mr Ali Khan, with a hunting knife, threatening to 'cut [his] Paki heart out'. At the time of the offence he was in breach of anti-social behaviour and curfew orders imposed only two weeks earlier for possession of crack cocaine.

Stephen Shah of Southmead Residents' Action today said

3

that Wills was 'a well-known teen terror and a menace whose death should stand as a lesson to all young hooligans'.

Bristol Evening Post

Danny Wills's short stain of a life had come to an end shortly before dawn on a glorious spring morning: Saturday 14 April. He was, perhaps by fated coincidence, aged fourteen years and as many days, earning him the dubious honour of being the youngest prison fatality of modern times.

No one – apart from his mother and the oldest of his three sisters – shed a tear at his passing.

Danny's six-and-a-half-stone corpse was wrapped in white plastic and lay on a gurney in a corridor of the mortuary of Severn Vale District Hospital over the weekend.

At eight o'clock on Monday morning, a consultant pathologist, Dr Nick Peterson, a lean, marathon-running forty-five-year-old, glanced at the bruises rising vertically from the throat and decided it was suicide, but protocol required a full autopsy nonetheless.

Later that afternoon, Peterson's brief report landed on the desk of Harry Marshall, Severn Vale District Coroner. It read:

I
Disease or condition
directly leading to death   (a) **Asphyxiation due to strangulation**

Antecedent causes   (b) **None**

II
Other significant conditions contributing to the death but NOT related to the disease or condition causing it   **None**

Morbid conditions present but in the pathologist's view NOT *contributing to death*	*None*
Is any further laboratory examination to be made which may affect the cause of death?	*No*

Comments
This fourteen-year-old male was found in his locked room at a secure training centre, hanging by a noose improvised from a bed sheet. Vertical bruises on his neck, absence of fracture to the hyoid bone and localized necrosis in the brain are consistent with suicide.

Harry, a world-wearied man of fifty-eight who struggled with his weight, mild angina and the financial burden of four teenage daughters, duly opened an inquest on Tuesday 17 April which he immediately adjourned pending further enquiries. He sat again two weeks later on 30 April, and, over the course of a day, took evidence from several staff employed at the secure training centre. Having heard their mutually corroborative accounts, he recommended to the eight-member jury that they return a verdict of suicide.

On the second day of the inquest, they obliged.

On Wednesday 2 May Harry decided not to hold an inquest into the death of fifteen-year-old drug user Katy Taylor and instead signed a death certificate confirming that she died as the result of an overdose of intravenously administered heroin. This was to be his last significant act as Her Majesty's Coroner. Thirty-six hours later, on waking from an unusually restful night's sleep, his wife found him lying stone cold next to her. The family doctor, a long-standing friend, was happy to attribute his death to natural causes – a coronary – thereby sparing him the indignity of a post-mortem.

Harry was cremated a week later, on the same day and in the same crematorium as Danny Wills. The operative charged with sweeping ashes and bone fragments from the retort of the furnace into the cremulator for fine grinding was, as usual, less than conscientious; the urns handed to the respective families contained the mingled remains of several deceased. Harry's urn was emptied in a corner of a Gloucestershire field where he and his wife had once courted. In a touching impromptu ceremony, each of his daughters read aloud from Wordsworth, Tennyson, Gray and Keats.

Danny's remains were scattered in the crematorium's Garden of Remembrance. The marble plaque set among the rose bushes read 'Beauty for Ashes', but in deference to every religion except that which had provided these words of comfort and inspiration, the Bible reference had been chiselled out.

Harry would have smiled at that, would have shaken his head and wondered at the small, mean minds who decreed what portion of the truth others should know.

TWO

JENNY COOPER, AN ATTRACTIVE BUT not quite beautiful woman in her early forties, sat wearing her determined, resistant face opposite Dr James Allen. The community psychiatrist must have been at least ten years her junior, Jenny guessed, and was trying hard not to be intimidated by her. How many professional women could he encounter here at the small modern hospital in Chepstow – a one-horse town by anybody's measure?

'You've experienced no panic attacks for the last month?' The young doctor turned through the many pages of Jenny's notes.

'No.'

He wrote down her reply. 'Have any threatened?'

'What do you mean?'

He looked up with a patient smile. Noticing the neatness of his parting and his carefully knotted tie, Jenny wondered what it was about himself that he was suppressing.

'Have you encountered any situations which have triggered panic symptoms?'

She scanned back over the last few weeks and months: the tension of the job interviews, the elation of being appointed coroner, the impulsive decision to buy a home in the country, the exhaustion of moving without any help, the overwhelming guilt at acting so decisively in her own interests.

'I suppose – ' she hesitated – 'the time I feel most anxious is when I phone my son.'

'Because . . . ?'

'The prospect of his father answering.'

Dr Allen nodded, as if this was all well within his infinite experience.

'Can you be any more specific? Can you isolate exactly what it is that you fear?'

Jenny glanced out of the ground-floor window at the patch of garden, the green, sterile neatness defeating its purpose.

'He judges me . . . Even though it was his affairs that ended our marriage, his insistence that I keep up my career while trying to be a mother, his decision to fight for custody. He still judges me.'

'What is his judgement?'

'That I'm a selfish failure.'

'Has he actually said that to you?'

'He doesn't have to.'

'You say he encouraged you in your career . . . Is this a judgement you're passing on yourself?'

'I thought this was psychiatry, not psychoanalysis.'

'Losing custody of your son is bound to have stirred up all sorts of difficult emotions.'

'I didn't lose him, I consented to him living at his father's.'

'But it's what he wanted, though, wasn't it? Your illness shook his trust in you.'

She shot him a look intended to signal that was far enough. She didn't need a thirty-year-old quack to tell her why her nerves were shot, she just needed a repeat temazepam prescription.

Dr Allen regarded her thoughtfully, seeing her as a case – she could tell – to be cracked.

'You don't think that by taking this position as a coroner you're in danger of overstretching yourself?'

Jenny swallowed the words she would like to have hurled at him and forced a tolerant smile.

'I have taken this position because it's predictable, safe, salaried. There's no boss. I answer to no one.'

'Except the dead . . . and their families.'

'After fifteen years in childcare law the dead will be a welcome relief.'

Her answer seemed to interest him. He leaned forward with an earnest expression, ready to explore it further. Jenny cut in: 'Look, the symptoms are easing all the time. I can work, I can function, and mild medication is helping me to regain control. I appreciate your concern, but I think you'll agree I'm doing everything to get my life back on the rails.' She glanced at her watch. 'And I really do have to get to work now.'

Dr Allen sat back in his seat, disappointed at her reaction. 'If you gave it a chance, I'm convinced we could make some progress, perhaps remove any danger of you having another breakdown.'

'It wasn't a breakdown.'

'Episode, then. An inability to cope.'

Jenny met his gaze, realizing that young and gauche as he was, he was enjoying the power he had over her.

'Of course I don't want that to happen again,' she said. 'I'd love to continue this discussion another time, you've been very helpful, but I really do have to leave. It's my first day at the office.'

Assured of another date, he reached for his diary. 'I've a clinic here a fortnight Friday – how about five-thirty, so we can take as long as we need?'

Jenny smiled and pushed her dark brown hair back from her face. 'That sounds perfect.'

As he wrote in the appointment he said, 'You won't mind if I ask you a couple more questions, just so we've covered ourselves?'

'Fire away.'

'Have you deliberately purged or vomited recently?'

'You've been thorough.'

He handed her an appointment card, waiting for her answer.

'Occasionally.'

'Any particular reason?'

She shrugged. 'Because I don't like feeling fat.'

He glanced involuntarily at her legs, reddening slightly as he realized she had spotted him. 'But you're very slim.'

'Thank you. It's obviously working.'

He looked down at his notebook, covering his embarrassment. 'Have you taken any non-prescription drugs?'

'No.' She reached for her shiny new leather briefcase. 'Are we finished now? I promise not to sue.'

'One final thing. I read in the notes from your meetings with Dr Travis that you have a twelve-month gap in your childhood memory – between the ages of four and five.'

'His notes should also record the fact that between the ages of five and thirty-five I was relatively happy.'

Dr Allen folded his hands patiently on his lap. 'I look forward to having you as a patient, Mrs Cooper, but you should know that the tough defences you have built for yourself have to come down eventually. Better you choose the time than it chooses you.'

Jenny gave the slightest nod, feeling her heart beginning to thump, a pressure building on either side of her head, her field of vision fading at the edges. She stood up quickly, summoning sufficient anger at her weakness to push the rising sensation of panic away. Trying to sound casual but businesslike, she said, 'I'm sure we'll get on very well together. May I have my prescription now?'

The doctor looked at her. He reached for his pen. She sensed him reading her symptoms, too polite to comment.

*

Jenny picked up the pills from the dispensary and popped two with a mouthful of Diet Sprite as soon as she climbed into her car, telling herself it was only first-day jitters she was feeling. Waiting for the medication to hit, she checked her make-up in the vanity mirror and for once was mildly encouraged by what she saw. Not bad, on the outside at least; wearing better than her mother was at her age . . .

After only seconds she felt the pills begin to work their magic, relaxing her muscles and blood vessels, a warmth spreading through her like a glass of Chardonnay on an empty stomach. She turned the key in the ignition and drove her ageing Golf out of the car park.

With Tina Turner blasting from the stereo, she crawled through the queue of traffic to the roundabout on the edge of town, joined the eastbound M4 motorway and pressed her foot to the floor. Driving into the sun, she flew across the three-mile sweep of the old Severn Bridge at eighty miles per hour. The twin towers, from which the bridge was implausibly suspended by nothing more than steel cables a few inches thick, seemed to her magnificent: symbols of unbreakable strength and promise. Glancing out over the bright blue water stretching to a misty horizon, she tried to look on the positive side. In the space of a year she had endured an emotional collapse which forced her to leave her job, survived a bitter divorce, lost custody of her teenage son and managed to start afresh with a new home and career. She was bruised but not broken. And determined more than ever that what she had endured would serve only to make her stronger.

Jockeying through the traffic into central Bristol, she felt invincible. What could that psychiatrist know? What had he ever survived?

To hell with him. If she ever needed pills again, she'd get them from the internet.

*

Her new office was in a fading Georgian town house in Jamaica Street, a turning off the southern end of Whiteladies Road. Having struggled to find a parking space nearby, she approached it for the first time on foot. It couldn't be called grand. Three doors from the junction with the main road, it stood between a scruffy Asian convenience store and an even more down-at-heel newsagent's on the corner. She arrived at the front door and looked at the two brass plates. The first and second floors were occupied by an architect's practice, Planter and Co.; the ground floor was hers: HM Coroner, Severn Vale District.

It sounded so formal, so Establishment. She was a forty-two-year-old woman who had tantrums, read trashy magazines in bed, listened to reggae and smoked cigarettes when she'd drunk too much. But here she was, responsible for investigating all unnatural deaths in a large slice of north Bristol and south Gloucestershire. She was the coroner: an office which, according to her limited research, dated back to the year 1194. Feeling the temazepam glow begin to recede, she fished out the bunch of keys she had received in the post and unlocked the door.

The entrance hall was drab and painted a sickly light green. A dark oak staircase wound up to the first floor and beyond, its grandeur spoiled by the industrial grey carpeting which covered the uneven floorboards. The dreary effect was completed by the wall-mounted plastic signs which guided visitors upstairs or left to the door, partially glazed with grubby frosted glass, marked 'Coroner's Office'.

The interior of her new domain was even gloomier. Shutting the door behind her, she flicked on the strip lights and surveyed the large, dingy reception area. She made a mental note to redecorate as soon as possible. An elderly computer and telephone sat on a desk which looked older than she was. Behind it stood a row of grey filing cabinets of similar vintage and a dying cheese plant. On the opposite side of the room were two sagging sofas set at right angles around a low, cheap coffee table on which were arranged a selection of tired *Reader's Digest* magazines. The high point was a tall sash window overlooking a spacious light well in which the architects upstairs – she presumed – had placed two potted bay trees and a stylish modern bench.

There were three internal doors: one led to a functional, recently modernized kitchenette, another to the cloakroom and the third, a solid, original feature, to her office.

The modest fifteen by fifteen room could only have belonged to a middle-aged man. In the centre sat a heavy Victorian desk scattered with files and documents. More files and disorganized papers were stacked on the floor. A dusty venetian blind hung over what should have been a splendid shuttered window overlooking the street.

Two walls were taken up with floor-to-ceiling bookshelves lined with the *All England* and *Weekly Law Reports*. The remaining wall space was hung with traditional prints of rural and golfing scenes and a matriculation photograph from Jesus College, Oxford, 1967. Jenny studied the faces of the long-haired students dressed in their academic gowns and white bow ties and picked out Harry Marshall – a slim, playful teenager pouting sideways-on to the camera like the young Mick Jagger.

She spotted a half-drunk cup of coffee sitting on the mantelpiece above an elderly gas fire. Some ghoulish instinct made her pick it up and study the thin film of mould floating on the surface. She imagined Harry, heavy, breathing through his mouth, sipping from it hours before his death, and for a fleeting moment wondered what the bookends of her own career might be.

Her eye was caught by a blinking light on the desk. An answerphone which looked like a relic from the 1980s had two messages. She put down the cup and pressed the play button. The voice of a distressed young woman fighting tears crackled out: 'It's Simone Wills. The things they said about me in the paper aren't true. None of it's true . . . And I *did* call the Centre and tell them how Danny was. That woman's lying if she says I didn't . . .' She broke off to sob, then continued tearfully, 'Why didn't you let me give evidence? You told me I'd have my say. You *promised*—' The machine bleeped, cutting her off short.

The next message was also from Simone Wills. In a much more controlled, determined voice, she said: 'You got it wrong, you *know* you did. If you haven't got the guts to find out what happened, I'll do it myself. I'm going to get justice for Danny. You're a coward. You're as bad as the rest of them.' Clunk. This time Simone beat the machine to it.

Danny Wills. Jenny recalled reading about the young prisoner who had died in custody. She had the idea that his mother was a drug addict, one of the feckless underclass she had grown so accustomed to in her previous career. Hearing her angry voice brought an unwelcome sense of déjà vu. As a lawyer whose daily routine consisted of wresting neglected children from their incapable and occasionally abusive parents, she had had her fill of hysterical emotion. As coroner, Jenny had hoped she would be at a dignified arm's length from the distressed and grief-stricken.

'Hello?' A female voice called out from reception. 'Is that you, Mrs Cooper?'

Jenny turned to see a woman in her early fifties with a neat bob of dyed blonde hair standing in the doorway. She was short, substantial without being overweight, and wore a beige raincoat and smart navy business suit, her skin suntanned against her white blouse.

'Alison Trent. Coroner's officer.' The woman gave a guarded smile and offered her hand.

Jenny smiled back and shook it. 'Jenny Cooper. I was beginning to wonder if you were still here.'

'I haven't like to come here since Mr Marshall died. I didn't know if I should disturb anything.'

'Right.' Jenny waited for further explanation, but Alison offered none. She sensed awkwardness, hostility even, coming from her. 'So, if you haven't been here, who's been handling the caseload for the last four weeks?'

'I have,' Alison said, sounding surprised and a little indignant. 'I don't work from here. My office is at the police station. Didn't they tell you?'

'The police station? No. I just assumed—'

'I'm ex-CID. Perk of the job – they give me an office. A bit nicer than this one, I'm afraid.'

Jenny looked at her with a half smile, realizing that here was an employee who thought she was returning to business as usual. From what she had already seen, that couldn't be allowed to happen.

'I suppose I should let you settle in before dumping any files on you,' Alison said. 'Not that there's much on at the moment – just the usual from the hospital, a couple of road deaths.'

'You can't have been signing death certificates?'

'Not personally. I phone Mr Hamer, the deputy in Bristol Central. He's been giving me the OK and I pp them for him.'

'I see,' Jenny said, forming a picture of this cosy arrangement. A deputy coroner in another part of the city, not even troubling to look at the files, taking the word of a retired police officer that no further investigation was required. 'I don't know what you've been told, Mrs Trent, but it was made plain to me by the Ministry of Justice that I was to overhaul this office and make it part of the modern Coroner's Service. The first step will be to bring it all under one roof.'

Alison was incredulous. 'You want me to work from here?'

'That would make sense. I'd like you to fetch over whatever

you have at the station as soon as possible. Make sure to bring the file on Danny Wills. And I'd like to see any current files this morning – get a taxi if needs be.'

'Nobody said a word to me,' Alison protested. 'I can't just leave. I've been there five years.'

Jenny adopted her most formal tone. 'I hope you won't find this process too trying, Mrs Trent, but it has to be done. And quickly.'

'Whatever you want, Mrs Cooper.' Alison turned abruptly, marched out into reception and headed for the outer door.

Jenny leaned back against the desk and took stock. Another thing she hadn't counted on: a difficult subordinate, doubtless jealous and aggrieved for a hundred different reasons. She resolved to stamp her authority from the outset. The very least she needed to get the job done was the unquestioning respect of her staff.

Time to prioritize. The office was badly in need of a clean, but that would have to wait. The most pressing task was to wade through Marshall's papers and see what needed attention.

First she needed coffee. Strong coffee.

She found a Brazilian café around the corner on Whiteladies Road, Carioca's, which sold take-out ristretto and small, bite-sized custard tarts. She bought one of each and was back in harness within ten minutes.

Next to the desk on the floor she found a stack of twenty or so manila case files, each of which contained a death certificate signed in the last few days of Marshall's life. They all seemed to be routine cases, mostly hospital deaths, waiting to be absorbed into whatever manual filing system Alison operated.

On the surface of the desk were two disorderly heaps of files. The first contained papers and receipts relating to the office accounts. A letter from the local authority – the body which, due to a quirk of history, employed the coroner and paid his or her salary and expenses – reminded Marshall that this year's figures were overdue.

The second consisted of a random selection of cases, some of them years old. On top of the pile was a clear plastic wallet stuffed with newspaper cuttings dating back to the early 1990s, all reporting on cases Marshall had investigated. He had marked passages on most of them. Some were carefully cut out, others roughly torn, but all were dated.

In the midst of all this Jenny unearthed a collection of personal correspondence weighted down by a crusty bottle of writing ink: credit card bills, bank statements, a reminder from the dentist. She weeded out the junk, gathered the rest together and searched for an envelope large enough to take it. She rummaged through the untidy desk drawers, finding broken pencils, paperclips and accumulated detritus, but no envelopes. Having ransacked all of them and ready to give up, she noticed a further shallower but much wider drawer set back under the lip of the writing surface. She tugged at the handle. It was locked. She glanced around for a key and spotted the plastic desk tidy, which held a selection of chewed ballpoints. She upended it and among the dust and small change found what she was looking for.

She pulled the drawer open. There were envelopes sure enough, in all manner of sizes, but also one of the now familiar manila files. She quickly stuffed a Jiffy bag with the correspondence, scribbled 'Mrs Marshall' on the front, then opened the file.

Uppermost on the slender pile of documents was a copy death certificate dated 2 May. It was a Form B: notification by the coroner to the Registrar of Births and Deaths and Marriages that, having held a post-mortem, an inquest was not considered necessary. The deceased was named as Katherine Linda Taylor, aged fifteen years and three months, of 6 Harvey Road, South-mead. Place of death was recorded as Bridge Valley, Clifton – the spectacular gorge spanned by the Clifton Suspension Bridge. Jenny's immediate thought was of the many suicides who jumped from it each year, but cause of death was recorded as 'intravenous overdose of diamorphine'. The Certificate for Cremation section had been left blank save for the word 'burial'.

Intrigued, Jenny turned over to find a two-page police report handwritten in turgid, ungrammatical prose by a Police Constable Campbell. A member of the public had chanced on Katy's partially decomposed body in shrubbery some thirty yards from the main road. She was found in a seated, hunched position with an empty hypodermic syringe at her side. The dead girl had been reported missing by her parents seven days previously and had a history of truanting, absence from home and minor crime.

She wasn't prepared for what came next: a Xeroxed copy of a police photograph picturing Katy's body where it was found. A small, slender figure dressed in jeans held up by a wide, white belt, high-heeled sandals to match and a short pink T-shirt. Her delicate hands, mottled with decay, hugged her bony knees. A mop of untidy blonde hair hung forward, obscuring her face. Her chin rested on her chest.

Jenny gazed at the image for a long moment, horrified, absorbing every detail. It was the colour of the teenager's skin which fascinated her: the brilliant white of her sandals against the mouldering flesh. Her mind created a picture of the scene had the body not been found until weeks later: would there still be tissue, or just a skeleton inside the clothes?

Banishing the image, she turned the page, expecting to find a copy of the post-mortem report, but there was none. Strange. The pattern in every other file she had seen so far was the same: police statements, post-mortem report, death certificate. And why was the file locked away in a drawer?

Although she had spent the best part of the last three weeks boning up on coronial law, Jenny felt in uncertain territory. She opened her briefcase and brought out her already well-thumbed copy of Jervis, the coroner's standard textbook and Bible. It confirmed what she had suspected. Section 8(1) of the Coroner's Act 1988 required an inquest to be held where the death was violent or unnatural. There was no more unnatural death than a possible suicide or accidental overdose, so how could Marshall have certified it without going through the lawful procedure?

She checked the dates: body discovered 30 April, police report 1 May, death certificate signed 2 May. She recalled that Marshall died later in the first week of May. Perhaps he was already feeling unwell and was cutting corners. Or maybe he simply wanted to spare the dead girl's family the ordeal of an inquest. Either way, failing to hold one was a flagrant breach of the rules. Just the sort of practice all coroners were being instructed by the Ministry of Justice to stamp out.

Alison returned an hour later. Jenny felt the waves of resentment crashing over her even before she pointedly knocked on the partially open door.

She tried to sound cheerful. 'Come in.'

Alison hefted a heavy nylon holdall into her office and dropped it on the floor.

'That's everything I could find that's been dealt with since he died. The ones in the blue files at the top are still open. We get about five deaths a day on average, sometimes more.'

'Thanks. I'll try to get through them.'

'I've arranged a van, but he can't do it till tomorrow afternoon. There's half a dozen filing cabinets. I don't know where you think you're going to put them.'

'I'm sure a lot of it can go into storage,' Jenny said, refusing to acknowledge Alison's martyred tone. 'As long as we have the last couple of years' worth on site. We'll be computerizing the system more or less immediately anyway.'

'Oh?'

'You must have worked with computers?'

'Only when I couldn't avoid it. I've seen how they go wrong.'

'There's a standard system all coroners are being required to use. In future GPs and hospital doctors will notify us of all deaths by email, not only the ones they can't write certificates for. You know Harold Shipman managed to murder two hundred and fifty of his patients and not one of their cases crossed the coroner's desk?'

'That wouldn't happen here. We know all the doctors on our patch personally.'

'That's been part of the problem.' Jenny drove the point home: 'I hate bureaucracy more than anyone, but abusing trust was the reason he got himself into the record books.'

Alison frowned. 'I suppose I couldn't have expected to carry on just as we were. It's only human nature to want to change things.'

'I hope we'll get on well, Mrs Trent.' Alison's face remained stony. 'I've heard great things about you. My interview panel said Mr Marshall found you indispensable. I'm sure I will, too.'

The older woman softened a little, the tightness leaving her face. 'I apologize if I seem a little tense, Mrs Cooper.' She paused. 'Mr Marshall and I had become good friends over the years. He was such a nice man. Concerned for everyone. I hadn't been in here since . . .' She trailed off, a slight catch in her voice.

'I understand.' Jenny smiled, genuinely this time, and Alison smiled back.

The tension between them eased. An unwritten truce was declared.

Alison glanced at the empty cardboard coffee cup on Jenny's desk. 'Fancy another? I'm just going to get one for myself. Sorry there's not much in the kitchen. I'll pop out and stock up on supplies later.'

'Thanks.' Jenny reached for her handbag in search of her purse.

'It's all right, I'll get them.'

'No, I insist.' Jenny brought out a twenty-pound note and handed it to her. 'That should cover the other things, too.'

Alison hesitated briefly before taking the money, then folded it gratefully into her raincoat pocket. 'Thank you, Mrs Cooper.' She ran her eyes around the room. 'I expect you'll want to smarten this place up. Hasn't been touched for years.'

'I'll live with it for a couple of days, see what inspiration strikes.'

'Harry always said he was going to redecorate, but he never quite got round to it. Pressures of life, I suppose – a wife and four daughters all at school and university. He was an old father, too.'

Jenny remembered the photograph of Katy Taylor. 'Before you go, Mrs Trent—'

She reached for the file.

'Alison is fine.'

'Of course—'

'Don't worry, I'll call you Mrs Cooper. I'm happier with that anyway.'

'Whichever you prefer,' Jenny said, relieved she'd been spared the embarrassment of insisting on her formal title. She couldn't abide being called by her Christian name at work. She opened the file and produced the death certificate. 'I found this locked in a drawer.'

'I remember. The young girl who took the overdose.'

'Two things seem odd about it. There's no post-mortem

report, and where there's a possibility of suicide, surely there should have been an inquest.'

Alison reacted with surprise. 'The police made no suggestion of suicide. Junkies are always accidentally topping themselves.'

'It's still an unnatural death.'

'Mr Marshall never liked to upset families where there was nothing to be gained from it. What would be the point?'

Jenny chose not to embark on an explanation. It was going to take more than a brief lesson on the Coroner's Act to re-educate her officer.

'What about the post-mortem report? He can't have signed a death certificate without seeing one.'

'He never had any choice. We're lucky if we see a written report three weeks after a death. The pathologist would phone him up with his findings after the p-m, the paperwork would arrive whenever.'

'Three *weeks*?'

'We are talking about the National Health Service.'

Alison's phone rang. 'Excuse me.' She fished it out of her pocket and answered. 'Coroner's officer . . . Hello, Mr Kelso . . . I see . . . Of course. I'll let Mrs Cooper know straight away . . . Yes, she's just started. Will do.' She rang off and turned to Jenny. 'That was an A&E consultant from the Vale. Fifty-four-year-old homeless man dead on admission. Suspected liver failure. Post-mortem this afternoon.'

'And a report next month?'

'I'll give you the morgue's number if you like. You can give them a ring and introduce yourself.'

She reached for a scrap of paper and wrote down a Bristol number. 'That'll get you through to Dr Peterson's answerphone – the consultant pathologist. He's usually pretty good at calling back.'

Jenny glanced again at the file and felt an uneasy stirring in the pit of her stomach. Whatever Marshall's motives may have been, his handling of the case was negligent at best and it was her responsibility to clear up his mess.

'No, I think I'd better pay him a personal visit, see if we can't speed things up a bit.'

'You can try,' Alison said. 'Do you still want the coffee?'

Jenny got up from her chair and grabbed her handbag. 'I'll wait till I get back.'

'Have you been to a mortuary before?'

'No.'

'Just to warn you – it might be a bit of a shock. Wild horses wouldn't drag Mr Marshall down there.'

Alison waited until she heard Jenny's footsteps disappear through the front door of the building, then sat quietly at her desk for a long moment before reaching into her briefcase and drawing out a thick, bound document. She turned through its pages, her eyes flicking anxiously towards the door as if fearing that at any moment she might be seen. At the sound of voices on the stairs she hurriedly closed it again and returned it to her case. Long after the voices had gone she remained in her chair, staring across reception into the office where Harry Marshall should have been, her eyes burning with tears that refused to come.

THREE

JENNY SIPPED THE WARM DREGS of her Diet Sprite, one hand on the wheel, as she drove the four miles to the hospital in slow-moving traffic. Edging through road works at walking pace, sandwiched between a truck belching fumes and an impatient Mercedes, she felt her heartbeat begin to pick up, a tightness in her chest, her 'free-floating anxiety' as Dr Travis, her previous psychiatrist, had termed it, close to the surface.

Highly strung. Stressed. Nervous. Call it what you like. Ever since the day almost exactly a year ago that she dried in court, had to sit down midway through reading out a banal medical report to a bemused judge, the most mundane of anxiety-making situations could trigger symptoms of panic. Waiting in a supermarket queue, travelling in an elevator, sitting in the hairdresser's chair, crawling through traffic: any situation from which there was no immediate escape could make her heart pound and her diaphragm tighten.

She went through her relaxation routine, breathed slow and deep, felt the weight of her arms tug at her shoulders, her legs sink into the seat. The anxiety gradually subsided, retreating to its hiding place in her subconscious, but leaving the door open a chink. Just so she wouldn't forget it was there.

Arriving at traffic lights, Jenny tossed her empty can into the passenger footwell and rummaged in her bag for the temazepam. She shook out a single tablet and swallowed it dry, angry at her dependence. Other people survived traumas without living on pills, why couldn't she? She tried to console herself with the fact that in the three months since she decided to quit being a courtroom lawyer her symptoms had eased significantly. No dark unwanted thoughts. No full-blown panic attacks.

One day at a time . . .

Approaching the large, modern, brick-built hospital that looked like another of the anonymous business units that surrounded it, she endeavoured to be rational, to accept that the stress of a new job would temporarily cause her to be more anxious. She would use the pills while she adjusted to her new responsibilities, then, in a week or two, wean herself off them again.

But as she parked up and walked across the tarmac to the hospital building her mind refused to still. Disturbing, unformed images played under the surface. What if her psychiatrists were right? What if there was a secret horror in her childhood that would continue to haunt her like a malevolent ghost until she somehow summoned the strength to confront it?

Damn. She had thought she was over this.

She caught her reflection in the glass of the revolving door: a smart, confident woman in a business suit. A professional. A presence. Give it a little more time, she told herself, and it'll dissolve like a bad dream.

After ten minutes of wandering along crowded corridors, many doubling as wards, with grey-faced patients stranded on trolleys, Jenny realized there were no signs to the mortuary. She queued at the reception desk, too self-conscious to pull rank on the ragtag of enquirers ahead of her. Most looked poor, old or confused; a heavily pregnant young woman gripped her stomach in obvious pain. The receptionist, a tense woman with nicotine-stained teeth, dealt increasingly impatiently with each one, one hand fidgeting with a pack of cigarettes as she struggled to give complicated directions around the building with the aid of a faded plastic map no one could follow.

The mortuary was situated in a separate anonymous, single-storey building at the rear of the hospital complex. There was no reply when she pressed the buzzer. She tried again. Still no response. On her third attempt a young Filipina cleaner answered, wearily wiping her hands on grubby, sleeveless overalls. Jenny tentatively asked where she could find Dr Peterson. The girl shrugged and waved her in, saying, 'No speak English, sorry,' and went back to flopping her mop across the tiled floor.

Jenny stepped inside, proceeded along a short corridor and pushed through swing doors into an open lobby area, off which were two semi-glazed office doors and a set of slap doors. A water cooler and a snack vending machine stood in the corner. She glanced through into the offices but no one was home. Following the sound of voices, she nudged through into a wider corridor, at the side of which were parked half a dozen or more gurneys, each carrying a corpse wrapped in white plastic. Then the smell hit her: powerful disinfectant mixed with a heavy, sweet odour which caught the back of her throat.

A tall, wiry, dark-featured man wearing stained surgical scrubs came through a door to her right. Pulling off a face mask, he gave her a look of pleasant surprise. 'Can I help you?'

Jenny straightened, tearing her eyes away from the row of dead bodies. 'Hello. Jenny Cooper, Severn Vale District Coroner. I'm looking for Dr Peterson.'

'That's me.' He smiled, tiny lines creasing around his eyes.

Jenny instinctively offered her hand. 'Pleased to meet you.'

'I wouldn't recommend it – best if I wash up first.' The

smile again, almost boyish. 'Coroner, hey? Can't remember the last time I had one of you down here. Harry Marshall even managed to avoid it after he died. Shall we talk in my office?'

'Sure.'

Peterson led her along the corridor. As he walked, he pulled off his scrubs, revealing a neat-fitting polo shirt, and tossed them along with the mask into a laundry bin. He was slim for a man of his age, but vain, Jenny suspected. He arrived at a door with corpses parked either side of it and held it open. 'After you.' Jenny glanced uneasily at the bodies. Peterson said, 'Best patients in the NHS – been waiting for hours and not a cheep out of them.'

She managed a faint smile and stepped into his modest office. There was a window on to the hospital car park, shelves laden with textbooks, box files and several indistinct objects floating in jars of formaldehyde. Peterson stepped over to a stainless-steel wash-hand basin and proceeded to scrub his hands vigorously with strong-smelling liquid soap.

'Have a seat.' He nodded towards a single chair next to the desk. 'Just taken over the reins?'

'First day at the office.' She glanced around the room, her eye caught by the only picture on the wall: a framed postcard picturing a dead weasel slumped over a tiny desk, a miniature revolver in his paw, 'if you can call it that. I get the impression my predecessor had let things slide a little.'

Peterson rinsed the suds from his skin and shut off the tap. 'I don't know, Harry Marshall seemed a capable sort to me – not that I saw him very often.' He tugged a paper towel out of a dispenser. 'Always found him a pleasure to deal with.'

'Not one to get hung up on formalities.'

He balled up the wet paper towel and tossed it into the bin, a vaguely amused look on his face. 'That sounded a little loaded.'

'Merely an observation. At the beginning of last month you

conducted a post-mortem on a fifteen-year-old girl, Katy Taylor. We're well into June and my office hasn't received a report from you.'

'You'll have to jog my memory.'

'Small blonde girl. Suspected heroin overdose.'

'I remember. Yes – partially decomposed. What we call a stinker.'

'Really.'

'I informed Marshall of my findings over the phone.'

'Which were?'

'She mainlined some close-to-pure heroin. I must get a couple like it every month.'

'Was there any possibility of suicide?'

'You can never rule it out.'

'Then Marshall was obliged by law to conduct an inquest. Any idea why he didn't?'

'I'm just a pathologist. I tell the coroner the cause of death and that's where my responsibility ends.'

'My officer says you seldom produce a report within three weeks of post-mortem.'

Peterson smiled patiently. 'Mrs Cooper, Jenny – I share a secretary with five other consultants, all of whose patients are still drawing breath. I'd love to get reports out to your office more quickly, but there's a better chance of one of those stiffs out there getting a hard-on.'

Jenny fixed him with the look she would give an evasive witness. 'Why don't you type them yourself?'

'Find me another three hours in the day and I'd be glad to.'

'In future I won't be signing death certificates without sight of a written report.'

'Then I suggest you take it up with the managers of this place. God knows, I've tried.' He glanced at his watch. 'Talking of which, I've got a meeting with the bastards any minute. I'm going to have to leave you.'

'I'm serious, Dr Peterson. That means bodies won't be released to undertakers for burial.'

'*What?*' Peterson let out a laugh. 'Do you want to see my fridges? They're stuffed in three deep as it is.'

Jenny rose from her chair. 'Then why don't you try storing them out in the car park?' She gave him a disarming smile. 'My guess is you'll have a secretary in no time. I look forward to reading the report.'

Alison had left a note saying, 'Gone to fetch more stuff from the station', and four death report forms, all of them patients at the Vale. Jenny ate a take-out salad at her desk and studied the new cases. The first was the homeless man who had died from suspected liver failure in a cubicle in A&E. She didn't know much medicine yet, but she knew enough to realize he would have left this world in agonizing pain, probably on a trolley waiting for overstretched junior doctors to decide which one of them would draw the short straw. The second was a woman in her seventies who had been admitted with emphysema and promptly contracted a hospital infection. The third was a male, sixty, dead on arrival having suffered a suspected heart attack, and the fourth an unmarried Pakistani girl of nineteen who had haemorrhaged while giving birth in a public park.

She imagined them all stacked up on top of one another in Peterson's fridge and felt a momentary sense of dread.

Her desk phone rang, a welcome interruption.

'Jenny Cooper.'

A confident young woman said, 'Tara Collins, *Bristol Evening Post*. Are you the new coroner for Severn Vale?'

'Yes?'

'Hi. I wrote a piece a few weeks back about a boy who died in custody, Danny Wills. Your predecessor handled the inquest.'

'Uh-huh.' Jenny tried to sound noncommittal, wary of reporters even though in family law she had had few dealings with them.

'Marshall died three days after the jury returned a verdict of suicide.'

'So I understand.'

There was a brief pause on the line. 'His GP wrote out a death certificate stating cause of death as a coronary, but as far as I can make out no post-mortem was performed.'

Jenny sensed she was being drawn into something. 'I'm afraid I don't know any more than you do, but if the GP was satisfied as to his cause of death—'

'How could he have been? Marshall only had mild angina. He had an ECG in February.'

'What exactly is it that you want, Ms Collins?'

'Don't you think it strange that only three days after conducting an inquest into the death of a fourteen-year-old prisoner in a privately run prison, the coroner died suddenly and didn't even undergo a post-mortem?'

'I've just taken over here. I don't know much about the Wills case – only what I read in your paper, which wasn't exactly sympathetic to the boy, as I recall.'

'My copy got subbed . . .' Tara Collins trailed off.

Jenny waited for her to continue.

'Marshall was a busy man before the inquest. He was taking statements from the staff at Portshead, the prison escort service, the Youth Offending Team, and then he pushed the whole thing through in a day. He only called four live witnesses and went back on his promise to let the boy's mother give evidence.'

It was Jenny's turn to pause for thought, acutely aware that anything she said was in danger of appearing in this evening's paper. She tried to change the subject. 'How do you know about his ECG?'

'A source. I can't tell you who.'

'And his discussions with the family?'

'I've been in close contact with Mrs Wills since Danny died. Marshall promised her no stone would be left unturned. He was giving her regular updates until three days before the full hearing. Then he went silent. Never spoke to her again.'

'Well, I suppose there could be any number of explanations. I'd have to look at the file before forming a view, but if the family are dissatisfied with the inquest the normal course is to seek legal advice.'

'There's no legal aid for inquests and bugger all chance of getting any to challenge the outcome of one.'

'Mr Marshall's death was very unfortunate,' Jenny said, straining to remain patient. 'I'm sorry for his family and even more so for the family of Danny Wills, but my job is to make sure that as of now this office is run in a modern, efficient and open manner. I want to make sure that in future families feel fully satisfied by the inquest process.'

'Did you read that from a script, Mrs Cooper? It sounded like it.'

Jenny bristled. 'Do you want me to respond, Ms Collins, or are you simply trying to make a point?'

The journalist was quiet for a moment. When she spoke again she had her emotions back under control. 'I apologize . . . But having covered Danny's case, it seems to me that the truth never made it into the open. Not by a long way. And then there's Marshall's death . . .'

'What about it?'

'Doesn't it strike you as rather more than coincidental?'

'Given that it was due to natural causes, no.'

'His behaviour leading up to the inquest was pretty peculiar.'

'Never having met him, I couldn't possibly comment.'

'So you won't be looking at the Wills case again?'

'It's been dealt with. I have no power to do so.'

'What about Section 13 of the Coroner's Act 1988? You can ask the High Court for permission to let you hold a fresh inquest.'

Jenny felt the muscles in her throat tighten. She swallowed, resisting a powerful urge to slam down the receiver. 'Since you've been researching the law, you'll know that only happens where there's compelling new evidence.'

'If you look for it, you might find it. Goodbye, Mrs Cooper.'

Jenny slowly lowered the receiver on to the cradle, adrenalin coursing through her veins. Half a day into the job and a journalist was already trying to catch her out. Family lawyers had to cope with weeping mothers and violent fathers in court, but the press were excluded. No case she'd conducted had ever attracted an inch of newsprint. Dealing with the media was another thing she'd have to learn on the job. Tara Collins was obviously working an angle, so she'd have to be ready for her and on top of the facts. She found the Danny Wills file and started to read.

The Form of Inquisition recorded the jury's verdict of suicide. In the narrative section, the foreman had written: 'Between 2 and 4 a.m. the deceased tore a strip from his bed sheet, tied one end to the bars of the window and, standing on a chair, tied the other end around his neck, then kicked the chair away, causing death by strangulation.'

There were statements from the maintenance man who discovered the body, the two secure care officers who were on duty in the house unit that night, a security guard who testified to the continuing malfunction of the CCTV system in the unit, the medical staff who examined Danny on his admission, the director of Portshead Farm and the case worker from the Youth Offending Team who had dealt with him before he was sentenced. A copy of the staff rosters for the week leading up to Danny's death had been carefully gone through: there were personal phone numbers next to each name and ticks, she assumed, Marshall had made as he worked through them.

Near the back of the file was an aerial photograph and detailed plan of the secure training centre which Marshall had annotated. It was a small prison in an exposed field on the south Gloucestershire side of the Severn estuary, midway between the Severn Bridge and Oldbury nuclear power station, four miles to the east.

Portshead Farm consisted of five buildings positioned around a central yard area and a playing field. The entire complex was surrounded by a twelve-foot concrete wall topped with razor wire and surveillance cameras. At the entrance were the reception and medical centre in which new inmates were examined and, if necessary, housed in one of several observation cells before being certified fit for transfer to one of the two single-sex house units. The fourth building contained classrooms in which trainees underwent a crude form of education. The fifth, nearest the playing field, was the canteen, which doubled as a gymnasium.

The centre was equipped to hold up to a hundred trainees between the ages of twelve and seventeen. While child custody had virtually ceased to exist in some parts of Europe, Britain's appetite for incarcerating children was increasing. Over four thousand were currently imprisoned, nearly five times the number of its nearest rival, France.

To cope with the ever-rising numbers, the government had created the Youth Justice Board, a quango charged with commissioning places for young offenders. Private companies would bid to build and run new secure training centres and the board would pick the winners. Portshead Farm was owned and run by UKAM Secure Solutions Ltd, a company with a portfolio of correctional facilities across the USA and now the UK. UKAM's business was security: concrete, bars, wire, cameras and attendant personnel. Catering, cleaning, laundry, healthcare and education were all subcontracted out. For this burgeoning industry the growing army of young inmates was very good news indeed.

In an uncharacteristic fit of conscientiousness, Marshall had written a longhand note listing the salient points in Danny Wills's recent history. Jenny worked her way through it.

Danny came from a large and dysfunctional low-income family. His mother seemed to be the one constant, but had numerous drugs convictions of her own. His own lengthy record began at ten – the age of criminal responsibility – suggesting that he had started lawbreaking well before.

He had convictions for possession of marijuana, amphetamines and crack cocaine, ABH, criminal damage and a violent disorder. Two weeks before his death he had been given an Antisocial Behaviour Order and ordered to wear an electronic tag to enforce a curfew. Three days in, he cut the tag off 'as a prank' and was hauled before the Youth Court for breach. The Youth Offending Team recommended community service; the court gave him four months' detention and training.

On 4 April Danny was received into Portshead Farm. The medical examiner, Nurse Linda Raven, noted that he was 'difficult, obstructive and offensive' and during the standard strip search he had threatened 'to fucking kill himself'. Judged a potential suicide risk, he was placed in an observation cell, dressed only in a sturdy, one-piece gown which Marshall described as 'like a horse blanket', where he remained for three days before being introduced to the male house unit.

Once transferred, Marshall recorded that Danny refused to attend classes and was reduced to the lowest level of privileges, bronze, which meant only three pairs of underwear per week, no television or confectionery. He lived this way for six days, only leaving his room to eat in the canteen and to shower. It was on his seventh night in the house unit that he died.

A final note, added in a different pen, recorded the fact that Danny's mother had telephoned the director's office several times immediately after the sentencing hearing to express her concern about her son's state of mind. Marshall's last note read: 'Director failed to respond to calls.'

Jenny flicked back through the file and found the director's statement. Mrs Elaine Lewis, MPhil, MBA, wrote that Danny had been subjected to the same rigorous and thorough-going checks as all other new trainees, and had benefited from the special attention of the highly trained secure care officers on his house unit. She regretted not having responded to Mrs Wills's 'alleged' telephone calls, but emphasized that in any event there was nothing more that she or her staff could or would have done for him.

Jenny closed the file with the same feeling of depressed resignation she had felt countless times during her years dealing with the troubled, self-destructive young. She could picture Danny vividly: violent, struggling, spitting, lashing out at and abusing the staff, consumed with self-loathing. Shoved in a tiny cell without clothes or dignity, a plastic meal tray passed through the inspection hatch, an uninterested face glancing in each half-hour, a tick in the box: a claustrophobic nightmare.

What the system did to young offenders was, in her long experience, far more calculatedly brutal than anything most of them had done on the outside. To remove all love, affection and human contact from kids at their most vulnerable was barbarism of a kind she had never begun to understand. She let out a weary sigh. Having staked her future on leaving all things child-related behind, the irony of being pitched straight into an adolescent's death wasn't lost on her.

So much for moving on.

She heard Alison arrive back in the outer office and exclaim in surprise. She appeared in the doorway clutching a sheaf of papers. 'Didn't you see this on the fax, Mrs Cooper? It's the Katy Taylor post-mortem report.'

She handed the still warm sheets of paper across the desk.

'About time,' Jenny said, and glanced at Peterson's conclusion: heroin overdose.

'I shouldn't count on him making a habit of it. Just trying to impress you, I expect. What would you like me to do first? I was thinking of clearing out those old filing cabinets.'

'That'd be good. But before you do – I had a call from a Tara Collins at the *Bristol Evening Post*. Ring any bells?'

Alison thought for a moment and shook her head.

'She covered the Danny Wills inquest. She seemed to know quite a lot about Mr Marshall's investigation.'

'He never mentioned her.'

'What was your involvement with the case?'

'Very little really. I was on leave the last week of April – my husband was poorly. My first day back was the start of the inquest.'

'How did Mr Marshall seem?'

'His normal self. A bit quiet, I suppose. Why? What was this reporter saying?'

Jenny considered her words carefully. 'She had the impression he conducted a very thorough investigation but hurried the inquest rather. She seemed to think there was something suspicious about it.'

'He didn't like to make a meal of inquests. Never did. He said it only upset the family.'

'You knew him better than anyone else – was there anything about the case that was troubling him?'

'Like what?'

'I've only looked through a few of his files, but he does seem to have worked quite hard on this one. And from the messages the mother left on his answerphone it's clear she felt let down. He seems to have gone back on a promise to let her give evidence.'

'I can't imagine him making promises. That just wasn't in his nature. He gave relatives sympathy, that's all. He was very skilled at dealing with the bereaved.'

'You don't think that in this case he might have made an exception, decided to get a little more involved than usual?'

'I've no reason to think so. You've seen the papers – there's nothing improper, is there?'

Jenny shrugged. 'Nothing obvious.'

'That's what I thought.' Alison seemed twitchy. The subject had stirred something in her, Jenny could feel it.

'This reporter clearly thinks there's an untold story and I got the impression she intends to pursue it. If there is anything to be unearthed I'd rather get to it first.'

She met Alison's gaze, no doubt in her mind now that her officer had something to tell her.

Alison looked down at the floor. 'I want you to know that in all the time I knew him, Mrs Cooper, I only had respect for him. He put people first. He could be almost too kind to them. Sometimes the phone in here would never stop ringing – I suppose because he was so calm and reassuring . . . He was always professional, but now and again, I saw it in him, he'd get involved. He'd start to brood, go into himself. That's partly why I took my leave when I did: he'd become grumpy as hell, quite honestly. Snapped my head off one day; I answered him back, I'm afraid.' She faltered, only just holding at bay the tears Jenny could see were close to coming.

'You were fond of him, weren't you?'

Alison flashed her a look. 'Not like that, Mrs Cooper.'

'I didn't mean—'

'We were good friends, that's all. We were getting on each other's nerves, so I took my holiday.'

'And when you came back?'

'He was quiet . . . but I could tell he was sorry for losing his temper. We just carried on where we left off.'

'He didn't talk to you about the case?'

'He mentioned how upsetting it was. The mother was very distressed in the courtroom, of course – kept calling out. I had to escort her outside at one point.'

'He didn't express any feelings about the verdict?'

'Only that it was what he expected. For what it's worth, I don't think the jury could have done anything else.'

Jenny glanced around her dreary office, beginning to get a sense of how Marshall might have been feeling in his last days. Stuck in here by himself, wanting to help a grieving family but frightened to put his head above the parapet. A wife and four daughters at home, and dealing with Alison, who clearly had feelings for him beyond the professional. A lot of competing emotions. Men weren't good with those.

Jenny said, 'And you're quite sure that there was no connection between the Wills case and Mr Marshall's death?'

'What kind of connection?'

'I don't know.'

'Harry had a heart condition, we all knew that. You only have to work here for a few months to realize how many men in their fifties drop dead without warning. Anyway, reporters are all vermin in my experience. Ignore her, that's my advice.'

'I think I ought to have a word with Mrs Wills, at least. If only to check that nothing was missed.' She saw Alison stiffen with indignation. 'I'm not suggesting for a moment—'

'I can assure you, Mr Marshall would have done everything he could.'

Realizing there was nothing more to be gained from the conversation, Jenny said, 'I'm sure you're right. I do appreciate how difficult the last few weeks must have been.'

Her placatory tone caused Alison's eyes to redden. Embarrassed, she hurriedly excused herself, saying she was going to make tea.

If, after Tara Collins's call, Jenny needed further evidence that there was something amiss about the Wills inquest, the atmosphere in the office at that moment was it. She listened to Alison stifling quiet sobs as she busied herself in the kitchenette, filling the kettle and clattering cups. Her grief was palpable.

Coroner. The title sounded so grand, so removed from the ordinary. But sitting at her desk, the air thick with suppressed, painful emotion, she could have been a child again, hiding in her bedroom, trying to shut out the sound of her parents' incessant arguing.

Why did life always pitch her into the middle of other people's crises?

Jenny had always resisted notions of fate, but reaching again for Danny Wills's file she felt that somehow this was meant to be; that the dead boy was touching the deadness in that secret part of her where the darkness lay.

If she had learned one thing from her 'episode' it was never to ignore her instincts. Turning once more through the pages, she knew that while their bones had been ground to dust, neither the young prisoner nor Harry Marshall was yet at rest.

FOUR

THE BROADLANDS ESTATE WAS A network of tired-looking streets. Prefabricated houses dominated, built some time postwar with little care and even less thought to future residents. Now nestled in the crook between the M5 motorway to the west and the M4 to the north, the low distant rumble of traffic was ever present.

As sinks go, Jenny thought, it was not too bad. If the highrises of east London, Birmingham and Glasgow were the seventh circle of hell, this was only the second or third, but it smelt of poverty. Not a single dwelling was maintained. Litter hung in the breeze and collected under bushes, slouching kids buried in sweat-top hoods clustered on corners smoking, the schools they should have been attending an irrelevance to their lives of drugs, sex and petty crime.

While practising childcare law Jenny had visited many such places and she always came away shocked by the narrowness of the inhabitants' world. It was as if the streets immediately around them were the limits of the far horizon. She had long since concluded that it was the simple crushing boredom of life on estates like these which sucked the hope out of people. There were no challenges, only the law to kick against.

She parked outside the Wills's address, checked the car doors were locked and walked up the short path to the front door. A broken baby buggy and faded plastic toys littered the tiny front lawn.

A bony coffee-coloured man with beads in his hair answered the door in a grubby T-shirt and boxers. A powerful waft of marijuana followed in his wake.

Jenny glanced over his shoulder at two pre-school children still in their pyjamas, both of them white. 'I'm Jenny Cooper, the new Severn Vale coroner. I'm looking for Simone Wills.'

The man stared at her with swollen, bloodshot eyes. 'She's not here.' He moved to shut the door.

Jenny stuck her foot over the threshold. 'I just want to talk to her for a minute. It's important.'

'Piss off.'

He kicked out at her foot with his bare toes, misfired and caught them on the corner of the jamb. 'Shit.'

Jenny suppressed the urge to smile.

'Who is it, Ali?' The woman's voice called through from the back. Jenny saw her shape appear in the doorway at the far end of the hall, stick thin, a joint in her hand.

Ali, rubbing his stubbed toes on the back of his bare calf, said, 'Bitch here for you says she's the coroner.'

Jenny called through, 'I just need a few minutes, Mrs Wills. Sorry to disturb you at home.'

Simone disappeared for a moment, then came back down the hall minus whatever she had been smoking, stepping over the kids. She yelled at Ali, 'Get those two upstairs and changed.' He backed off, giving Jenny a look that said he wouldn't forget.

Simone stepped out on to the doorstep in bare feet beneath her frayed jeans saying, 'You can't come in now. It's a mess.' She glanced up and down the street, checking for who might be watching. She had dark rings around her eyes but still managed to be pretty, a vulnerable look about her. Built like a bird, the loose flap of skin showing over her belt the only sign she had borne six children. 'What do you want?'

'You heard Mr Marshall died shortly after the inquest?'

'Yeah. Can't say I'm that sad about it.'

Jenny watched her run nervy fingers through her hennaed hair. 'I picked up the answerphone messages you left him. Didn't he call you back?'

Simone shook her head. 'Didn't want to know me, did he? Before the inquest it was all promises, then nothing. I never even got to speak in court.'

'What would you have said?'

'Like I kept telling him – I phoned the centre the day Danny went down. I called five times to tell them he wasn't right. He'd never been inside before. I knew he couldn't take it.'

'That was in your statement, at least. Did Mr Marshall put it to the director when she gave evidence?'

'Yeah. She said she never knew about the calls, her secretary must have taken them.'

'Is that who you spoke to?'

'I guess.'

'Did she say that even if she had received your calls Danny wouldn't have been treated any differently?'

'Yeah. She was a bitch. A real hard fucking bitch.' Simone ran her eyes over Jenny's suit. 'Dressed like you. What do you want anyway?'

Jenny said, 'Would you like to talk somewhere more comfortable, Mrs Wills? I'll buy you coffee. Why don't you put on some shoes?'

Simone chose a coffee chain in the mall at Cribbs Causeway. Jenny followed her along the walkways and up escalators, thinking she could have found her way around the shopping centre blindfold. Simone looked at all the shop windows, checking out the new season's clothes in Next and some coloured plastic orbs in the Gadget Shop she said were the iPod speakers Ali wanted. He wasn't exactly her partner she said, more of a friend she was still getting to know, though she wasn't sure how much he liked kids.

Being in the mall seemed to relax her. Stopping to take in a display outside Knickerbox, she said she felt like a different person whenever she got away on her own – free.

Jenny bought them cappuccinos and muffins in Soho Coffee, a café decorated to look like it belonged in Manhattan. They sat opposite one another at a table beneath a poster of the Empire State Building, Simone sucking the froth off her coffee with a spoon.

She told Jenny that Danny was her oldest. His dad was a Trinidadian guy from St Pauls she went out with when she was fifteen. Getting pregnant was the reason she left home and went to live in a flat on her own. She'd tried to bring him up right, but different men kept letting her down, nothing in her life ever seemed to get set and Danny didn't cope well with change. He'd calmed down for a while when she got married to the father of her fourth, but Jason, her now ex-husband, got hooked on crack and was in and out of prison. With no man around, Danny fell in with boys on the estate who were always out thieving. By the time he was nine he was too strong for her to stop him going out of the door. Trapped at home with the young ones, what could she do?

Most of the times Danny went to court it was for stupid things. He wasn't a wicked boy, he was just out to impress the other kids. It was either that or get beaten up by them. His problem was he always got scared when he got arrested and would put his hand up to anything to get bail. The police took advantage: half his record was for things he hadn't done.

When the court tagged him, she remembered him starting to fret that the other kids were calling him gay for staying at home. He came back from school with a black eye and two cracked teeth and wouldn't leave his room all evening. That's when he cut off the tag. He was arrested next morning.

He was scared shitless spending a weekend in the police station – though he'd never admit it – but once he'd got bail he was OK again: a couple of nights inside had earned him respect. Simone had hoped the shock would bring him to his senses. Justin, his case worker from the Youth Offending Team, talked about community service or a supervision order, maybe spending Saturdays on a mechanics course, but the magistrates wanted him assessed for custody. Danny's brief said it was just to scare him. It worked – that's when the real change in him happened.

'What kind of change?'

'He went quiet, wouldn't talk to Ali or me, kept fighting with his younger brothers. He was smoking a lot, couldn't stop him, but I saw he'd been burning himself.'

'With cigarettes?'

'Yeah. Scabs all up the inside of his arms.'

'Did you speak to him about it?'

'I tried. He hit me. Never done that before. Ali weighed in and he smacked him, too. Nearly broke his nose. That was the night before he was sentenced – had to threaten him with the police to stop him breaking his curfew again. He was crazy, but I guess he was afraid.'

'Of what?'

Simone looked down at the table and pushed some spilled grains of sugar around with a teaspoon. 'What no one got was that Danny was just a little kid. He'd fight and curse, but I know all he wanted was for things to be right . . . And I never gave him that.' She lifted her dark green eyes. 'He knew he couldn't handle going away. The thought of it terrified him.'

'You were his mother, what did you think would happen to him?'

Simone drew a careful circle in the sugar. 'What would you think?'

'You were there in court when he was sentenced?'

'Course.' She set the spoon down on her saucer. 'But he never said a word to me. I tried to see him before they put him in the van, but they said I wasn't allowed.' She paused and rubbed her eyes with the heel of her palm. 'I knew there was something wrong with him. I knew he'd try to hurt himself . . . I just knew.'

Jenny handed her a clean napkin and waited while she blew her nose, thinking about the director of Portshead Farm, Elaine Lewis, telling her secretary she didn't take calls from mothers. She imagined an unmarried woman on the lower rungs of the corporate ladder, the secure training centre her testing ground: make it run under budget for two years, get promotion, then try to knock out a baby before the hormones dried up.

When Simone stopped sniffling Jenny asked whether she saw or spoke to Danny during his time at Portshead Farm.

'They wouldn't let me the first weekend, they said he was being assessed. So I fixed to go the next Saturday afternoon, the 14th. Justin said normally kids could make phone calls home, but getting a phone card was a privilege you had to earn – that's why Danny couldn't call that week.'

'So you had no contact at all?'

Simone shook her head.

'Did Danny know you were coming on the Saturday?'

'I don't know. No one could say . . . I don't think he'd've done it on the Friday night if he did know.'

'Why do you say that?'

She twisted the napkin in her fingers. 'It's a feeling. I can't explain it. Like he wouldn't have done it if he hadn't felt so alone.'

'A mother's instinct?'

'If you had kids you'd know what I mean.'

Jenny said, 'I have a teenage son,' but didn't add that he had chosen to live with his father.

Moving on, she asked when Mr Marshall had first got in contact. Simone said it was late Saturday morning, only about an hour after two policemen came to the house to tell her that Danny was dead. She couldn't remember much about it except that he'd said something about a post-mortem. She didn't get to see Danny's body at the hospital mortuary until Monday morning. They hadn't even dressed him in his own clothes: he was in the crappy blue tracksuit they must have given him at Portshead.

It was some time on the Tuesday when she met with Marshall in his office. He gave the impression he was very sorry, made her a cup of coffee himself and asked her lots of questions about Danny's past, how come he'd ended up in custody. Marshall said Portshead Farm should have taken very special care of a boy that young and he wouldn't rest until he knew every single detail of what had happened, from the moment he was sentenced until the moment he died.

'Did you meet with him again before the inquest?'

'No, but he called me several times, said he was making progress.'

'Did he give you any details?'

'He said it would all come out at the inquest. He promised me he'd get justice for Danny.'

'He used those words?'

'Yeah. "*I promise.*" And he said I could give evidence about the phone calls.'

'Then what?'

'You tell me. Didn't hear from him again.'

'Any idea why?'

Simone's gaze drifted off across the café to the shops beyond. 'The papers started writing things about me, said I was a bad mother. Reporters were phoning the house with all sorts of lies. One of them asked was it true Danny was a crack baby. Another one said I was lying about my age and I'd got pregnant with him when I was thirteen. They were just making it up.'

'When exactly did these calls start coming?'

'The middle of that week.'

'But Marshall wouldn't have known about them.'

Simone shrugged.

It made no sense. Why get enthused about a case, then back off so dramatically?

Jenny said, 'A journalist named Tara Collins called my office today. She seemed to be on your side.'

Simone lightened a little. 'She's OK. At least she came and talked to me.'

'She thinks the inquest left a lot of questions unanswered.'

'It was all over in a day and a half. Didn't answer anything.'

Jenny sat back in her chair and studied Simone's tired face, blotches showing under the harsh fluorescent light. A welfare-dependent, dope-smoking mother of six whose idea of a good time was a shopping mall. But something about this young woman had touched her. At the very least she deserved some closure, some peace of mind.

'Simone, I'd like you to think hard about this – do you think the jury were right to return a verdict of suicide?'

She looked puzzled by the question. 'What else would it have been?'

'You see, the job of the coroner is to determine the cause of death, and once a verdict has been given you need a very good reason, usually new evidence, to reopen a case. Even then you need the High Court's permission. If there was something badly wrong with the way Mr Marshall handled the case or if some important new facts turned up, of course I'd do everything I could.'

'So you're not going to do anything?'

'You told me you thought Danny killed himself. What else do you want to know?'

'Why he was left alone. Why they wouldn't let him talk to his mother. Why he was kept in a cell for three days with no clothes. Why they didn't listen to me when I told them what would happen . . .'

All perfectly good questions, which, Jenny didn't doubt, the transcript of the inquest would show Marshall had asked. She needed fresh evidence but had no excuse for spending time and money going to look for it. All she had was a bad smell and a local journalist in search of a story.

Jenny said, 'I'll tell you what I'll do. I'll go through Danny's file and make a list of every question that Mr Marshall should have asked but didn't. We'll take it from there.'

Simone gave her a look of weary indifference. She pushed up from the table. 'Whatever.'

Jenny wound down the car windows and let the warm wind blow through her hair as she crossed the bridge into Wales. Leaving the expanse of the estuary behind her and driving along the narrow road that snaked seven miles through the forested gorge from Chepstow to Tintern, she felt the rush of being enveloped by nature at its zenith. July and August were mellowing and fading months; June was the pinnacle of life. Through breaks in the trees she caught glimpses of the woodland canopy on the opposite side of the valley, an undulating sea of every shade of green.

Driving away from her responsibilities for the night, she felt light and liberated. Simone Wills and all the dead people were safely on the other side of three miles of water in another country. Another world.

Shutting the door at the end of the day was something she'd worked on with Dr Travis. He'd told her that, in common with so many women, she was a perfectionist who couldn't rest until everything around her was in order. When work was a daily round of chaos, loose ends and uncertainties, it was only a matter of time before a personality like hers would collapse under the pressure. He taught her techniques to help deal with professional guilt. She had learned to accept that she was neither indispensable nor responsible for the outcome of every case.

But despite all her efforts, the deep-seated unease that seeped up from her subconscious refused to vanish. Divorce hadn't cured her, nor had removing herself from the stress of family law. She could take away the anxiety with pills or retreat to lush countryside, but the root of her problem – though mostly buried – stuck fast.

Trying to concentrate on the moment as Dr Travis had taught her, she rounded the corner into Tintern to see the ruined abbey casting a majestic shadow over the meadow. Although only the shell of the building remained, its elegance and permanence, its resilience nearly five hundred years after Henry VIII sent his troops to destroy it, never failed to inspire her. Not even the tourist coaches and cars that swarmed around it on summer weekends could diminish its beauty. If it could endure against all the odds, so could she.

Taking in the view, the splendour of the landscape, its history and vitality, Jenny momentarily felt the kind of peace and lightness she remembered from her teens. A high no pills came close to giving.

She turned left at the Royal George Hotel and drove the final mile up the switchback single-track lane lined with ancient hedgerows to Melin Bach, Welsh for 'little mill', the two-bedroom stone cottage she had bought impulsively at auction and moved into only a fortnight ago. The previous owner was an eighty-five-year-old woman, Miss Preece, who had lived there all her life and who had changed little since her father died decades before.

The cottage was fronted by an overgrown garden in which hollyhocks, leggy lavender bushes and overgrown roses vied with the weeds and foot-high grass which she had yet to tackle. The low drystone wall which separated it from the lane was in need of repair, and her parking spot – the entrance to an old cart track which led round to the back – was so rutted and full of nettles that she could barely get across it in heels without twisting an ankle or being stung.

It was perfect. Untamed and full of possibilities.

At the rear of the house there was a quarter-acre of overgrown lawn, the remains of a vegetable garden and a roofless stone shed backing on to a brook which had once been the saw mill. Until the early 1950s, a neighbour had told her, Miss Preece's father had earned his living working a water wheel-driven bench saw, turning oak and beech butts from surrounding woodlands into roughly milled timber. Shire horses hauled in wagons along the track and drank from the stream. The iron rings where they were tethered could still be seen rusting in the crumbling mortar of the mill walls. Put a spade in the ground anywhere nearby and you'd turn up old horseshoes, some of them ten inches across.

Jenny's vision was to bring it back to what it once was. To tame the weeds, grow her own food and maybe rebuild the mill and water wheel to power the house. She already had a pile of books next to her bed with titles like *Living Off-Line* and *The Smallholder's Guide to Electrical Generation*. Once she had got the place straight, she saw herself living two distinct lives: one in the city, surrounded by people and their travails, and the other here, in peace and fruitful labour.

Whether she would ever share this life with anyone, what the ultimate point to it was, were issues for later. She was in recovery from a failed marriage and a crashed career and was trying to wean herself off medication. She would take it a step at a time, enjoy the achievements of each day and hold on to the belief that eventually the fragments of her life would rearrange themselves into a picture that made sense.

With these hopeful thoughts in mind, she turned a hefty iron key in the front door and stepped inside. A smell of wood ash from the grate greeted her and she felt the reassuring solidity of well-worn flagstones beneath her feet.

The interior of the cottage was compact, but the ceilings were high enough for a tall man not to have to stoop under the beams, and the windows were sufficiently wide to avoid it ever feeling gloomy. In the entrance hall was a narrow staircase leading up to the two bedrooms and bathroom. The former parlour, which she had already arranged as a study, was through a door to the left. To the right was a snug sitting room leading to the kitchen at the back, which still had a Belfast sink, solid pine cupboards and a coke-fired range. A washing machine crammed in by the back door was the only concession to modernity. Eventually she intended to knock the kitchen and sitting room into one and build a conservatory, but there was something pleasing about the quaintness of the current layout. Her ex-husband, an ambitious, intolerant heart surgeon, would have hated everything about it. An old, unruly, inconvenient house like this would represent the sum of all his fears. What's to admire about the past? he'd say. It stank, was full of disease and you were lucky to make forty.

David had always insisted on living in the suburbs in a modern home with a new car on the drive each year. His idea of heaven would be to live forever in a dust-free environment. Coming home to Melin Bach, Jenny couldn't understand how it had taken her sixteen years of marriage to realize that was her idea of hell.

She dropped her briefcase in the study, went upstairs to throw on jeans and an old shirt, then went in search of a glass of Rioja and the last of the evening sun.

She sat sipping her wine at the old scrub-top table she had dragged to the spot in the middle of the lawn from where you could see the sun set on Barbadoes Hill. She listened to the wood pigeons in the chestnut tree beside the mill and the sound of the brook chasing over the stones. She couldn't believe her luck. Less than three weeks ago home had been a rented apartment in a new-build near Aztec West on the fringes of Bristol.

She'd have to get Ross over to stay soon, when the spare room was straight. He'd love it here once he'd got used to the quiet. He was in the middle of his GCSEs so she hadn't seen much of him for a couple of weeks. After she split from his father Ross had been to stay a few weekends at her apartment but had got bored and they'd argued. That made up her mind to wait until summer before reviewing the situation. Once he saw Melin Bach she was sure he'd come and live with her while he was in the sixth form. She could drop him at college on her way into town and bring him home in the evenings. Unlike his father, she wouldn't mind if he brought girls back or drank the odd beer. They could relax here together, finally get to know each other.

Thinking about Ross gave her a tight knot in her stomach: a feeling of grief mixed with unrequited longing. She didn't normally call him on Mondays – Wednesdays and Fridays at eight were the usual times – but she couldn't wait that long. She wanted to tell him about her new job and how much she was looking forward to having him over. She didn't want to seem needy – he hated that – but he'd want to hear her good news.

The third glass of wine gave her the courage to fetch the phone and dial his mobile. It rang several times, then clicked to voicemail. Damn. She could try the landline but would probably get David and a slice of his heavy sarcasm.

What did it matter? She'd just give it back to him.

'Hello?' A cautious woman's voice she didn't recognize answered.

Assuming she'd misdialled, Jenny said, 'Oh . . . is Ross there?'

The voice said, 'I'll just go and see.' She sounded young, but older than a teenager.

Jenny listened to her set down the receiver and call out his name, not like a girlfriend would, but uncertainly. She heard David, a hurried conversation between them she couldn't make out, then his voice barking down the line.

'Jenny?'

'I was wanting to speak to Ross – his mobile's off.' She tried to sound calm.

'He's over at Max's. They're revising together, or so he claims.'

'OK. I'll try him again later.'

'You remember it's parents' evening on Wednesday? You are expected.' He spoke to her how she imagined he spoke to his subordinates in the operating theatre.

'I'll be there.' She couldn't resist: 'Who was that who answered the phone?'

A pause. 'Deborah. I don't think you've met. I'm sure you will.'

'She sounds very young. A nurse, is she?'

What else could she be? David hadn't had a life outside the Frenchay Hospital in nearly twenty years.

He sighed impatiently. 'I'm entitled to pursue my life and you yours. I expect I'll see you on Wednesday.'

'I took over as coroner today.'

'Excellent. I hope you make a success of it.'

She knew she shouldn't rise to it, but his patronizing tone made her want to kick him, hard. 'If I'm anywhere near as good at my job as you are at bedding young women, I expect I will.'

'Move on, Jenny.'

He hung up on her. His dismissal, as ever, absolute.

She threw down the phone, cursing him, her eyes filling with angry tears. She gulped down the rest of her wine, furious that he was still having this effect on her. She didn't even have feelings for him any more, apart from loathing.

'Hello there.'

She looked round to see an unfamiliar male figure coming up the cart track, knee deep in nettles.

'Mrs Cooper?'

'Yes.' She sniffed hurriedly and wiped her eyes. Shit. A visitor was all she needed.

He waded towards her. Somewhere in his upper thirties, his faded red shirt hung loose over his jeans. His face was weathered and unshaven, a man who worked outdoors.

'Steve Painter – I live over the hill, Catbrook way. Mike down at the Apple Tree said you might be looking for a bit of a gardener.'

'Oh? Who's Mike?'

He made it out of the undergrowth on to the unkempt grass and glanced around.

'He's who you go to to find out what you're doing. They talk faster than you can think round here.' He turned his gaze to her. He wasn't bad-looking close up. Flat stomach. Strong arms. 'It could certainly do with it. I'm not too expensive if you're interested. A day or so would deal with the worst of it.'

Jenny tried to work out what it was about the stranger that surprised her, and realized it was his voice. It had a touch of the local accent – a mixture of Welsh borders mixed with the more rustic Forest of Dean – but sounded educated. The way he looked at her, too: polite, but on her level.

'How much is not too expensive?'

'Nine quid an hour.'

'*Nine?*'

'Seven fifty.'

'All right. Deal. When do you want to start?'

'Tomorrow morning? Early?'

'OK. I'm afraid I haven't got much in the way of tools.'

'I can bring everything I need.'

'Great.' Jenny looked at him, wondering who this man was she had just agreed to employ. He could be anyone. She'd never even been to the Apple Tree. 'Have you got any references? Anyone I could call to vouch for you?'

He smiled and rubbed his head. His hair was sandy brown, bleached by the sun. 'Someone I haven't robbed? Let's see . . . You could try Mike.'

She picked up the phone. 'What's his number?'

He shrugged. 'Wouldn't know. I don't have one of those things.'

'No phone?'

'Nope. I try to live off my bit of land, mostly. It's OK till you need to pay the council tax or fancy a beer. I guess that makes me a hypocrite.'

'Sounds ambitious. What do you grow?'

'This and that. Hey, look – I didn't mean to disturb you. I'll see you in the morning.'

He turned to go.

'I'll probably be gone by quarter to eight.'

'That's fine. I won't expect a welcoming committee.'

He raised a dirt-brown hand in a lazy wave and drifted

back the way he had come, disappearing around the side of the house. Jenny heard an engine cough reluctantly into life. The vehicle sounded elderly. She caught a glimpse of it through a gap in the hedge as it moved off up the lane: an open-topped Land Rover with a keen-eyed sheepdog riding in the back.

She poured another glass of wine. Trying to make it last, she watched the sun go down and the ash trees stirring in the breeze. She thought about her new gardener over the hill. Why would an intelligent man live out in the woods without money or a telephone? What kind of woman would put up with him, no new clothes or gadgets in the house? She'd only lived in the country for fifteen days and had already learned two unexpected things: no matter how remote your home there was no such thing as privacy, and the people were more complex and interesting than she had imagined. Living with space around them, they seemed somehow freer to be themselves.

She had intended to be in bed with the lights out by ten-thirty, but by ten her head had started to clear and her thoughts were racing over the events of the day. With no prospect of being able to sleep without pills which would leave her groggy in the morning, she sat down in her study, switched on a bar of the electric fire and took both the Danny Wills and Katy Taylor files out of her briefcase.

Flicking once again through the pages of Danny's file, she began to understand how Marshall had embarked on a crusade, then gradually lost heart. From the case worker in the Youth Offending Team through to the director of Portshead Farm, everyone appeared to have done their job and ticked the right boxes. The fact that a disturbed fourteen-year-old boy had hanged himself while in state custody was shocking, but hard to pin on any one individual.

Jenny wanted to believe that had she conducted the inquest she would have rooted out some rotten management practices, but picking through the statements it was hard to see exactly where fault lay, except with a government that allowed a child to be imprisoned in the first place.

And Simone Wills had to take her share of the blame. How many times in his fourteen years had Danny felt she cared more about him than smoking a joint or knocking back a few more vodkas with her latest boyfriend? Maybe this had been Marshall's thought process, too? Setting out to make a noise, then realizing that the only person who could really have made a difference was a lost cause; that he could no sooner get justice for Danny than raise the dead.

At least the Katy Taylor file contained a genuine procedural irregularity she could correct. She would be considerate to her parents, but a full inquest would have to be held: modern coroners were obliged to act rigorously in the public not the family's interest.

For the second time that day she struggled through the original police report, written in tortuous longhand by a constable who knew neither punctuation nor where to place capitals. It mentioned that Katy was suspected by unnamed 'Local Youths' to have been paying for drugs through prostitution and that she had cautions for possession of marijuana and shoplifting. Nothing unusual about that, but the constable didn't seem to have investigated how she had ended up six miles from home with a syringe full of smack: most addicts would shoot up down the nearest alley. Plus her sandals had spiky heels – there was no way she could have arrived there on foot. Even the stupidest policeman must have suspected that someone had driven her to such a secluded spot.

The fact that the report was silent on this matter didn't altogether surprise her. The cash-strapped police were savvy enough to put their money wherever the media interest was. A dead celebrity in the bushes would have brought out the full forensic team; a clean-cut DI would have given hourly updates for the rolling news. A dead nobody whose parents were happy not to have their grief paraded on TV got an illiterate PC.

Still, it wasn't good enough. Jenny closed the file with a decision to find out who Katy had been with before she died. If the police didn't like it, tough.

She slept badly. Outside, a tawny owl competed with a vixen which screeched like a screaming baby. She dreamed she was in her childhood home, paralysed by furious shouting and the crashing of doors; in her dream she pushed her thumbs into her ears and pressed on her eyelids until she saw stars.

The nightmares rolled on through the restless small hours: she started awake as a faceless murderer unsheathed a knife and thrust it at her guts. Collapsing into the pillow, her heart thumping against her ribs, she looked over at the clock and saw it was nearly seven a.m. Slowly coming to, she became aware of a noise outside the window: metallic scraping.

She swung out of bed and anxiously hooked the corner of the blind back with her finger. Steve, his back to her, stood over by the cart track stroking a sickle with a sharpening stone. He tested the blade with his thumb and started into the weeds with big, relaxed strokes. Not a trace of tension in his frame.

FIVE

Thank God for temazepam. She arrived at the office to find Alison agitatedly directing removal men who had brought in half a dozen filing cabinets and were now filling the rest of reception with document boxes.

Jenny was barely through the door when Alison turned to her accusingly and said, 'I told you there was nowhere to put it all, Mrs Cooper.'

'We'll rent some storage and archive what we don't need.'

'And who's going to pay for that?'

'We managed to pay for an office at the police station.' She grabbed her mail from the tray on Alison's desk. 'Could we have a word?'

Alison hurled some instructions at the removers and followed Jenny into her office.

'The chief super was surprised that you were moving me, to say the least. We've always found it a mutually beneficial arrangement. My ex-colleagues are often helping out.'

'And what's in it for them?'

'Mr Marshall and I uncovered several murders over the years that would never have got to the police otherwise. There was a man who poisoned his wife with insulin, a girl who smothered her baby . . .'

Sorting her mail, Jenny said, 'The difference between the police and the coroner is that the police chase convictions, the coroner chases the truth. One doesn't necessarily follow from the other.'

'I was a detective for twenty years and I never saw a false conviction.'

'But did you always find the truth? And once you had a suspect, did you even want to find it?'

'You're not a fan of the police, Mrs Cooper?'

Jenny opened her briefcase and brought out the Katy Taylor file. She handed it to Alison. 'Did you read the constable's report before Mr Marshall signed the death certificate?'

'I usually do.'

'She was found six miles from home wearing high-heeled shoes. Why wasn't there a detailed search of the area? Why no forensics? Why no investigation into how she got there, who brought her, where the drugs came from? And if the police decided they had other priorities, why didn't Marshall ask those questions?'

'He'd have had his reasons.'

'You were working for him at the time; what do you think they were?'

Alison fingered the corner of the file. 'I didn't discuss the case with him in detail—'

'He must have said something.'

'Only that Dr Peterson was sure it was an overdose and that Detective Superintendent Swainton in CID was happy with that.'

'So he had a heads-together with the police?'

'He would have spoken to them, of course.'

'And if Swainton was content to mark it down as accidental that was good enough for him?'

'It wasn't like that. He had a very good relationship with the CID. They trusted each other.'

'I see.' Jenny was getting the picture: Marshall didn't tread on CID's toes and in return he got an ex-copper with an office at the station to do his legwork. 'In this case I'm afraid his trust wasn't justified. I'm revoking the death certificate and starting again, with a proper investigation this time.'

'What am I going to tell CID?'

'It's nothing to do with them.' She grabbed a legal pad and slotted it in her briefcase. 'I'm going to pay a few visits, talk to her family. You can stay and sort this place out. And expect a call from Josh at the Ministry of Justice.'

'Josh?'

'He's setting up our IT. We'll have a brand new wi-fi system up and running by the weekend.'

Jenny pushed out of the door before Alison could protest. She'd give her a week to see if she was capable of change. If not, she'd have to go.

The mortuary assistant said Dr Peterson was mid-autopsy and had another three to get through by lunch. If she needed to see him she'd have to talk to him from the viewing gallery while he worked. Jenny said fine, whatever it took to reach the great man. The assistant directed her to a door along the corridor.

She had expected something a little more removed from the action. The gallery was no more than a raised section of the autopsy room, divided from the dissection area by a waist-high wall. The smell was overpowering: blood, faeces, disinfectant and rot. Covering her mouth, she saw Peterson, no more than eight feet away from her, lifting the heart and lungs from the wide-open chest cavity of a grossly obese middle-aged man. She looked away, fighting the urge to gag as he dumped the organs on the stainless-steel counter directly beneath where she was standing.

'Twice in two days, Mrs Cooper? To what do I owe the pleasure?'

She breathed through her mouth, telling herself it was only

disinfectant and formaldehyde she was smelling, not decomposing flesh. 'I got your report yesterday. Thank you.'

'Don't think it'll happen every time.' He held a slice of lung up to the light. 'See that? Threaded through with lines of black soot. He wasn't even a smoker. That's atmospheric pollution – lived most of his life in London. Everyone in the south-east has lungs that look like they've been on thirty Bensons a day.'

Unable to help herself, she glanced over at the dark pink, spongy slab he was holding up for her benefit. Sure enough, the surface was speckled with tarry spots.

He slapped it on the counter and went back to work, slicing like a sous chef. 'Ever watched an autopsy before?'

'No.'

'If you feel the need to vomit there's a plastic bucket up there somewhere. And if you feel light-headed, make sure to sit down. I had a female student fall right over the front last month. Landed in a pile of sliced liver.'

'Thanks for the warning.'

'No problem.' He glanced up at her, eyes smiling over his mask.

Jenny swallowed against the nauseous sensation rising in her throat. She was coping mentally, but her body was desperate to leave. She'd have to get this over with quickly or take up the offer of the bucket. 'I'm here about Katy Taylor. I'll need a detailed statement from you.'

Moving on to the second lung, Peterson said, 'I gave my findings in my report.'

'It's not just your findings I want. I need to know what contact you had with Marshall and the police. How you were briefed, what was said. Anything at all you can remember.'

He carefully studied another section of lung, prised open the trachea with callipers and peered inside. 'To what end, exactly?'

'The death was hardly investigated, not in any meaningful sense. I'll be finding out why.'

Peterson placed the callipers in a kidney dish and rested both hands on the counter top. 'If you're implying that I've been involved in something improper, Mrs Cooper, I'd appreciate hearing it straight.'

'Until I've investigated I've no idea whether anyone acted improperly or not.' She sucked in another breath; she could even taste the air in here. 'But what I do know is that a fifteen-year-old girl died in circumstances which merited more than a two-page report from a constable and half a dozen lines from a pathologist four weeks after the event.'

'If I were you, I'd try the job on for size for a few weeks. You might find the system works better than you thought. Start throwing your weight around, you'll make enemies you never even dreamed of.'

'That's your philosophy, is it? Keep your head down and don't rock the boat.'

That smile behind the mask again. 'Tell you what, Jenny, why don't we start again? How about we meet up for a drink one night and I'll give you the benefit of my experience – off the record, of course.'

Jesus. It had only taken him two *days*.

'I'd rather you spent the time writing your statement.'

'And if I have nothing to say?'

'I won't believe you.'

She turned to the door.

Peterson said, 'Ever seen an aortic valve?'

She glanced back over her shoulder. He was holding a bloody heart in his hand. 'A flap of tissue not much thicker than your thumbnail. All it takes is for the tiniest piece of cholesterol to break free and jam it, you're dead.'

'Your point being?'

'Perhaps you should be a little more philosophical? Spend a few days down here and you'd come out with a whole different view of the world.'

'You're not kidding.'

Andy and Claire Taylor lived in a 1930s ex-council semi with a mock-Georgian front door and geraniums in hanging baskets either side of it. Their street was less than a mile from the estate Jenny had visited the day before, but the houses and public areas here were cared for. There were no truants on the street.

She found both parents at home. Andy, who was a clerk of works in a construction company, had taken a day's leave to go with Claire to the hospital that morning. She'd been off sick since Katy died. Her doctor said it was probably depression that was causing the crippling abdominal pains that kept her awake at night, but was sending her to have a barium meal to rule out a tumour.

All of this came spilling unprompted out of Andy, a stocky, hospitable man with kind, conscientious eyes. While Claire sat silently next to him on the sofa hugging a cardigan around her waist, he gabbled like a man who'd been rescued from a life raft after weeks adrift. Claire, with her hollow cheeks and pale, freckled skin, looked like she was still drowning, barely recognizable as the woman in the family photographs arranged on the mantelpiece.

When Andy eventually paused for breath, Jenny explained the reason for her visit. Mr Marshall had acted too hastily in signing a death certificate. She was investigating prior to holding a formal inquest into Katy's death.

Claire looked up and spoke for the first time since her mumbled hello. 'He told us there wouldn't have to be one.' She turned to Andy. 'Didn't he? When we went to his office.'

Andy reached for his wife's hand. 'Yes.'

Jenny adopted her best bedside manner. 'I'm afraid he was wrong about that. Obviously he was trying to avoid putting you through any more unpleasantness, but where there is any possibility that death wasn't due to natural causes, by law an inquest must be held.'

Andy said, 'What does that mean?'

Claire tugged her hand away from his and pulled the cardigan tighter around herself.

'I'm not for a moment suggesting that Katy's death was caused by anything other than an accidental overdose, but the circumstances were such that other possibilities have to be ruled out.'

Claire said, 'She didn't do it on purpose. I know she didn't. I told him.'

'Part of my task is to determine her state of mind. Whatever you have to say is important evidence.'

'Evidence? What are you talking about? Mr Marshall told us this was all done with. He phoned up and said so.'

'I'm sorry—'

'I'm not listening to this. We're not interested.'

'I appreciate how you must feel—'

'No, you don't. How could you? Will you please leave?'

Andy put a hand on Claire's shoulder. 'Love—'

'Get off me.' She pushed up from the sofa. 'I didn't ask for any of this. Why can't you just leave us alone?'

'Mrs Taylor—'

Claire hurried to the door, slammed out into the hallway and ran upstairs. Andy got up to go after her but gave up halfway across the room as a bedroom door crashed shut, shaking the whole house.

He turned, embarrassed. 'She's been like this ever since we lost Katy.'

'I understand.'

He sat back down on the sofa, out of words now, despair on his face.

'It would help me a lot if you could fill in some of the background, Mr Taylor.'

'What do you want to know?'

'As much as possible. I saw in the file that Katy had some criminal convictions in the last couple of years.'

He lowered his head. 'We moved here when she'd just turned thirteen – that's when it all kicked off. The kids she was hanging out with were all into drugs and stealing. We tried to keep her on the straight and narrow but every time we put our foot down she ran off. Don't know how many times we've had the police out looking for her.'

'Where did she go?'

'Off with friends. She'd never say who.'

'Male or female friends?'

Andy shook his head and looked up at the many photographs of his dead daughter on display. A slight and extremely pretty blonde girl with a knowing look in her eye. The latest photo, a school portrait, showed a beautiful young woman who would have turned heads everywhere she went. 'Some of them must have been boys, in the last year at least, because she got herself on the pill. Who they were, I couldn't say.'

'Did the police ask you about any of this? Speak to her friends, check her mobile phone?'

'They asked a few questions, but once they knew she'd injected they seemed to make up their minds it was an accident. They said it happens all the time.'

Jenny gave him a moment, then said, 'What do you think she was doing out in Bridge Valley by herself?'

'It doesn't take a lot of working out.'

Jenny recalled the police photograph of Katy's body, the

little top that stopped short of her navel, the tight jeans and high-heeled sandals. Slim, stunning, sexy and in need of a fix.

'You think she was selling herself to feed her habit?'

The muscles tensed in Andy's jaw. 'We never thought it had gone that far, but apparently friends of hers had seen her getting into cars . . . I know it sounds like we were bad parents, but you can't begin to understand how out of control she was. We tried locking her in her bedroom, but she jumped out of the window. She was wild. It was like she was possessed.'

'Who were these friends who saw her getting into cars?'

He seemed at a loss. 'Kids who hang out down by the rec – the police would tell you.'

Jenny could see from the set expression on his face that he was close to breaking down. She didn't want to make him suffer more than she had to, but couldn't leave without some information about the police investigation. 'Mr Taylor, do you remember the name of the police officer who liaised with you after her death?'

'I think it was PC Campbell, Helen Campbell – the same girl who arrested her before she went inside.'

'Inside?'

Andy, surprised, said, 'Yeah. She got three months for breaking a woman's nose. Robbing for drugs again.'

'Oh . . . For some reason I hadn't picked that up.'

'Back in February. That's the craziest thing about it. The people from the Youth Offending Team said once she was inside they'd get her clean. Get her off before she was hooked for good is what they promised. Two days before she was sentenced she went AWOL and turned up in a gutter somewhere. We were all night in the hospital, wondering if she was ever going to wake up.' His voice started to shake. 'When she did, she promised me, never again. But as soon as she was out . . .'

Jenny gave him a moment. 'Where did she spend her time in custody?'

'Up there by the Severn Bridge. Portshead Farm.'

'When did she get out?'

'My wife's birthday – 17 April.'

The filing cabinets were stacked two high against one wall, the archive boxes in neat piles next to them. A vase of flowers stood on the windowsill and there were fresh magazines on the coffee table. At least Alison was making an effort, even if there was no sign of her.

All the way back in the car Jenny had been making mental lists of witnesses she wanted to depose, questions that needing answering. Her mind was buzzing. She searched Alison's desk for a paper and pen and started to write it all down. The phone in her office rang. She dashed through, writing as she went, and snatched up the receiver, jamming it against her shoulder.

'Jenny Cooper.'

'Tara Collins, *Bristol Evening Post*. We spoke yesterday.'

Her heart sank. 'Yes?'

'You met with Mrs Wills yesterday.'

'I'm very busy right now. What is it that you want?'

'She got the impression that you weren't interested in her son's case.'

Jenny stopped writing and tried not to erupt. It was an effort. 'Then she's mistaken.'

'But you're not going to investigate?'

'Ms Collins, I have a job to do, so do you. I'm happy to talk to the press on issues of public interest, but I will not be making daily reports on my activities. If you'll excuse me—'

'If you're looking for new evidence, I can tell you where to start.'

Jenny sighed, a whisker away from losing her temper.

'Darren Hogg was the security guard responsible for monitoring the CCTV in both the male and female house units that night. He said in his statement that two cameras covering the corridor in the male unit had been out for a week and were waiting to be repaired. Marshall spoke to the repair company, who said the fault was only reported on the 14th, the morning Danny died.'

Jenny didn't remember seeing any such statement. She said, 'I told Mrs Wills I'll be reviewing the file in detail. Of course I'll look into any anomalies.'

'It won't be in the file – Marshall never took a statement from them. And another thing: Kevin Stewart, the care officer who says he reported Danny's toilet blocked the night before he died – he wasn't asked why he didn't move him to another room. There were two free in the male unit that night. When I spoke to Smirski, the maintenance guy who found him, he said he couldn't remember when Stewart reported it. Marshall didn't even call Smirski at the inquest.'

'When I've had a chance to look at the transcript—'

Tara Collins interrupted again. 'The point is, Mrs Cooper, a care officer was meant to look through the inspection hatch of each child's room every half-hour. Those allegedly broken cameras could have verified whether the inspections were made. If the blocked toilet was reported that morning, Smirski was being set up to find the body.'

Jenny knew where Collins was heading: a finding of death by neglect, a gross failure of the system to provide the basic care which would have prevented Danny's suicide. The kind of finding that would rock the Ministry of Justice and make her the most unpopular coroner in the country.

And all she'd wanted was a quiet life.

'I'll be honest with you, the reason I'm not letting this story go is that I met Danny Wills a couple of times when I was writing a piece on the Youth Offending Team. He was a bright kid. He'd come up with these phrases, like he described himself as a "lost soul". You got the feeling that with a bit of help he could have pulled himself clear. He was bright . . . Not very professional of me, but there you are.'

Jenny felt her hostility towards Tara Collins begin to subside. 'I've known a lot of kids like that myself. Look, I appreciate you bringing this to my attention. I'll look into it. I will.'

'Can I tell that to Mrs Wills?'

'I'd be grateful if you left it to me.'

Tara Collins was quiet for a moment, then said, 'I think it's only fair to let you know this, Mrs Cooper. I've received information that you haven't enjoyed the best of mental health recently.'

Jenny heard herself say, 'I beg your pardon?'

'It's one of those difficult judgement calls you have to make as a journalist – deciding where the public interest lies. Oh, well . . .'

The line went dead.

She couldn't believe it. Not even the Ministry of Justice knew she'd been seeing a psychiatrist. If it got out she'd not only lose her job, she'd risk prosecution for fraud. *Medical conditions that could affect your ability to carry out the office of coroner* – she remembered writing 'none', convincing herself that the lie was justified, that a new career was her passport to getting well.

'Everything all right, Mrs Cooper? You look a bit dazed.' Alison was standing in the doorway, studying her with a concerned expression.

Jenny replaced the receiver, trying to hide the fact that her heart was racing. 'That journalist again. Did they bother Mr Marshall much?'

'He'd never speak to them. Called them parasites.'

'I think I agree.' Jenny needed a temazepam, now, and wished Alison would go so she could take one.

'I hope you don't mind – I probably missed Josh's call. I've been at the station.'

'Right.' Jenny masked the anxiety beginning to grip her with a smile. She glanced at her watch. 'I'm just going out to grab some lunch. How about we get together at one-thirty and go through what happens next?' She reached for her handbag.

'Before you go – I had a chat with one of my former colleagues in the CID about Katy Taylor.'

Shit. There was nothing for it. 'Yes?' Jenny reached non-chalantly into her bag and took out a small bottle of Evian and her pills, careful to keep her hand over the label while she unscrewed the container. She saw Alison observing her in the way of a police officer, her eyes fixed on her face, watching her hands with peripheral vision.

'He wasn't very happy about the investigation either. It certainly looked like she might have been with someone when she died, but there was no evidence of force or assault, and the fact that she was already using meant that proving her death wasn't an accident was going to be virtually impossible. If there was even a hint of a struggle it would have been a different story.'

Jenny swallowed a pill with a mouthful of water, sure that Alison had noticed the tremor in her hands. 'What does this detective think should have been done?'

'For one thing they had evidence she was on the game, so any punters she'd been with could have been nicked for sex with a minor. Then there was the fact that there was no spoon, lighter or ligature found with the body – all things that might have had someone's dabs on them. All they found was a syringe with her prints on it.'

'So we're pretty sure she wasn't alone?'

'The scene could have been disturbed by someone after she died and before the body was discovered, but my friend's pretty sure there was a man involved. Who knows, he could even have been a dealer who traded her drugs for sex – out-of-the-way place like that.'

Jenny felt the temazepam seep into her system and her heart start to slow. Her rational mind began to regain control. 'Suspected underage sex, possible manslaughter. What more does it take to get an investigation going?'

'It's still technically an open file.'

'Meaning?'

'They'll investigate further if evidence comes to light, but no one's being paid to go looking for it.'

Jenny said, 'I met her parents this morning. I don't get the feeling they'd have put any pressure on for a big investigation. The way Katy had been going for the last couple of years, I think they were half expecting it.'

'I heard she'd been inside for a few months. Same place as Danny Wills, wasn't it?'

'Not that much of a coincidence, considering it's the only secure training centre this side of the city.'

'Still,' Alison said, 'makes you wonder.'

They exchanged a look.

'I know. But what, exactly?'

Alison shrugged. 'Drugs, pimps, gangs . . . All the scum that prey on kids like that. They were both from the same part of town – you can bet there's some connection.'

'And it was Detective Superintendent Swainton who made the decision not to look further?'

Alison nodded.

'And it was purely about resources?'

'That would be the obvious reason.'

She was clearly insinuating something that Jenny was meant

to get, but didn't. Another police trait: assuming other people thought as deviously as you did.

'Could there be any other?'

'Not that I can think of. Unless he was afraid of upsetting another investigation . . . or if he'd been sat on for some reason.'

'Why would anyone have sat on him?'

Alison shifted uncomfortably from one foot to another. 'If the person she was with was an important informer, for example, or someone prominent.'

'Is that what you've been told? Don't tell me she was having sex with an MP.'

'No. No one's said anything like that, apart from the idle gossip that goes round. He probably had more work on than his officers could cope with.'

Jenny could see the conflict in her, the loyal detective versus the decent, homely woman as troubled by Katy Taylor's solitary death and the inadequate police response as she was. Alison probably had children, most likely grown up by now, but their teens can't have been that long ago. Another thought struck her: yesterday Alison had defended the sainted Marshall to the hilt, now she was intimating that he'd been part of something shady. It would have taken more than idle gossip to knock him off his pedestal.

'Then I suppose,' Jenny said, 'that if for whatever reason the police didn't go after whoever was with Katy, Mr Marshall must have been persuaded to do the same?'

Alison stood very still, then, without warning, her eyes filled with tears. Holding herself rigid, she said, 'I loved Harry Marshall, Mrs Cooper, not as a lover, but for three years he was the best friend I'd ever had. Something happened to him in those final weeks . . . He was in a fury over the Danny Wills case. I'd never seen him like it. He said he was going to shake the citadel to its foundations. But when I came back from leave he was so depressed he'd hardly speak to me.' She paused, collecting herself. 'Then on the Thursday night the phone rang at home. I answered, but the caller hung up. I checked – it was Harry's home number. He never called me from home. I should have phoned back, but I didn't like to – it was nearly midnight ... And the next morning, he was dead.'

The floodgates finally opened. Jenny guided Alison to a chair and handed her tissues as six weeks of silent suffering gave way to wails of grief.

SIX

DRIVING HOME AT THE END of only the second day of her new career Jenny felt the first twinges of nostalgia for family law. Courts were traumatic but had the virtue of being impersonal. Her relationship with Alison was already becoming uncomfortably intimate. And while she was watching her officer weep for her lover who never was, she had realized that there was now no question of replacing her, at least not in the short term. Not only had she inherited a tangled mess of dubious cases, it was left to her to deal with the emotional fallout.

The story of her life: everybody's needs before her own. Surrounded by powerful personalities – her parents, her husband, numerous bosses and judges over the years – the real Jenny Cooper had yet to step forward. Forty-two years old and still no territory to call her own.

The train of self-pitying thoughts persisted all the way home and she pulled up to Melin Bach with a dull headache and a nagging anxiety which would only be cured by a large glass of wine. She was almost at the front door before she realized that the front garden was transformed. The weeds had gone, the grass was mown and the foxgloves and hollyhocks either side of the porch now stood in freshly dug borders. Lavender and peonies she hadn't known were there had emerged from the jungle. She dropped her briefcase and wandered around to the back along the cart track, now tamed and tidy, and found a lawn, a little rough but mown in stripes, stretching from the back of the house to the stream. A path of evenly spaced flagstones set into the turf had been uncovered, leading from the kitchen door to the stream's edge; and by the stone wall bordering the field going downhill to the left of the house, rosemary, sage and thyme bushes had emerged from a thicket of briars and nettles.

She stood for a long moment and took in her new domain, now seeing it as a working place where generations of women had walked the path to the stream in all weathers to fetch water and wash clothes, and with callused hands had gathered herbs on summer evenings like this. She pictured a mother standing with an aching back and heavy woollen skirts thinking of the freedom she might have enjoyed a distant twenty miles away in the city, never imagining that her homestead would one day be a refuge for a woman who had been given freedoms she could never have dreamed of.

On the scrub-top table was a note weighed down by a rusty horseshoe. It read: 'Got a bit carried away and worked till seven. Hope it doesn't look too drastic. Steve.' Too coy to mention payment, but he was letting her know that he'd worked more hours than she'd left money for. She had cash in her purse but he hadn't left his address. 'Catbrook way' was all he'd said, and no telephone.

Why not see if she could find him? It was a nice evening and she had yet to explore the tangle of lanes which wound through the woods on the west side of the valley. It would be an adventure. She decided to leave the wine until later and keep good relations with the gardener.

She put on a white linen blouse with her jeans and faded blue canvas trainers, checking in the bedroom mirror that she didn't look too citified. She changed her mind about the trainers three times before settling on a pair of Caterpillar work boots she'd bought before the move, picturing herself digging vegetables and chopping logs. They were pristine, straight out of the box, but the solid weight of them on her feet felt right, grounded. As a final touch, she bunched her hair in a black elastic. She checked her reflection: rural but businesslike, not trying to look sexy but still feminine. No less self-conscious now than when she was sixteen.

She drove off up the hill, the single-track lane following the stream up the steep-sided valley lined with dense oak and beech. Here and there she passed cottages set in small clearings at the side of the road, but none scruffy or bohemian enough to belong to a thirty-five-year-old backwoodsman. She spotted several rough tracks that looked like they might lead to dwellings deeper in the woods, but all too rutted to risk negotiating in her Golf. Emerging at the other side of the small forest she circled back across the reed- and gorse-strewn heath and trawled the rectangle of lanes around the hamlets of Whitelye and Botany Bay: she was only three miles from home as the crow flies but had travelled nearly fifteen.

She considered knocking on someone's door to ask for directions, and even pulled up outside a ramshackle-looking farmstead with a sign advertising eggs and local honey, but was gripped by a shyness which prevented her from stepping out of the car. It was the same affliction that since her 'episode' had often seized her before going to a dinner or cocktail party: a dread not of meeting other people, but provoked by the thought of doing so. When it struck, without a drink or a pill, she couldn't get outside of herself. Even the most insignificant of small talk became an ordeal; when she spoke her own voice would echo in her head as if she was hearing herself from a great distance, her cheeks would burn, her diaphragm tighten and her heart pound. With Dr Travis's help she had learned to control these symptoms by consciously relaxing, but it was the fact that the simplest of encounters could prove so difficult which infuriated her. It made her feel so foolish, such a child.

Angry with herself, she started off down the lane back towards the north end of Tintern. As her self-critical thoughts escalated into a torrent of rage she picked up speed. With the high hedges and verges bursting with waist-high grass and cow parsley, the chances of seeing oncoming traffic were zero. It was an old Ford tractor towing a load of freshly cut silage that met her coming around a hairpin. The tractor driver saw her first and pulled sharply into the gateway of a field. Jenny rounded the bend and was faced with an implausibly narrow gap between the hedge and the trailer. Instinct took over. She jerked the wheel sharp left, smacked her wing mirror on the trailer as she skimmed by with inches to spare and fish-tailed to a halt, her left wheels jammed in a ditch hidden by the long grass on the verge.

She sat, dazed for a moment, aware that the car was leaning and stuck. There was a knock on the driver's window. She turned, startled, to see a ruddy-faced old farmer smiling in at her, several of his teeth missing. She lowered the window.

'In a hurry, were you, love?'

'I'm sorry—'

'Lucky I saw you coming.'

'I don't know what happened. I must have been miles away.' She felt a sudden urge to cry but fought hard against it. 'Is your trailer all right?'

'He's fine.' The old boy glanced over her car. 'Looks like you might have got away with it, too. I've got a rope in the back – I'll tug you out.'

'I'm so sorry . . .'

The farmer grinned, only four brown teeth in the whole of his mouth. 'You're Mrs Cooper, aren't you? I've heard you're one to look out for. Still, you won't be doing that again, eh?'

Fifteen minutes later and having suffered no more than a broken mirror and wounded pride, Jenny drove carefully up the track lined with silver birch leading to Ty Argel, where, the good-natured farmer had assured her, she would find Steve 'still skulking in the woods'. She rounded a bend and pulled up outside a small farmhouse. There was a dirt yard in front in which stood his elderly Land Rover, assorted tools, building materials and a handful of chickens. Jenny climbed out, glad of her boots, and was met by an exuberant sheepdog running towards her, barking loudly. Dogs were one thing Jenny wasn't frightened by. Her grandparents had owned three of them. Patting her thighs, she said, 'Come on, then. There's a good girl.' The dog, sensing a friend, jumped up and planted two dirty paws on her shirt. Jenny pushed her down and ruffled the fur on her head, making the kind of baby noises all dogs love.

'He's a boy. Alfie.' Steve appeared from the stone barn at the far side of the yard, an axe in his hand. He dropped his roll-up and ground it underfoot as he walked over.

'He's very friendly.'

Alfie rolled on his back, feet in the air. A sign of complete trust.

'Unless you're the postman. Can't stand anyone official, can you, Alf? Just like his owner.' Steve crouched down and joined Jenny in stroking the dog's belly. He was in bliss.

Steve glanced at her boots. 'Come dressed for work, I see? I've got five ton of logs in there need splitting.'

Jenny smiled, noticing his smell: sweat and rolling tobacco, strong but not offensive. 'I figured I owed you some overtime. The garden looks great, by the way.'

'You should have seen it years ago when Joan Preece was still fit. It was beautiful, but sort of natural.'

'Hopefully it will be again.'

'The thing about gardens, they take a lot of attention. Don't touch them for weeks at a time they get resentful.'

Jenny pulled some notes out of her jeans pocket. 'I'm sure I'll need some regular help, if you're interested.'

'Sounds dangerously like a job to me.'

'I'll leave it up to you.' She offered the money.

He stood up from stroking the dog. 'If you're sure?'

'I didn't come all the way over here and drive into a ditch to stroke your dog, nice as he is.'

Steve smiled and stuffed the money into his hip pocket. 'Cheers.' He ran his eyes over the Golf, scratches all along the nearside. 'I can see you've been giving the hedge a trim. What happened?'

'Nearly ran into a tractor up the lane. Luckily he was decent about it and towed me out of the ditch.'

'Wasn't an old lad with no teeth?'

'Could be. Said his name was Rhodri something.'

'Glendower. That's him. Keep your doors shut tonight – he's got a real thing for the ladies.'

'I could hardly contain myself.'

'Since his wife died he's had most of the women up this valley. Promises them all half his farm.' He smiled. 'Let me get you a beer. I'll show you round.'

He fetched two bottles from the pantry – he didn't have a fridge, he said – and gave her a tour of the homestead. It comprised twelve acres of mostly coppiced woodland in which he cut logs and grew a variety of trees which he sold to a commercial nursery. At the back of the house was a vegetable garden where he raised produce which he supplied to local shops. He didn't offer to show Jenny inside, saying he was still working on the house, but from the glimpses she caught through the downstairs windows she saw a tidy but stark interior: solid floors and wooden furniture he might have made himself.

Leading her between the rows of produce, he rolled another cigarette – somewhat guiltily, she noticed, hiding from her whatever he had in his tobacco tin – and told her about some of the local characters. There was Dick Howell, an alcoholic accountant who lost his job, his wife, then took to living in the back of his estate car while he drank what was left of the money he had stolen from his clients. He'd camped out in Steve's barn for a while, then went to live with a woman old enough to be his mother. And there was Andy the carpenter, a young guy who went to do a job for a couple who had just moved down from London and never left; two years later the three of them were still sharing the same house. Some nights they'd all come to the pub together.

Listening to him talk, she found herself weighing him like a lawyer would a witness, thinking, was his calmness genuine or did it come from what he smoked?

She said, 'So what's your story?'

Steve stopped by the crooked wooden gate leading from the vegetable garden to the yard and took a slow pull on his beer. 'It's not the life I planned, that's for sure.'

Jenny leaned back against the fence. 'And what was that?'

'I was at architectural college in Bristol. Bought this place in my fourth year with money my dad left me. Had big plans for it. Then I met a girl . . .' He set his bottle on the gatepost and started to roll a third cigarette, a pained expression on his face. 'She was an art student. Talented, but mad. We fell in love, moved out here and fought like hell.' He broke off to strike a match and took a deep draw. 'Couple of years of that and I'd sort of let the studying go. She got high and threw herself in the river a couple of times, then took off with some bloke she met in rehab in Cardiff. Last I heard she was out in Thailand or somewhere.'

'What was her name?'

'Sarah Jane. Sounds innocent, doesn't it? He tugged his T-shirt down across his left shoulder revealing a jagged scar that ran almost to his neck. 'Did that with the kitchen knife. Could've killed me. Had the best sex ever the next day.'

Jenny tried to hide her embarrassment. 'How long were you with her?'

'Five years. And I've had another five here on my own since. Quiet sometimes, but at least there's no one trying to kill me.' He spotted Alfie stalking a chicken in the yard and called out to him to leave it alone. The sheepdog scuttled away. 'You got me sounding sorry for myself, now – it's not like that. Life's good.'

'You'd be the envy of a lot of people.' She swallowed the last of her beer. 'Thanks for the drink. If you fancy more work you know where I am.'

He lifted the gate, sagging on its hinge, and let her through into the yard. As she headed back to her car, feeling light-headed from the beer and wondering whether she was safe to drive, he called after her, 'I'll see you next Tuesday.'

Jenny got to the office the next morning with the aid of only one temazepam, determined to put her relationship with Alison on a professional footing. Having slept on it, she could see two distinct explanations for Marshall's failure to hold an inquest for Katy Taylor and his lack of passion in conducting the inquest into Danny Wills's death. Either improper pressure had been brought to bear on him, which like all conspiracy theories, was unlikely, or else there was a far more human and personal reason. Having suffered the ravages of a minor emotional collapse, she had an all too vivid insight into what a major one might be like. Marshall's behaviour during his final few weeks bore all the hallmarks. A man struggling with depression would be moody and listless; the Danny Wills investigation might have caused him to rally briefly, only for the clouds to gather again once he realized the futility of his task. By the time Katy Taylor's file landed on his desk he had probably lost all will. Slumped in despair after twenty years of processing the dead, there would have seemed little point in mounting yet another inquest in which the outcome – accidental death – was a foregone conclusion.

Clipping up to the front door in a new pair of heels, this straightforward conclusion felt liberating. She would hold an inquest into Katy's death and properly explore the possibility of suicide or homicide, politely but firmly calling on the relevant police officers to account for their actions. Meanwhile, she would review the evidence in Danny Wills's case and come to a conclusion as to whether the drastic step of seeking leave from the High Court to conduct a fresh inquest was justified. Both courses of action were entirely proper, uncontroversial and exactly what the Ministry of Justice would expect of a diligent new coroner. She filed all paranoid thoughts of dark forces away and went to work feeling a good deal saner.

She entered reception to find Alison hovering by her desk. Jenny glanced at her watch. It was only eight-thirty.

'Good morning, Alison. You're early.'

Alison's eyes flicked apprehensively towards Jenny's office. 'Mr Grantham's here to see you. I told him to wait inside. It's still a bit of a mess out here.'

'Grantham?'

'From the local authority. Head of legal services.'

'Oh, OK.' She vaguely recalled the name from one of her interviews and wondered what he could want. All meaningful control over the coroner's office, and there was not a lot of it, was exercised by the Ministry of Justice. 'Are we expecting him?'

Before her officer could answer, a stocky man somewhere in upper middle age emerged from the inner office. He was dressed in a blazer and grey flannels and wore what Jenny assumed was a golf club tie. He hoisted his heavy cheeks into an insincere smile.

'Mrs Cooper, good to see you again.' He extended a plump hand, which she felt obliged to shake. 'Thank you, Alison.'

Turning to Jenny, Grantham said, 'I won't keep you a moment. I know how busy you must be.'

'Yes,' Jenny said, doing a bad job of hiding her irritation.

'Shall we?' He gestured towards her office as if it were his own.

Jenny turned to Alison. 'Bring me through any overnight reports, would you?'

'Will do, Mrs Cooper.'

Taking her time, Jenny stepped into the room ahead of Grantham and gestured him to one of the two visitor's chairs while she stood behind her desk and proceeded to unload papers from her briefcase.

'What can I do for you, Mr Grantham?'

'A good job, I hope. I was on your interview panel.' He remained standing, still vying for dominance.

'I remember.'

'It was a close-run thing. Several very good candidates.'

Not reacting, she calmly placed her briefcase on the floor, sat down in her much bigger chair and looked up at her unwelcome guest with a professional smile.

Grantham tugged the thighs of his trousers up an inch and took a seat, his eyes travelling around the room. They settled on a vase of dahlias Alison had placed on the windowsill. 'I can see the woman's touch.' He seemed to find the thought of a female coroner amusing. 'And you're making yourself very busy already, I hear.'

'That's what I promised to do.'

'Of course. But, how shall I put this? . . . I'm sure none of us would want this office to get a reputation for upsetting people unnecessarily.'

She looked at him quizzically. 'What are you referring to, exactly?'

'I know you're only just getting your feet under the table, but we do try to keep the various public services in our district working in harmony.'

'I'm afraid I'm not following.'

'I hear you've been talking to Dr Peterson at the Vale.'

'Yes.'

'Like I said, Mrs Cooper, in Severn Vale all our public services are encouraged to support each other. That's our ethos, and it works very well.'

'It certainly wasn't working for this office. My predecessor was routinely waiting three or four weeks for post-mortem reports. Obviously death certificates couldn't wait that long to be signed, so he was forced to act improperly, in a way, in fact, which could result in a coroner being summarily removed from office.'

She observed Grantham suck in his cheeks a little, resenting being lectured but without a ready response.

'Coroners are under so much pressure to investigate every unnatural death thoroughly, we simply can't afford to cut corners.' She went in for the kill. 'But quite frankly, I can't see that my discussions with the pathology department at the Vale are any of your concern.'

'My department pays for the coroner. It's everything to do with me.'

'I think you'll find the law is against you on that.'

'I'm trying to be polite, Mrs Cooper, but the fact is each department relies on the cooperation of every other. If you have a problem I will happily help guide you to the appropriate channels. That's what I'm here for.'

'If you can help get post-mortem reports to me on time I would be more than grateful.'

'I'll have a word.'

'Thank you.'

'There is just one other matter—'

They were interrupted by a knock at the door. Alison came in with a sheaf of overnight reports, placed them on the desk and retreated. Jenny picked them up and skimmed through, giving Grantham only half her attention.

'I understand from Alison that you're planning to hold an inquest into the death of that young addict?'

'Katy Taylor . . . Yes. There should have been one a month ago.'

'I'm not here to tell you how to do your job, but really, is this strictly necessary? From what I heard, the family aren't asking for it, and you know what a meal the press make of these things.'

'It's absolutely necessary. Why else would I be doing it?'

Grantham sighed and knitted his fingers together. 'Then I'll leave you with something to think about. Harry Marshall was a good friend of mine, a very good friend. He never held an inquest when he didn't have to. And in all the years he ran this office we never had a single complaint.'

He heaved himself up from his chair, wished her good day and let himself out. She heard him saying a friendly goodbye to Alison and her replying with a, 'Goodbye, Frank.' Jenny waited until he had exited into the hall, then went out to confront her.

'Did you know he was coming?'

'He phoned me last night and said he would be.'

'And you didn't call me?'

'It was after nine.'

'How did the Katy Taylor inquest come up in conversation?'

'He asked me about it. He must have picked up the gossip from the station.'

'And you didn't think to clear it with me before telling him my business?'

'He is the boss.'

Jenny took a deep breath. 'Wrong. We answer to the Ministry of Justice, not to him. Understood?'

Alison gave an uncertain nod.

'And while we're on the subject, maybe you can tell me about this informal network of public servants who seem to be trying to make each other's lives as easy as possible.'

'It's just that everyone knows everyone. And Frank Grantham's very well connected. He's on a lot of committees.'

'Masons, Rotary . . .'

'That sort of thing.'

'And he's frightened of me upsetting his friends in the police by holding an inquest which might show them up?'

'I wouldn't know.'

'Alison,' Jenny said, 'when you said that Detective Superintendent Swainton might have been sat on, who were you thinking of?'

'No one in particular . . . just someone more senior.'

'Are you and Grantham friends?'

'Not particularly . . . I know his wife, though. We play golf sometimes.'

'And where does Dr Peterson fit into the social scene?'

'I think he and Harry might have been on the same charity committee, raising money for cancer research. I know Frank does a lot of that sort of thing, too.'

It was all becoming clear. Severn Vale District might take in a large slice of north Bristol, but it ran like a small country town. Doctors, policemen, civil servants, the coroner all woven into the same fabric. Very useful if your face fitted, but also adept at covering up friends' mistakes. Jenny felt the certainty with which she entered the office twenty minutes earlier slipping away. Suddenly anything seemed possible, no scenario too far-fetched. It wasn't implausible to conceive of Katy Taylor being hired for sex by a local Establishment man, or Marshall being leaned on to save the reputation of Portshead Farm Secure Training Centre. Jenny wanted no part of it; more than that, if such a sleazy system existed, she wanted it exposed and dealt with.

'OK. I'm going to open the Katy Taylor inquest tomorrow morning.'

'Tomorrow?' Alison sounded shocked.

'Before our witnesses have a chance to get their stories straight. I want summonses issued this morning to Dr Peterson, the investigating officers and whoever was handling her parole at the Youth Offending Team.'

'What about the family? Shouldn't we give them more notice?'

'I'll deal with them.' Jenny marched towards her office.

'Mrs Cooper?'

She wheeled round. 'Yes?'

'Where are you planning to hold it?'

She stalled for a moment. The question was obvious, yet it hadn't occurred to her. Severn Vale was one of the majority of coronial districts which didn't have a dedicated courtroom; coroners had to book venues when needed. Some of her colleagues were still forced to hold court in the function rooms of leisure centres and church halls, slotting in between kids' birthday parties and quiz nights. The only legal restriction was an ancient prohibition on holding inquests in public houses.

'Where did Marshall hold his inquests?'

'Usually in the old county court, but it's just been sold for flats.'

'What do you suggest?'

'We used Ternbury village hall occasionally. It's cheap.'

'A village hall? Is that the best we can do?'

'At a day's notice? There's an upstairs room in my local Indian.'

It took Jenny a moment to realize that Alison was being sarcastic. 'Fine. We'll go with the village hall.'

The rest of the morning was spent dealing with the overnight death reports. A Polish lorry driver had crashed into a bridge on the M4, having apparently fallen asleep at the wheel. It took an hour to track down and inform the appropriate authorities in Gdansk, and shortly afterwards Jenny received a call from a hysterical woman she presumed to be the widow who couldn't speak a word of English. She wept incoherently on the line for more than fifteen minutes while Alison tried and failed to locate a translator. Next was a four-year-old girl who had died at home from advanced leukaemia. The GP was prepared to sign a death certificate but the parents were insisting on a post-mortem, convinced their child had been contaminated by radiation from the nearby decommissioned Berkeley power station. Jenny granted them their wish, if only to give them peace of mind.

Her afternoon was largely taken up with calls to bemused consultants at the Vale explaining that she wouldn't be writing death certificates for their recently deceased patients until she had received written post-mortem reports. After eight such encounters she received an angry call from a senior manager, Michael Summers, who complained that their mortuary was already full to overflowing. Jenny told him that hiring a secretary for the pathology department would be far cheaper and more environmentally friendly than a fleet of refrigeration lorries.

At five-thirty, just when she thought she could turn to planning tomorrow's inquest, Alison arrived with six more death reports, all of them old people who had died in nursing homes that day. Alison was puzzled by them. Ninety-nine out of a hundred such deaths were attributed to natural causes and had certificates signed by GPs. Mr Marshall had hardly ever got reports like this. Jenny asked Alison to phone round the coroners in the four districts neighbouring hers and her suspicions were confirmed: only she had been hit by this new phenomenon. Further enquiries revealed that an email had been sent to local surgeries from the Severn Vale Primary Care Trust recommending that all but the most mundane deaths be referred to the coroner. After only three days in post, her enemies were organizing to bury her in paperwork.

Grantham's visit and subsequent interference had stirred up her anger, the one emotion powerful enough to displace her anxiety. She responded by firing off an email to all local doctors, informing them that they would shortly be required to submit details of all recorded deaths to her office electronically, and to ignore the trust's recent instruction. She was damned if a puffed-up petty bureaucrat was going to frustrate her work. Jenny flicked through her copy of Jervis and read up on the common law offence of obstructing a coroner: if he tried anything else she could have him arrested.

It was gone eight by the time she found a parking space near to Ross's school and arrived, perspiring, outside the gymnasium where the parents' evening was being held. The temazepam she had taken mid-afternoon was wearing off and her heart was galloping. She pushed her way through a stream of parents flowing in the opposite direction and made it to the doors as her ex-husband came out. Forty-six now, but still thirty inches around the waist and good-looking, almost unfairly so, he was wearing one his most expensive bespoke suits, determined, as always, to let the other parents know that his son wasn't attending a comprehensive school for want of money.

David looked at her in the pitying way he had perfected in the early years of their marriage. 'Prompt as usual.'

'It's only just gone eight.'

'Our appointments were at seven-thirty. I emailed you last week.'

'Oh. Did you?'

'You didn't miss anything. These clowns wouldn't know potential if it ran up and bit them on the backside.'

'What did they say?'

'Does it matter? You know my views on this place.'

'He's in the middle of exams.'

'According to his teachers he'll be lucky to pass any of them.'

'Why haven't you told me any of this? You must have known there was a problem.'

'You had enough of your own. I didn't want to add to your burden.'

'Well, what does Ross say?'

'Very little. He usually just grunts and disappears upstairs, plugged into something.'

'You live under the same roof, you must have some idea what's going on.'

'I'm afraid I don't have your powers of insight.'

Jenny felt her throat tighten. 'Look, I didn't come here for an argument, David. I'm sorry I was late, but it sounds like it's Ross I should be talking to, not his teachers.'

'Then why don't you come over for lunch on Saturday?'

'To your place?'

'It is his home. If you can bear it, I thought we might put

on a united front, try to talk to him like responsible parents for once.'

Resisting the urge to call him a spiteful prick, Jenny said, 'If you think it'll help. Will *she* be there?'

'Deborah and I are together. If you've got a particular objection—'

'Whatever. As long as Ross is all right with her.'

'They get on rather well, actually.'

'Pretty, is she?'

David gave a look that said he wasn't going to dignify that with an answer. 'Shall we say one o'clock?'

'Fine.' She felt a stab of guilt at her cheap shot. 'Sorry.'

There was an uncomfortable pause.

David said, 'Quite a job you've landed yourself. How did you wangle that?'

'I'd like to think I was the best candidate.'

'Don't let it get on top of you, will you? Ross is probably going to need you in the next few years.'

'I've every intention of being there for him.'

'Good.' He nodded abruptly and strode off. Jenny stood and watched him. Even the way he walked was arrogant.

No wonder she had fallen off the edge.

SEVEN

TERNBURY WAS NO MORE THAN a large cluster of houses set amid fields of rape and barley seven miles north-east of Bristol. The village hall was a glorified tin shack that stood at the edge of the green. Decorated with faded bunting and a banner proclaiming the forthcoming village fête, it was about as far removed from a seat of justice as any building Jenny could imagine.

She arrived early to find Alison, dressed in a black two-piece suit, already setting out trestle tables and ancient wooden folding chairs to resemble a court. The hall, not much larger than the average classroom, had a floor of worn, bare boards; the walls were of dark, nicotine-stained pine cladding. At one end was a small stage, at the opposite end a shuttered serving hatch. Its smell – of old timber, mildew and stewed tea – flung Jenny back to the Sunday school she had been forced to attend, a place she associated with fear and a vague sense of guilt. Miss Talbot, the acidic spinster who presided, had been one of those Christians whose life's mission was to stamp out all joy.

Responding to Jenny's subdued reaction, Alison said, 'At least it makes people feel at home.' She straightened the table beneath the stage that would serve as Jenny's desk. 'Mr Marshall always liked it here, said it reminded him of his childhood.'

'I can see why. Is there anywhere I can put my things?'

Alison pointed to a door at the side of the stage. 'There's an office through there. Shall I bring you a cup of tea? I've got the urn going.'

'Thanks.'

Jenny went through the door and into a little room boasting an old desk and chair and a number of tea chests containing what looked like the costumes for the annual pantomime. A small window looked out across a large, flat field and in the near distance the Severn and the Gloucestershire hills beyond. Despite the rural setting and the quaintness of the hall she felt a rising sense of claustrophobia. She had avoided sleeping pills and slept badly; she'd been awake since five a.m. Her chest felt constricted and she hadn't managed any breakfast. The pill she had taken an hour ago had barely touched her anxiety and had left her feeling sluggish. An uneasy sensation: on the edge of her nerves but at the same time physically exhausted.

She took a deep breath, repeating a mantra Dr Travis had taught her: *my right arm is heavy.* She let it hang loose, felt its weight, then moved her focus to her other arm, trying to breathe deeply down into her stomach. After a minute or so she felt her heart begin to slow. Relief. She opened her eyes and, taking care to move in an unhurried fashion, unloaded the papers, textbooks and legal pads from her briefcase.

She sat at the desk and turned through the pages of cross-examination notes she had carefully prepared. Unlike a regular criminal or civil court, a coroner's inquest was not a competition between competing cases. It was an inquiry, led by the coroner, into the circumstances surrounding a death. The coroner questioned all witnesses personally before allowing other interested parties to cross-examine. The rules of evidence were very relaxed. Leading questions and hearsay were perfectly permissible. The single objective was to unearth the truth.

Jenny found herself staring at the pages of neat handwriting, seeing the words but unable to take them in. Last night in her study she had been clear-headed and confident. Now her mind crowded with unwanted thoughts and concerns. Her attempts to focus were thwarted by humiliating and doom-laden scenarios. She tried Dr Travis's routine again, but her arm refused to relax and her heart began to pick up speed. Sweat trickled down her back and from under her arms.

There was nothing for it: she grabbed her handbag and brought out the temazepam. With shaking hands, she pushed down the lid and twisted, but with too much force. Pills tumbled out across the desk and scattered across the floor. Damn. She grabbed two off her notebook, swallowed them dry, then tried to scoop the others back in the jar. The door swung open. Alison entered carrying a mug of tea. Jenny looked up with a start.

Alison trod on one of the pills, then saw others strewn across the floor.

'I spilled some aspirin—' Her words came out in a panicky burst.

Alison set the mug on a clear patch of table. 'Are you sure you're all right, Mrs Cooper?'

'Headache. I was up late working.'

Alison glanced at the little white pills, 'T-30' stamped clearly on the front of each of them. It wouldn't take an ex-policewoman to work out they weren't painkillers. 'We've got a good hour before we get under way,' she said with almost maternal reassurance. 'The police are sending a Mr Hartley QC to ask questions on their behalf, but the family have chosen not to be represented. The young man from the Youth Offending Team called to say he's on his way, but I've heard nothing from any of the police officers or Dr Peterson. I assume they'll be along.'

Jenny took a gulp of the hot tea. 'They'd better be. I'll be issuing warrants for their arrest if they're not.'

'At least I've got a full complement of eight jurors, and the landlord of the local pub's been put on notice to be ready with sandwiches.'

'It's like organizing a village social club.' Jenny collected the last of the pills from the desk and dropped them in the container, beyond caring what Alison thought of her taking tranquillizers – half the population had been on them at one time or another.

'Do you mind if I offer you a little advice, Mrs Cooper?'

'Fire away.'

'In my experience of inquests it always seems to work best when the coroner keeps things low key. Witnesses are much more forthcoming when everyone's relaxed.'

'I'll do my best.'

A pause, then Alison said, 'And I'm sorry about the other day. I shouldn't have got emotional. It wasn't very professional of me.'

'It's been a difficult time.'

'Yes.' Alison stood in silent reflection for a brief moment, turned to the door, reached for the handle, then glanced back over her shoulder. 'Do be careful, Mrs Cooper.'

At nine-thirty Jenny emerged from her office feeling back in control – the two pills seemed to have settled her, but she wasn't prepared for the sight outside: the hall was full to bursting and already stuffy. Wearing an usher's gown over her suit, Alison called out, 'All rise,' and the room stood in unison. Four rows of chairs at the back of the hall were occupied by journalists, members of the public and the pool of jurors. Among them she spotted Mr and Mrs Taylor, Andy, dressed in a suit, clutching Claire's hand; Mrs Taylor was even whiter than Jenny remembered her. Set slightly apart from her desk and at forty-five degrees to it was a trestle table at which sat two lawyers, one a young man in his early thirties Jenny took to be a solicitor, the other a dapper man in his fifties wearing a dark navy chalk-stripe suit and the starched shirt collar of a barrister. Opposite the lawyers' desk was a smaller table which would serve as the witness box, on which stood a tape recorder, the coroner's budget not stretching to a stenographer. Alison occupied a chair by the stage to Jenny's right, a position which gave her a clear view of the entire hall.

Jenny gave a brief, formal nod and took her seat. As the assembled company followed her lead, she noticed another suited figure darting through the door and finding a place at the very back: Grantham.

She folded her hands neatly in front of her. Her nerves were holding steady. 'Good morning, ladies and gentlemen.' She glanced at the note of the counsel's name Alison had left on her desk. 'I understand you're here on behalf of the Severn Vale Constabulary, Mr Hartley.'

Giles Hartley QC rose to his feet at a measured, theatrical pace and addressed her in precise, public school tones. 'Yes, ma'am, and I am instructed by Mr Mallinson.' Mallinson, his instructing solicitor, gave the customary nod. 'But before we begin, ma'am, might I raise a question of law?' He continued without waiting for an answer: 'If my understanding is correct, the unfortunate death of Katy Taylor was, following a post-mortem examination on Tuesday 1 May, certified as being due to an overdose of the drug commonly known as heroin. A finding having been made, one questions the validity of this hearing, pleasant though the journey here this morning was.'

A ripple of sycophantic laughter travelled round the hall.

Jenny was expecting a shot across the bows and was ready and primed. 'I'm sure you've read the 2001 case of *Terry* v *Craze*, Mr Hartley, in which the Court of Appeal held that a coroner is entitled to hold an inquest even after a death certificate has been issued, where evidence gives rise to reasonable cause to suspect the deceased died an unnatural death.'

'That is precisely the issue, ma'am. The death was unnatural and the coroner, Mr Marshall, certified it as such. He may have erred in failing to hold an inquest, but that does not give you jurisdiction to hold one now. The correct procedure must surely be for you to request leave of the High Court before embarking on this fresh inquiry.'

Hartley had a point, but only a slender one. Jenny had read and re-read the authorities and was prepared to stand her ground. Let Hartley run off to the Court of Appeal if he wanted, she wasn't going to be strong-armed into abandoning now. 'Mr Marshall was indeed wrong to sign a death certificate and I consider it void. No formal finding of fact having been made, I am therefore not only entitled, but legally *obliged*, to hold this inquest. I will not be persuaded otherwise. Thank you, Mr Hartley.'

She turned to Alison, who looked impressed at her opening salvo. 'May we have a jury please, Usher?'

Disgruntled, Hartley resumed his seat. While Alison called up the eight jurors from the back of the room, he leaned over to Mallinson and whispered instructions. The younger lawyer scuttled to the door and disappeared outside, pulling out his phone.

Jenny scanned the faces in what passed for the public gallery while the jurors took their places in a row of seats along the wall opposite the lawyers' table. There was no sign of Peterson or any police officers. Mallinson must have gone to let them know that they would have to come to court after all. Jenny looked over at Hartley impatiently tapping his fountain pen on a legal pad. Did he really think she would be derailed that easily? She watched him crane round and exchange a glance with Grantham, and, as if sensing that he'd been caught out, pick up some papers and pretend to read.

She'd won the first skirmish, but was under no illusions that Grantham and his friends planned to make her life as difficult as possible. She felt a knot of tension in her chest, then fear. The one time Marshall had dug too deep, she reminded herself, he hadn't lived to tell the tale.

The first, and only, witness to have answered his summons at the allotted hour was Justin Bennett, a young social worker attached to the Severn Vale Youth Offending Team. Jenny's son would have called him a crusty. He was white, twenty-four, no more than five seven and wore his dark hair in matted, shoulder-length dreadlocks which he had tied back into a ponytail for the occasion. He had several rings in each ear, a nose stud and another ring through his bottom lip which either caused or enhanced his lisp. He sat uncomfortably in the witness chair in a khaki-coloured suit and open-necked shirt. A young man, Jenny thought, in a state of some confusion: working for the forces of law and order but trying to pass on the street for a drug dealer.

She questioned him in the same patient manner she would have done a surly teenager: 'In early March of this year Katy Taylor received a twelve-week detention and training order for mugging an eighteen-year-old woman.'

'Yes.' Justin mumbled his answer, looking anywhere but at her.

'Could you try and speak up please, Mr Bennett. The jury needs to hear you.'

He gave a defensive nod, his cheeks flushing.

'In the course of the attack she broke the victim's nose and stole thirty pounds to buy drugs.'

'That's right.'

'After six weeks in Portshead Farm Secure Training Centre she was released from detention on 17 April and placed under your supervision for the remaining six weeks of her sentence.'

'Yeah.'

'What did that supervision involve, exactly?'

'She had to go to school every day, she was on a seven p.m. curfew and she was meant to go to RA twice a week.'

'RA?'

'Recovery from Addiction. She came out of Portshead clean and she was meant to stay that way.'

'How were these conditions enforced?'

'She was on voice verification. She'd get a phone call on her home number at seven-fifteen every night and the computer would check the voice print to make sure it was her.'

'Did she have to attend personal meetings with you?'

'Twice a week after school before RA.'

'Sounds like a tough regime.'

Justin didn't answer. Jenny suspected he didn't know what *regime* meant.

'But she was only out five days before she went missing.'

'Yeah.'

'How many times did you see her in person during this period?'

'Twice. On Wednesday the 18th for an appointment, and just in passing on Friday before her RA. She was due to see me again on the Monday, the 23rd.'

Jenny wrote down his reply and in brackets added ('well rehearsed').

'Did she stick to her curfew?'

'Mostly. She was late in on the Friday night, I think.'

'But she turned up for RA?'

'Yes.'

'Did you know or suspect that she had been prostituting herself to buy drugs?'

'I did read that on her file.'

'Did you discuss it with her during the Wednesday appointment?'

'No, I don't think so.'

'What did you talk about?'

'I explained the terms of her contract to her, took her voice print and gave her all the information about the course. It was more admin than anything.'

'Admin? Weren't you meant to be there as an emotional support, Mr Bennett? Surely discussing the reasons for her previous offending and prostitution was pretty fundamental, especially given that she was only fifteen.'

Justin turned a darker shade of pink. 'It was just an initial meeting.'

'I see. And do you have any knowledge of any friends, acquaintances or anyone who might have supplied her with heroin?'

'No.'

'You never asked who she bought from?'

'We never ask young offenders to inform. It's our job to win their trust.'

In five minutes of questioning she felt she had extracted all she ever would from Justin Bennett. He reminded her of so many social workers she had encountered in family law – a couple of years into the job they realized their struggle to right the wrongs of society was futile, got compassion fatigue and turned into clock watchers. Ask the requisite questions, tick the boxes and get out of the office by five. Justin showed every sign of fitting the mould.

'Thank you, Mr Bennett, no more questions.' She looked over at Hartley, who shook his head. 'You may stand down. Leave the building if you wish.'

Justin bolted from his seat and straight for the exit, avoiding the gaze of Mr and Mrs Turner. He was already shrugging off his suit jacket as he pushed out of the door.

The only other witness to have arrived was Police Constable Helen Campbell, a nervous, overweight young woman who had trouble moving one thigh in front of the other; she didn't look capable of tackling determined criminals. Her hands shook as she read the oath, stumbling over the words. Several members of the jury looked surprised at this and exchanged glances. Jenny knew how the young officer felt, and, adopting her most unconfrontational tone, proceeded to question her gently.

PC Campbell had been first on the scene at nine a.m. following a call from a member of the public. She was alone in the patrol car as her partner had rung in sick. Still alone, she taped off the immediate area around the body and called in CID, who arrived an hour later with a small forensics team. It was raining hard and had been for several days previously. By one p.m. forensics had drawn a blank and she was given the job of arranging an undertaker to remove the remains to the Vale mortuary. Later that afternoon she met Mr and Mrs Taylor at the hospital and arranged for them to identify their daughter's body. Before ending her shift she wrote a longhand report of the day's events which she handed to Detective Superintendent Alan Swainton, the officer in charge of the investigation. She heard no more about it until two days later, 2 May, when she learned that CID were satisfied the death was due to an accidental overdose and that the coroner had released the body for burial.

Jenny paused for a moment and considered the evidence PC Campbell had just given. A young, clearly substandard officer had been first to arrive at a potential murder scene. It had taken an hour for detectives and scenes of crime officers to arrive. Although Campbell was barely literate, she had been charged with writing the report to the coroner. Jenny made a note of these thoughts, then turned back to the police constable.

'Would you consider it unusual for an officer of your relative inexperience to be left in charge of a potential murder scene for a full hour and to have been given the responsibility of writing the report to the coroner?'

'Not really, ma'am.' PC Campbell spoke in her thick Bristol accent, growing a little more confident now. 'We were that stretched, it was a question of whoever was free to do it.'

'Did you offer to write the report or were you asked to?'

'I had to write a statement about finding the body anyway. It was Detective Superintendent Swainton who asked me to send it to the coroner's office.'

Out of the corner of her eye, Jenny noticed Hartley listening closely to this exchange. Alison, too, was on the edge of her seat. Jenny recalled her speculation in the office before she broke down: that Swainton had been sat on, that Katy might have been consorting with someone prominent, or even a police informer, someone neither the police nor Marshall wanted – or dared – to touch.

'Constable, could you tell the jury exactly how and by whom Katy's body was discovered?'

'A woman walking her dog, a Mrs Julia Gabb, found her. Actually the dog did. He'd run off and the lady found him by the body.'

'Did she walk her dog there every day?'

'She said she hadn't been to that spot for a week.'

'Presumably, a lot of other people walk there too?'

'A few do, yes.'

'So, even though the body was out of sight of the road and the footpath above, it might be considered strange that it wasn't discovered before?'

PC Campbell shrugged. 'I couldn't say.'

Jenny picked up her copy of the police photographs of Katy's body at the scene and studied them again. The corpse was under the cover of a large shrub, a laurel or a rhododendron. She recalled from her childhood haunts on the north Somerset coast that such shrubs appeared impenetrable from the outside, but once you were through the outer leaves, there was invariably a secret den in the middle. How would Katy, a thoroughly urban girl, know that? Why go to such lengths to find somewhere to take drugs?

'Tell me, PC Campbell, did you find anything at the scene to suggest that this was a place where people commonly injected drugs or entertained prostitutes – any needles or condoms on the ground?'

'Only the one syringe next to Katy.'

'Is this a place known to the police as somewhere these activities commonly occur?'

'Not particularly.'

'Would it be fair to say that it's a remote place, only really accessible by car?'

'Yes.'

'And Katy was wearing high heels?'

'She was.'

'It seems unlikely she got there by herself, doesn't it?'

'It does, really.'

'Which leaves us with two possibilities: either she went to this place with another person while she was alive, or her body was placed there after she was dead.'

'All I did was write a report, ma'am. I'm not an investigator.'

'No.' Jenny glanced at the jury, registering their suspicion. 'Wait there, PC Campbell.'

Hartley rose to his feet with a saccharine smile, a gold tooth glinting in the upper corner of his mouth. 'Just a couple of questions, Officer. I presume you were first on the scene because you were the closest officer at the time the alarm was raised.'

'That's correct.'

'And being first to arrive you were obliged to write a report of what you had found.'

'Yes, sir.'

'And you have no idea how Katy Taylor came to be in that place, do you?'

PC Campbell stalled for a second, before conceding, 'No, sir.'

Hartley shot the jury another smile and sat down again, pleased with himself.

Right on cue, Peterson arrived, together with a uniformed police officer who, from the row of pips on his shoulder, Jenny took to be Detective Superintendent Swainton. Both men looked indignant at being hauled away from their busy lives to an obscure corner of the Gloucestershire countryside. Jenny felt a small swell of satisfaction at being able to wield such power over them.

She called Detective Superintendent Swainton forward first. A tall, broad-shouldered man of around fifty, still sporting a full head of dark brown hair, he was an imposing physical presence and gave the impression of being impatient to get back to far more important matters. His manner was abrupt and confident, unintimidated by Jenny or her court. Immediately she found his confidence unnerving. Bennett and Campbell had been soft witnesses; here was a man determined to match her.

'Officer, you were in overall charge of the investigation into Katy Taylor's death?'

'I was.'

'When did you arrive at the scene?'

'Approximately an hour after Constable Campbell. My team and I had been up all night dealing with an armed incident over near Stroud.'

'Did you regard the death as suspicious?'

'Initially. But when the post-mortem report came it was clear she had died of a heroin overdose.'

'But that finding couldn't tell you whether she had administered the fatal dose herself or if someone else had assisted, or even forced it on her.'

'There was no evidence from the pathologist of any physical

force having been used against her.' He turned to address the jury directly, determined to deliver the last word on the matter. 'Of course we couldn't rule out the possibility of manslaughter, or indeed murder, but there was no physical evidence on which to base such an assumption. In that situation we hand the case over to the coroner but continue to keep the file open in case any further evidence comes to light. That is what we have done, and no evidence of third-party involvement has yet arisen.'

'So you do accept the possibility that she was killed either accidentally or on purpose by another person?'

'Of course, but we can only do what we can with the resources available to us. We probably have a dozen or more accidental overdose cases like this every year. If we treated every one as a potential murder we'd need twice the number of detectives we have.'

'Katy Taylor was a vulnerable fifteen-year-old girl with a history of drug taking and prostitution. Surely if anyone was going to be taken advantage of by a predatory man, it was her.'

'I would agree with you.'

'So why didn't you investigate the circumstances more fully? Why not concentrate resources on trying to pinpoint her last known movements, who she was with?'

'Believe me, we tried, but prostitutes are not people inclined to help the police. My officers have appealed for information and will receive anything anyone has to say in the strictest confidence, but the fact remains there is to date no evidence of violence having been used against her.'

'What about the possibility that her body was positioned where it was after her death?'

'Firstly, the body had been well soaked with rain over several days, preventing the recovery of third-party DNA, and secondly, the pathologist confirmed that the pattern of rigor mortis and the pooling of blood in the parts of her closest to the ground were consistent with her having been in that position since she died.'

'How did he inform you of that? It's not in his report.'

Swainton glanced at Dr Peterson, sitting in the front row of the gallery. The question had broken his stride and the jury sensed it. The Detective Superintendent cleared his throat and said, 'I had a detailed telephone conversation with him on the afternoon of 1 May, after he had conducted his examination. It was as a result of this that I decided to hand the file over to the coroner's office.'

'Only twenty-four hours after the body was found.'

'As I've explained, it didn't mean we were closing our file, only that there were no obvious grounds to suspect foul play.'

'You didn't consider her death worthy of even a few days of concentrated investigation?'

'At the time we were dealing with several brutal homicides and serious sexual assaults.'

'In other words, it wasn't a priority.'

'Compared with others, no, it wasn't. It felt like a case more appropriately handled by the coroner's office.'

Jenny sat back in her chair and considered the implications of Swainton's evidence. If he was to be believed, the police were simply too undermanned to give every death the attention the public would expect. Obvious and brutal homicides took precedence; those that were problematic or obscure went to the bottom of the heap. And to counter allegations of neglect, they claimed cases remained active when the truth was they were buried as deep as the victim. It was a good time for killers who had the wit to cover their tracks.

Jenny said, 'What kind of investigation did you expect the coroner to carry out?'

Detective Superintendent Swainton nodded, as if he had been waiting for this question. 'I must confess I was surprised that a death certificate was issued without an inquest being held, especially given Katy's troubled history. She was meant to be under close supervision by the Youth Offending Team.'

His attempt to pass the buck was delivered with admirable understated sincerity. Jenny imagined he had been planning his move ever since the summons landed on his desk yesterday afternoon.

'Did you query this with the coroner, Mr Marshall?'

'No, ma'am. I wouldn't consider it my place to do so, and by the time I found out, unfortunately, he had died. But I have to say, I am very grateful that you are now giving Katy's death the attention it deserves.'

Charm itself. Swainton had skilfully avoided all responsibility and somehow handed it back to her. She felt a sudden, childish urge to retaliate. Alison had read the signals and was giving her a warning look. Jenny ignored her. 'The question remains, Officer, why you and your force spent barely more than a few hours investigating the death of a fifteen-year-old girl. It seems so extraordinary that one has to wonder if there wasn't a sinister reason for it.'

Hartley leapt to his feet. 'Ma'am, I really must object. Detective Superintendent Swainton has given a perfectly rational account of his decision.'

'It may appear rational to you, Mr Hartley, but I have to say I am far from satisfied.'

She had the bit well and truly between her teeth. Alison stared hard at the ground, while Hartley dropped back into his seat with an expression of barely suppressed fury.

'I'll be more precise, Officer. Did you come under any pressure to back off from this investigation?'

'No, ma'am, I did not.'

The several reporters in the gallery were scribbling in unison, hanging on every word.

'Was there ever any hint or suspicion that Katy had been

consorting with someone your force may have had reason to protect, an informer, for example, or someone prominent?'

Swainton fixed her with a cold, level look. 'Absolutely none whatsoever. And with the greatest of respect, ma'am, I deeply resent that suggestion.'

Feeling herself diminish under his gaze, Jenny thanked him for his time and tried to regain her composure while Hartley asked some easy questions designed to repair the damage. She could have kicked herself. Not only had she sounded impetuous, she had shown her hand too soon. If Swainton did have anything to hide, he would now move heaven and earth to keep her from finding it out. She felt the familiar knot forming beneath her diaphragm, a pressure either side of her forehead: the drugs were wearing off. She waited impatiently for Hartley to finish his final question and called a brief adjournment.

Jenny bought herself a few minutes alone, telling Alison she had to make some calls. She brought out her bottle of temazepam and a metal nailfile she carried in her handbag and cut three tablets in half. It was a procedure she hadn't carried out since the dark post-episode months when each day in court was a desperate struggle. She wasn't anywhere near as anxious as she had been then, but she had no fall-back position; there was nowhere to run and hide if she could no longer cope. During those desperate times she had learned that each half-dose would keep her steady for an hour. Now the clever part: a tube of Polo mints, the only edible item considered acceptable in a British courtroom. She carefully unwound the foil package, extracted six, jammed half a pill in the centre of each and rewrapped them.

No one would ever know.

*

Detective Superintendent Swainton had left the building, leaving Peterson to face the music alone. Grantham, too, had disappeared, adding to Jenny's suspicion that the two of them were in cahoots. Peterson sat in the witness chair with the air of a man resigned to having his day ruined. The flirtatious smile was gone. He looked tired and seemed to carry the weight of the corpses backing up along his mortuary corridor on his narrow frame.

'You conducted a post-mortem on the body of Katy Taylor on the morning of 1 May, approximately twenty-four hours after it was discovered. Is that correct?'

'Yes. That's right.'

'What did you know about the circumstances of her death?'

'Only what PC Campbell had told me, that she was found in a seated position with a syringe next to her.'

'What did your post-mortem reveal?'

'The first issue was time of death. The condition of the tissue told me she had been dead for somewhere between five and seven days, but beyond that it was impossible to say with any accuracy. The body arrived in an almost foetal position, but once clothing had been removed it was clear to see that blood had pooled in the buttocks and lower abdomen and feet and ankles – the areas closest to the ground – indicating that she had been in a seated posture before death. Examination of the internal organs showed she'd suffered a cardiac arrest consistent with a drug overdose. I ordered an expedited haematology report and it confirmed the presence of a hefty dose of undigested diamorphine – heroin. It was impossible to say how much she had injected, but I've had several similar cases over the last six months, which suggests there's some particularly pure heroin doing the rounds. I hear it's got very cheap lately.'

'Could you say whether she had injected it herself?'

'No.'

'Do heroin users usually inject themselves?'

'Yes, unless they are particularly inexperienced.'

'Could you tell whether Katy was an experienced heroin user?'

'She didn't have any of the obvious signs: emaciation, for example—'

Jenny glanced up and saw Andy Taylor half raising his hand, trying to catch her attention. Jenny nodded to him and gestured Alison to go and see what he wanted. 'Hold on a moment, please, Dr Peterson.'

Alison leaned over to Andy Taylor. Both he and Mrs Taylor spoke animatedly in whispers, adamant about something. Alison returned to Jenny and relayed their message: Katy took marijuana and cocaine but always protested that she and her friends didn't touch heroin. The night she had ended up in hospital was as a result of smoking crack, which she wasn't used to. It made sense: heroin was a complicated drug to use intravenously, getting the needles together was a problem in itself for a fifteen-year-old girl. A pinch of coke was a much easier high.

A sudden and very obvious realization hit. She turned back to Peterson. 'Am I right in assuming that, to be fatal, this dose of heroin probably went straight into a vein?'

He considered the question for a moment. Jenny thought she detected a flicker of alarm. Perhaps his mind was going in the same direction as hers. 'I'd say that was more than likely.'

'And a girl unused to injecting heroin would struggle to find a vein alone, wouldn't she? We've all had experienced nurses misfire trying to take blood samples?'

Jurors nodded in recognition.

Peterson was forced to concede. 'It's not the easiest thing to master.'

'But once you *have* mastered it, an accidental overdose becomes increasingly unlikely – is that fair to say?'

'I suppose so.'

'What I'm driving at, Dr Peterson, is that it is more likely than not that Katy was injected with a fatal dose by a third party who knew what they were doing.'

'It's possible.'

'There are tests, aren't there, which could have told you whether she had taken heroin before? Hair analysis, for example.'

The pathologist stirred uncomfortably in his chair, crossed, then uncrossed his arms. 'Yes.'

'Did you perform those tests?'

'No.'

'Why not?

He shook his head vaguely. 'They didn't seem relevant.'

Jenny wanted to come back with a smart remark but this time managed to resist the urge. There was a thought nagging somewhere in the recesses of her mind, a connection she wasn't quite making. Then it came to her: fingernails. She had read enough pathology in the few weeks since her appointment to know that while DNA might degrade very fast when exposed to the elements, fibres did not. If Katy had been forcibly drugged, the chances are she would have fought back and in the process collected fibres from her attacker's clothing under her nails. Either the police Forensic Science Service or a Home Office pathologist could take scrapings and order detailed tests to determine the provenance of any recovered fibres. All of this was expensive, of course, and now every aspect of police work was tightly budgeted, such tests would be rare.

'Dr Peterson, did you take scrapings from under Katy's nails in order to test for fibres or foreign DNA?'

'No. I wouldn't do that unless specifically asked by the police. It would require liaison with the Forensic Science Service.'

Jenny bet the police hadn't troubled themselves to test for fibres, either. Even if they had, she wouldn't trust their results. She was stuck in an evidential hole. Both the police and Peterson had done just enough to cover themselves, but neither had done enough to prove exactly how Katy died. There were tests which should have been ordered but weren't, tests which even over a month later could still be done if she was prepared to take a very drastic step.

Jenny looked over at the tortured faces of Andy and Claire Taylor and reached for her mints.

She retreated to her office and gathered her strength while, on the other side of the door, Alison directed the jurors across the village green to where they would find lunch waiting for them in the pub. Listening to their cheerful chatter as they stepped out into the warm afternoon, she tried to collect her fractured thoughts. The knock at the door came before she was ready. She turned with a start.

'Come in.'

Alison opened the door, held it back for Andy and Claire, and followed them in. Claire looked even more pallid than she had earlier, traumatized by her morning in court.

Andy was putting on a brave face, but his expression was strained and weary, Claire's depression taking as much out of him as the inquest itself. He said, 'Mrs Trent said you wanted to talk to us.'

'Yes . . . Sorry. I'd offer you a seat but it's rather cramped in here.'

He shrugged. 'It's all right.' He looped his arm around Claire's middle, realizing that they hadn't been summoned to hear good news. She said nothing, her eyes unfocused, turned towards the window.

Jenny said, 'I know you both understand that the purpose of an inquest is to determine as far as possible the precise cause of death. You've heard the evidence as I have, and I expect you've come to the same conclusion as me – that neither the police nor the pathologist did everything they could to find out whether Katy was alone or with someone else when she died, or even whether her death was accidental.' She hesitated. Even tranquillized, she could feel her heart banging against her ribs. 'I'm afraid that my predecessor, Mr Marshall, failed to have certain tests carried out on Katy's body which could shed a lot of light . . . Apart from testing for fibres, he could have ordered hair analysis. That would have shown what drugs Katy took and when – hair is like a chemical calendar. That information could help us with finding out where the drugs came from, maybe even *who* they came from . . . Those tests could still be carried out.'

Claire looked up sharply, tears in her eyes. 'No. You're not touching her. I'm not letting you.'

Alison gave Jenny a look that said, 'I told you so.'

'Mrs Taylor, we need to find out if there was anything untoward about your daughter's death.'

'I knew you'd want to do this. I *knew*. I'm not having Katy disturbed. It's not right.' She tugged away from her husband's side.

Andy said, 'Love, just listen—'

'There's nothing to hear. I didn't want any of this. It's not doing anyone any good. Why can't you just leave her alone?' Fighting tears, she made for the door, forcing Alison to step aside.

Andy grabbed her wrist. 'Claire . . .'

'You can go to hell. I'm not having it.' She yanked free and fled, sobbing, out of the door.

Jenny said, 'Mr Taylor—'

He cut her off. 'This is all wrong.'

'If you'll just let me explain. I'd rather have your coopera-tion—'

'Tell that to my wife.' He followed Claire out of the door, slamming it hard behind him.

Jenny stared into space. She felt like a driver who'd just run down an innocent pedestrian, as if the Taylors' distress was her fault.

Alison said, 'You're not really going to dig her up?'

'I don't think I've got any choice.'

'What do you think you're going to find?'

'I don't know. That's the point. I need a Home Office pathologist outside the area, someone who's not involved in the local mafia.'

'It'll have to be Wales, then. There's Professor Lloyd at Newport.'

'Fine. I'm going to order an exhumation. I'd be grateful if you'd make arrangements as quickly as possible.'

'Are you sure about this? An exhumation . . . Mr Marshall never—'

'Maybe if he had, we wouldn't be here now.'

'If you want my advice, I'd leave this decision until later . . . when you've had a chance to calm down.'

Jenny snapped. 'If I want your advice I'll ask for it.'

Alison stiffened and turned to the door with exaggerated calm. 'Whatever you think best, Mrs Cooper.'

EIGHT

SHE DIDN'T ANNOUNCE THE REASON for the adjournment. She intended, if at all possible, to keep the exhumation secret and away from the public gaze. When Hartley stood up and demanded to know the reason they were being sent away until Monday morning, Jenny said, 'To carry out further enquiries.' She was under no obligation to tell him or the jury and he deeply resented the fact. As she left the hall he was in a huddle with his henchman, Mallinson, and two others who had appeared over the lunch break. She guessed they were lawyers from the Severn Vale District Hospital Trust, hurriedly summoned to consider the implications of Peterson's incomplete post-mortem. Hartley would be asking for notes and records, desperate to isolate and destroy any incriminating evidence.

Outside the hall Grantham was sitting in his Mercedes – a fancy car for a town hall public servant – with a phone pressed to his ear. He glanced furtively at Jenny as she passed. She considered stopping and asking him what business he had being at her inquest, but managed to restrain herself. In the ten minutes they had had face to face in her office she had learned all she needed to know about him: he was a little man with an even smaller mind and a big opinion of himself. It was no use talking to a person like that; she would have to show him through her deeds who was boss.

*

Her bullishness was short-lived. Back at the office she picked up an email from Josh at the Ministry of Justice to say that the IT department was overstretched and he wouldn't be able to install her new system for over a month. And spewing out of the fax machine were another dozen death reports and a terse letter from the finance department at the local authority demanding the coroner's accounts for the previous year.

Jenny sat at her desk, looked with a sense of foreboding at the heap of untidy papers that Marshall had optimistically called 'the books', and decided that her time was far too precious to waste in tedious administration. She moved the papers on to the floor, out of sight. Alison could deal with them later.

Reading through the latest batch of local deaths and with her medication wearing thin, each brief, impersonal description conjured its own tragic story. Male, twenty-eight, chronic asthmatic, suspected respiratory failure. Male, eighty-five, partially decomposed body discovered on kitchen floor, cause unknown. Female, fifty-three, alcoholic, suspected brain haemorrhage. Female, forty-one, psychiatric outpatient, fall/jump from ninth-floor balcony. Here were the one in five of the population whose corporeal journey ended on the mortuary slab; to whose humiliating ends it was Jenny's task to afford some small measure of dignity.

After just four days as coroner she was already the earthly representative of fifty traumatically departed souls. Knowing only snatches of their stories, she nevertheless felt their presence. Many times during the long hours in Dr Travis's office spent trying to fathom the nature of the unexplained dread which slithered through the gloomy recesses of her mind, she had described it as a fear of death. The psychiatrist had urged her to summon childhood memories of viewing the bodies of her grandparents, hoping that such memories would hold the key, but they didn't. She had tried to explain that the sensation was something far greater than that: a feeling of all-encompassing doom. He told her that lots of anxiety sufferers used the same language to describe their symptoms. Sometimes she could believe that she was simply suffering from a common ailment, but there were occasions – and she never dared tell him this – when she truly believed that what had broken down was not her nervous system, but the delicate barrier that separated everyday life from the reality of evil.

During the worst times, while David had slept soundly next to her, she would reach for her leather-bound confirmation Bible and look for words to send her peacefully to sleep. It would always fall open at Matthew 7:14: *strait is the gate and narrow is the way which leadeth unto life, and few there be that find it.* She would close her eyes and pray in earnest, for the first time since she was a child, that she would find the narrow way and be delivered from her suffering. Divorce had brought some relief, leaving her job a little more, certainly enough that she hadn't felt the need to pray for several months now, but almost without conscious thought, she had gravitated to a new career that dealt only with the sum of all her fears. Sitting at a dead man's desk, dealing only with the dead, she dared to ask herself whether those prayers were somehow in the process of being answered; whether she had been led to this place for a purpose.

With an effort, she forced her mind back to the present and composed a series of emails on her laptop, requesting post-mortems for the recently deceased. It was strangely comforting to reduce these horrors to a series of administrative tasks. It gave her back a sense of control. Perhaps, she thought, all people who dealt in death were in fact secretly terrified by it.

She had cleared her desk sufficiently even to contemplate the accounts when Alison returned. She had been speaking to a trusted undertaker, Mr Dawes, about the practicalities of exhuming a body. It was a very uncommon procedure which he had performed only twice in his thirty-year career. The form was to do it at night, after the cemetery gates were shut. The police usually liked to be present, although there was no necessity for it, and some relatives liked to be nearby. Having a clergyman to hand was also considered advisable. Dawes and his men would arrange for a mechanical excavator to dig most of the way down but the final few feet of soil would be removed manually. If everything went to plan the coffin could be out of the ground within an hour. The undertakers would then transport it to the hospital mortuary in Newport.

Keeping it businesslike, Jenny asked what sort of condition the remains would be in. Alison said Katy was buried in a solid coffin which would hardly have deteriorated at all in just over a month. The body itself would have further degraded, but most of the tissue would still be available for examination. As modern coffins were pretty much airtight, decomposition took many months. Dawes had told her that it could take up to ten years for a corpse to skeletonize.

Jenny instructed her to make the necessary arrangements and returned to her computer to draft the warrant ordering the exhumation to take place the following night.

Alison said, 'You're absolutely sure you want to go ahead?'

Jenny opened her copy of Jervis and turned to the index, looking for 'exhumation'. 'It's not a question of wanting to, I don't have any choice. I didn't directly accuse Swainton or Peterson of negligence, but that's what it amounts to.'

'It does seem very soon in your career to be doing something as drastic as digging up a body.'

Jenny found the page she wanted and looked up. There was more than concern on Alison's face; she looked troubled, perplexed. 'You said to me that something happened to Harry Marshall in his final weeks, those were your words. The last act he performed as coroner was writing a death certificate in this case when he should have held an inquest. Think about what that means.'

'He obviously wasn't feeling well. It could have been a mistake . . . Maybe he couldn't face holding another inquest?'

'The night he died he called you at nearly midnight. I didn't like to say anything, but years ago something like that happened to me. I had a university friend who'd been depressed and took her own life. She knew I was worried about her, but hours before she did it she told me she was OK, on the mend.'

'You don't know that's what happened.' There was a note of panic in Alison's voice.

'No. But if he did know he was going to die, he did everything bar leaving an explicit instruction to ensure that his successor took the case up. He signed a death certificate which couldn't pass without question and he locked the file away in his drawer. Even if he thought he would be back at work the next morning, what was the file doing in there? Who was he keeping it from?'

'Not from me.'

'Right. And no one else has access to this office, do they?'

Alison shook her head.

'So unless there's something more you think I ought to know, I'll continue to apply the law and see where it leads.'

There was no reply on the Taylors' number but somewhere on the file Jenny found a note of Andy's mobile. He answered it against the background roar of heavy machinery, saying he'd come to work the late shift out on some groundworks at Sharpness. When Jenny asked if she could see him or his wife in person he said she could come and meet him on site, he had a break at seven p.m.

*

Jenny found her way across an unfamiliar part of the south Gloucestershire countryside and picked up temporary signs that directed her along lanes beside the estuary to the construction site. It was situated within sight of the concrete sarcophagus which was the former Berkeley nuclear power station. The evening was overcast and the air hung heavy with mist and faint drizzle. A brooding sky merged with the murky grey water of the Severn racing out to sea on a low tide.

She crept along a section of unmade road and arrived at a Portakabin serving as site reception next to a ten-foot-high wire fence adorned with signs warning that the area was patrolled by dogs and security guards. On the other side of the wire, bulldozers were creating a roadway, no doubt destined for the anticipated Berkeley II. Permission had yet to be granted for a new nuclear power plant at the site, but local opinion was in no doubt that it was on its way. Jenny's view on the issue was straightforward: if they were so safe, why not build them in the middle of London?

A security guard in hard hat and reflective jerkin directed her to park on a muddy patch of gravel and summoned Andy Taylor to the gate via his walkie-talkie. Jenny climbed out of the car and looked out at the river while she waited for him. Although it was June the wind was cold; her light mac did little to keep her warm or the rain from cutting through to her skin. She took a perverse pleasure in huddling in a minor gale watching a flock of geese flying upstream in perfect formation, a feat of grace and beauty unmatched by human beings.

Andy Taylor drove up to the site entrance in a pick-up truck and stepped out of the cab wearing wellington boots and an orange fluorescent jacket over suit trousers, shirt and tie. He walked along the inside perimeter of the wire and stopped near to Jenny, the fence between them.

'If I go past the gate I have to sign out and back in again. Causes problems.'

'Fine.' She could tell he was keen to get whatever needed to be said out of the way, his eyes darting over to the Portakabin as if their meeting was somehow illicit. 'I wish there was some other way of doing this, Mr Taylor . . .'

He looked at her with a face of stone. A gust of chilly wind whipped across their faces. 'When's it happening?'

'Tomorrow night. Eleven p.m. You're entitled to be there if you wish.'

He shook his head. 'For God's sake, don't tell my wife. I'll deal with her.' He turned back towards the truck.

Jenny said, 'She blames herself, doesn't she? Any mother would.'

Andy stopped and spun sharply back round to face her, raw emotion now shining in his face. 'We worked all the hours God sent to get a house near a good school, Claire doing nights, whatever it took. And what happened? Our thirteen-year-old daughter got screwed and screwed and drugs pushed at her until she was dead. My wife does *not* blame herself. We blame the teachers, the police, the politicians, every last God-damned one of those self-righteous bastards who spend their lives telling other people what's best for them but can't tell right from wrong. That's who we blame.'

He wrenched open the door of the truck, jumped in and took off in a shower of mud and grit.

The rain picked up and heavier, darker storm clouds descended. The sky split with lightning and traffic inched at snail's pace across the Severn Bridge, warning signs flashing in the semi-darkness. Jenny gripped the steering wheel with both hands, rigid with tension. Halfway across she hit a bank of fog. The crawling train of cars ahead of her disappeared into nothingness. She flicked on the radio and tried to distract herself with music, but the banal tunes weren't enough to dislodge her mounting panic. Her heart raced, every breath was an effort, the road swam in front of her eyes. Convinced she would be swept off the bridge and hurled into the boiling river below, it was all she could do to keep creeping forwards, but somehow she clung on and made it to the far side.

Climbing the slip road from the motorway, she broke through to the light and her claustrophobic symptoms began to ease. She was flooded with relief that she hadn't succumbed to a full-blown panic attack, but despaired that the prospect had returned to haunt her. Dr Travis would have said it was a sign of excessive stress. She felt it more as a kind of psychic disturbance which had begun that morning before the inquest convened. It was as if, over the course of the day, she had been shaken by a mental earthquake which had opened up dark, bottomless cracks large enough to swallow her.

She tried to make sense of it. At the heart of her anxiety was something dreadful but vaguely familiar. It carried a mood of complete despair. She held the word 'despair', as Dr Travis had taught her. What image came to mind?

It was Katy. The photograph of her sitting balled up in the bushes. It resonated with a state she remembered from her own adolescence, of storming out of the house and walking aimlessly for miles and miles, her rage and insecurity distilling into numbness and an overwhelming desire for release.

It felt self-indulgent to equate her own juvenile emotions with the dead child's, but it caused Jenny to question whether, if someone had approached her in that state and offered her a syringe full of heroin, she would have taken it willingly.

The answer was no. Even in her bleakest moments, the spark of life had always been strong in her. Instinctively, she felt Katy was the same. Despite her wildness, she was well dressed, energetic, ferocious. Something told her, and it was nothing more than a gut feeling, that Katy wasn't ready to die.

The atmosphere around her, and around Danny Wills, was of heavy but not inevitable tragedy.

That's what she was feeling: the horror and injustice of life cut short. Isolating this thought, she felt an overwhelming pang of loneliness. The valley, hanging with low, dark clouds, had become forbidding and ominous, the oak woods a place where restless souls wandered in confusion. She put her foot down harder on the accelerator. Alone on the twisting road, every shape in the hedgerow was now a threatening presence, every shadow a ghost. She glanced at a flicker in the rear-view mirror, half expecting to see a figure in the back seat, ready to feel powerful fingers tightening around her neck. The imaginary presence grew so strong she glanced over her shoulder to check for him; when he wasn't there she felt sure he had ducked beneath her seat. She reached around with her left hand and felt the empty space. She knew it was paranoia, her imagination playing tricks, but that didn't make it any less real. She slammed the steering wheel with her fist in frustration: she was forty-two years old and as haunted by invisible spectres as an infant.

As she rounded the corner into Tintern, her phantoms retreated, leaving her feeling drained and stupid. She swung left up the hill towards home, trying to cram her mind with some reassuringly trivial thoughts. Was there food in the fridge? What needed doing in the garden? No. Damn. She had meant to call in at the supermarket in Chepstow. All she had at home were some tins, pasta and a limp lettuce. And she was out of red wine. Tonight was not a night she could manage without a drink.

With alcohol on her mind and contemplating the twelve-mile round trip to the supermarket, she slowed to pass the cars parked in the lane outside the Apple Tree. Normally she would never have considered going into a pub by herself, but among the vehicles she recognized Steve's Land Rover. If he was there she could just about face going up to the bar to buy a bottle of wine to take home. And right now her need was outweighing her shyness.

The bar was pleasantly busy. No music, a relaxed hum of conversation. The decor was basic but pleasant, wood floors, upturned barrels serving as tables at which groups of men stood with pint glasses, several private booths where couples were eating hearty meals. She moved unselfconsciously through the friendly crowd and approached the bar. She squeezed into a space next to two jovial, sturdy men who looked and smelt as if they had spent the day with cattle. She caught the eye of a young, dark-haired woman who was taking money at the far end of the bar. She noticed that the customer, whose face was hidden behind a vertical beam, reached out and touched her hand as the transaction took place, the young woman not resisting, rather letting his fingers linger, as if reluctantly accepting a gesture of apology. As she turned, pensive, Jenny saw that it was Steve she had been serving. He saw her and raised a hand in greeting, his eyes flitting between Jenny and the girl. She sensed a situation, or at least an awkward frisson between them.

Jenny asked for a bottle of red wine, whichever was one up from the cheapest, and studied the girl as she fetched it from a rack under the counter. There was none of the joy of youth about her. Her body was slender, but not well looked after; her hair, which could have been a feature, was scraped back behind her ears. She sketched an imaginary biography: locally raised, bright enough for university but in love and pregnant at eighteen. Ten years later she was single, struggling, desperate for a man to rescue her but too proud to acknowledge the fact.

Jenny noticed the girl looking her over as she came back with a bottle of Chilean red, wondering what a woman in a city suit was doing in here alone. The look said this was her territory and other women who might be after the same prize as her weren't welcome.

But maybe she was just imagining it. Her mind was still racing. It was going to take most of the bottle to calm it down. Jenny thanked her politely and threaded her way back towards the exit.

'Hey!'

She glanced back and saw Steve coming after her, a half-empty pint glass in his hand. He caught up as she reached the door.

'Hi.'

'Steve.' She noticed the girl behind the bar look over at them as she took another customer's order.

'I promised a mate of mine I'd pass a message on to you. Name's Al Jones – he's got a load of flagstones would make a great patio for you at the back. They just came out of an old chapel.'

'I'm not sure I can stretch to a patio right now. I'm happy enough with the grass, especially now I can call it a lawn.'

'He'll do you a good price. Fifteen quid a flag – you won't beat that.'

'You do a pretty hard sell for a man who doesn't work.'

'Just a thought. No pressure.' He took a mouthful of beer. 'Can I get you a drink?'

'Maybe another time.'

'It's your money. You might as well get the benefit.' He noticed her unconscious glance towards the bar. 'Annie's an old friend of mine. Not the friendliest – had a rough time with her ex, drank the mortgage money and knocked her about.'

'Does anyone have any secrets around here?'

'Nope. And what they don't know they'll only make up.' He smiled. 'We're already up to God knows what as far as the gossips are concerned, so there's no point turning me down on their account.'

'Great. I thought this was a friendly place.'

'No one means any harm.' He nodded towards a spare booth. 'Indulge me. I want to hear about this job of yours.' He smiled, innocent and engaging.

'I can't stay long.'

'Drink?'

'Bloody Mary. A large one.'

She sat with her back to the bar, out of Annie's line of sight. Her touch of hands with Steve was more than old friends give each other, it told a whole story: Annie wanting more than occasional sex from a part-time boyfriend and Steve, addicted to the single life, in no mood to commit.

He came back with her drink and a whisky for himself and slid into the seat opposite, close to the wall, she noticed, where Annie would strain to see. 'So, you spend your days finding out how people died.'

'Sort of. But, come to think of it, I don't recall telling you what I do for a living.'

'You're still not catching on, are you? I knew who you were a fortnight before you moved in. *Attractive divorcée from Bristol, just appointed coroner.*'

'What else did they say about me?'

'You really want to know?'

'Try me.'

'Husband's a fancy doctor, ran off with a nurse.'

'Wow. Almost right.' She rolled the ice cubes around her glass and took a large gulp. 'It was nurs*es*, actually.'

'They got some things wrong – said you had kids.'

'I do have a son. He's fifteen, lives with his dad in Bristol.'

'Oh. Sorry.'

'It's OK. It's no secret. It just suited us that way. He's got exams, didn't seem right to move him.'

'Must be tough.'

'Of course.'

'Look, I didn't mean to—'

'Forget it. Actually I'm hoping he'll come and live out here soon. I think he'll like it.'

'There aren't many nightclubs.'

'Bristol isn't far, and he can have his friends over to stay. Maybe I'll turn the old mill building into a bunkhouse.'

'I know a good builder.'

'I'm sure you do.' She took another sip, the vodka finding its way into her system, beginning to take the edge off.

'I asked her to make you a good one.'

'She did.'

His eyes flicked in the direction of the bar. 'We're not an item. Just friends.'

Jenny nodded, unsure how to respond.

'You can imagine what it's like in a small village. Easy for things to get intense.'

'So I'm learning.' It began to dawn on her that he was actually quite drunk, not so that he was slurring his words, but the brakes were definitely off.

'We went out a few times after she split with her husband but it was never going to work. She wants *stuff*. I'm not interested in that. That's why I live up in the woods. Keep things simple.'

'Do you think you ever can?'

'You don't know if you don't try. You must have come out here looking for something.'

'I guess.'

'Have you found it?'

'Too early to say. I hope to.'

He took a glug of whisky and looked at her over the rim of his glass. 'Do you mind if I say something personal to you, Jenny?'

She was sure he was going to say it anyway, so why bother to object. 'Go ahead.'

'There's something sad about you. I saw it in your face in the garden.'

'I'd just been on the phone to my husband.'

'Still in love with him?'

'No. And it's none of your business.' She meant to sound serious, but it came out tongue-in-cheek. She blushed, then laughed, trying to cover the fact.

'Just a bit then, huh?'

'No. Not at all. He's an arrogant sod.'

'I get the picture.'

He was teasing her now. She couldn't work out how she'd let herself get so friendly with someone she hardly knew.

'We have nothing in common. He spent years stifling and judging me and all the time he was bedding any woman who'd say yes.'

'Sounds like a real gentleman.'

She took another large mouthful. 'And still he expects me to tip up at his house for lunch this weekend and sit there while his twenty-five-year-old girlfriend simpers around him like a grateful servant.'

'That was heartfelt.'

'You did ask.' Jenny looked at her glass: it was empty.

'Another?'

'Better not.'

'You look like you could do with it.'

'I've got a bottle of wine to sink in front of the TV.' She started to slide out of the booth.

Steve said, 'Do you believe in karma?'

'What do you mean?'

'Annie over there's been telling me for months I'm storing up bad karma, never doing anything for anyone else.'

'Tell her you made a good job of my garden.'

'I'll make a confession – I took a long look at you before I came over. I was standing over there in the weeds while you

were on the phone. You're right, he does sound like a bastard.'
He looked at her curiously, as if she posed him some kind of
challenge. 'How about if I offered to come with you to your
husband's?'

'Why would you do that?'

'Moral support. Might even earn me some good karma.'

'You hardly know me.'

He swallowed the last of his whisky. 'It doesn't feel that
way to me. Does it to you?'

Jenny said, 'I'll think about it.'

She took her bottle of wine and made for the door.

Steve called after her, 'Give me some notice if you want me
to shave.'

NINE

THIN RAIN SLANTED OUT OF a moonless sky and beat down on the gaudily decorated graves in the new arrivals section of the public cemetery. Several policemen in uniform stood at the locked gates. An undertaker's van and a number of private vehicles, one containing a miserable-looking clergyman sipping tea from a Thermos flask, were parked on the access road near to where the excavator was working. The whole scene was illuminated by an array of temporarily erected arc lights.

While she waited, Jenny walked along the row of fresh tombstones under cover of an umbrella. Some of the graves were staked out with mini picket fences and in-filled with coloured gravel; most bore photographs of the deceased. It had been nearly twenty years since she had spent any time in a cemetery and things had changed. Religious messages had all but disappeared; the memorials were shrines to ordinary lives with golf clubs, favourite pint pots and statuettes of Frank Sinatra cemented to them. The afterlife, where it was referred to, was envisaged as a kind of Disneyland with an easy-listening soundtrack, a place where the departed would forever mingle in a cosy lounge bar.

No fear of God or the devil here.

Alison approached, wrapped up in an ankle-length Driza-Bone and matching hat. 'We're about ready for the final removal, Mrs Cooper.'

Jenny followed her back along the row of headstones as two of Dawes's men lowered a nervous young gravedigger into the oversized hole and handed him a spade. He thrust it into the sticky soil and hit the coffin lid with a hollow, splintering thud. Dawes, a drawn-looking man in a black suit and raincoat, called out to him to be careful, and motioned him to scrape the soil off gently, miming how it should be done. The young man's courage failed him briefly, and then, averting his eyes, he drew his spade cautiously across the shiny veneer lid. There was scarcely room for him to stand clear of the coffin at the sides; no one seemed to have worked out how big the hole would have to be in order for the gravedigger to get straps underneath to lift it. As the undertakers discussed their dilemma, Jenny noticed the car headlights drawing up at the cemetery gates. A policeman approached the driver's window.

Alison said, 'Oh no. Please don't let it be the parents.'

The policeman stepped back to the gate and unlocked it, waving the driver through.

'What's he doing now? I told them no one else was to come in.'

Jenny said, 'I'll go. You stay here and make sure they don't make a mess of things.'

She strode across the wet grass to meet the large black saloon which was pulling up next to the undertaker's van. It was a Mercedes she'd seen before. Frank Grantham climbed out. Jenny caught up with him before he made it on to the grass.

'I'm going to have to ask you to leave, Mr Grantham. I gave strict instructions that no one was to come in.'

'What do you think you're doing here, Mrs Cooper?'

'Section 23 of the Coroner's Act—'

Grantham shouted over her. 'That's what I thought we hired – a coroner, not a bloody grave robber.'

Jenny strained to remain calm. 'I don't have to answer to you, but this is a legitimate and necessary investigation. I am merely doing what my predecessor for whatever reason failed to do.'

'I'll tell you what it is, it's disgusting.' Jenny could smell alcohol on his breath. 'And no way is my department paying for it, so you might as well stop right now.' He looked enraged enough to hit her.

'I've asked you once, now I'm telling you – you are not permitted to be here. Please leave or I'll have to ask the police to remove you.'

'This is council property. I'm as entitled to be here as you.'

'This operation is under the jurisdiction of the Crown. Any attempt to obstruct it is a criminal offence.'

Grantham sneered, the rain plastering loose strands of his dull grey hair to his forehead. 'You've lost your marbles, madam.'

He pushed past her and set off towards the grave. Jenny chased after him. 'How dare you? How *dare* you? Who do you think you are? Get out.'

'If anyone should be packing up, it's you.' He called out to Dawes and his men, 'Stop what you're doing.'

Confused faces looked up as he bore down on them. Alison stepped forward. 'Frank?'

Jenny grabbed hold of the sleeve of his anorak, stopping him in his tracks. She erupted. 'Maybe you've got a problem with women in positions of authority. Well, get used to it, I'm the coroner here and what I say goes. Get the hell out of this cemetery or you'll be spending the night in a police cell.'

Grantham looked at her in dumb astonishment. 'You're unhinged.'

'If you're not gone within one minute, I'm filing charges of obstructing a coroner in the course of duty and contempt. Your choice.'

Grantham looked at Alison, expecting her to come to his rescue.

Jenny said, 'See Mr Grantham out, would you?'

Grantham said, 'I thought you were more sensible than to get mixed up in this sort of nonsense, Alison.'

Quietly, but firmly, Alison said that perhaps it would be better if he were to let the coroner get on with her work.

Grantham shook his head. 'I don't believe this. I do not believe it.'

Jenny turned to Alison. 'He doesn't seem to have got the message. Fetch one of the police officers.'

Alison hesitated for only a fraction before reaching into her pocket and bringing out a walkie-talkie.

'All right,' Grantham said. 'But I'm warning you, Jenny, this is going to land you in deep trouble. The Ministry of Justice is going to hear about this.'

'They certainly will.'

He gave her a look of utter contempt and marched back to his car, slipping several times on the mud. It was a small, drenched, pathetic figure that climbed into the driver's seat and reversed erratically towards the gates.

Jenny said, 'What did he think he was doing coming here? He's got no right to interfere with a coroner's investigation.'

'You'd have to know him. He's used to being king of his own little castle. If he doesn't like something, he thinks he can just weigh in.'

'Did Marshall have to put up with this?'

With a note of regret, Alison said, 'I'm afraid he wasn't very good at standing up to bullies.'

Jenny turned back to the grave, where the men were still standing idle, waiting for instruction. 'Who told you to stop? Come on, I want this coffin out and away from here.'

She woke from a heavy, dreamless sleep at ten a.m. It was nearly two when she had got back from the cemetery, jumpy and agitated. She had lain awake, starting at every sound, until at nearly four she knocked herself out with two sleeping pills. It took her a moment to realize it was the telephone that had woken her and it was still ringing. She heaved herself out of bed and groped for her bathrobe. More asleep than awake, she stumbled downstairs, wondering who could be so desperate to want to reach her on a Saturday morning. She pushed through the door into the study, and lifted the receiver.

'Hello.'

'Good morning, Mrs Cooper. It's Tara Collins from the *Post*. We spoke earlier in the week.'

How could she forget?

'Sorry to call you at home. Your number was in the book.'

'Is it? It shouldn't be.'

'I'm calling to ask if you want to make any comment on the exhumation of Katy Taylor. I believe it happened last night.'

'Who told you that?'

'I'm afraid I'm not at liberty to say. You understand.'

No, she didn't, but it was foolish to think such a rare and ghoulish event could have stayed out of the papers. Someone along the line would have picked up the phone and sold the story for a few hundred pounds. Probably one of the gravediggers, perhaps even one of the policemen at the gate.

She knew she would have to say something to avoid idle speculation or a sensational headline such as 'Coroner silent on reason for exhumation'. She said, 'In order to determine the cause of death the body will be re-examined and exploratory forensic tests carried out. I am not looking for anything in particular, merely making sure that my investigation is thorough.'

'I understand she died five days after being released from Portshead Farm.'

'That's when she went missing.'

'It doesn't strike you as any sort of coincidence?'

'I deal in factual evidence.'

'You do know Danny Wills and Katy knew each other? They'd both been to drug awareness classes with the Youth Offending Team. Justin Bennett dealt with them both.'

Jenny tried to maintain the professional front, but a disturbing sensation was moving through her. 'As I said, I'm not in the business of speculating.'

'Off the record for a moment,' Tara said, striking a conspiratorial tone, 'don't you think it's a connection worth looking into? I'd go in there and try and find kids who knew them both if I could, but I've no access. You have.'

Even half awake she wasn't going to fall for the off-the-record routine. 'You'll appreciate that my investigation will proceed a step at a time. I can't say any more than that.'

'Hear that?' Jenny heard a faint click. 'That's my tape recorder switched off, swear to God. None of this is going into print. Look, I appreciate you've got a problem reopening the Danny Wills case when there's already been an inquest, but what you're doing now is a way into it. Believe me, I've spoken to kids who've been in Portshead – there's drugs, sex, the place is rotten. You think street gangs are bad, in there there's no escaping them. No one comes out better. Anything could have happened to her inside. We're talking about a drop-dead-gorgeous fifteen-year-old prostitute with a drugs problem – talk about easy meat.'

The crawling sensation worked its way up Jenny's spine and over her head. What Tara was telling her made perfect sense, of course. She'd spent most of her career despairing at the parlous state of the institutions that were meant to look after vulnerable kids, but the prospect of taking them on and digging that deep filled her with dread: it was precisely the mire she'd hoped becoming a coroner would drag her out of. Andy Taylor had hit it on the head out at the building site when he said the system couldn't tell right from wrong. There was something almost demonic about criminal teenagers; they were compelling, frightening and unpredictable. It took an iron will and a ferocious moral sense to deal with them, but rarely had she met a man or woman in the field who possessed those qualities.

Jenny said, 'Last time we spoke, Ms Collins, you threatened me. I appreciate these are emotive cases, but I won't be told what to do by you or anyone else. I will do my job as best I can. No proper line of enquiry will remain unexplored. Now, if you'll excuse me, I need to have some breakfast.'

'Just one more question—'

Jenny put down the receiver. She expected the journalist to ring straight back, but the phone remained silent. She walked through to the kitchen with her head already full of possible connections between Katy and Danny Wills, none of them pleasant. Tara Collins's call had certainly woken her up.

Halfway through her second cup of strong coffee and after she had scribbled pages of questions in a notebook, she remembered her lunch date with David and Ross . . . and Deborah. She had spoken only briefly to Ross on the phone last night as she was on her way to oversee the exhumation and he was heading out with friends, allegedly to a bowling alley. He'd been monosyllabic on the subject of his exams and even more taciturn about today's lunch. Who could blame him? David had probably issued grave warnings about a 'family conference' and a 'serious chat', some of the stock phrases he would utter in the same doom-laden tones he must use on his poor patients about to undergo bypass surgery. She pictured the scene around the dining-room table and cringed.

A third cup of coffee and half a temazepam only cancelled each other out. She threw on some old clothes and went out into the garden to see if it would make her feel any better.

In only three days the grass had already grown several inches and the weeds on the cart track were doing even better.

Either she would have to find the energy and the inclination to mow and slash every week of the summer or it was going to cost her a small fortune in labour. She breathed in the mild, damp air. Everything was still wet with last night's rain and now the sun had finally made it out clouds of steam were rising. It was as humid as a rainforest; the garden felt heavy and oppressive, every leaf and blade of grass seemed to bend under a burden. She wandered over to the ruined mill building, leaned back against the cold stones and watched the brook. The water was a good six inches higher than usual and full of dirty brown silt. It had swollen from a harmless paddling stream to a minor torrent capable of drowning a child.

It infuriated her that David could make her so frightened. He was only a few years older than she was yet had always managed to feel like her father, far worse than her father, in fact, who was now a frail old man in a Weston-super-Mare nursing home. In all their years of marriage she had never managed to attain an equal footing; she was always the junior partner, always in the wrong. Only on the issue of Ross's education did she get her own way. She was adamant that he would go to the local comprehensive and grow up among children who didn't take wealth and advantage for granted. She had to admit it hadn't been an unqualified success and the school's failings provided David with a stick he never missed an opportunity to beat her with, but at least Ross hadn't become arrogant or removed. Exams could always be taken again.

She retreated back indoors, took a shower and spent the best part of an hour trying to put together an outfit that would let her hold her own against the inevitably attractive Deborah without making it look as if she had tried too hard. She ended up in a pair of smart, close-fitting jeans and a black top that showed just a hint of cleavage. She put on a plain silver necklace – one she'd bought for herself since the divorce – and matching earrings. With a little skilful make-up she looked ten years younger and quite sexy, the kind of woman who'd eat a twenty-five-year-old floozy for breakfast. She slipped on a pair of plain black heels that gave her an extra three inches; she'd stand almost eye to eye with David.

Dressed for battle, she teetered downstairs and stopped for a final check in the hall mirror. She barely recognized the face that stared back at her. It looked strong, confident, mature, but behind the mask she was a bag of nerves, and what made it worse was that David would know that. Almost everyone else in her life thought she'd merely grown tired of courtroom advocacy and had opted for a change; he knew the truth, that inside she remained an emotional cripple.

As she fetched her car keys and double-checked the doors and windows, panic set in. All the usual symptoms bubbled up and took hold. She considered drifting through the day doped up to the eyeballs, but her rule had always been no pills at the weekend. She'd broken it this morning almost without thinking; more pills now would mean she was dependent. Months ago, when she was in a much weaker state, she had sworn that wouldn't happen. She pushed herself out of the front door and got as far as the car, but couldn't get in. What she felt was dread: she simply couldn't face the day. She slammed her fist on the roof. *What was wrong with her?* She was going to discuss her son's future but she was so screwed up and self-absorbed she couldn't get beyond her own insecurities.

Shit. Shit. Shit. She was an addict. She'd just have to drug herself and limp through life as best she could. As long as she saw Ross safely into adulthood she would have done her job. That was all that really mattered, her one responsibility. Everything else was irrelevant. She took out her bottle of pills, forced down the lid and twisted. She had only three left. How had that happened? She remembered the spillage in the office at the village hall. Half her supply had disappeared down the cracks in the floorboards. She'd meant to order some more online but it had slipped her mind. Now it would take until Tuesday to get them in the post and she'd need at least two to get her through Monday. That left her just one for today. If she took it now it would have worn off by lunchtime, but she couldn't even face the drive unmedicated, let alone the ordeal to follow.

She thought about phoning to cancel, pleading work, but David would see straight through that. Part of her knew this lunch was a test he was setting her: could she, a woman who until recently was seeing a psychiatrist twice a week, really claim to have got her life back? Could she be trusted to make decisions about their son's future?

She held the pill in her hand in an agony of indecision. A glossy new Toyota pick-up drove past in the lane and tooted, a vaguely familiar figure raised his hand in a wave. It was Rhodri Glendower with a lady friend in the passenger seat. Jenny smiled and waved back, touched at the neighbourly gesture. Rhodri was probably dining out on the story of rescuing her from her ditch, but she had no doubt he would help her out again if the need arose. It's just what decent people did.

The Toyota disappeared up the road, leaving her with the crazy thought that perhaps the answer to her dilemma lay with another of her well-meaning neighbours. Steve had had a few drinks when he made his offer to accompany her but he had seemed sincere.

What had she to lose? He could only say no.

What he said was sure, just give him a minute to throw on some clean clothes and run a razor over his face. Just like that, not a hint of surprise. He left her at the foot of the stairs stroking the dog and shouted down that there was a beer in the larder if she wanted it, he didn't mind driving.

She took him up on it. Five minutes later she was sitting in the passenger seat of the Golf, a little tipsy from the Grolsch she was still drinking and listening to Bob Marley on the stereo as Steve rolled a cigarette while steering with his wrists. He was wearing a collarless white cotton shirt and a crumpled linen suit with canvas boots, an outfit that looked like it had served him well over a number of years. Just smart enough to make him look arty without being unkempt.

He said, 'You looked so surprised. I was expecting you.'

'Then you must know me better than I do. I wasn't intending to ask you.'

'Really?' He licked the paper and glanced over at her as he popped the cigarette in his mouth.

'Really.'

He brought a box of matches out of his jacket pocket. 'Any objection?'

'Go ahead. Your funeral.'

'I'll remember you in my will.'

He lit his cigarette and opened the window a couple of inches. Jenny didn't say so but she liked the smell of smoke. It took her back to her student days, when the world seemed full of endless possibilities and responsibilities were still way beyond the horizon. Instead, she said, 'So you're doing this for your karma?'

Steve took a draw and blew the smoke out of the crack. 'That and because I like you.' He saw he'd embarrassed her and said, 'I don't mean like *that* . . . I like you. It was just the feeling I had when I met you. I thought we could be friends.' He gave an apologetic smile. 'Sorry. I should choose my words more carefully. I guess it's what comes of living alone – you forget how people react to things.'

She called David from her mobile to let him know she was bringing a friend, but got Deborah. She said it was no problem, there was plenty to go round. When they pulled into the neat brick driveway and parked alongside David's Jaguar, Jenny saw him peer out from the sitting-room window to get a glimpse of the opposition. In the ten seconds before he answered the front door he had pulled off his V-necked sweater and pushed up the sleeves of his shirt to reveal his sinewy forearms made hard from years of squash and work-outs in the gym he'd built in the cellar.

He opened the front door with a manly, 'Hi.'

Jenny, still glowing from the beer, said, 'David, this is Steve, a neighbour of mine. Deborah said it would be fine.'

'No problem at all. Pleased to meet you, Steve.' He gave him a powerful handshake.

Jenny could see him taking in the scruffy suit and shoes and visibly relaxing. He could deal with other men only as long as he could feel superior.

Steve said, 'Good to meet you, David. I thought she could do with a driver – almost went under a tractor the other day.'

Jenny said, 'He's been very neighbourly.'

'Excellent.' David scanned the younger man one more time and gestured them indoors. 'Let me get you both a drink.'

He led them through into the large, expensively decorated open-plan kitchen diner, which incorporated a conservatory overlooking a large but orderly back garden. The house managed to be both extravagant and soulless, as spotless as an operating theatre, the furniture tasteful, modern and expensive, but with no flourishes or quirks. It was devoid of ornaments or any other objects that might attract dust; the few paintings were modern and abstract. It was what an interior designer might call peaceful and what Jenny would call dead. The garden, too, had been cropped of life: a manicured kidney-shaped lawn fringed with evergreen shrubs. Nothing that would make a mess or do anything as frivolous as flower extravagantly or shed leaves. She had lived here with David for over ten years and it had never felt like home.

Deborah was a petite blonde nearer thirty than twenty-five and was busy at the kitchen peninsular unit, wearing a blue stripy apron over a pretty, high-waisted summer dress. Just David's type, and with a kind, submissive smile. A woman whose main desire in life is to please her man. She was welcome to him. Deborah wiped her hands on the apron – one Jenny now recognized as an unwanted Christmas present to her from David's mother – and scurried out to greet them.

'Hello, Jenny. I'm Deborah.'

Jenny said, 'Hi.' They touched hands, Deborah too unassertive to shake. 'This is my friend, Steve.'

Steve said a bright hello and leapt straight in with a kiss on the cheek. Deborah seemed to like it.

Blushing a little, she said, 'Lunch won't be a minute – I got a bit behind with the rice salad.'

'No problem.'

'Ross should be around somewhere. Shall I call him?'

David, over by the gleaming fridge pouring glasses of Pinot Grigio, said, 'He'll certainly be well rested. I only managed to turf him out of bed half an hour ago.'

'I'm sure you did it very nicely,' Jenny said.

Before David could retaliate Steve stepped in neatly. 'Twelve-thirty's not bad for a fifteen-year-old. I remember making it until at least four.'

'My son's not quite that lazy.'

Deborah gave a sugary smile as she carried a bowl of rice salad over to the table. 'Teenagers. We were all the same.'

A moment of awkward silence followed as David handed round the glasses. Jenny could tell he was desperate to know who and what Steve was to her, but was too wary of her reaction to dive in with direct questions. Over the years he had come to regard her as irrational, unpredictable and prone to unacceptable outbursts. His main priority would be to avoid a scene in front of Deborah at all costs.

It was she who broke the impasse. 'David tells me you're living near Tintern. It's beautiful over there.'

'Makes a change from the city.'

Steve said, 'The people are bloody weird. Strangers turn up at your door asking for work.' He gave Jenny a look.

She was grateful for his cue. 'Steve's got a farm over the hill. He sorted out my garden. If the weeds had got any taller I wouldn't have been able to see out of the windows.'

Wary again, David said, 'Oh. What sort of farm is it?'

'It's more of a smallholding. Been ten years up there trying to lead the good life.'

David looked baffled. 'You mean self-sufficient?'

'That was the idea. It almost works.'

Jenny said, 'He was an architect.'

'Not quite. I dropped out in the final year.' He nodded towards the garden. 'Mind if I go outside for a smoke?'

David shook his head and motioned towards the garden. Deborah quickly rummaged in a cupboard and came out with a saucer which she handed to him. 'Ashtray.'

'Thanks.' He stepped out of the French doors on to the pristine patio, sliding them closed behind him.

Deborah glanced at David and gave Jenny a nervous smile. 'I'll go and see where Ross has got to, shall I?' She hurried out to the hall, leaving them alone together.

David creased his face into a smile, waiting for her explanation.

'He's just a friend. He offered to keep me company, that's all.'

'Did I say anything?'

He didn't have to. Jenny could read his thoughts perfectly. She'd got herself a young dropout for a boyfriend as a childish rebellion against him, the high-pressure life they had led and the maternal responsibilities she had failed to bear. She couldn't face a lengthy explanation. He wouldn't believe the truth anyway.

'What about you and Deborah? Is it serious?'

'It seems to be going in the right direction.'

'She and Ross get on?'

'She's very good with him. More patient than I am.'

Jenny wanted to say, that's because she's hardly more than a teenager herself, but held off. She was determined to stay level, in control. David was going to see a different side of her today. She was here as an equal.

He said, 'How does it feel being a coroner? I must say, it's not a job I ever imagined you in. You always said you never wanted to be a judge.'

'It's nothing like being a judge. I'm more of an investigator. Judges referee competing arguments; I have to find the truth.'

'Stressful?'

'Nothing I can't cope with.'

'Your health must have improved.'

'I'm fine.'

He nodded, looking almost pleased for her. 'I'm glad.'

She felt like a fraud. She was still popping pills and starting at shadows. The subtext of David's questions was: *I hope for your sake you're not kidding yourself. Cracking up in the Coroner's Court really would be the end of your career.* She had butterflies in her stomach and minor palpitations. She took a large mouthful of wine and wondered if she shouldn't have taken the temazepam after all.

Deborah reappeared with Ross in tow. He was dressed in baggy jeans and a long-sleeved T-shirt and his hair, dark like hers and shoulder-length, was still flat on one side from where he'd been sleeping.

David grunted in disapproval. 'Couldn't find a comb?'

'No. Hi, Mum.'

'Hi, sweetheart.' She gave him a hug which he didn't return, self-conscious in front of Deborah and his father.

He noticed Steve on the patio stubbing out his cigarette. 'Who's that?'

'Steve's a neighbour of mine.'

'Yeah, right.'

'He offered to drive me, that's all.'

Ross shuffled over to the table. 'What's for lunch?'

Between them, Deborah and Steve made a brave effort to keep the small talk rolling throughout the meal. They discussed her work as a senior theatre nurse, her three sisters, who were all settled down with children and couldn't understand why she hadn't done the same, and the blessings of internet shopping. As far as Jenny was aware, Steve didn't own a computer but you wouldn't have known. She and David strained to chip in with light and uncontroversial observations, but Ross remained largely silent and surly at the end of the table. She had worried on the way over that he would react badly to her bringing Steve – she hadn't had a boyfriend since her divorce – but he seemed too deeply buried in himself to care.

By the time Deborah was serving strawberries and meringues David had drunk enough to tackle the subject they had gathered to discuss.

Never the diplomat, he launched in without notice. 'Well, Ross, I can't say I was very impressed with those so-called teachers of yours. If I was in any doubt that you should do your A levels elsewhere, that parents' evening settled it.'

Jenny, tense, said, 'We haven't actually decided that's what's going to happen.'

'What if I'm happy where I am?'

David topped up his glass. 'The thing is, even today, if you want to read medicine at university you need straight As.'

'I never said I want to do medicine.'

'You told me—'

'You told me that's what *you* wanted.'

'He doesn't have to decide this minute, does he?' Jenny said. 'The issue is whether he's in the right school. He's got to be somewhere he's happy.'

'I told you. I want to stay where I am.'

David sighed. 'It's a sink, Ross. They don't have any ambition for you. They treat you the same way as the kids from the council estate. If you got a job as the manager of a supermarket they'd think it was a success story.'

Jenny said, 'Can we not get emotive?'

'It's his entire future we're talking about. You don't get second chances at education. This is a decision that will affect him for the rest of his life.'

'You think I don't know that? I'm not stupid.'

'I didn't say you were.'

'That makes a change.'

Deborah said, 'Home-made meringue with strawberries, anyone?'

Steve handed over his dish with an eager 'Yes, please.'

'Ross?'

He shook his head and pushed his plate away.

Jenny said, 'Why don't we leave this until after? None of us wants to get in a state over it.'

'What's the point? No one ever listens to me anyway.'

David said, 'That's not true, Ross. We're your parents, for goodness' sake. If we didn't make the best decision now you'd blame us for the rest of your life.'

'Yeah, you know best about everything, don't you?' He got up from his chair and headed for the French doors.

'Ross? Where are you going?'

'Nowhere.'

He slammed out on to the patio and strode off up the garden, taking refuge on the area of lawn beyond the shrubs, out of sight.

David, who had been staring at the table in an effort to avoid erupting, looked up and started out of his seat. 'I can't allow that kind of behaviour.'

'Leave him. Please. Just give him a moment.'

'You want him to get away with that? What sort of message does that send?'

Deborah and Steve exchanged a look. She said, 'Why don't you have these strawberries first? He'll calm down in a minute.'

David grunted and reluctantly sat back down. 'Why you didn't let me send him to Radley in the first place . . .'

Jenny dropped her spoon and glared at him. Steve shot out a hand and put it on her knee. She pushed it away. 'Why didn't I? They might have made an even better job of screwing him up than we have.' She shoved away from the table and went after Ross.

She found him sitting on the bench in the secret part of the garden she had insisted on when they'd had it landscaped soon after they moved in. The fantasy had been of little moments à deux, hidden from the nanny and next door by a dense hedge of conifers and from the three adjacent gardens by a semi-circular screen of bamboo. She and David had sat here together perhaps once. Its main use had been as a place to storm off to and sulk.

'Any room for me?'

He shrugged, then moved over a touch, making a space. She sat next to him, neither of them saying anything for a moment. She knew how he felt: being judged by David was crushing. It had been bad enough as a wife, as a son it must be devastating.

'Sorry these things always end up so bad-tempered. I didn't

mean it to . . . You know what your dad's like. He doesn't realize how harsh he sounds.'

Ross picked distractedly at a splinter of wood. 'You don't have to make excuses for him.'

'He's concerned for you, that's all.'

'Huh.'

Jenny studied his face. Even in the six months since she'd left home he'd changed. You couldn't call him a boy any more. He was a young man, six foot tall and with his father's athletic build. He'd be a real catch one day, but still had several painful years of confidence building ahead of him.

'I haven't spoken to your dad about this, but I was wondering if you might like to come and live with me while you're at sixth form.'

'Go to college over there? Forget it.'

'No, in Bristol. I'd drop you off on my way in. You'll be able to drive yourself soon, anyway.'

He glanced up at her, wary. 'You'd get me a car?'

'Nothing flash, but yeah, why not? You could have friends to stay . . .' God, she was being manipulative, but she couldn't help it. It was working. She had his attention for the first time in months. 'Are you still seeing Gina?'

'Lisa.'

'Sorry—'

'S'all right.' He continued picking at the bench. She watched him turning the offer over in his mind, weighing the inconvenience of living out in the wilds against escaping from his father. 'You mean she could come over at weekends and that?'

'Whoever you want, as long as they're not too crazy.'

She seemed to be winning. He nodded. 'I'll think about it.'

'So what about sixth form? Your dad wants you to go to interview at Clifton College.'

'I'm not moving. Anyway, why would they want me?'

'He went there.'

Ross kicked at the weedless turf. 'You're really selling it to me.'

'He thinks you'll get the best teaching.'

'I don't want a life like his. He hasn't even got one.'

Jenny's phone rang. She took it out of her jeans pocket and checked the screen, it was Alison. 'Won't be a moment. It's work.' She clicked the answer button. 'Hello, Alison.'

'Sorry to disturb you, Mrs Cooper – Professor Lloyd just called. He's done the post-mortem on Katy Taylor and wants to talk to you.'

'Can't he call?'

'He asked if you could go over and see him. I think he wants to show you something.'

'Now?'

'That's what he said.'

'OK. Tell him I'm coming from Bristol. I'll be about an hour.'

Ross got up from the seat.

Jenny said, 'I'll call you when I'm on my way,' and rang off. 'Ross, I've finished. Let's talk.'

'You've got to work.'

He started back to the house.

The lunch had achieved nothing. No decisions had been made about Ross's future and David and Jenny had parted on acrimonious terms. Ross refused to come out of his room to say goodbye and only one of Deborah's meringues got eaten. If it hadn't been for Steve, Jenny felt sure it would have ended in an ugly scene. She had always hated the house and the swanky kitchen, but seeing another, younger woman so at home there had made her feel irrationally excluded and resentful. She was wearing *her* apron, for God's sake, and cooking with *her* pans. And now the dutiful, domesticated Deborah would be sent upstairs to talk Ross round as the voice of reason.

Steve had managed to survive the ordeal on only one glass of wine and was now gallantly chauffeuring her to Newport while she sat staring out at the motorway in moody silence.

'I can see why you two split.'

Jenny was looking at cows standing in a field, wondering whether they ever got used to the traffic. 'Why's that?'

'Every time he poured wine he put a stopper back on the bottle.'

'I didn't notice.'

'You're so used to it you don't see it any more. And when they cleared the plates he made her rinse them down before putting them in the dishwasher. Didn't even say anything, just with this look he gave her.'

'Did she?'

'No question.'

'He's a control freak.'

'I guess you wouldn't want a flaky heart surgeon.'

'Someone must appreciate him.'

Steve thought about that for a moment, then said, 'Can I ask you something? What's it like having sex with a man like that?'

'You shouldn't be having those kind of thoughts, it's bad karma.'

TEN

STEVE REFUSED HER OFFER TO come with her to the mortuary in Newport General, an imposing Victorian building on a hillside overlooking the city. She left him in the car smoking a cigarette, listening to *The Best of Jimi Hendrix*, and promised she wouldn't be long. Steve said to take as long as she needed, he wasn't in any hurry.

The mortuary was in the traditional place, down in the basement through an unmarked door which had to be buzzed open for her. She had read that while body snatching was rare, stealing of jewellery, particularly rings from corpses, was commonplace. There were stories of fingers cropped off with secateurs. The Newport mortuary, like that at the Vale, had a storage problem. Following signs to the autopsy room, she passed along a badly lit subterranean corridor. Stretched out down the wall to her right was a line of gurneys parked nose to tail, each carrying a familiar, body-shaped white plastic envelope. She tried not to look, concentrating instead on the tangle of exposed pipes and wires which snaked along the wall to her left: the ragged arteries of the ageing hospital. Her footsteps echoing off the grubby tiled walls was the only sound.

A door opened ahead of her. Professor Lloyd, an eccentric-looking man in his sixties, burst enthusiastically out of his office in shirtsleeves. He had an unruly shock of white hair and a bent pair of half-moon spectacles balanced on a small, sharp nose.

'Mrs Cooper?'

'Yes.'

'So glad you could come. It's been most interesting, really most interesting. Would you like to come and see?'

'Um—'

'Not squeamish, are you?' He laughed. 'Hold on.'

He darted back into his office and re-emerged with two sets of clean scrubs and latex gloves. He thrust one of each at Jenny.

'The post-mortem report your officer sent me, the one Peterson wrote, is that really all he said?'

'Yes. Why do you ask?'

'You'll see. But I have to say I'm most surprised, I always used to think of him as very thorough.'

He yanked on his gloves and scrubs at double-quick speed and hurried across the corridor. 'She's in here.'

He pushed through slap doors into the autopsy room. Jenny was hit by a draught of fetid air. Pulling on her scrubs, she took a deep breath and followed him in.

The body was so decomposed as to no longer appear human. Aside from the overpowering smell, it was more akin to one of the mummified remains in a museum cabinet than a fresh corpse. It lay uncovered on the table. The skin, where it was intact, was black or a dark mossy green; as the muscles and subcutaneous fat beneath had decomposed, it had the appearance of having melted across the skeleton. The fleshy tissue of the breasts and thighs had collapsed entirely and rotted through to the bone. The hands retained their slender shape, but the skin had broken away and started to slough off at the wrists and slide over the fingers.

All of this was bearable, just, but the sight of Katy's face made Jenny recoil. Her hair was still blonde, but the scalp was peeling from the front of the skull. The eyelids had all but been eaten away, as had the eyes, leaving two grisly hollow sockets. The cartilage of the nose was virtually intact, but the softer tissue of the lips had decomposed, revealing even white teeth which appeared fixed in a clenched grin.

Apparently oblivious to the smell, Professor Lloyd leaned over the body and closely studied what remained of Katy's features. 'I only wish I'd got a look at her before. Never mind – at least I've got some of the picture.'

Jenny placed a gloved hand over her face and took a breath through her mouth. 'What did you find?'

'Let's put it in context. We know the primary cause of death was an overdose of heroin, but if I'm right what we're really looking for is some clue as to what went on before it got into her bloodstream.'

She nodded, wishing he'd get on with it.

He picked up a slender instrument that looked like something with which a dentist might scrape out a cavity and used it as a pointer. 'The first thing I noticed was a chip out of this front tooth.' He tapped the left of her two front teeth.

She steeled herself and looked. Sure enough there was a chip perhaps two millimetres wide off the bottom left-hand corner.

'The edges are jagged, suggesting a very fresh break. Anything could have caused it, of course, but – ' he reached over to the steel counter next to the sink and picked up a kidney dish, which he waved under her nose – 'there's the missing chip itself. Guess where I found it?'

'I've no idea.'

'In the back of her mouth, between her molar and her cheek. The normal human reaction is to spit out any foreign body in the mouth, but it was still there, which I would say is a pretty good indication that she was hit, and with some force.'

'When?'

'Obviously not long before death. And for the fragment still to be in her mouth I would say there is a strong chance either she was unconscious when it happened, or the blow, or blows, rendered her so.'

'Why didn't Peterson spot it?'

'To be fair to him, one doesn't pay the teeth much attention during a routine p-m, sometimes none at all. None of us exactly has the luxury of time.' He placed the kidney dish carefully back on the counter. 'So, we have a possible blow. Now we need evidence to corroborate. Even in its present state the body has yielded us not one but two further clues.' He pointed to the right shoulder, which, Jenny now noticed as she walked around to the other side of the table, had been substantially dissected, revealing the joint. 'I was looking for evidence of a struggle and I found it. You'll have to look carefully for this.' He poked his pointer at the mid-section of the joint. 'Two of the glenohumeral ligaments have been wrenched from the bone.'

Jenny saw some stringy bits of tissue but couldn't have identified them as ligaments.

Professor Lloyd was becoming increasingly excited. 'This is consistent with a violent wrenching injury, such as when the wrist is forced up the back. And then there's the hair.' He set down the pointer and, gently taking hold of the skull in two hands, tilted it to the right. 'You see?' He pointed a finger at a bare, black patch of scalp. 'There's a clump of hair missing. It's a good inch across. Your officer says it wasn't found by the police at the scene.'

'No. I've seen no record of it.'

'Her hair is quite long. It wouldn't be immediately obvious, but when you look at it in context you begin to build up a picture – her wrist forced up her back, the assailant pulling so hard on her hair that a handful comes out. As it wasn't found near the body, this violence may well have taken place elsewhere.'

'And the blow to the face?'

'More likely to have taken place at the scene, or it could all have happened at once. Impossible to say.'

'Before she was injected?'

'Yes . . .' Professor Lloyd straightened up, fixing her with an intense, serious gaze. 'The final thing: our lab was good enough to test her various samples this morning and they came up with some interesting results. As you know, hair gives us a sixty- to ninety-day chemical history of the body. We found that Katy had taken marijuana and cocaine regularly, almost without interruption throughout that period, but no heroin. Blood and tissue samples are somewhat less reliable at this stage, but heroin was detected and a high concentration. We estimate in the region of 2,000mg.'

'Meaning?'

'Enough to kill a small horse.'

Jenny forgot about the smell. What she had now was evidence of murder.

She said, 'Is there any way of telling if there was any sexual violation?'

Professor Lloyd gave a regretful smile and shook his head. 'I am afraid there are some secrets the dead take with them.'

'How do you think she died?'

'In all likelihood struggling against a very brutal and determined assailant. Someone armed with a massive dose of heroin who planned his actions very deliberately.'

'Could you have a report for me by tomorrow and be able to give evidence to my inquest on Monday morning?'

'Certainly.'

Jenny looked at the body and thought of the smiling photograph on Andy and Claire Taylor's mantelpiece. What was it about beautiful young girls that made men kill them?

All she told Steve was that she was dealing with the unexplained death of a fifteen-year-old girl. He didn't buy newspapers and she hadn't seen a television in his house, so it was a safe bet he hadn't heard about the case. Unlike some lawyers, she had always taken her duty of confidentiality seriously. As coroner it was even more important. Experience had taught her that you could trust no one with professional secrets, not even loved ones. David, too, for all his faults, had never blabbed about his patients. They hadn't done pillow talk. In the last few years they hadn't done much in bed at all.

Steve let her sit there without disturbing her thoughts about sex, death and what it meant for her to find herself caught in the middle of a gruesome killing when all she had wanted was a quiet life. She had chosen certainty, a job and a house that would see her through several decades, but in the space of a week she had found herself in the midst of chaos and she was anxious. Anxious in that deep-down, stirring-of-the-silt way she had been in the months before her breakdown. It was like the melancholy which seeped into the mind when a thunderstorm had yet to come over the horizon: you felt its pressure on your spirits long before you knew what was coming. And it pierced all the layers: there was no state of happiness, joy, drunkenness or drugged-up dopiness that could deliver escape. It tugged like a heavy stone tied around your neck.

Steve turned off the dual carriageway and took off across country, traversing the side of the wide Usk valley heading towards the ridge that separated it from the Wye valley on the far side. It was a deep green, barely populated landscape of fields and meadows divided by dense hedgerows and dotted with coppices that hadn't changed in hundreds of years. He wound down his window and breathed in the fresh air that smelled of cow parsley and ripe grass.

He said, 'I don't think I could live without that. That's what I hated most when I lived in Bristol – the smell of the place.'

Jenny, trying to push her dark thoughts aside, said, 'I know what you mean.' She wound her window down and put her face to the rushing wind, closing her eyes.

'You want to go for a walk? There's a place up here I'd like to show you.'

'In these shoes?'

'I put some boots in the back.'

'You did? When?'

'When we were leaving. I knew you wouldn't have brought any.'

'You don't know my size.'

'I can tell from the look of you. You're a six, like my ex.' He leant an elbow on the open window, at ease with the world. 'What's the problem – you got something better to do?'

They parked in a gateway at the top of a hill, near a hamlet he said was called Llangovan. He reached into the back seat, where he had stashed a carrier bag containing two pairs of ankle-high leather work boots. 'She left them behind on purpose, said if she took them they'd only remind her of wallowing in the mud like a peasant.'

Jenny, never comfortable in other people's cast-offs, removed her heels and eased a bare foot into the stiff leather. 'That was her story.'

'What do you mean?'

'No woman likes to think she'll be forgotten.'

He took her along a footpath around the edge of a field of sheep, skirting a wood that stood on the summit of the hill. As they walked he pointed out landmarks and talked about trees, the way that oak and beech were planted side by side so that the wide canopy of the beech would starve the oak of light and force it to grow a long, straight butt with no branches shooting out and spoiling the grain. Much of the Wye valley was planted for ship's timber and charcoal to fuel the wire and iron works that had stood alongside the river in Victorian times. When the industry died the woods survived. It was a rare and beautiful part of the world where nature had reclaimed a once industrial landscape; he took it as a sign of hope.

They stopped at the highest point of the field and sat on the grass to take in the view across the fifteen miles to the soft purple silhouette of the Brecon Beacons. The vast expanse of sky had many moods: patches of clear blue interspersed with puffs of cumulus and clusters of heavy-laden, slate-grey rain clouds. Their shadows drifted lazily over the fields, giving and taking away the sun. Now and then a bright shaft of light would penetrate the thicker clouds and shoot a golden column down to earth. Steve said it was called 'God light'; you saw it on sentimental greetings cards but with good reason: nothing a human being could ever make would be as beautiful. Perhaps that was the reason he'd given up architecture – his buildings would only spoil what couldn't be improved.

Jenny said, 'You're quite a romantic, aren't you?'

He stretched back on the ground, squinting at the sky. 'Someone has to be.'

'Can you really be happy not having any money?'

'Yes and no.'

'Why don't you go back and qualify, do some ethical work? Everyone wants green buildings these days. You'd be rich.'

'I'm thinking about it.' He rolled over and leaned up on one elbow, looking at her. 'Or should I say, you've made me think about it.'

Jenny, feeling a flutter of shyness, said, 'What have I done?'

'Nothing in particular . . . You just reminded me that there's a world out there.'

She pulled at the grass with her fingers, nervous with him

looking at her. Any moment she was expecting him to reach out and touch her and she hadn't a clue what she'd do if he did.

He sat up, legs in front of him, leaning back on his hands. 'You find it hard to relax, don't you? Can't you just enjoy the view?'

'I've got a lot on my mind.'

With a hint of a smile he cupped a hand to shade his eyes and looked out over the valley. 'I'll give you one less thing to worry about – I'm not trying to have sex with you. I'll be honest, I wouldn't say no, but I think we could get along fine without.'

Jenny, flustered, said, 'That's admirably direct.' God, she sounded uptight.

'I thought you'd appreciate it.' He smiled, got back to his feet and brushed himself down. 'Guess you'll be wanting to head back.'

He held out his hand. She hesitated a moment, then reached up and took it, letting him pull her up.

She sat in front of her laptop late on Saturday night. The website she chose was based in Ireland. She paid extra to have the pills couriered over the weekend. She arranged to pick up the package from the company's depot in Avonmouth at eight a.m. on Monday so she wouldn't have to give her home address or risk being without pills until Tuesday. She'd sign the docket with an unintelligible scrawl. The only thing that would link her to the technically illegal purchase was her credit card records, but the website promised the entry on her statement would read *Gifts by Mail*. She had ordered ten bottles of 30mg tablets, telling herself that was all she was ever going to need.

ELEVEN

THE ATMOSPHERE IN THE HALL was edgy, bordering on hostile – a two-temazepam occasion. The ranks of journalists had swollen to fill up two of the four rows of seats and a news van sprouting satellite dishes had arrived outside. Andy and a deathly pale Claire Taylor had been joined by several grim-faced friends and relatives. Hartley and Mallinson had laden their table with an impressive array of files and law reports. Grantham was nowhere to be seen, but Dr Peterson had responded to his second summons and was seated next to an earnest young woman with a blue legal pad on her knee whom Jenny took to be a solicitor. Alison had informed Detective Superintendent Swainton that today's proceedings might be of interest to him but she had met with a curt response: he was too busy to attend and so were his officers.

Professor Lloyd strutted to the witness chair in a three-piece suit and badly knotted bow tie, relishing his moment in the spotlight. He placed his reading glasses carefully on his nose to read the oath card and recited the words with excessive precision.

Early on Sunday morning Jenny had received by email his careful and thorough report. Only she and Alison had seen it. She had decided not to circulate copies until after he presented his findings in open court, wanting to see Peterson's reaction and catch Hartley, as far as possible, unawares. Her plan was to spend the morning hearing the forensic evidence and any explanation Peterson could offer for his failure to spot what Professor Lloyd had found so easily. The next stage was to look for possible perpetrators. A further summons was on its way to Justin Bennett and to the senior care officer in charge of female trainees at Portshead Farm. Jenny wanted to know how Katy Taylor had managed to keep up her intake of marijuana and cocaine during her time in her care.

Before beginning her examination of the witness, Jenny turned to the jury and explained that, as they might have gathered from the local press, the reason she had adjourned proceedings on Thursday was so that Katy Taylor's body could be exhumed and re-examined by a Home Office pathologist. This was a senior pathologist with special expertise in detecting evidence of crime who was frequently called on to conduct post-mortems on behalf of the police or the coroner. The jurors listened with earnest expressions. The novelty of their strange public duty in a remote village hall had faded. Their frowns and nods told her that these eight citizens were now feeling the full weight of their responsibility.

She addressed Professor Lloyd. 'Professor, you are the Home Office pathologist for the city of Newport in the county of Gwent?'

'I am.'

'Did you, on Saturday 23 June, carry out a post-mortem examination on the body of Katy Taylor?'

'I did.'

'And did you write a report dated 23 June, detailing your findings?'

'I did.'

She glanced at Peterson. He was sitting very still, but his eyes were wide and apprehensive, a man who knew his reputation was on the line.

'Before we go into the detail, Professor, would you please read the jury your summary.'

'Certainly.' Alison stepped forward and handed him a clean copy. He cleared his throat, paused, then read aloud: 'While I agree with the findings of my colleague, Dr Peterson of the Severn Vale District Hospital, that the immediate cause of death was a massive overdose of diamorphine (heroin), in the course of my examination I have found substantial and compelling evidence of serious and violent physical assault . . .'

There was a sound in the public gallery, somewhere between a faint gasp and a dull moan. Jenny looked up to see Andy Taylor clasping Claire's hand between both of his. Dr Peterson tugged nervously at his cuff. His solicitor was urgently noting every word.

'This evidence is in three parts. Firstly, the glenohumeral ligaments of the right shoulder had been wrenched from the bone, indicating that the right arm had been pushed with some force up the deceased's back. This would have been extremely painful and it is hard to conceive of an innocent explanation. Secondly, a clump of hair, approximately one inch in diameter, had been traumatically wrenched from the rear left occipital area of the scalp – ' he pointed to an area between the top of his neck and the back of his left ear – 'leading to the reasonable conclusion that it was pulled out during a physical altercation. It is notable that the missing hair was not discovered with the body.'

Jenny saw the look of suppressed desperation cross Peterson's face. She longed to know what was in his mind, whether he had simply missed or deliberately overlooked the evidence of violent death.

'Thirdly, there was a small chip out of the left of the two front teeth. The edges were jagged, suggesting a recent trauma. I recovered the chip itself from between the deceased's cheek and gum. In my opinion she received a powerful blow to the front of the face. The fact she had not swallowed or spat out the chip indicates that she was unconscious or insensible either before or as a result of the blow.'

Claire Taylor sobbed. A woman who looked like she might be her sister passed tissues down the line. The faces of the friends and family were pictures of grief, bewilderment and betrayal. Peterson stared, expressionless, at the floor in front of his chair.

The hall listened in sombre silence – interrupted only by Claire Taylor's sniffles – as Jenny led Professor Lloyd through the fine detail of his findings. He described how the dose of heroin had been so massive that had Katy tried to inject it herself, she would have been dead or unconscious before the syringe was half empty. He was convinced that a third party had administered it, perhaps even two people: one forcing her arm and grabbing hold of her hair while the other stuck in the needle.

Jenny asked, 'What do you make of the photographs the police photographer took of her body where it was found?'

'She must have been placed in that position. As I have said, it would have been impossible for her to inject that much heroin, then set the syringe down by her side. I would have expected to find the needle still in her arm, the syringe half full.'

'Is there anything else about the photograph that strikes you?'

'Her clothing seems remarkably ordered given the level of violence to which she had been subjected. I can assume the attack on her was very swift and vicious. And well planned.'

'You think this was premeditated?'

'Acquiring and preparing that amount of heroin takes some doing. I think it fair to say that anyone with that degree of know-how would have been well aware that such a large dose would kill her.'

She then took him through the results of the hair analysis test. It confirmed beyond doubt that this was the only dose of heroin Katy had received, at least in the ninety days before her death. He agreed with Dr Peterson's finding that she had probably been dead for five to seven days or thereabouts when she was found and that, because of the onset of rigor mortis, it was more than likely that she was placed under the bush in a seated position very soon after she died.

Jenny noted that this meant Katy had probably died on Tuesday 24 April, two days after going missing from home. She needed to know where Katy had been on the night of Sunday 22 and Monday 23 April and who she had been with. The two days she spent missing were critical.

Jenny finished her examination of Professor Lloyd by asking how it could be that he and Dr Peterson had arrived at such different conclusions. He thought for a moment, then, after a further studied pause, said, 'Initially I was inclined to take a charitable view. The standard blood tests he ordered were less precise than the analysis I have carried out, so he wouldn't have known with as much accuracy how much heroin was in her system – that I can understand. He is a man under great pressure of work who probably conducts half a dozen post-mortems each day, but in my opinion, in a case where a violent death was even a remote possibility, a reasonably competent pathologist should have carried out a more detailed examination than he did.'

'You're surprised that he didn't find the chipped tooth?'

'Moderately.'

'And the missing hair?'

'Perhaps a more understandable oversight.'

He glanced across at Peterson without a hint of remorse or

embarrassment. Jenny knew what this meant: his words may have been calculated to sound reasonable, but what he was really telling her was that his colleague had been careless at best, negligent or even complicit in the deliberate concealing of evidence at worst.

'Thank you, Professor. If you would be kind enough to wait there, Mr Hartley may wish to ask you some questions.'

Hartley, who was still writing a longhand note of Professor Lloyd's closing remarks, took his time to finish, glanced over the page as if reassuring himself of an obvious conclusion, and rose, with no particular sense of urgency, to his feet.

'Professor,' Hartley began, 'is it correct that you carried a full forensic examination of the body of Katy Taylor at the request of the coroner, Mrs Cooper?'

'Yes.'

'And you were therefore mindful of the fact that you were looking for, and might well find, evidence leading to the conclusion that Katy's death was suspicious.'

'I'll agree only with the first part of your question.'

Hartley smiled. 'And if I understand you correctly, you have concluded that it is more likely than not that her death was suspicious.'

'I have.'

'Thank you, Professor.' Hartley turned to Jenny. 'Ma'am, I'm sure I do not have to remind you of rule 26, subsection (1) of the Coroner's Rules 1984.'

Still a little shaky on the fine detail of the Coroner's Rules, Jenny opened her copy of Jervis with a sense of foreboding.

'It states that if the chief officer of police requests the coroner to adjourn an inquest on the ground that a person may be charged with murder or manslaughter in relation to the death, the coroner must adjourn the inquest for a period of twenty-eight days. As the chief constable's representative, I hereby request such an adjournment with immediate effect.'

Jenny glanced at the rule, checking that it read as she thought it did. 'Mr Hartley, this rule applies only where the chief officer of police envisages charging a specific individual. It is designed to prevent two judicial processes occurring at the same time. As there is no suspect, I presume, who is about to be charged with Katy Taylor's murder or manslaughter, I am fully entitled to continue with this inquest.'

'I have been instructed that in the light of this evidence, the CID wish to reopen their investigation. It is customary in those circumstances for the coroner to adjourn and await the outcome of criminal investigations and proceedings, if there are any.'

'Mr Hartley—'

'If you'll allow me to finish, ma'am.'

Jenny conceded and let him continue.

'The function of the adjournment serves a dual purpose. Not only does it prevent the police investigation suffering in any way from the publicity this inquest may attract, it will also ensure that when this inquest resumes, both you and the jury will have the benefit of any evidence obtained by the police. I have a number of authorities here to support my argument if you wish to see them – ' he waved in the direction of a hefty pile of photocopied documents – 'but I think you'll agree, this is primarily a matter of where the interests of justice lie. Surely that *must* be with the resumption of the police investigation.'

'I'll adjourn to consider your submission, Mr Hartley.'

Jenny rose and retreated, with her copy of Jervis, to her office. She turned up the Coroner's Rules again with a sinking sensation. Hartley was correct. The police had the right to request an adjournment where there was a chance that a person – who need not be specified – might be charged with an offence relating to the death. If she were to refuse the police could ask the Director of Public Prosecutions to intervene and request one. Again, she didn't have to comply, but she risked creating a major diplomatic incident.

The rules and procedure had a straightforward and simple purpose: to ensure that the police investigated crimes and coroners investigated causes of death. Where a coroner's investigation turned up evidence of a crime, the spirit of the regulations, if not a strict interpretation of them, required her to stand aside while the police took over. Her inquest would resume either when the police decided that no crime had been committed or that no one was to be charged, or if a suspect was charged, at the conclusion of the criminal trial.

The problem was, what happened when the coroner didn't trust the police? If, for whatever reason, they failed to do their job properly, she was the only backstop. No one else had the necessary capacity or resources to demand answers.

There was a tap on the door and Alison entered. 'Are you all right? You looked like you'd seen a ghost when he asked for the adjournment.'

'I knew he was planning something. He didn't lug that many books to court for show.'

'He's right, though, isn't he? You can't carry on if CID have got an active inquiry.'

'I could, but it wouldn't make me very popular with the Ministry of Justice.' She sighed. 'What do you think's going on?'

'You've shown them up, Mrs Cooper. Nobody likes that.'

'What about your theory – that Detective Superintendent Swainton was being pressured?'

'I don't know . . . I was probably just being emotional. I know a lot of the boys in CID. I can't see any of them going easy on a case like this, especially after the second post-mortem. What you need to know is what Katy was up to in the couple of days before she died, that's what they'll be trying to find out.'

'You honestly believe we can trust them, even after whatever happened to Harry Marshall?'

Alison glanced over her shoulder at the door, checking it was shut fast. 'The way I see it, you could turn them down, but apart from Professor Lloyd's findings you've nothing to go on. The jury *might* come back with a verdict of unlawful killing, but where does that get you – you still need the police to find the perp.'

'What do you suggest?'

'Give them their adjournment and use the time to sniff around, take a few more statements – they can't stop you doing that.'

'And meanwhile the truth gets buried deeper?'

'There are a couple of blokes in CID, old friends of Harry's. I'll have a word, see what they've heard.'

Jenny considered the alternatives. Apart from potentially scuppering her career, refusing the adjournment might lead her nowhere fast. What she wanted was the unvarnished truth, and Alison was right, there was little chance of hearing it in open court during the next two days. And if the police really were involved in a cover-up of some sort, the chances of her unearthing the facts by herself were non-existent.

Jenny resumed her seat at the head of the hall. Hartley looked at her expectantly, a battery of legal authorities at the ready in the event her decision didn't go his way.

'I have considered your application on behalf of the chief constable, Mr Hartley, and I'm prepared to adjourn for fourteen days.'

Hartley rose with a satisfied smile. 'Thank you, ma'am.'

'However, before I do so, I would like to hear again from Dr Peterson. Would you come forward, please?'

She gave Hartley no time to object. He exchanged a look

with Mallinson, who shrugged, as if to say they had nothing to fear.

Peterson's solicitor leaned forward and whispered words of instruction to him. He got up, walked to the front of the hall and sat in the witness chair, fixing his eyes on Jenny.

'Dr Peterson, you have heard Professor Lloyd's evidence. Do you have any explanation for why you failed to note the three factors which led him to conclude that Katy Taylor died a violent death?'

In a calm, even voice with a well-judged hint of apology, he said, 'Professor Lloyd was quite correct to say that I was handling, and still am handling, an enormous caseload. Now and again things are missed which shouldn't be. The police informed me that Katy Taylor had died from a suspected drugs overdose and my findings confirmed that. It was not suggested to me that her death was violent, therefore I didn't carry out the detailed investigations Professor Lloyd was briefed to do. Dissection of the shoulder, for example, is not a common procedure in a post-mortem.' He glanced over at Professor Lloyd, who was seated in the front row of the public seats. 'I am grateful to my colleague for sharing his findings and to you, ma'am, for requesting a second examination. And for the sake of Miss Taylor and her family, I sincerely hope the police investigation is successful. They have my deepest sympathy.'

Back in the small side office, Jenny packed her books and papers into her briefcase with a sense of anticlimax. After all the anxiety and anticipation she had managed only one and a half days in court. She felt for Claire and Andy Taylor. First the shock of an exhumation, then hearing that their daughter had probably died a violent death and now an adjournment. Their agony must seem endless.

When her outrage at what had felt at the time like a cynical ambush by Hartley began to subside, she concluded that she had probably made the right decision. She had a breathing space in which to interview witnesses in her own time and to try to gain an understanding of what Marshall's reasons were, if any, for not holding an inquest in the first place. Perhaps she had been too swift to imagine a conspiracy, too easily swept up in the emotion of a teenager's shocking death. Snapping her briefcase shut, she made a decision to go about her investigation in as detached and professional a manner as she could. She was the coroner, an impartial, clear-headed, determined investigator of the truth.

Pulling on her raincoat, which, judging by the increasingly frequent spits of rain against the window, she was likely to be glad of, there was a knock on the door behind her. 'Come in, Alison.' She glanced out of the window, drawn by a flash of lightning in the distance. 'Everything sorted out?'

A voice answered, 'It's Tara Collins.'

Jenny wheeled round to see a woman in her upper thirties, a little over five feet tall, with fierce, determined eyes and short dark hair. She was smartly but not expensively dressed in a trouser suit. Jenny recalled seeing her sitting in court that morning and had assumed she was a lawyer of some sort – the journalists had distinguished themselves by their scruffiness and frequent yawns.

'Have you got a moment?'

'I can't discuss the case—'

'It's not about the case, not directly at least. I spoke to your officer and she said it would be all right.'

Jenny was cautious. 'It'll have to be brief . . .'

Tara stepped fully inside and closed the door behind her. 'I was at home writing a piece on Katy's exhumation and this inquest when I called you on Saturday. Ten minutes after we finished the police turned up and arrested me on suspicion of credit card fraud. It's a complete joke. I've been framed. I spent the weekend in a police cell. They bailed me at six this morning. I'm in court first thing tomorrow – I'm supposed to have defrauded Western Union of $25,000.'

'Have they got evidence?'

'Apparently my laptop has been used to wire money to someone in New York I've never heard of. The cash was purchased with stolen credit card details which I'm meant to have entered on the Western Union website. The really sweet bit is that the US authorities could apply to have me extradited. Whoever thought this one up really put some effort in.'

'Who was the complainant?'

'Tip-off, that's all they'll say. And they took my computer and back-up drives. All my work's on there, research notes, interview transcripts. Everything.'

Jenny felt a numb sensation spreading from the tips of her fingers. 'Is there any particular reason you think this is related to Katy's case?'

'I've been making a few calls, trying to work out how well Katy and Danny knew each other. I told you they'd been to the same drug awareness class run by the Youth Offending Team back in December.'

'Where did you get that?'

'A girl called Hayley Johnson. She was a friend of Katy's, similar lifestyle but a touch older – she's eighteen.'

'She sounds interesting.'

'I'll see if I can find her again – she's a bit hard to pin down, moves around a lot.' Tara ran a hand through her tight hair and let out a sigh of frustration. 'Look, I want you to know I'm not usually one to get paranoid. If you think I'm crazy, I'd rather you just told me straight so I can give you some more detail.'

Jenny shook her head. 'I'll believe you. Have you got good lawyers? They should be able to check the history of those transactions.'

'I'll be working on it, don't worry.'

'So, what I can do for you, Ms Collins?'

Tara said, 'Don't let go of this thing until you find an answer.'

TWELVE

TWO TEENAGERS HAD DIED AND, according to Tara Collins, not only were their deaths linked, but someone very determined and very organized was trying to prevent an investigation. These were powerful claims and Jenny was struggling to make sense of them. Just as she was getting her own irrational fears under control, the journalist's visit had unnerved her again. She told Alison nothing of what Tara had said and sent her off to buy new furniture for the office instead. She wanted time alone to think.

Back in Jamaica Street she locked the outer door between reception and the hallway, closed the venetian blind at her office window and sat in artificial light with a legal pad and pen. There was the usual crop of daily death reports to deal with, but they would have to wait. Unless she made a plan, her anxiety would mount until she could no longer function. She started to note down her thoughts.

Professor Lloyd's evidence had proved to her satisfaction that Katy was violently restrained, hit in the face and injected with a lethal dose of heroin. This might or might not have taken place where her body was found, but it seemed likely that it had happened elsewhere and her body was dumped or, more accurately, carefully arranged in the dense undergrowth. This meant that her attacker or attackers had a good deal of local knowledge – the location was obscure – which might support the theory that she was murdered by a man who used prostitutes; but why the violence if she was a willing sexual participant? In any event, her death probably took place on Tuesday 24 April and she went missing from home five days after her release from Portshead Farm. The police would now be concentrating their efforts on tracing her movements and contacts during that time. With a bit of luck, Alison would get inside information from her former colleagues and they would be able to stay abreast of developments. If evidence turned up which for some reason the police suppressed or failed to pursue, Jenny would investigate personally.

Without drawing too much attention to herself, she would quietly develop a few lines of enquiry of her own. She wanted to speak to Mr and Mrs Taylor to find out if they had any clue where Katy might have been on the missing two days. Perhaps they knew more than they had admitted and for reasons of their own had chosen to keep certain things to themselves. Now they knew how their daughter had met her end they would surely be willing to part with anything they had. She also wanted to speak to Justin Bennett again, to the senior care officer at Portshead Farm and to Hayley Johnson, Katy's elusive friend, who, Tara had told her, moved from squat to squat, taking drugs and selling sex to pay for them.

So far so good. She had witnesses to seek out and interview, evidence to gather. Solid, practical actions: tasks that a competent coroner would be expected to perform.

Turning over a page she wrote down three names which represented all that was disturbing and intangible about the case: Danny Wills, Peterson, Harry Marshall.

Danny's connection with Katy was one she could legitimately explore. As they had met in the past and as the evidence proved Katy had taken drugs while at Portshead Farm, it was logical to suppose there might be some drugs-related connection between them. Perhaps they were both in debt to the same pusher. Collecting money by violent means, even murder, was becoming commonplace in the city. Hayley Johnson might be able to help with an insight into the teenage underworld. It was one Jenny knew to be labyrinthine in its complexity and operatic in its melodrama; its loyalties, fears and feuds could only be understood with inside knowledge.

Peterson's post-mortem examination remained an enigma. Even setting aside the fact that he didn't commit his report to paper until she forced him to, it was suspiciously brief. He had been very skilful in praising Professor Lloyd in court – he almost had her convinced that he merely made an innocent mistake – but her impression of him was not of a man who was slapdash. She had met plenty of lazy professionals in her time, people content to mark time until retirement, but none of them had still been athletic in their mid forties. He might be exasperated by, even resigned to, the failings of the NHS, but he still had the bright eyes of a man open to a new challenge. Katy's case couldn't have failed to spark his interest. And if he had spotted signs of violence he must have had a very compelling reason not to mention them. Next to his name Jenny put a large question mark.

Harry Marshall presented another problem. A man who generally swam with the flow, but who, only a few weeks before signing Katy's death certificate, in flagrant breach of the regulations, had been threatening to shake the citadel to its foundations. She drew a connecting line between his name and Peterson's. They had been close colleagues. They operated on trust. Harry had taken Peterson's word and their old school system had ticked over for years. It seemed probable that Peterson was in some way involved in whatever had taken place, or at least had an inkling, but he was unlikely to talk. Still in mid-career and doubtless with a wife and family to support and protect, he would do all in his power to safeguard his position.

Harry too, had dependants, everything to live for. There was no reason to think his death was anything other than tragically untimely, but still, there was a sense that it was more than mere coincidence. Even heart attacks were rarely entirely random events. Delve deep enough and you could usually find something which had triggered a feeling of depression or hopelessness in the deceased; how many men died in the immediate aftermath of retirement? Jenny paused, put down her pen and sipped at the cup of tea, now nearly cold, which sat untouched on the desk. Harry's disorganized files and papers still lay on the floor either side of her, and in them, possibly, might lie some small clue.

She pushed her notes aside and lifted them on to the desk. The accounts file still waiting for her attention was too dull even to open. She dropped it back on the floor and turned to Harry's collection of newspaper cuttings in search of a common thread. She leafed through them. Now and again he was mentioned or quoted: there were cases of industrial accidents, road deaths, hospital operations gone tragically wrong, several deaths in custody, a brutal beating to death of a young black man by police officers and numerous spectacular suicides. The most recent cuttings related to Danny Wills's death. In all of them Danny was portrayed as a dangerous young criminal whose end was to be expected, even applauded. One article, written by a journalist determined to tar Simone Wills's name, pointed out that she had failed to register the names of the fathers of three of her children, quoting an acquaintance who implied their fathers had most likely been Simone's dealers.

The fact that Harry had bothered to read and cut out these articles at all said something, but Jenny couldn't decide what. It might only be that he still possessed a streak of vanity – the Mick Jagger pout in his college photo suggested it – and the cuttings boosted his ego. There were no articles, however, about Katy Taylor's death. Even though the discovery of her body had been reported widely, he hadn't clipped a single cutting. Perhaps his failure to shake the citadel to its foundations in the Danny Wills inquest had temporarily deflated his ego. Or perhaps his mind had been on other things.

Alison arrived back from her shopping expedition and bustled in with the news that she had taken Jenny at her word and ordered two new desks and executive chairs that were so smart they were going to put the rest of the office to shame. She'd made a few calls on the way and arranged for some decorators to come and quote, people she'd used on her own house who'd give them a good price.

Jenny let the stream of trivia wash over her and then, when Alison had finished, said, 'I'd like you to get hold of Harry Marshall's medical records.'

Alison seemed shocked by the request. 'What for?'

'I'm not sure.'

'But you haven't got any power to. You're not investigating his death.'

'No, but I'm investigating Katy's, and his motive for writing her death certificate is something I need to understand.'

'He wouldn't have done anything wrong on purpose, Mrs Cooper. He wasn't like that. He was a decent man.'

Gently, Jenny said, 'I understand your feelings towards him and I promise I'll deal with this sensitively. They may turn up nothing.'

'What do you want me to tell the doctor?'

'I'll give you a letter requesting that he produce Mr Marshall's notes. He's under a legal duty to comply. If there's any problem give me a ring and I'll talk to him.'

Alison, muted now, said, 'What about the decorators?'

'We'll see them another day.'

*

Steadied by her third pill in ten hours, Jenny crawled through slow traffic to the Taylors' house. She rang the bell three times and was about to give up when Claire answered the door. Her hair was rumpled, as if she had been lying down. She was wrapped in her usual cardigan and was shivering slightly. Her face was thinner, too, as if she hadn't been eating.

'Sorry to disturb you, Mrs Taylor. I thought I should explain the situation. Is your husband home?'

She shook her head, burying her hands in her cardigan pockets, arms pressed in closed to her sides.

'I could come again when he is.'

Claire thought about it for a moment, then took a step back from the door, Jenny's invitation to come inside.

She followed her along the short hallway to the kitchen. Breakfast bowls and cups lay unwashed in the sink. The atmosphere was heavy and airless, all the windows firmly closed. Claire motioned her to a chair at the small dining table. Jenny thanked her and took a seat. Claire remained standing, in the corner by the stove, putting as much distance between them as she could.

'You understand that I've adjourned the inquest to allow the police time to reopen their inquiry.'

She nodded.

'In the meantime, I'm afraid Katy's body will have to remain at the mortuary, in case the pathologists need to run any more tests.'

Another nod. Every second spent in Jenny's presence was clearly painful.

'I'll also be conducting some enquiries of my own. I'm particularly interested in finding out who Katy might have been with when she disappeared from home.'

Claire shrugged, an almost indifferent gesture. 'She never told us where she was. Could have been anywhere.'

'Does the name Hayley Johnson mean anything to you?'

Jenny could see that it did and that the associations weren't good. Claire said, 'I think I heard her talk to her on the phone. One of her druggy mates, I expect.'

'You don't know where I might find her?'

'Andy told you where the kids hang out, down the rec . . .'

'Is that where Katy used to go?'

'Sometimes . . . I think there were older kids involved, too. Girls with their own flats and that. Katy couldn't wait to get a place on her own.'

Jenny offered a smile, relieved that Claire was at last beginning to open up a little.

'Did Katy have a mobile phone?'

'Andy wouldn't let her. She had one once but we got a bill for three hundred quid. That was that. Whether she bought one out of her own money, I don't know. I think it all went on drugs.'

'Can you remember what happened on the Sunday, Mrs Taylor – I'd like to know about the last time you saw Katy.'

Claire looked out of the window, her body language becoming defensive again. Jenny waited. It was some moments before she spoke.

'She'd kicked up on Saturday night about this curfew, but we managed to keep her in. Andy and I went to bed about eleven. She was already down. I was up at half-six next morning and she was gone. That was the last we saw of her.'

'Was it a big argument on Saturday night?'

'No more than usual.'

'Did Katy take anything with her, a bag, clothes?'

Claire shook her head. 'Not that I could see. Just what they found her in. She might have had a coat.'

'What happened to Katy if she hadn't taken drugs for a while?'

'She got difficult, argumentative. She'd hit and scratch, swear . . .'

'Is that how she was on Saturday?'

'It was just shouting, quite mild really. The fact she actually stayed in . . . we thought the curfew was working, that she was going to stick to it.'

'Had you seen a change in her since she came out of Portshead?'

'Yeah . . . She was quieter. Definitely quieter. That's the thing . . .' She broke off and wiped her eyes with her cuff. 'We both really thought we were getting somewhere.'

'I'm sorry to put you through this, but it's very useful for me . . .'

Claire nodded and reached for a roll of kitchen towel.

'Did you go looking for her on the Sunday?'

'We walked down to the rec, that was about it . . . Thing is, we couldn't do anything. We went through all this with social workers the last few years – you can't use physical force against your own kid. If Andy tried it she'd just threaten him with Childline or the police. She'd call them both without even thinking. We've had police here, social services, all treating us like we're the ones at fault . . . Of course I wanted to shove her in the car and drive off to the Highlands or somewhere we could get her straight, but you daren't. You're frightened of your own child . . .'

Jenny said, 'Would you mind if I had a look in Katy's room?'

Claire shrugged. 'Opposite the top of the stairs.'

Jenny left Claire in the kitchen and climbed the narrow staircase to the small landing. Four doors led off it. One, ajar, was to the marital bedroom; the curtains were drawn, the bed unmade. She opened the door opposite her and stepped into a tidy single room. Her first reaction was surprise. There was the usual collection of schoolgirl posters on the walls, hair-dryer, make-up on the dressing table that doubled as a desk, a TV, stereo, some books. It could have been the room of the girl who was top of the class. It didn't smell of cigarette smoke, she hadn't disfigured the wallpaper, the collection of magazines on the shelf was relatively innocent. The clothes in the wardrobe were hung up neatly and folded in orderly piles. Jenny opened drawers and stooped down to look under the bed. It was the same everywhere: nothing that screamed, or even suggested, that she was a delinquent.

She heard Claire come up the stairs and stop out on the landing. 'You don't mind if I don't come in?'

'No.' Jenny had a final glance around and stepped out to join her. 'It's very tidy, Mrs Taylor.'

'She was, mostly . . . Part of her was still our little girl. I don't think she knew what she was. Drugs, friends she felt she had to impress, I don't know what it was got hold of her.'

'You haven't touched it since?'

'No. That's how she left it.'

'Was that usual?'

'She'd kept it nice since she came home on the Wednesday. It was like she was trying to make an effort.'

'Had she taken drugs in that time?'

'Not that I knew about. And I could normally tell from looking at her, but she seemed clean. Saturday night, that's when I imagine she got the craving . . . That's the only thing I can think of.'

It made sense. For all her wildness, Katy came from a solid home. She knew what family life was and how normal people lived. Even for a girl who'd learned to turn tricks to pay for drugs, six weeks in Portshead Farm would have come as a shock. Yes, it did make sense that she would have tried to behave when she came out. And when you've been used to taking drugs every day, four days without a fix is when the need would become acute. She could imagine her pacing the floor in the small hours, tidying her room, wanting to get straight again, desperate to make it up to Mum and Dad and all the while fighting the irresistible urge to get high.

Jenny said, 'Did Katy ever mention a boy by the name of Danny Wills, about a year younger than her?'

'Danny Wills who hanged himself at Portshead?'

'Yes.'

'She knew him. They were at the same primary school, Oakdene, up in Broadlands. He was trouble even then.'

'Did she spend time with him recently?'

'Not before she went away as far as I know. When she came out she said she'd seen him in the canteen before he died. Said he looked in a bad way, like he'd been fighting. She said there were a lot of fights there.'

'Did she say any more?'

'No . . . Why?'

'My office dealt with his case.'

Claire looked at her mistrustfully. 'Katy may have been bad, but she wasn't in the same league as him. He was out of control when he was eight years old. She had a proper home, parents who loved her.'

Jenny had touched a nerve. 'I can see that. I can see that you loved her very much. I will find out what happened to her, Mrs Taylor. I promise you.'

The unseasonal rain had returned and the recreation ground, a grand title for a tired, unkempt two acres of public park, was largely empty. Jenny turned up the collar of her mac and went in search of dissolute teenagers. There were none to be seen. She found their cigarette ends, empty beer cans and alcopop bottles and, by the benches in the corner furthest from the gate, several used condoms in the untended flower beds. It was depressing but not shocking, only a few degrees worse than she had been. She'd drunk her share of alcohol, smoked joints when they were on offer and probably would have given cocaine a whirl if the right boy had waved it under her nose. There was sex, too, but under slightly more savoury conditions, and mostly in the belief that it was the route to eternal love.

Making her way across the wet grass to the exit, she spotted two girls, aged around fourteen or fifteen, who came into the park, clumsily lit cigarettes and swaggered in her direction en route to the benches. Both wore a semblance of school uniform, one had a phone pressed to her ear.

Jenny addressed the taller of the two, the one without the phone, a dark-haired, mixed-race girl with a pretty face. 'Excuse me. Did you know Katy Taylor?'

'What d'you say?'

'She was the girl who died at the end of April. She used to hang out here.'

The girl struck an aggressive pose, cocked a hip. 'I don't know what the fuck you're talking about.'

'Hayley Johnson?'

The other girl came off the phone and said to her friend, 'What does she want?'

Jenny said, 'I'm trying to find people who knew Katy Taylor. I'm the coroner. I'm investigating her death.'

The girl with the phone said, 'We don't know shit,' and walked on. Her friend followed, stepping in close to Jenny and bumping her with her shoulder.

Jenny fished in her jacket pocket, pulled out a card and set off after them. 'Look, there's money in it. A hundred pounds for anyone who can tell me where Katy was on Sunday 22 or Monday 23 April. I also want to speak to Hayley Johnson. You see her, give her my number.'

She offered her card to the taller girl. 'It looks like she was murdered. You could be a lot of help to me.'

The two girls traded a look, their bravado wearing a little thinner.

'Take the card. Think about it.'

It was the phone girl who reached out and snatched it, then tossed it on the ground.

It was nearly eight p.m. and she was still at her desk. She had cleared today's death reports – already becoming inured to the gruesome details – and was contemplating opening the accounts file to see just how big and dreary a task awaited her. She had managed to lift it on to the desk and open the cover when she heard the outer door opening and Alison call through, 'Hello? Mrs Cooper?'

'In here.'

She appeared in the door clutching a large brown envelope. 'The surgery had passed the records back to the main archive at the hospital. We were lucky to get hold of them – it took the girl ages. They were bagged up, ready for the shredder.' She handed the package across the desk.

Jenny opened it and pulled out a crumbling cardboard file. Marshall's name and date of birth were written on the front in the kind of cursive script that hadn't been used for decades.

Alison said, 'They go right back to when he was six months old.'

Jenny turned through the fragile pages, smiling at the neat, perfunctory entries made by the Marshall family doctor: 'Cough, moderate. Reassured mother (fussing) not whooping.' 'Complains of stomach aches – only on week days!'

'The later stuff is mostly about his blood pressure. He was taking statins for his cholesterol.'

Jenny turned over a chunk of dusty pages and found the most recent entries. She could sense Alison's jumpiness.

Harry had visited the doctor approximately every six weeks

for the last two years to have his cholesterol measured, and the trend was mostly downwards. His final reading, a month before he died, was a respectable four point five, two points lower than what she would have expected from a coronary victim. The final entry was dated Friday 27 April, just short of a week before his death, and three days before the Danny Wills inquest. It read: 'Symptoms of depression, feelings of being overwhelmed, insomnia, TATT, anxious about ability to function at work. Advised long summer holiday in order – agreed. 4 x 50mg Amitriptyline for two weeks then review.'

Alison said, 'What does TATT mean?'

'Tired all the time. These are classic symptoms of depression. He prescribed a sedating antidepressant, quite a high dose.'

'I thought so.'

'Have you spoken to Mrs Marshall about this?'

'No. Why would I?'

Jenny slid the notes back into the envelope. 'Maybe I'd better.'

'What for?'

'For one thing, it would be useful to know how many pills he had left from his prescription.'

'No. You mustn't.'

Jenny looked at her, surprised at the sharp note of alarm in her voice.

Alison said, 'Let me talk to his GP first. There's no point upsetting Mrs Marshall and his girls.'

'Alison, there's something you've got to understand. I am going to find out what happened to Harry Marshall, and if it's relevant information it will become public. I am not and never will be in the business of protecting anyone's reputation if that stands in the way of justice.'

Alison fixed her with an accusing glare. 'You may be

grateful for your friends one day, Mrs Cooper. And real friends are there even after you're gone.'

The phone rang at nearly midnight, waking Jenny with a jerk from her first, fitful dozes of the night. Unexpected calls always made her think something terrible must have happened to Ross. He had barely more than grunted during their twice-weekly conversation last Friday and it left her feeling empty and rejected. She gripped the banister as she went downstairs, fighting the effects of half a bottle of red and a sleeping pill. She lurched into the study, barely able to focus as she picked up the receiver.

'Hello?'

'It's Alison, Mrs Cooper. I didn't know if I should disturb you—'

'What is it?'

'I spent most of the evening with Mrs Marshall, talking. She's still very upset, of course . . . I did manage to mention the tablets, but she didn't know about them. I looked them up. They're ones you're not meant to mix with alcohol, but Harry was still having his gin and tonic in the evening. We think he might not even have picked up the prescription.'

'She didn't find any drugs bottles in his clothes or anywhere?'

'No. Nothing, Just his statins – he kept them in a drawer in the kitchen.'

'Did you mention the phone call he made to you the night he died?'

'I didn't like to.'

'Anything else?'

'Not really. Like me, she'd noticed he was out of sorts, but he didn't really talk to her about his work much. She says it depressed her.'

No wonder Harry liked his gin so much. Alone all day with the dead and no one to offload to in the evenings.

'OK. Thanks.'

'So what do you think?' Alison sounded genuinely hopeful that Jenny would say that was an end to it, that Harry's death was tragic but clearly natural.

Jenny said, 'I'll think about it. Goodnight, Alison.'

She set down the receiver and sank into the upright chair at her desk. The room was spinning slightly. Through the haze, she tried to picture what this information meant. Either Harry had so much gin on top of his antidepressants he accidentally nudged himself into a coronary, or he swallowed his entire prescription, flushed the containers down the toilet, picked up the phone to Alison to say goodbye – perhaps even to make a declaration of love – and ran out of courage at the last minute. As the pills began to seep into his system he climbed the stairs, changed into his pyjamas, bade his wife goodnight and quietly lay down to die.

THIRTEEN

AFTER SEVEN GOOD HOURS' SLEEP Jenny decided to face the world on a single tablet, which she snapped in half. One half with breakfast, one saved for lunch. She toyed with taking no more with her, but wasn't ready to let go of the security blanket just yet. Instead she zipped them away in the furthest recess of her handbag, making it an effort to get to them.

Her first stop was at the offices of the Severn Vale Youth Offending Team, a dreary 1970s building that stood in the middle of a row of convenience stores, nail bars and take-aways, only a few hundred yards from the Broadlands Estate. There was no reply when she arrived at nine a.m. and she had drunk two cups of tepid coffee in the greasy spoon opposite before she spotted a slouching figure that looked like Justin unlocking the front door at gone half past.

He took a long time responding to the buzzer, four attempts in all.

'Who is that?'

'Jenny Cooper, Severn Vale District Coroner. I've a few more questions I need to ask you, Mr Bennett.'

'Right . . . I'm about to see a client.'

'I'm sure the client can wait.'

'Can't we fix a more convenient time?'

Jenny lost patience. 'I'm conducting a major inquiry, Mr

Bennett. You are under a legal duty to comply. Please let me in.'

There was a brief pause. The door-release sounded.

Justin's office was as she expected. Poky, untidy and tucked away at the end of the first-floor corridor. He sat apprehensively behind his desk in jeans and a Lil' Kim T-shirt and tried to look busy, shuffling coffee-stained papers into a heap.

'What can I do for you?'

'I'm trying to find out where Katy Taylor was and who she was with on the days before her death.'

'No idea. I only saw her once after she came out of Portshead, on the Wednesday . . . apart from passing her in the corridor on the Friday.'

'When she went to her Recovery from Addiction class?'

'That's right.'

'In this building?'

'Upstairs. We have a meeting room.'

'Uh huh.' Jenny brought a legal pad out of her briefcase and turned to a blank page. She noticed Justin looking at it, wary. 'You said in evidence you talked about the terms of her contract on that Wednesday. Did you talk about her time in Portshead?'

'I probably asked her how she managed. I don't remember our exact words.'

She jotted a note. 'Did she tell you she was taking drugs all the way through, marijuana and coke? They seem to have been in plentiful supply.'

'No. She didn't mention that.' He crossed and uncrossed his arms, having problems finding a comfortable position.

'She was here before Christmas, wasn't she, on a drugs awareness course? She was on a supervision order that time for possession with intent to supply cannabis resin.'

'I believe so.'

'Did you have dealings with her back then?'

'Not directly. I knew of her – her name came up in team meetings, that's all.'

'Was the fact that she might be selling sex discussed?'

'I think so.'

Jenny made a note and looked up. 'Can I see her file please? I'd like to take it with me.'

'What, now?'

'As she's dead, I can't think you've any more use for it.'

'I'll have to get authority. My boss is in shortly.'

'The only authority you need is mine, Mr Bennett. The file please.'

Justin rose hesitantly from his chair and went to a filing cabinet. Jenny kept her eyes on him, checking that he didn't try to weed out any documents. He removed a slender wallet file and handed it over the desk. She opened the flap and took out the handful of papers, no more than twenty separate sheets. All of them were tick-box forms apart from a typed report written prior to her sentence. She skimmed through it and didn't learn anything she hadn't already known.

'Don't you write down any personal observations?'

'I don't tend to, no.'

'Why not?'

He shrugged. 'It's just not how it's done.'

Jenny glanced through the forms. They were all designed to ensure that criteria were met, meetings attended and appropriate actions taken. The young offender was often referred to as the 'client'. There was the odd scribbled note, but the accent was on keeping it all as impersonal as possible. These soulless, bureaucratic pro-formas said this agency was more concerned with protecting itself and its employees than its clients. One of the documents was Katy's contract with the Youth Offending Team in which she promised to keep her curfew, go to school, arrive punctually at meetings and attend Recovery from Addiction classes. There was also a clause about understanding her responsibility to society, respect for others and our laws. Fine words.

Jenny slotted the papers back in the file. 'Do you have any idea who Katy was associating with when she came out?'

'No.'

'Didn't you talk to her about that? You must have a lot of local knowledge.'

'As I tried to explain to you in court, my job is to win the young person's trust, not to act as an authority figure.'

'And you earn this trust how?'

Her question caught Justin off balance. He stammered, 'I try to make them see me as someone they can talk to . . . honestly.'

'But you don't ask questions.'

'Building trust is a process.'

Jenny wanted to say, *and meanwhile she's out on the streets getting herself killed*. 'Tell me who you think she was associating with.'

'I can't say. I don't know.'

She was fast losing patience. Even as a lawyer several steps removed from this street-level work, she got to know personalities and reputations. Justin was part of the neighbourhood, all he did every day was meet its most persistent teenage criminals.

She held him in her gaze. 'Why are you lying to me, Justin?'

His cheeks flushed red and his Adam's apple rose and sank in his throat. 'I'm not. I don't know who her friends were . . . She wasn't very open with me.'

'Really?' She kept her eyes on him. 'She was an associate of Danny Wills, wasn't she? When they were younger they were at school together, they were in the same drugs awareness class here last December, and they met again in Portshead. He died while she was in there.'

'She didn't mention him.'

'He was one of your "clients", too, wasn't he?'

'Yeah . . .'

'You didn't think to say what a shame about Danny? Had she seen him at Portshead? Was she upset?'

'We didn't talk about him.'

Jenny let him sweat for a moment. She didn't know what to make of him. Was he a liar or just a natural-born bureaucrat already skilled in the arts of self-preservation?

'What time of day did you meet with Katy on the Wednesday?'

'At the end of the day. Around five, I think.'

'That explains a lot,' Jenny said, and let him reach his own conclusion. She shut her legal pad and opened her briefcase. 'I'll take Danny's file, too.'

She read through it sitting in her car, which was parked outside a bookmaker's where old white men and jobless young West Indians seemed to be forging an unlikely common bond. A permanent cluster stood outside smoking cigarettes, finding plenty of things to joke about. The file didn't contain many laughs. It was thicker than Katy's but just as impersonal. It held almost no clue as to who Danny Wills was apart from the list of offences he had committed. No one perusing the pages would have gleaned any insight into the mind of an unhappy teenager who grew up without a father or any security. The good news for Justin Bennett and his bosses was that the form marked 'Reoffending Behaviour' wouldn't be getting any more ticks. There was no box to record a death; if they were deft enough Danny could even make it into the annual statistics as a success.

What troubled her most was the lack of personal information – the kids' interests, friends, skills. It felt like the only public official who had made a genuine attempt to understand him was Harry Marshall when he compiled his pre-inquest report. What she had found this morning made her angry. Without thinking, Jenny took out the half-tablet she had saved for later and swallowed it. Washed down with a mouthful of Diet Coke, it made her feel a little better, but not much.

She watched the men outside the bookmaker's, happy low-life, all smoking, friends together. It struck her how quickly friendships must be made in prison. A frightened child like Katy or Danny couldn't have avoided being drawn to a familiar face in the canteen. They must have spoken.

She opened her legal pad, turned to the chronology she had roughly begun to compile in the back pages and drew circles around the significant dates:

> 14 April – *Danny found dead*
> 17 April – *Katy released from Portshead*
> 22 April – *Katy goes missing*
> 27 April – *Marshall prescribed antidepressants*
> 30 April – *Katy's body found*
> *Danny's inquest opened*
> 1 May – *verdict of suicide returned*
> 2 May – *Marshall writes Katy's death certificate*
> 3/4 May – *Marshall dies*

She stared at it, trying to fit Marshall into the equation. Simone Wills had said his mood had changed about three days before the inquest, about the time when he saw his doctor. Alison had said he'd been out of sorts for a while before then, probably up and down with symptoms; but could an event have triggered his decision to get hold of pills? Katy Taylor was missing at the time, dead in fact, but as far as Jenny knew her name would have been unknown to Marshall until Monday 30 April, when her body was discovered.

She tried the lawyer's trick of looking at the facts from

every angle, plugging in 'what ifs'. A big one loomed out at her from the page: *what if* Marshall had found a connection between Danny and Katy between the 22nd and the 27th? And *what if* he knew or suspected she was dead? If he had made a link, if it was something overwhelming that he simply couldn't fight, it would explain both the feebleness of his inquest into Danny's death and his avoidance of an inquest into Katy's. And then there was Tara Collins. She hadn't given up digging on either of them and was now facing spurious criminal charges. There had to be a common factor.

Simone Wills had a two-year-old boy on her hip and his three-year-old sister at her feet. She stood in the doorway with uncombed hair in the baggy top and sweat pants she had slept in. All three of them looked in need of a wash.

'Can you spare a moment, Mrs Wills?'

Simone sighed and shook off the three-year-old, who was tugging at her leg. 'If you don't mind the place being a bloody mess.'

'Five minutes and I'll be out of your hair.'

Resigned, Simone led off along the hallway strewn with toys and children's clothes and took Jenny into the sitting room. It hadn't seen much cleaning in a while; there were dirty plates and crisp packets on the three-piece suite. She plonked the two-year-old in a playpen and cleared a space on the sofa. The boy screamed and shook the bars while his sister poked at him from the other side with him a plastic sword.

'Ignore them. They'll scream their heads off no matter what you do.'

'You've got your hands full.'

'Tell me about it. On my own now as well.' She brought a packet of cheap cigarettes out of her pocket. 'Ali's gone.' She tugged one out and lit it.

'Oh. I'm sorry.'

'I'm not. He was crap with kids. Where he comes from, kids make a noise they beat the living shit out of them. I told him if he tried that with one of mine I'd have him arrested for child abuse. Called me a white whore.' She took a drag, held the smoke in deep for a full count. When she blew it out it was almost clear, filtered through her lungs. 'He's Egyptian. Won't be going with one of them again. I'd rather have a Jamaican any day.'

Jenny nodded in sympathy, spotting Ali's new iPod speakers sitting on top of the TV.

Simone smiled and coughed. 'He forgot to take them with him. He can stuff it, it was my money.'

Jenny said, 'I promised you last week I'd read Danny's file. I did. I've got some questions. Did he ever mention a girl called Katy Taylor? You might have read about her. She was in Portshead at the same time as him. She died a week after she got out.'

Simone's expression became serious. 'I knew Katy. She was at Oakdene Primary with him. Family used to live here, then moved out. Turned bad, didn't she?'

'She had problems. What do you know about her?'

'Danny never mentioned her, but I've seen her around the estate a few times.'

'With?'

'Not really sure. A gang of girls one time. I can't keep up with them.'

'Hayley Johnson?'

Simone looked blank. 'Never heard of her.'

'When was the last time you saw Katy?'

'Not since she was out . . . January, February?'

It wasn't much, but it was something. Katy had gravitated back to where she had been at primary school, probably hanging out with old classmates. She could put Alison or her friends in the police to work finding out who they were.

'The other thing is about Mr Marshall. You said he changed before the inquest, went quiet on you.'

Simone took a short, angry puff on her cigarette. 'That's right.' The kids were screaming louder, looking for attention. She shouted at the younger one, 'Shut up, Sam.'

He took no notice. He had the little girl's fingers inside the bars and was trying to bite them.

Jenny waited for a gap in the yelling. 'What was the last conversation you had with him?'

'God, this noise.' Simone put her hands over her ears, trying to think. 'On the phone . . . on the Friday.'

'Can you remember what about?'

'Our social worker, Ruth Turner, wanted to speak to him. She'd tried phoning but he hadn't got back to her.'

'Who's she?'

'She looks in on the kids and that. Never had much to do with Danny, it was mostly the young ones, but it was her who wanted him seen by a psychiatrist.'

'When?'

'Before he went to Portshead.'

'What did Marshall say?'

'He'd give her a ring. Don't think he did, though.' She found an empty Dr Pepper can on the floor and used it as an ashtray.

'Have you got a number for her?'

'Somewhere . . .'

'I'll find it. She works out of the family centre, does she?'

'Yeah.' She snapped at the toddler, 'Sam, if you don't bloody shut up I'll get Ali back.'

He stopped screaming and let go of his sister's fingers.

'Thanks, Simone. I'll leave you to it.' Jenny got up from the sofa, the tacky carpet sticking to the soles of her shoes.

Simone said, 'Oh. There's something I forgot to tell you last time, 'bout what happened before the inquest.'

Jenny stopped in the doorway. 'Yeah?'

'You know the press found out all about my past record and that? They also found out about these two having been in care when they were tiny.'

'They could have got that from one of your well-meaning neighbours.'

'Maybe. But the day before the inquest, the Sunday, the cops came round and turned the place over. Said my twelve-year-old, Scott, had been seen dealing.'

'Did they find anything?'

'No way. He's not like his brother. Goes to school and everything. The kid was terrified – they had him down at the station for three hours.'

'You were lucky Ali didn't have a stash in the house.'

'He did. Guess who had to walk around with a two-ounce wrap up her half the day? A Jamaican would have swallowed the lot and no one would have known the difference. They can even turn a police raid into a party, those boys.'

Jenny smiled. 'I thought you said Danny's dad was from Trinidad?'

'Trinidadians are different. They're right villains.'

It must have taken a dozen attempts to track down Ruth Turner's number through the council's switchboard but eventually a hassled-sounding woman answered her mobile with a lot of traffic noise in the background.

Jenny, sitting in her car still outside Simone's, said, 'Is that Ruth Turner?'

'Who's this?'

'Jenny Cooper. Severn Vale District Coroner.'

'*Who?*'

Jenny raised her voice and gave her name again.

'Oh. Right.' She calmed down. 'What can I do for you?'

'I'd like to talk to you, this morning if possible.'

'Oh . . . I'm out of the office, between appointments.'

'I'll drive over and meet you somewhere. Whatever you want. It's urgent.'

Ruth Turner took a moment coming back to her, then said, 'I'm coming back through Clifton in half an hour. Do you know Dino's?'

'I'll find it.'

The social worker took closer to an hour to arrive at the little Italian café, leaving Jenny to deal with Dino, who kept trying to offer her the lunch menu, giving her a look over his moustache which said he could do her something extra special.

Forty-two was an interesting age. If you dressed up you were still a young man's fantasy, but old guys tried their luck with you as well, ones with pot bellies and facial hair. She thought about Steve for the first time since the weekend. It had felt good having someone solid next to her at David's. 'Solid' – the word just popped into her head, but it didn't seem to square. Steve had opted out of life and was wasting his talents grubbing around for gardening jobs. That wasn't solid. Still, it was nice to know a good-looking younger man was attracted to her. She wondered what would have happened had he reached out and touched her while he was lying there on the grass.

'Mrs Cooper?'

Jenny popped out of her daydream and saw a woman of about her own age, carrying too much weight and mumsy-looking. Dyed auburn hair everywhere, no make-up.

'Hi, Ruth.' Jenny gestured to the chair opposite.

Ruth called out to Dino by the counter, 'Skinny latte, Dino.'

He gave a backwards flick of his forehead, not returning her smile. She hung her oversized handbag, which doubled as a briefcase, over the back of the chair and dropped into the seat with a dramatic sigh.

Jenny didn't want to hear about her busy morning, so got

straight to business. 'I'm looking into the death of Danny Wills. I believe you are the family's social worker.'

'Yes, but I thought the inquest was all over with.'

'That depends. My predecessor wasn't a well man when he conducted it. I've got to make sure he took account of everything he should have.'

'I'm afraid he never answered my calls. I would have liked to speak to him.'

'That's what I wanted to ask you about. What happened there?'

'I hadn't been with the Wills family for that long, only a couple of months, but Simone had told me about Danny and his pre-sentence report and how he was reacting, getting depressed. Well, given what a difficult time he'd had, I thought he ought to have a psychiatric assessment before the court considered putting him in custody.' She paused and sighed again. 'I don't know if you have any idea how long these referrals take, Mrs Cooper—'

'I was in childcare law for fifteen years. Head of North Somerset's legal team.'

'Then you'll know.' She seemed relieved. 'I put in a request to one of my colleagues and I called the Youth Offending Team, what's-his-name?'

'Justin Bennett.'

'Yeah.' She gave Jenny a look: *that one*. 'He said he'd see what he could do, but nothing happened. Two weeks went by and the next thing I know Simone's calling me in a panic, saying they've just sent him into custody and she was frightened he was going to hurt himself.'

A lumpy young waitress appeared with Ruth's coffee. Dino was busy greeting a couple of pretty twenty-somethings who'd just arrived, giving them the pick of the tables. Ruth took a mouthful and wiped the foam off her lip with the back of her hand. 'I was up to my eyes that day – I had a care hearing going on – but I called the reception centre at Portshead a few times and finally got through to someone there. Actually, I think she was a nurse.'

'There's a nurse called Linda Raven mentioned on his file.'

'That rings a bell. She said he would be given a psychiatric assessment as part of the reception procedure. I said, would that be by a psychiatrist? She said, no, but the procedures were perfectly proper. That's all I could get out of her.' She broke off, her expression telling Jenny she felt guilty about her role in this. 'I'm afraid I didn't have time to pursue it. You know what it's like when you're in court . . . When I heard Danny had hanged himself I tried to call Portshead again, but no one would speak to me. I finally got through to the local health trust out there and they said they weren't currently providing psychiatric services to Portshead Farm because of a dispute over contracts. As far as I could make out the trust and the company that runs Portshead couldn't agree on how much having a psychiatrist on call was going to cost.'

'What happens to an inmate with a psychiatric problem?'

'Good point. All their medical staff come from a private company. A psychiatrist should be part of the package. I'd argue every child should be seen by a psychiatrist on reception, but it's not required.'

'Danny was put in an observation cell for several days dressed in something my predecessor described as like a horse blanket.'

'That's their idea of psychiatric care, I'm afraid. That's what I wanted to be looked into at the inquest. I wanted to tell Mr Marshall that if there had been a psychiatrist there they might have spotted the signs and done something – at least put him on medication.'

'Did you think of writing to him with this information?' Jenny asked.

'You know what it's like, you're trying to do a hundred

things at once.' Her phone rang. She pulled it out of her handbag and took a call about a child whose GP suspected she had been deliberately scalded by her mother.

Jenny finished the dregs of her double ristretto and tried not to judge the social worker too harshly. At least she was still in the system, sticking at it. She hadn't cracked up and tried to hide away.

While Ruth got deeper into her harrowing call, Jenny ripped a corner from a page of her legal pad and wrote, 'Please could you put what you've told me in writing and send it over?' She pushed it across the table, together with a business card. Ruth gave her the thumbs up. Jenny left a five-pound note on the table and headed out of the door while Dino was busy taking an order. He looked up and winked at her she passed. Loud enough for him to hear, Jenny said, 'Creep.'

Alison was tackling the accounts, her desk swamped with receipts she was attempting to arrange into piles by month. Jenny hadn't crossed the doormat when she picked up a thick handful of papers and said, 'Seven today.'

Juggling her briefcase, handbag and take-out sandwich, Jenny flicked through the overnight death and yesterday's post-mortem reports. 'At least Peterson's got his act together. He's getting his reports out in twenty-four hours.'

'Too good to be true. It won't last.' She emptied out another envelope of miscellaneous receipts, letting Jenny see what she was having to endure.

'I appreciate you going through all that stuff.'

'Someone has to.'

Jenny gave a flat smile and headed to her office.

'Don't you want to know how the police are doing, Mrs Cooper?'

Jenny stopped at the door and turned. 'Have you heard anything?'

'Vice Squad think they might have found some pictures of her hanging around Broadlands Estate on the Monday. They're not very clear, so CID are going to send them down to the lab.'

'Alone or with someone?'

'That's all I know, and I'm not meant to know that.'

'I appreciate it. Really.'

Alison gave a stoical nod and went back to her receipts. Jenny nudged open the door of her office with her shoulder, thinking she'd been working with her officer less than a fortnight and knew only two things about her, that she was married and had been in love with Harry Marshall. There were lots of questions she ought to ask her, but Alison never gave her the chance. It seemed deliberate and almost perverse, as if she was embarrassed by what Jenny already knew about her but at the same time determined to let her know she was still suffering.

Jenny's late lunch was a pill and the last dried-out sandwich in the shop eaten hurriedly at her desk. Skimming through the early edition of the *Post* she found a two-inch report on Tara Collins's court appearance. It said she had been remanded on bail on charges of credit card fraud and would appear again in a fortnight's time. It made no mention that she was a reporter on the paper or that she violently protested her innocence. Even medicated, reading the article made her anxious. She hadn't given Tara a lot of thought in the past day, but there it was in black and white: she was looking at five years in prison. And for what – investigating two suspicious deaths?

She pushed her paperwork to one side and booted up her laptop. After her meeting with Ruth Turner she had enough to set the procedural wheels in motion to seek a second inquest into the death of Danny Wills. The law was straightforward. Under section 13 of the 1988 Coroner's Act the High Court could quash the verdict in a previous inquest and order a new one if the original was unsatisfactory through insufficiency of enquiry, or if new facts or evidence had come to light. That much was simple: Marshall had refused to call a witness who had vital evidence about the lack of psychiatric care both before and after Danny was sentenced. There were two obstacles in the way: the court would have to be persuaded that there would be a different result if the inquest were reheard in a proper manner, and before she could even get to court, she needed the Attorney General's permission to proceed.

This layer of bureaucracy had to be negotiated carefully. The Attorney General was a politician with special responsibility for the public, for which read *government*, interest. Any application which smacked of emotion or outrage or which spelled potential embarrassment wouldn't even make it past the low-grade civil servant who opened the envelope. Jenny's letter would have to be as dry as dust and focus on one unanswerable objection: the family social worker had tried and failed to get a psychiatric assessment for a mentally ill teenager. He was sent to an institution which placed him on suicide watch but still did not have him psychiatrically examined. Had this evidence been heard, a verdict of death caused by gross negligence would have been highly likely.

She drafted, then read and re-read her legalistic letter and tried to conceive of how the Attorney General, part of an administration which claimed to put children first, could possibly refuse her request. She couldn't. The facts were too stark; it would have to get through.

The grass had started to sprout daisies again and weeds were reappearing among the herbs. It was gone eight and she could barely pull the cork out of the bottle, let alone contemplate gardening. As it was Tuesday, she had half expected to come home and see that Steve had been again. Secretly, she had hoped she would find him still here, turning to greet her with that smile.

She filled the large glass up to the top so she had to sip a quarter-inch off before lifting it to her lips. A couple of mouthfuls and it was two-thirds empty. What did it matter? No one was watching. She filled it up again. She'd make the second glass last. The wine was good. A Chianti. Why not just enjoy it?

After another refill she could have been sitting in her own private paradise. The leaves on the ash trees glittered, the sky was the colour of the Mediterranean. When you could feel this good on your own, who needed company?

The second bottle was a screw top, cheap French red. Not bad, though. She was relaxed, enjoying herself. She felt like a cigarette and remembered an emergency pack she kept in the bottom kitchen drawer. She lit one off the electric stove and wandered back outside, a glass in her hand, not feeling the cold at all. Sitting in her garden at sunset, her bare feet on the wet grass, a stream running by, what could beat it? Forget Steve. If she ever wanted a man, she could do much better.

She woke in the semi-darkness. Her skull was splitting and she was shivering. She looked around, disoriented, and realized she was still at the scrub-top table on the lawn, two empty bottles in front of her. She lurched inside. Her phone was blinking on the kitchen counter. She snatched it up and struggled to focus: *Missed call. Ross 20:25.* Shit. How had that happened? What was the time? She looked over at the clock – ten to four.

As she hit the pillow, the birds struck up. Thousands of the little bastards.

FOURTEEN

SHE MADE IT TO HER desk by ten a.m., loaded up with aspirin, temazepam and caffeine. Fortunately, Alison was out of the office, so wasn't there to see what a wreck she was. Jenny would have been angry with herself had she had the energy, but she was shattered, every slight movement making her head pound. It was a deep, rotten hangover that bitter experience told her would last all day and into tomorrow. Forcing herself to throw up several times had had no effect. She felt too sick to eat and her lungs were sore from the ten cigarettes she had smoked. The last time she had been in this state was the morning after she left David. How had it happened?

Sitting on her desk was a print-out of a report Ruth Turner had emailed through, repeating the story she had told yesterday, a neat stack of receipts bulldog-clipped together and a manual ledger in which Alison had attempted to enter them. With it was a long note full of queries which needed answering and a detailed form which had to be submitted to the council's auditor. She pushed the accounts aside and turned instead to the fresh stack of reports she had picked up from Alison's desk. It contained the usual collection of depressing hospital cases, a woman of ninety who had choked on her dentures and a thirty-five-year-old farm worker who had fallen into a slurry pit, cracked his head and drowned.

Just what she needed. Reading about death in a cesspool.

She tried to lose herself in work, but as she read Dr Peterson's post-mortem reports she could smell his autopsy room. Fighting a wave of nausea, she headed out to the kitchenette to make more coffee. While she was leaning against the counter trying to calculate how many more aspirin she could safely take, Alison arrived, busy and excited.

'They got the tape back from the lab. They think they've got a sighting of Katy at eleven o'clock on the Sunday evening getting into a blue car, a Vectra.'

Jenny tried her best to sound bright. 'They can't be certain?'

'It's bit grainy, apparently. A security camera outside some flats.'

'Any chance we could get a look?'

'They haven't gone public yet. We're not meant to know. You could call Swainton and ask him how it's going.'

'I'll give it some thought. I don't want to make him any more defensive.'

Alison, relieved, said, 'I've got a feeling they'll get a result.'

Jenny stirred a second spoon of instant coffee into her cup. 'At least we haven't had any more trouble from Grantham. I don't know what his problem was.'

'You. He likes to be in control.'

'You sound as if you've heard something.'

Alison reached down a mug, not wanting to be drawn.

Jenny said, 'What is it?'

'Nothing in particular ... But it just looks bad for him, doesn't it? Everyone knows he and Harry were close. If there was something wrong with the way Harry handled Katy's inquest it'll reflect on him.'

'Too bad.' Jenny took her coffee and headed for her office.

'Did you pick up the message from the Attorney General's office?'

'No.'

'I left it with the accounts. They're sending someone down to talk about your letter. I booked them in for midday.'

Her headache was no better when Adam Crossley arrived five minutes ahead of schedule; if anything, all the fluids she had taken had made it worse, swollen her brain. Crossley, an ambitious, ex-military type in his late thirties, was bright and alert, refreshed after a ride down in first class at taxpayers' expense. To make the day even jollier he had brought a young colleague. Kathy Findlay was an attractive, bookish young redhead who sat in a corner taking verbatim notes. During the obligatory pre-business chit-chat, Crossley explained he was a criminal barrister who had been headhunted to take a two-year contract with the AG's department to help steer through a programme of radical change. He spouted a lot of management speak about 'streamlining' and 'concentrated focus', but what it amounted to was that the department was being brought under political control. Forget the law, he could have said, in future politics was going to come first.

As soon as he said 'criminal barrister' Jenny had him pegged. Not bright enough for commercial law, probably scratching a mediocre living prosecuting and destined only, if he got lucky, to serve out his final years on the Crown Court Bench. A low-level lawyer hungry for a fragment of power.

Niceties over and already presuming to use her Christian name, Crossley said, 'I've read your letter, Jenny – it raises some very significant points.'

'That's why I wrote it.' Her hangover was making her tetchy.

'Do you have a copy of Mrs Turner's evidence?'

She handed the statement across the desk. Crossley sat in silence for a full minute, reading it in detail. Kathy Findlay tapped her pen on her legal pad and glanced around the room with a look of mild disgust.

'Very interesting,' Crossley said. 'May I keep this for my records?'

'Sure.'

He tucked it into his file. 'You do appreciate that rehearing an inquest is quite a drastic step. The Attorney General would have to be convinced that an alternative verdict would be highly likely to result.'

'A secure training centre took in a boy whose family social worker told them needed to be seen by a psychiatrist, but they didn't do it. They didn't even have access to a psychiatrist because of a contractual dispute. That to me seems a clear breach of their duty of care.'

'But how sure can you be that seeing a psychiatrist would have made any difference? The boy might still have killed himself.'

'A psychiatrist might have had him sectioned or medicated.'

'Plenty of people properly diagnosed as medically ill kill themselves.'

Jenny felt a fuse blow. 'We're talking about a children's prison operating without access to a psychiatrist. Doesn't that concern you?'

'It's certainly regrettable, but I'm not altogether persuaded—'

'Perhaps a coroner's jury would be.'

Crossley eased back in his chair and knitted his fingers, the smile replaced with a frown. 'This is what I was concerned about, Jenny, that you had become personally involved in the case. I note your background is in family law.'

She could have jumped over the desk and punched him. 'What concerns me, Mr Crossley, is that someone's sent you down here scared that I'm about to embarrass the government by exposing gross flaws in the private prisons it's so keen on.'

'You're giving every impression of partiality, I must say.'

'The coroner is not an impartial judge like those you are familiar with in the Crown Court, she is an inquisitor with one overriding duty: to discover the cause of death. My predecessor failed to call vital witnesses. If you choose not to give me leave to ask the High Court's permission to examine this again, I really will embarrass you – I'll seek judicial review and it'll be all over the press that your department tried to stand in my way.'

'You're imputing a very disreputable motive to us, verging on the paranoid.'

'Well, tell me I'm wrong.'

'In the light of Mrs Turner's statement I can see that we might be sympathetic to your application, but you'll understand that we're concerned that any inquest conforms to the highest standards. You'll be under a good deal of scrutiny from the Ministry of Justice.'

'Their time might be better spent scrutinizing their prisons.'

'You're really quite angry about this, aren't you?'

'Danny Wills was a sick child. Who wouldn't be?'

Crossley gave an uncomfortable smile. 'If you really are intent on hearing this inquest again you can at least conduct it in dignified surroundings. Call the Ministry – they'll find you a proper courtroom. We can't have the public thinking we're running a third-world system.' He rose from his chair. 'I hope we understand each other.'

Alison showed Crossley and his young companion out and recommended an Italian restaurant where they'd be sure to get a table for lunch. Through the partially open door to reception Jenny could hear her, calling him *Mr* Crossley, and wishing him a pleasant journey back to London, doing everything she could to repair the damage.

Alison appeared a few minutes later with a handful of printed emails. She gave her a look that Jenny now recognized, the one that said she was concerned when what she actually wanted was to give her opinion. 'I do hope they let you go ahead, Mrs Cooper.'

'They've got no choice. If they refuse, I'll go straight to the High Court, seeking judicial review.'

That look again. 'You seem tired.'

'If you've got something to say, just say it.'

'You did sound rather aggressive.'

'He was the aggressive one. I was honest.'

'This will be the only chance they give you, you know that.'

'I can't think of a better case to take it on, can you?'

The call came as two delivery men were manoeuvring a desk through her office door. She was jammed up against the bookshelves, pleading with them to be careful as they trod files underfoot and knocked lumps out of the paintwork. She snatched the phone before one of them tripped over the wire. 'Jenny Cooper.'

'Mrs Cooper, it's Isabel Thomas, Ross's Head of Year.'

'Oh, hello.'

'I'm afraid we've had a situation. Ross is all right, but he's rather the worse for wear.'

'Oh . . .' Her heart was bouncing off the back of her throat. 'What's happened?'

'We're not sure exactly. A member of staff found him at lunchtime. He's intoxicated.'

'Drunk?'

'No. I think it's some kind of drugs. As you know, school policy is to inform the police—'

'Please don't do that. It's completely out of character.'

'I'll hold off this time, but my feeling is that this has been going on for a while.'

'No one's said anything.'

'It's just an impression, that's all . . . Look, I've got him here in my office. I tried to contact your husband—'

'*Don't*. I'll be right there.'

FIFTEEN

THE IRONY WASN'T LOST ON her as she swallowed another pill before venturing into the building. Schools filled her with dread at the best of times: the sense of judgement which suffused them. Her footsteps reverberated around the scruffy corridors. The air was stale, heavy and smelt vaguely of bleach and the lasagne that had evidently been served for lunch. She passed classrooms, some orderly, others bordering on riotous, in which teachers pleaded with unruly children to be quiet. It brought back memories of her own schooldays in a precious girls' grammar: always on edge, waiting for the sharp reproach or hurtful jibe. It had felt like a prison. She had hoped Ross's experience would be less pressured, but she could feel the tension in the air. Different, but no less intimidating.

Isabel Thomas, a brisk, impersonal woman in her early thirties, was hovering in the corridor outside her office, talking into her phone. When Jenny approached she rang off and glanced at her watch as if to say, *what took you?*

'Mrs Thomas?'

'He's in here, but I just wanted a quick word.' She ushered her several yards along the corridor out of earshot. 'Ross won't say anything, but I'm pretty sure he's been smoking cannabis. Another member of staff found some roaches and he had papers and tobacco in his pockets.'

Jenny felt a wave of relief. 'At least it wasn't anything worse.'

'Some of his teachers have noticed that he's been a bit vague in lessons recently. I see from the register that he's had a large number of absences this year.'

'Really? I'd no idea.'

'So he's not been staying at home?'

'I don't think so . . . Actually, he lives with his father most of the time.'

'You separated earlier this year, didn't you? It's often a crisis point for teenagers.'

'We will deal with it. I'm sure it's just a phase.'

'I'd recommend you get him some professional help if you can. Normally this sort of thing would result in immediate expulsion.'

'You can't. We don't even know what happened.'

'I've had to tell the Head. It's her decision, but in Ross's case I think she might be persuadable.'

'So what's his status?'

'She'll call you, but you can presume he's suspended until further notice.'

'He's still got exams to sit.'

'He'll be allowed to sit them, just not to remain on school premises.'

'This is such an overreaction.'

'I'm sorry it was your son, Mrs Cooper, but it can happen to anyone.' She gave her a look of faux sympathy. 'You'd better take him now.'

Ross lay back in the passenger seat, his eyes half closed, as Jenny climbed into the driver's seat. He looked peaceful, not at all rattled by the events of the afternoon. She looked at him: he was profoundly stoned, probably feeling on cloud nine.

'Where do you want to go – home or my place?'

'Wherever. You decide.' The words drifted out of him.

She considered the alternatives. Whichever she chose, the day would end in an ugly confrontation with David blaming her for ruining their only son. It made sense to take Ross back to his own house, where he could sleep off the dope, but it would send a message to his father that she couldn't cope. And if there was to be a showdown she would prefer to be on her turf and not have Deborah as an audience.

Ross dozed as she drove away from the city and headed out on the motorway towards the Severn Bridge. She called Alison and told her he had been taken ill and she wouldn't be back in the office until the morning. More than happy to be proved indispensable, Alison promised to hold the fort and fax any vital paperwork to her at home. By the time they reached Chepstow, Ross was in a deep sleep. When they pulled up outside Melin Bach Jenny tried to shake him awake, but he wouldn't stir. So she pulled further up the cart track and left him in the car.

It was nearly six o'clock when he woke from his torpor and staggered out on to the cart track. Jenny came out of the kitchen with her second pot of coffee and saw him leaning against the bonnet, light-headed and trying to figure out where he was.

'How are you feeling?'

He scratched his head. 'Rough.'

'Come and sit down. I'll get you a cup.'

He sloped over to the table rubbing his eyes, avoiding her gaze. She went back into the kitchen to fetch a mug and some biscuits. Coming down from that big a high, he'd be ravenous.

She let him sit in peace while she pulled weeds out from around the herbs and nipped the dead heads off the semi-wild roses. She wanted to let him know he wasn't being judged, that she wasn't an ogre like his father. Neither said a word for more than ten minutes, but she could feel him gradually lift out of the deep trough he'd woken in. She would never have said it, but she felt she understood his mood, better than he did. Like her, he was sensitive and self-conscious. If he felt under attack he'd retaliate and say things he didn't mean. If he felt accepted he'd open up and let her in.

He broke the silence first with a muttered, 'Sorry.'

Jenny straightened up from her weeding and turned with a smile. 'It's OK.' She came over to the table, wiping her muddy hands on the jeans she had changed into while he was sleeping. 'Feeling any better?'

He nodded, his face set in a tired frown.

'What do you think of the place?'

He looked up from the table and glanced around, screwing his eyes up against the bright, early-evening light. 'Different.'

'Like it?'

'Yeah. It's cool.'

They sat in silence for another moment, then Jenny reached out and touched his hand. 'You're not feeling ill?'

'I'm fine.' He pulled his hand away. 'Have you spoken to Dad?'

'I left a message for him.'

'Does he know?'

'Mrs Thomas got to his secretary first. I told him you were with me and we'd call him later.'

'Shit . . . Am I suspended?'

'While the Head decides what to do, but you can take your exams. Mrs Thomas thinks we can persuade him to let you stay, if you want to.'

'Don't know what I want.'

Jenny said, 'I'm not going to lecture you about drugs, after all the legal sort I've taken over the years, but if you could tell me what was going on . . . '

She waited for him while he stared into his empty coffee cup. 'Had some weed, that's all.'

'Where d'you get it?'

He shrugged. 'A mate. What's it matter?'

'Any particular reason?'

He thought for a moment, then shook his head.

'Was it anything to do with the weekend? You know I'm sorry about all that.'

'I don't know . . . Don't know why I did it. Just felt like it.'

She believed him. But she also believed he wanted to escape the hell of having his father pressuring him into becoming something he wasn't.

'You don't have to do what your dad says. It was easy for him, he always wanted to be a doctor. It takes longer for some people to decide.'

Ross, silent, picked at the biscuit crumbs on the plate.

'As far as I'm concerned, you can decide to be what you like, when you like.'

'A dropout?'

'Within limits.' She attempted a smile but didn't get one back. 'Look, I meant what I said about coming to stay here. I think it would be fun if you came here this summer. You could think things through without any pressure.'

'You don't like Deborah much, do you?'

'It's nothing to do with her. I haven't had a proper place till now.'

'Dad didn't rate that bloke you brought either.'

'Steve's just a friend. He does the garden.'

Ross glanced at the ankle-high grass. 'Right.'

'It's true.'

'I don't care. At least he's not half your age.'

'If I was in a relationship with anyone, believe me, you'd be the first to know.'

'Well, if you do, try and keep the physical stuff out of sight – it's pretty gross watching a fifty-year-old bloke groping—'

'OK, I get the picture.' She tried to wipe it from her mind. 'I know it's tough with your dad and me, but you understand I always wanted to be with you, don't you?'

Ross looked down at the table. She sensed the wave of emotion that came over him. 'Yeah.'

They lapsed into silence, Jenny suddenly feeling very guilty, furious at herself for cracking up when she did. Two more years and he would have been off to university, ready to strike out on his own. After a while, she said, 'So will you come at the end of term?'

'If you want.'

'And you'll promise me you won't smoke any more of this stuff?'

'I thought you weren't going to give me a lecture.'

'I wouldn't be much of a mother if I wasn't worried.'

'It's a bit late for that now. Damaged goods, aren't I?'

She looked at him, hurt, trying to decide if this was genuine or bravado and wondering what she could ever do to make things better.

They both turned at the sound of a powerful engine roaring up the lane. David's BMW 7 Series pulled up behind Jenny's Golf. Ross flinched as he jumped out and slammed the door.

Jenny said, 'I'll deal with him.'

David strode across the grass, still in his suit trousers, shirt and tie. Jenny got up to face him, the moment she had been dreading all day. She'd prepared half a dozen good lines to head him off, but couldn't recall a single one. 'Don't be angry, David, we're working it out.'

He stopped next to the table, his face travelling through several different emotions before settling on a strangulated reasonableness. 'I'd no intention of getting angry. If things need talking about I always believe in doing it rationally.' He looked Ross over, appraising him like a patient. 'Feeling a bit lousy, I expect?'

'He's not too bad.'

He motioned to a chair. 'May I?'

'Go ahead.'

David took a seat next to Ross and opposite Jenny. The avuncular smile he affected was unnerving. 'Quite a place you've got here. Certainly peaceful.'

Jenny regretted all the coffee she had drunk. Her nerves felt suddenly raw. 'I was saying to Ross he might like to spend some time here in the summer.'

'Why not? Might do you some good to get out of town.'

Ross stared at the table.

David looked at him, recognizing familiar signs. 'We're not going to get to the bottom of this unless you talk to us, matey.'

Jenny said, 'I think maybe we should give him a bit of time.'

Ross jumped up and flung down his chair. 'Why do you always talk about me like that? I'm not a fucking child.' He stamped off across the grass, got into the back of David's car and slammed the door.

David said, 'Just what I need. Six straight hours in theatre and I get a phone call saying my son's a drug addict.'

'He smoked some dope. It's not the end of the world.'

'It could be the end of his education.'

'Don't be so melodramatic.'

'What do you suggest we do – nothing? He's not the only kid in the world to have divorced parents.'

'He's sensitive.'

'Tell me about it.'

'Why doesn't he stay here for a few days?'

'While you're off at work.'

'You're at work, too.'

'Deborah can take some time off.' He got to his feet. 'She's got a sensible head on her shoulders.'

Jenny, stung, said, 'I hope so. If our son's anything like his father—'

'Don't be so bloody childish.'

Jenny stood by the stream and listened to David's car going down the hill, feeling his fury in every rise and fall of the engine, imagining Ross in the back, numb, staring out of the window. Feeling trapped but too scared to stand up to his father, preferring oblivion to taking him on. It was exactly how she had felt when it had started to come unstuck. David had treated her like one of his more neurotic patients. When she would break down or try to describe the frightening sensations that seemed to come from nowhere, he would see her as a set of symptoms to be suppressed. He never once asked about her deeper thoughts or whether she was troubled by the past. He seemed only able to perceive life as a series of straight lines. Any deviation had to be hammered out.

There was an unseasonal chill in the breeze, the air smelt of wet earth. It added to her feeling of hopelessness. She was a failure as a mother and as an individual; so caught up in her own tangle of problems she couldn't care for her own son. When she dared look into the black heart of what lay inside her, it felt as if something truly evil, an entity she could only describe as a cancer, had taken hold. She felt it acutely this evening. Even the trees seemed malignant. Her mind kept replaying images from a recurring nightmare: she stood in the corner of a familiar, yet strangely off-kilter room in her childhood home, a crack opened in the wall in the corner revealing a pitch-black, terrifying secret space beyond that threatened to suck her in . . .

She walked back inside the house, trying to shake herself back to normality and shed the feeling of impending doom.

She reached for the wine bottle but, still hung-over, set it down again. She tried to cook but felt as if someone was watching her from outside the curtainless window. A sound from upstairs was a ghost, the old woman who'd lived here resenting her presence, moving her things. She picked up her pills but then worried that she'd pass out and wake in the dead of night with the old woman standing over her, smelling her fusty clothes and feeling her fury.

Gripping the kitchen counter, her heartbeat became footsteps on the boards in the bedroom above her. They shuffled towards the stairs and started to descend, both feet landing on a single tread before moving to the next. She turned to the door, her eyes on the latch, waiting for it to rise. There was a creak in the sitting room. She grabbed her car keys and fled out of the back door.

Although it was still June it was too cold for anyone to be sitting at the tables on the veranda in front of the Apple Tree. Jenny came to the door of the public bar and looked through the glass. The crowd was thinner than on her previous visit, a handful of men standing, a few couples at tables. Steve was sitting up on a stool, Annie coming to talk to him between serving customers. Jenny waited there, too scared to go in or to go home alone. She kept checking through the window, waiting for Annie to get distracted. It took an age. When eventually she ducked into the kitchen, Jenny stepped inside the door, caught Steve's eye, then stepped back out again. Hovering in the porch, waiting to see if he'd come, she felt like a schoolgirl. Stupid.

He came out, fishing tobacco and papers from his denim jacket, most of his attention on rolling a cigarette. She was sitting side on at one of the picnic-style tables and, now he was here, she didn't know what to say.

He said, 'How are you doing?'

'Sorry to disturb your evening.'

'I needed a fix anyway.' He spread tobacco across the paper, rolled it with one hand and licked it. 'They call it a free country. You try acting like it is – they'll put you in jail so fast, your feet won't touch the ground.' He cupped his hands and lit a match.

Jenny said, 'Haven't I heard that line before?'

Steve smiled. '*Easy Rider*.' He leaned back against the wooden rail and drew in the sweet-smelling smoke. 'It's a good movie, but Peter Fonda always looked like he'd brought a hairdresser along with him. Anyone who's worn a bike helmet knows what it does to your style.'

'I always just thought he looked cute.'

'I guess he was, but it was Nicholson who stole the show. An alcoholic lawyer in a sweat-stained suit wakes up in a cell, bribes his way out and takes off with motorcycle hippies . . . Then gets kicked to death in his sleep by rednecks.'

'The man who dared to be different.'

'Dangerous thing to be.'

Jenny looked at him in his mud-stained cargoes and faded green shirt, hair hanging down to his eyes, his expression saying he wasn't going to ask any questions, it was up to her.

She said, 'I got scared in my house.'

'Uh-huh.'

She sighed, wishing she didn't have to bore him with this. 'Ross got stoned at school. I had to bring him home this afternoon. My husband came for him, you can imagine . . . I was in the kitchen by myself, and I started thinking there was a ghost upstairs, it's crazy—'

'What kind of ghost?'

'The old woman who used to live there.'

'Joan? She wasn't the haunting kind.'

'I know it's all in my mind . . .'

He sucked on the cigarette. 'You've had a tough day. Anyone'd be jumpy.'

'I should go, stop bothering you.' She got up from the table and headed for the small flight of steps which led down to the path.

She had reached the bottom when he said, 'Hey,' and came after her.

She turned around. He pushed the hair from his face, saying, 'You want me to come and check the place over?'

'I've put you out enough already.'

'You pulled me off my stool to say that?'

Jenny glanced beyond him to the door of the bar. 'I think I'm OK now.'

'Sure?' He tossed his barely smoked cigarette aside, took a step towards her and looped his arms around her shoulders. 'I don't think you are.'

She leaned against his chest and felt his hand stroking the back of her head. 'I don't know what I am.'

'I've had too much to drive anyway. Give me a ride to your place, I'll be halfway home.'

It happened without either of them saying a word. She'd reached for his hand as they walked towards the front door, a gesture that let them both know what was coming next.

Afterwards they'd lain in the dark for a long while, their fingers touching. Then Steve had said, 'Has the ghost gone now?'

Jenny had said, 'I think so.'

'Good.' He'd eased out of bed and pulled on his Cargoes, his strong back to her in the moonlight. 'I'll be going, then. If I don't feed the dog first thing he'll eat my chickens.'

'You don't expect me to drive?'

'I'll walk. It's only a mile through the woods. I like listening to the owls.'

Then he'd pulled on his shirt, bent over and kissed her on the mouth. His last words to her before going: 'You're a beautiful woman, Jenny, you just don't know it.'

She listened to his footsteps as he set off up the lane and thought about what he'd said. With her illness, the joy in her had gone. She remembered the sensation as a prisoner might freedom, a past, unattainable thing. She wanted it back. She wanted out of the cell.

At least she was alive and could still lose herself in sex. At least she wasn't like Danny Wills, dead on the end of a knotted sheet. She pictured him, his boyish features, and Katy Taylor and Marshall. Three of them dead, hers the only heart still beating. She put her hand to her chest and felt the life in her.

She offered silent thanks and slipped into restless sleep.

SIXTEEN

THE NOTE ON THE KITCHEN counter said: *Not the answer to your problems but maybe a step on the way. Your call. Steve.* She read it over and over as she drank her coffee, trying to figure out what he meant, what she wanted him to mean. She decided he was probably as confused as she was, but more used to this kind of situation. Smart enough not to stay the night and have to face the awkward conversation in the morning.

'Your call'. The fact he put the responsibility back on her said that he didn't want it, that he was happy to be friends – *fuck buddies*, kids called it now – but not to think he was looking for anything more. But at the weekend he'd talked about his karma, wanting to help her, as if he felt fate had blown her his way. She didn't believe in karma, a *system*; life was more random than that. She believed in good and evil, spirits that drifted in and out of people's lives, perhaps for a reason, perhaps not.

She folded the note into her handbag, too superstitious to throw it away, deciding that she had enough on her plate without a relationship. Having a man in her bed was fun, a distraction. If she could choose the time it would be a good arrangement. Why not enjoy it for a while?

She took this thought with her into the car and was nearly at the bridge before she realized she hadn't taken a pill. Wow. Last night had really hit the spot.

David called her while she'd hit the stop–go into the centre of town. For once the sound of his voice didn't make her chest tighten. It helped that he sounded almost reasonable.

'Thanks for bailing Ross out yesterday. The Head just called me – he's technically suspended, but as it's exam time it won't make much difference. If we can reassure her it won't happen again she won't expel him.'

'That's something. How is he?'

'OK. We had a long talk last night . . . I didn't realize quite how badly the divorce had hit him. I suppose it's natural for kids to feel responsible in some way.'

'What did he say?'

'That it had upset him, left him feeling unsure of himself.'

'There's a lot we could do . . .'

David paused. 'I told him to get through the next few days and promised him the three of us would sit down together to talk about what happens next.'

The humble note in his voice amazed her. She couldn't remember the last time she had heard it. 'Where is he now?'

'Studying. Head down all day, he promised me. Look, I'd better go, I'm in theatre in ten minutes. Bye, Jenny.'

She pushed the red button on her phone, feeling a pang of jealousy. Ross had hardly spoken to her but had spent the evening opening up to David. Why couldn't he have told her about his insecurity? Did he see her as the sole cause of it? . . . Of course he did. She was the one who broke up the home, who had screaming fits and threw crockery. It made her want to cry, but that was precisely the reaction Ross would recoil from. He needed her to be strong, to get back fully in control of herself.

From now on she resolved to make that her task: to get a grip.

*

She arrived at the office shortly before Alison and found that their new desks had been neatly arranged and everything cleaned and tidied. It looked more professional already. She booted up Alison's vintage computer and checked her emails. First was a formal message from Adam Crossley saying that the Attorney General had considered her application for leave to apply to the High Court for a rehearing of the inquest into Danny Wills's death and decided to grant it, but on the strict understanding that it would be held in a professional court-room in Bristol Law Courts. Crossley signed off with a veiled threat: 'I trust that your investigation will be reasonable, thorough and temperate. We will observe with interest.'

Jenny dealt with her minor admin, then drafted the application to the High Court for an order to quash the verdict in the Danny Wills inquest and to mount a rehearing. She called the court offices in the Strand and badgered an official in the list office to fix an appointment before a judge for two days' time. With the Attorney General's leave, the hearing would be more or less a formality. She'd send junior counsel down to a judge in chambers who would read her affidavit and make the order.

She handed Alison the formal documents with instructions to have them couriered to the Royal Courts of Justice immediately. She planned to open the inquest first thing on Monday morning, taking everyone by surprise. Alison said she had already had a call from an administrator at the Bristol Law Courts saying he'd been contacted by the Attorney General's office, asking if a court could be made available.

It felt as if the system had decided that if they couldn't stop her, they would keep her under close scrutiny. Coroners had caused a lot of headaches in the recent past: the Princess Diana inquest had dragged on for more than ten years and got through five coroners, and the Oxfordshire coroner who dared to investigate the deaths of British servicemen whose bodies were flown back to his patch from Iraq found that the bodies were instead landed in the jurisdictions of colleagues more willing to accept the army's explanations. Jenny was not going to be forced into ignoring the ugly truth; she would expose it, but keep her poise and dignity. If the media latched on to her, she would present herself as elegant, determined and intellectual, never more than a trace of concerned emotion in her voice.

She asked Alison if she had heard any more about the police investigation into Katy Taylor's death.

'Only that they're still looking for the car. Could be false plates, which means they'll be trawling through every blue Vectra in Bristol. Could take days.'

'Have they got hold of any of Katy's friends? She won't have been out on the street on her own.'

'Not that I know of. Groups of kids are the toughest of all to get into.'

'There must be prostitutes working that area. If Katy was on the game—'

'They'll be trying, believe me, but there's no love lost there, either. You've got to have at least three girls killed before they'll start talking. Mostly they're glad the competition's thinning out.'

'Really?'

'Spend a few months on the street, Mrs Cooper, you'll be surprised how cheap life is.'

Jenny returned to her office with the overnight death reports but couldn't concentrate. Her thoughts kept drifting back to the teenagers whose paths must have crossed with both Katy and Danny Wills. Someone out there must know if there was a connection between them, or if Marshall had touched on something big enough to put him in water so deep death was the only way out. She turned over several morbid possibilities, but none of them squared the circle. If crime was at the bottom of this, why did Marshall baulk?

The only lead she had was the girl Tara Collins had mentioned, Hayley Johnson. After Tara had come to meet her at the inquest she'd been expecting a call but had heard nothing. The rational thing to do would be to mention Hayley's name to the police, but she still had a nagging distrust of them. She didn't fundamentally trust Tara either – for all she knew, she could be a credit card fraudster, and she hadn't flinched from threatening to expose Jenny's medical records – but to get to talk to Hayley she'd have to plump for one of them.

She decided to call the mobile number Tara had left with her at the village hall. It rang seven, eight times before a cautious voice answered.

'Tara?'

'Yes?' She sounded terrible.

'Jenny Cooper. How are you?'

'Not too good . . .' Her voice was shaky, all the confidence bled from it.

'The charges?'

'That and getting mugged last night. Somebody jumped me.'

'Who?'

'I didn't see. Stepped out behind me in the dark, hit me over the head right outside my house. I think there were two of them.'

'Any witnesses?'

'No. None that'll say anything.'

Jenny paused, weighing what she was hearing, careful to keep a distance, wary in case Tara was leading her on. 'What do you think they were after?'

'I had a bag. They didn't take it. All I can think is I've been trying to find out where these credit card transactions came from. A computer guy I've got on it thinks my ISP address was hijacked.'

'Someone stole your identity?'

'My online identity, at least. Stole some money, then dumped the evidence on my computer. I know it's what happened, but proving it's going to be tough.'

'Who do you think's behind this?'

'Put it this way, it was when I started asking questions about Katy Taylor that I got hit with the charges. Someone doesn't want me to make a connection.'

'Do you think it's safe to talk on the phone?'

'I doubt it.'

'Maybe we'd better meet.'

She pulled up in the supermarket car park in Bradley Stoke, the 1970s new town, now a suburb on the north-east fringe of Bristol. After five minutes a white Fiat Panda cruised past with Tara at the wheel. She spotted Jenny and pulled up in a space opposite, walking over with a limp, the left side of her face swollen up. Jenny leaned across and opened the door.

Tara climbed in with some effort. 'Must've cracked my hip when I fell.'

'Your face doesn't look too good, either.'

'Wrecked my chances of pulling for a couple of weeks.' She gave a painful half-smile.

Jenny wondered if men or women were her preference. An instinct told her the latter. There was nothing feminine about Tara and she had that distance some gay women have, emotionally at arm's length.

Jenny said, 'I wouldn't have dragged you here if you'd said.'

'Glad to get out of the house. I've been on paid leave since I was charged.'

'So much for innocent until proved guilty.'

'Who invented that myth? My credit cards got frozen, too. Police must have tipped them off. Bastards.' Her eyes scanned the car park, instinctively checked the mirrors, on her guard since being clubbed down. 'What couldn't you say on the phone?'

'I wanted to ask you about the girl you mentioned, Hayley Johnson. The police haven't got to her so far as I know and I'd like to speak to her first.'

'I've only met her once. She was working the street in Broadlands.'

'What else do we know about her?'

'Eighteen. Mixed race, comes from Plymouth, I think she said.'

'She knew Katy?'

'Said she'd seen her turn a few tricks, get in and out of cars. They'd spoken, nothing significant.'

'When did you find her?'

'About ten days ago, but she claimed not to have seen Katy since before she went to Portshead.'

'Did you believe her?'

'I don't know. She was kind of shifty, couldn't accept I wasn't a cop.'

'How did you track her down?'

'Just driving around. I've got to know the area.'

'I'd like to talk to her, see what she can tell me about the punters, cars they drive, whether Katy had any regulars.'

'You've got a particular car in mind?'

'Maybe.'

Tara looked at her, then out of the window, giving Jenny the impression she'd broken her trust by withholding information.

Jenny said, 'As far as I know, the police are looking for a blue Vectra. That's all we've got.'

Tara waited a moment before replying. This was Jenny

coming to her and Tara needed her to know it. 'Like I said, Hayley was hard to pin down. I was trying to win her trust.'

'Do you think you can get her for me?'

'That depends.' She gave Jenny a look, challenging her. 'What are you doing about Danny Wills?'

Jenny said, 'How can I trust a woman who threatened to publish my medical records?'

Tara tilted her head, conceding the point. 'We hadn't met.'

Jenny held her gaze, choosing to ignore what might have been the subtext of what she'd just said. 'I'm back on the case. And if it works out, next week I'll be opening another inquest.'

Tara looked surprised. 'I really was wrong about you.'

The list office excelled itself. Not only was she granted a swift hearing, it was listed in the Bristol District Registry of the High Court at nine-thirty a.m. on Friday morning, half an hour before court business normally commenced. Jenny arrived expecting to find an army of lawyers representing the Crown and UKAM, but UKAM were unrepresented and the Crown sent only the most junior and inexpensive counsel. Jenny's team consisted of a teenage clerk sent to hold the file by the modest firm of solicitors she had instructed, and an earnest young female barrister who looked as if she had sat up the entire night mastering the principles of coronial law. A solitary reporter sat in the gallery.

Mr Justice Aden Chilton, a ferocious intellectual snob with whom she had clashed many times in bad-tempered wrangles over the custody of various unfortunate children, barely acknowledged her when he swept into court in his full red robes and regalia. He said he had read the coroner's affidavit and was minded to grant the application if there were no objection. The grateful young counsel for the Crown shook his head, muttered, 'No, My Lord,' and the case was over.

Jenny glanced at the reporter and saw him yawn for the umpteenth time, showing no interest in taking a note.

She walked out of the courtroom and said goodbye to her bemused lawyers with a mounting sense of mistrust. A system which frequently conspired to keep troubled and desperate families in limbo for months had miraculously granted her wish in less than seventy-two hours. It seemed too good to be true, which meant it probably was.

It was only decent to have Alison phone ahead to give the staff at Portshead Farm half an hour's notice of her arrival, and for good measure she faxed a copy of the court order to the director's office. Her visit was irregular – coroners did not often visit the scene of a death and even less frequently presented themselves anywhere without an appointment – but she was within her legal rights. The wide-ranging common law powers of the coroner to investigate the cause of death entitled her to insist, with police back-up if necessary, on full cooperation from all potential witnesses and unlimited access to all relevant evidence. She had spent the previous night stooped over her textbooks until she was sure of her ground: Portshead Farm had no option but to open its doors to her.

She arrived in a cold, steady drizzle, weather which had hardly lifted for the entire month, and found there was no human being at the entrance to the secure training centre. She walked from the fenced car park along a paved walkway to solid steel gates watched over by a cluster of CCTV cameras perched on high poles. The outer concrete wall of the facility was high enough that only the roofs of the buildings inside the perimeter were visible. A little piece of urban hell in the English countryside.

She pressed the buzzer and got no reply. Only on her fourth attempt did a voice come over the speaker asking her to state her name and business.

'Jenny Cooper, Severn Vale District Coroner. I'm here to see the director.'

Silence. The voice came back several moments later, saying, 'There's no appointment on the system. You'll have to call the other party and have it logged.'

Jenny said, 'I'm a judicial officer on official business. The director has been notified of my arrival.'

'No appointment, no entry.' A click. Communication ceased.

She pressed on the buzzer for a full five seconds.

The voice returned, officious this time. 'Madam, you've been told the procedure.'

Staying calm, she said, 'Listen to me, whoever you are. Call the director's office and tell her Mrs Cooper, the coroner, is here. Either I'm on the other side of this gate in two minutes or you'll be having lunch in a police cell.'

Jenny waited, agitated, at the gate, feeling the effect of the pill she had taken earlier wearing off fast. There was no way she'd take another here under the cameras.

Several frustrating minutes passed before the gate opened. A woman of about her own age, dressed in a black, well-cut suit, stood on the other side of the threshold. Her immaculately styled hair and conspicuous make-up were explained by the mid-Atlantic accent in which she greeted her with a clipped, 'Good morning, Mrs Cooper. Elaine Lewis. What can I do for you?' She made no attempt to invite her in.

'I trust you received a call from my officer and a copy of the court order made this morning?'

'They were just handed to me. I've been in a meeting.'

'I've come to inspect the scene of death.' She stepped inside the gate. 'If you'd be good enough to have someone show me round.'

'All my staff are fully occupied. This is an extremely busy facility.'

'Then maybe you could show me yourself? As part of my investigation I'll need a detailed understanding of the procedures Danny Wills went through here.'

'That information has already been supplied.'

'I am conducting an entirely fresh inquest, Mrs Lewis. It's starting here, right now.'

Elaine Lewis appeared startled. 'I'm not sure I appreciate your tone.'

'You don't have to. You're under a duty to comply with all requests for evidence, including a full inspection of these premises.'

'This is news to me. I'll need to speak to our lawyers.'

'I'd rather look around without the need for a police escort, but if you want to push it that way it's up to you.' Jenny gave her a benign smile.

Icy, Elaine Lewis said, 'I'll see if my assistant is free.'

She turned and walked away at speed, signalling to one of the security cameras. Jenny followed at her own pace as the gate clunked shut behind her.

Elaine swiped her security tag across the reader and they entered through the main door of the reception centre, a brick-built two-storey building. To the left was an area signed 'Trainee Reception', the entrance to which was a solid steel door with a small observation window. Jenny caught a glimpse of a teenage boy on the other side, from the look of him no more than thirteen or fourteen.

Elaine Lewis said, 'You can wait here. Someone will be with you in a minute,' and swiped herself through a door leading to a corridor to the right, alongside which were signs that read 'Administration', 'Security' and 'Director'. Jenny was left a prisoner in an empty hallway. Ahead of her was a door that led on to a quadrangle around which were ranged the other buildings on the site, but it, too, opened only with a tag.

She hated being locked in anywhere and felt the familiar

stirrings of claustrophobia. She glanced at the walls and
ceilings, looking for cameras, and spotted only one, above the
door to the quadrangle. She turned her back to it, dipped into
her handbag and found a temazepam among several loose in a
zip pocket. She coughed, brought her hand up to her mouth
and slipped it in.

Her anxiety eased just from the feeling of the pill on her
tongue. She swallowed and her heart started to slow. She
stepped over towards the steel door and glanced in from a
distance, hoping she wouldn't be noticed. Three boys were
being seen by two nurses, one male, one female, both dressed
in prison medical style: tight buttoned waist-length jackets that
couldn't easily be grabbed. Two Asian boys of fourteen or
fifteen were sitting on plastic seats fooling around, while the
younger white boy was being processed. The male nurse was
peering into his ears as the female asked him questions she
read from a clipboard. She seemed impatient with his answers,
as if he wasn't following. Not liking having his ear poked, the
boy jerked his head away and the male nurse grabbed it with
one meaty hand, forcing him to hold it steady.

The door to the administration corridor opened and a
large, unenthusiastic young woman came through who said
her name was Sue and that Mrs Lewis had told her to show
Jenny round.

Thinking, who the hell do these people think they are?
Jenny said, 'I'm a coroner conducting a formal inspection. I
need full access to every area of this facility. We'll start with
the male house unit.'

Sue, a stone wall, gave her a flat look and moved, heavy-
hipped, to the door opening on to the quadrangle.

The house unit was a long, single-storey building with forty
matchbox-sized bedrooms, twenty on each side of the single
corridor. At one end of the unit was a fusty-smelling staff
room and trainees' common room with a TV set, at the other

the communal latrines and showers. Each room contained a bed, a steel wardrobe, a steel toilet bowl, a plastic chair and a writing table. All furniture apart from the chair was bolted down. Cell windows were permanently sealed and barred. Some cells contained personal effects – posters, a radio – but most didn't. Sue, who found communication of any sort an effort, said it was to do with the system of privileges. Only trainees who made it to gold got a radio.

The trainees were in class, so the unit was empty save for two young women cleaning. Jenny looked up at the ceiling and noticed the semicircular black domes which contained surveillance cameras. Sue said the monitors were all contained in a suite in the admin corridor near the director's office. She couldn't say how many staff would have been on duty the night Danny died.

Jenny looked through the toughened glass pane into the room where Danny had been found hanging. It was approximately ten feet long, six wide. The wardrobe stood at the end of the bed on the wall to her left, leaving a gap of less than a foot between it and the window. The toilet bowl was opposite, in the far right-hand corner; sitting on it, you'd be looking at the door. Hanging from the far left of the bars, jammed in tight to the wardrobe, Danny's body might have been partially obscured, but you'd have to have been blind not to have seen it from where she was standing.

They moved on to the female house unit. The layout was identical, the only difference being that there were doors on the toilet cubicles long enough to preserve some modesty and the showers had dividers between them. It wasn't much. There was no such thing as privacy here; nowhere a child could go and hide or lose herself to her imagination.

They crossed the quadrangle again and passed through the education block, where the trainees were divided into four classes. Jenny glanced through windows in the classroom doors: kids dressed in identical navy tracksuits and black plimsolls, teachers struggling to keep control. They had an energy you could feel: defiant and hostile.

Sue leaned with arms crossed inside the canteen door while Jenny looked around. Most of the time it was a gym, but at one end tables with benches attached folded down from the walls. Behind a serving hatch two female cooks, who were chatting in a Slavic-sounding language, were heating up frozen meals which were to be served in red moulded plastic trays: big hollow for main course, little hollow for dessert. Cups and cutlery were made of the same material.

Through the serving hatch she noticed a man coming up from under the sink with a spanner. He had a crew cut and rounded, stocky features, the same look about his eyes and cheekbones as the cooks. She remembered the maintenance man who had found Danny's body.

Jenny stepped up to the counter. 'Excuse me. You wouldn't be Mr Smirski?'

The man looked round. Jenny gave him a disarming smile and saw him run his eyes over her. 'No. Sorry.' He spoke with a heavy accent.

'Can you tell me where I can find him?'

The man shrugged. 'He went back to Poland.'

'When?'

He gave her a cautious look.

'I'm a coroner. I need to ask him some questions, about a boy who died here in April.'

He turned and said something to the cooks in what Jenny presumed was Polish, who then discussed it heatedly between themselves. She heard Sue's footsteps plodding towards her, coming to check what all the fuss was about.

Jenny said, 'He can't have been gone that long.'

One of the women seemed to win the argument and exchanged more words with the man, who turned to her and said they thought he left about three weeks ago.

'Any idea why?

The man translated and the women shook their heads. No one seemed to know. The man said, 'Polish people always come and go. That's how it is.'

Sue arrived at Jenny's shoulder. 'All right?'

Jenny said, 'I'll be taking further statements from your staff. I need to speak to Jan Smirski. He was a maintenance man here in April.'

Sue said, 'Maintenance staff are employed by an outside contractor. You'll have to speak to them.'

'I will.'

Last stop was the reception and medical centre. The female nurse was sitting behind the desk reading a magazine when Sue hit the buzzer. She flicked the switch letting them through, annoyed at being taken away from her celebrity gossip. Before Sue opened her mouth, Jenny announced herself as the coroner and asked whether she was Nurse Linda Raven, the person who saw Danny Wills on his admittance.

The nurse, a woman in her upper thirties, was almost good-looking, but she had hard grey eyes and found it difficult to smile. She said yes, she was, and reached under the desk, bringing out a file she said was Danny's. She added that the other coroner, Mr Marshall, had seen it when he came round in April. Jenny glanced through it, not afraid to let Nurse Raven and Sue wait in silence while she took her time absorbing the contents. She found nothing new, just the bare bones of Danny's assessment and the thirty-minute observation log that had been kept while he was held in an observation cell. The entries were brief and revealed little: *Trainee sitting on cot bench. Responded to greeting.* There were lots of questions Jenny would have liked to ask Nurse

Raven but they could wait for the inquest, better to leave her guessing.

She closed the file and tucked it under her arm. 'I'll keep hold of this. I'd like to see the cell in which Danny was held.'

Nurse Raven looked at Sue, who merely raised her eyebrows. What could she do? The nurse grabbed her security tag and crossed the tiled floor, swiped it over a reader and led Jenny and Sue through another secure steel door into a windowless corridor like those beneath many courts across the country: along the right-hand side a row of half a dozen cells, each with an observation hatch and a whiteboard on which the occupant's name was written in felt pen. It was hot in here, smelling of Jeyes Fluid and unwashed bodies. The male nurse Jenny had seen earlier examining the young boy was sitting in a glassed-in booth at the far end of the corridor watching a small television set.

Jenny said, 'How many have you got in here?'

Nurse Raven said, 'Just one at the moment.'

Jenny set off along the row of cells. One, two and three were empty. She stopped outside the fourth and saw a black boy lying on the cot shelf wearing a white paper gown that covered his body from neck to knees. Underneath it he was naked and barefoot, the gown cut off at the shoulders. The cell was empty save for a toilet bowl and a meal tray which lay untouched on the floor. He was the size of a man, but his features were still childlike, his skin smooth. He lay perfectly still, eyes half closed, staring at the ceiling, his hands folded across his stomach. The whiteboard said his name was 'Medway, Leonard'.

Jenny said, 'Has this young man been seen by a psychiatrist?'

'Yes. The contract has been agreed now. He's on anti-depressant medication.'

'What's wrong with him?'

'He made a suicide attempt in a police cell.'

'What's he in for?'

'About twenty-five TWOCs and assaulting a police officer.'

'What happened to the heavy gown Danny Wills was dressed in?'

'It's only needed if they're trying to harm themselves. Leonard's no trouble.'

The boy reached down under his gown, tugged it up a little and started to masturbate. Jenny looked away. Sue and Nurse Raven stood and watched for a moment.

Sue said, 'He can't be that depressed.'

SEVENTEEN

JENNY LEFT PORTSHEAD FARM WITH a feeling of frustration which, as she drove back towards town, grew steadily into a rage. She cursed at other cars hogging lanes on the motorway and honked at drivers slow away from the lights. She didn't care if they could hear her or see her gestures in the mirror. Screw them all.

Letting the anger fill her felt good. All the way through her inspection she had wanted to protest, to slap that fat, bone-headed moron Sue in the face and tell her, look, you've got kids held prisoner here, children with the bad luck to be born to people like Simone Wills. And what do you do? Lock them up and humiliate them, turn them into bitter, violent young men and women who just want to kick out and hurt some-one, anyone. Dealing with those people, the prick of a secur-ity guy, the self-important Elaine Lewis and the nurse who'd prostituted her profession to act as jailer, brought back mem-ories of years of impotent fury. Her mind filled with a pro-cession of long-forgotten faces and buried grievances: social workers who'd left kids to spend nights alone in police cells, too lazy to bail them out; staff in care homes who'd looked the other way while colleagues abused teenagers; judges who'd refused to criticize the system even when its failings led to violence and death. She knocked the bumper of the car behind when she parked and heard something crack, but didn't give a damn. If anyone crossed her now, she'd most likely hit them.

She thumped through the door into reception and immediately started dictating instructions to Alison. The inquest was going to start on Monday, Simone Wills was to be informed immediately. Elaine Lewis, Nurse Raven, Darren Hogg (the CCTV operator) and the secure care workers in the male house unit were to be summoned to attend. Elaine Lewis was to provide Jan Smirski's whereabouts and details of the trainees occupying the rooms either side of Danny's by close of business. The company who serviced the security cameras was to nominate a representative to come to court with a statement giving chapter and verse of when the cameras in the male house unit were reported faulty. When she had finished, she shoved through the door into her office and started on the pile of paperwork that had gathered on her desk, tearing through each death and post-mortem report like a prize fighter taking on all comers. For a highly productive two hours she felt furious and invincible. Nothing and no one would stand in her way.

Late in the afternoon Alison knocked cautiously and came in with some messages. Still pumped with adrenalin, Jenny listened impatiently, firing off responses as if her officer was wasting her time. Alison dealt with her patiently, wary of Jenny's dangerous mood. Minor matters dealt with, she said there was good and bad news from Portshead. The good news was they had provided an address for a sixteen-year-old burglar called Terry Ryan who had occupied the cell next to Danny's. She had spoken to Terry's mother, who said he could get to the inquest on Tuesday if he got bail on Monday – he'd been picked up on a bench warrant. The cell on the other side had apparently been empty. The bad news was that the company who employed Jan Smirski had no idea where he had gone. He had handed in his notice three weeks ago saying he had family business back home. He left no forwarding address. She'd tried googling him, but there were a lot of Jan Smirskis in Poland and the few she'd phoned didn't speak English. Jenny said to try harder, get his bank details out of the employer, do whatever a policeman would to find someone. Alison nodded, a touch resentful, then said she'd had an email from Grantham threatening to cut off their funding unless Jenny returned a full set of accounts within seven days.

'Why the hell haven't we got an accountant?'

'He won't pay for one.'

'Well, phone him up and tell him we're having one anyway.'

'I'd rather you made that sort of call, Mrs Cooper.'

'I'm not asking you, Alison, I'm instructing you. This is business. Just make the call.'

'And I'd rather you didn't speak to me like that, if you don't mind.'

'Like what?'

'As if I'm some sort of servant. I'm not. And when Mr Marshall ran this office he never once adopted that attitude.'

Jenny took a deep breath. 'I'm not adopting an *attitude*, I'm asking you to make a simple phone call. I couldn't care less what your relationship is with Grantham. This is a strictly professional matter and if he takes it personally it's his problem, not yours.'

Alison stood her ground, her expression saying she was going to get something off her chest. 'It's not about him, Mrs Cooper, it's about you. I don't like having to say this, but ever since you started I've found you extremely abrupt, and at times downright rude. You seem to be very angry, and in my experience that's not a helpful emotion in this job.'

'Well, as we're being honest with each other, I have to say I've found you obstructive and reluctant to take on new ideas, and you give every impression of not enjoying having me as your boss.'

'You haven't gone out of your way to make it a pleasant experience.'

'Maybe that's because I'm two weeks in and I've done nothing but shovel up the crap Marshall left me.'

'It was your choice.'

Jenny exploded. 'What do you expect me to do? Let it lie? Pretend Marshall did a good job? I don't care what your feelings were for him, he was negligent, for God's sake.'

'Oh, take a bloody pill.' Alison wrenched at the door handle.

'What did you say?'

Alison spun round. 'You clearly can't cope. Everyone knows you left your last job because you cracked up.' She walked out, the door slamming behind her.

'Come back here and apologize or you're sacked.'

Alison didn't reply. Jenny heard her grab her things and stomp out into the hall. Moments later there were angry footsteps outside her window, heading off down the street.

So what? She could do without her. She was sick of people telling her what she couldn't do.

It was nearly midnight and her blood was still up. She had spent the evening in her study at Melin Bach, trawling through the Danny Wills file, planning her cross-examinations and finding the holes Elaine Lewis wouldn't be able to plug. There was no doubt in her mind that her inquest would result in a verdict of death caused by gross negligence and want of care. It would see Elaine Lewis and her staff exposed to the full gale of media and public opprobrium. Questions would be asked in Parliament, criminal charges would follow. Her name would be synonymous with the fearless struggle for truth and justice. It didn't matter that her son had rejected her, or that Steve hadn't so much as left her a message. Nothing could shake her. She was a force of nature.

She poured half a tumbler of vodka over ice and drank it at her desk while she logged into the office email account. There was a reply from a low-cost airline saying a Mr J. Smirski had bought a one-way ticket to Poznan on 30 May but they had no Polish address for him; a Mr Mason from Sectec Ltd wrote to say he'd be at court on Monday and Ruth Turner confirmed that she would be attending. Annoyed about Smirski, Jenny looked up her powers to summon witnesses from abroad. The process was convoluted and required her to make an application through a civil court, whose jurisdiction, unlike hers, extended throughout the European Union. It could take weeks to get him to testify. She decided to chance going ahead without him; if the evidence wasn't firm enough she could always adjourn and track him down.

She continued to work furiously, pausing only to refill her glass. It was past two when, her mind still full of fighting talk, the alcohol won and she dragged herself upstairs to bed.

She had the dream about the crack in the wall of her childhood bedroom again. Only this time it was more detailed: there was a human creature in there, around the corner, out of sight. She imagined it as a man with a twisted face and musty clothes who at any moment would beckon her into the darkness and seal up the wall behind her so no one would ever know where he went. She turned her head towards the door and the safety of her parents on the other side, but her body refused to follow, her legs as heavy as granite. She felt the presence coming closer to the crack, heard it shuffling in the dust between the rafters. She wrenched at her legs with her hands but they stayed rooted to the boards.

On Saturday morning Jenny woke, feeling heavy and haunted, carrying a load that refused to lift as she washed, dressed and tried to make breakfast without any sudden movements. The day was dull and her mind was sluggish.

Several cups of coffee wouldn't shift the inertia. She tried sitting in the garden, but the shadows hung persistently around her.

The vividness of her dream sensations began to scare her. She remembered Dr Travis once telling her that the mind threw up disturbing images only when it was disturbed, that in themselves they meant little but were a warning sign that the brain was overloaded. She knew she was stressed, but tried to reassure herself with the thought that the last time this had happened she hadn't been as strong: she was still lying to herself that she could save her marriage. Things were fundamentally better now, she had reorganized, she knew where she was heading. What she was feeling was an aftershock, the unruly part of her mind testing her resolve. The answer was to lose herself, to throw everything into the inquest and emerge triumphant at the other end.

She went back into the kitchen, swallowed a temazepam and took a cup of herb tea to her desk. She didn't look up until nearly three, by which time the ghosts had finally crept away.

Alison was waiting in the lobby of Bristol Law Courts when Jenny arrived at eight-thirty on Monday morning. Dressed in a dark suit, she exuded an atmosphere of injured dignity.

'As I hadn't heard from you, Mrs Cooper, I thought it only proper that I should attend at least for today – that is, if my presence is required.'

'I think there are a number of things we need to discuss, don't you?'

'Now, Mrs Cooper?'

'I don't think that would be appropriate. We'll meet at the office after today's proceedings.'

'Very well. Will you be needing me in court?'

Jenny studied her face, her expression wounded and defiant,

emotion behind her eyes that she was struggling to hold in. 'Where did you hear those rumours about me?'

'The Bristol Central coroner's office knew all about you even before you arrived. Mr Hamer, the deputy there, told me you'd taken sick leave for stress after your divorce.'

'Grantham?'

'From what I hear he came under some pressure to allow your appointment.'

'From whom?'

'The word was you were a good lawyer. You'd done fifteen years' public service and the Ministry wanted more women coroners.'

'I see.'

The ease with which she was appointed was explained: her bosses in North Somerset had had a word with the powers that be and had helped ease her into a secure post. They'd got the Ministry on their side, played the female ticket and strong-armed a reluctant Grantham and his colleagues at the local authority to give her the job. It was nothing to do with her merits, it was a reward for long, badly paid years as a state-employed lawyer. And even though not a word had been said to her, somehow she was meant to understand this and toe the line in gratitude. The local authority and the Ministry were expecting a grateful, compliant coroner, and if she didn't play the game they could always explode the bomb of her psychiatric history and have her removed. They thought they had her on a leash.

Alison said, 'Shall I get the courtroom ready, Mrs Cooper?'

Mildly dazed, Jenny nodded.

Alison stepped towards the door, then paused and said, 'Still nothing to report on the Katy Taylor inquiry, I'm afraid. There was a murder and several rapes at the weekend – CID are pretty stretched at the moment.'

*

The courtroom, which normally hosted criminal trials, was small, modern yet formal. Jenny sat in a large, high-backed swivel chair several feet above floor level. Far from making her feel important, it made her feel responsible, part of the Establishment. There had been something vaguely subversive about the village hall; here she sat beneath the royal crest, surrounded by the trappings of office.

She looked out at benches packed with people. Simone Wills and several of her friends – women showing lots of tattooed flesh – sat at the front of the public gallery. Alongside them was Tara Collins, her bruised face now several shades of purple. Most of the other seats were occupied by journalists who had overflowed from the single press bench. Jenny estimated there were nearly twenty of them. Also in the public gallery were two suited figures: a middle-aged woman and a slightly younger, not unattractive man. She assumed they were civil servants of some sort, officials from the Ministry who had been assigned to assess her probity and impartiality. On the advocates' benches, representing UKAM Secure Solutions Ltd, sat her old friend Mr Hartley, obviously something of a regular at Bristol inquests. This time he was briefed by a glamorous young red-headed solicitor whose expensively bound lever arch files bore the name of a prestigious London law firm. Behind them sat several suits from UKAM, corporate men in striped shirts with suntans gained on the golf course. The Wills family was represented by a nervous trainee solicitor, scarcely more than a student, who was appearing pro bono in his capacity as a volunteer at North Bristol Law Centre. A jury of eight men and women, several obvious misfits among them, sat in the jury box. She suspected they were the dregs of the pool, shunted in her direction by canny jury bailiffs elsewhere in the building.

Her nerves steadied by 30mg of temazepam, she opened the

inquest by outlining the bare facts of Danny Wills's death. She explained to the jury that, as he had been cremated, further examination by a pathologist had not been possible. They would have to rely on the report of Dr Peterson, which stated that Danny had died from asphyxiation due to strangulation, having been found hanging by a strip of bed sheet from the bars of his cell window. Their job was now to listen to the evidence and to decide when, where and how Danny met his death. Possible verdicts might include accident – a completely unintended occurrence with a fatal effect; misadventure – a risk deliberately undertaken which led unintentionally to death; suicide; unlawful killing; an open verdict (where the evidence doesn't lead to a definite conclusion); and neglect – a gross failure to provide the basic necessities of life, including medical attention, to a person in a dependent position.

The first witness she called to give evidence was Simone Wills. Standing in front of so many people, Simone spoke in barely more than a whisper and was never far from tears, frequently having to stop to collect herself. Jenny nursed her through, encouraging her to talk directly to the jury. She told them all about Danny's time growing up, his troubled relations with the various men in her life, and how, despite her best efforts, he got drawn into petty crime until he finally received the inevitable custodial sentence. By the time she started describing her desperate phone calls to the director's office at Portshead Farm, she had the jury on her side. A woman in the back row dabbed her eyes as Simone said she knew, she *just knew*, that there was something badly wrong with her son. And when she recounted seeing the two policemen on her doorstep who had come with the terrible news, two more of the female jurors wiped away tears. This seemed to give her strength: at last she had moved people who mattered and they were feeling her pain.

Hartley said he had no questions for Simone, but skilfully proffered his condolences with such sincerity that an audible sob issued from the most tearful woman in the back row.

Ruth Turner arrived, flustered after dashing across the city from early meetings, just in time to be second in the box. A confident witness with many years of experience, she gave an unvarnished but compassionate account of the dysfunctional Wills family, painting Simone as a victim too: a young woman who'd struggled to build a secure home for her children but who had been let down time and again by feckless men. She described the young mother's anguish when during his first appearance before the Youth Court Danny was told to expect a custodial sentence, and how she had tried without success to get the Youth Offending Team to have him referred to a psychiatrist as part of his pre-sentence assessment. When she repeated the details of her phone call to Nurse Linda Raven – the one in which she was told there was no psychiatrist available, even to see a child who was suspected of harbouring suicidal tendencies – there were looks of outrage on even the most unpromising of the jurors' faces.

Jenny drove the point home. 'You're sure Nurse Raven told you there was no possibility of Danny being seen by a psychiatrist?'

'She said the local primary care trust had refused to provide one.'

'But there was nothing stopping the owners of Portshead Farm from paying for one privately?'

'Of course not.'

'As far as you know, even though Danny was placed in an observation cell for three days, he was never psychiatrically assessed?'

'That's correct.'

'What would happen in, say, a council-run children's home if a child in care was suspected of being suicidal?'

'We'd get them seen by a psychiatrist as soon as possible.'

'And if you failed to do so?'

'Obviously it would amount to serious neglect.'

'Is Portshead Farm obliged to provide psychiatric care?'

'It's a condition of its contract with the Youth Justice Board. There's no requirement to have every trainee assessed, but where there's a problem they're under a duty to have a psychiatrist come in.'

Hartley rose with the now familiar gold-toothed smile and asked Ruth Turner if Danny, as far as she knew, had a previous history of mental illness or disturbance? Ruth said no, he didn't.

Hartley said, 'Then on what basis did you telephone Nurse Raven and insist that he be seen by a psychiatrist?'

'Because of what his mother had told me.'

'Is Mrs Wills medically qualified?'

'Of course not.'

'Did she take him to her GP to express her concerns about his mental health?'

'She had six children.'

'And the oldest was about to go into custody for the first time. You'd think if her anxiety was that great she would have made him a priority?'

'We hoped the Youth Offending Team would have him seen.'

Hartley was the soul of patience. 'That does rather suggest your concern was more to keep him out of custody than for the actual state of his mental health.'

Hesitant, Ruth Turner said, 'In hindsight perhaps I should have made her take him to the doctor.'

'But you didn't. And nor did you persist with your request to have him seen by a psychiatrist after the one telephone call you had with Nurse Raven. You rather gave up on him, didn't you?'

She paused for a long moment. 'I have a very heavy caseload. I wish I had followed it up, but technically Danny was no longer my responsibility once he was in custody.'

'Such was your concern for his fragile state of mind that you washed your hands of him?'

'No. I did what I could in the time I had available.'

Hartley nodded and said, 'I'm sure we can all relate to that.'

As Ruth Turner stepped, deflated, from the witness box, Jenny felt as if she were staring into an abyss. It had never for a moment crossed her mind that the social worker's evidence could be used to bolster UKAM's position, but that was what had happened. Hartley had accused her of sentimental opportunism, of bleating about a psychiatrist without actually having the belief that Danny was ill. His point had even got home to the jury: there had been accusing looks in Simone's direction when they'd heard she didn't take Danny to the doctor. The weeping woman now wore a disapproving frown that said, *What sort of mother was she?*

Jenny took a gulp of water and called for Nurse Linda Raven to be sworn, telling herself that while Hartley was shaving the odds he still couldn't get around what happened in the house unit. There could be no excuse for not finding the body before morning.

Linda Raven read the oath with the same dispassionate, untouchable expression Jenny had observed in the reception centre. She answered her preliminary questions in a deadpan and unapologetic voice, confirming that she was the chief nursing officer at Portshead Farm, with overall responsibility for the medical assessment of trainees on reception. She had held the position for three years, since the facility opened, and prior to that had spent thirteen years working in the NHS, her last four as a senior staff nurse in the Vale Hospital's A&E department. When asked her reasons for leaving the NHS, she said she was attracted by the salary and the opportunity to enter management.

Jenny said, 'Could you describe the nature of the assessment you carried out on Danny Wills?'

'It was a standard medical questionnaire approved by the Department of Health and the Prisons Service. We take a basic history, ask if they're suffering from any physical or mental symptoms, whether they have any allergies. We also cross-reference with NHS records – if we can't get them online we call their surgery and talk to a practice nurse or doctor.'

'Is psychiatric assessment part of this process?'

'No. If there are any medical issues we get them seen by a doctor – we have surgeries twice a week. If it's more urgent there are on-call arrangements.'

'But there was no arrangement for psychiatric care at that time.'

'The company I work for has a contract with the NHS to provide a range of services. At that time, the local primary care trust withdrew funding for psychiatric services outside certain clinics. There was a dispute that lasted several weeks, during which time they refused to provide cover. We couldn't have had a psychiatrist if we'd asked for one.' Her answer was polished and well rehearsed, phrased in a way she wouldn't have come up with herself: *during which time.*

'Would you have liked Danny to be seen by a psychiatrist?'

'No. He didn't present with any particular problems – you can see from his file. It was a borderline decision whether to keep him under observation at all.'

'What led you to make that decision?'

'All trainees with a history of drug abuse are strip-searched to make sure they have no narcotics on their person. When my colleague attempted to examine him, Danny was obstructive and violent.'

'In what way?'

'Do you want me to repeat the exact language that was used?'

'Yes, please.'

'When my colleague, Nurse Hamilton, warned him that force could be used to carry out the search, he said, "Go ahead, you can fucking kill me. I'll fucking kill myself before I let you white niggers touch me." Once he'd said those words it amounted to a threat to self-harm. Our procedure was to keep him under seventy-two hours' observation.'

'Was he strip-searched?'

'Yes.'

'Was force used?'

'Two secure care officers contained him while Nurse Hamilton conducted the search.'

'Did that include an internal search?'

'It did.'

'And how did Danny respond?'

'Once the search was complete he was detained in an observation cell, where he continued to shout and swear for several hours before he calmed down.' Nurse Raven turned her head to the jury and said, 'I'd like to stress that after the search he did not make any further threats to kill himself.'

'But you took his initial threat seriously enough to dress him in a padded, knee-length sleeveless gown designed to prevent self-harm.'

'He'd been violent. It was a standard response.'

Jenny made no further progress. Nurse Raven's carefully prepared story, in which there were no obvious holes, was that Danny ended up under observation merely because he uttered a threat to harm himself which, although technically it made him a suicide risk, was in fact a hostile response to the indignity of having his rear end searched by a male nurse.

When he cross-examined, Hartley emphasized this point several times over, getting Nurse Raven to confirm that there was nothing else in Danny's behaviour which suggested he was a danger to himself.

When he had finished, Jenny asked: 'If there had been a psychiatrist available at the time, would you have had Danny assessed?'

'I doubt it. After the initial couple of hours he was perfectly cooperative. You can see that from the observation log.'

'But you had received a call from Ruth Turner, the family's social worker, saying that she wanted him seen by a psychiatrist.'

'Most trainees have got psychological problems, that's why they offend. We could keep ten psychiatrists busy. And in my experience of suicides, they tend to keep their plans to themselves.'

There were nods of recognition in the jury. In the public gallery Simone Wills was being comforted by a woman with 'Porn Star in Training' written in glitter across her tight top.

Jenny thanked Raven for her evidence and let her stand down, feeling the ground slipping further from under her feet. Hearing her last answer, she remembered how crafty her friend Cathy had been all those years ago. After being drunk for a solid week in which she claimed to have slept with ten men, she had spent several days in sober, self-imposed purdah, emerging from her bedroom in their shared flat neatly dressed, quietly spoken and repentant. That was the night she stepped under a train.

Jenny called the lunch adjournment and retreated to the charmless office at the back of the court grandly named the 'Judge's Chambers'. She couldn't face making small talk in the judicial dining room to which she had a pass for the duration of her inquest, and instead picked at a mini packet of shortcake biscuits which had been left for her on a trolley along with hotel-style sachets of coffee and a one-cup electric kettle.

The morning had moved her investigation no further forward. She felt naive and foolish for ever having imagined it could have turned out differently. Harry Marshall, who had been in the job for years, hadn't made a dent on UKAM. Less than two months ago he must have sat in a similar room coming to the same depressing conclusion: the system was geared so everyone got to avoid responsibility. That was why it worked it all. If a child or two died, what did it matter? Most didn't.

Alison, still frosty and maintaining her distance, came in with a message from Hartley. Elaine Lewis had been unavoidably detained and sought the court's permission to be excused attendance until tomorrow morning. Jenny said she would have preferred more notice, but could work around it. Privately, she was glad she wouldn't have to face her this afternoon. She was already feeling spent.

Alison said, 'That nurse was more confident than last time. I think they've been working on her.'

'I should say so.'

'Maybe the way Mr Marshall handled this case doesn't seem quite so strange to you now?'

She gave Jenny a look and left the room.

The afternoon started on a more promising note. A man named Vince Mason, an operations manager for Sectec Ltd, was next in the witness box. Producing a sheaf of computer printouts taken from the customer service log, he was adamant that his company hadn't been informed of any camera malfunction at Portshead Farm until nine a.m. on 14 April, a few hours after Danny's body had been discovered. Part of their contract with UKAM, he explained, was a regular three-monthly system check. His engineers had been in a fortnight before and found everything in full working order. What's more, they guaranteed that equipment would be fixed or replaced within forty-eight hours of a fault being reported. It was inconceivable that a camera reported broken would be down for a week.

Unfazed by Mason's certainty, Hartley asked him if it was possible that the security staff at Portshead Farm had reported the fault but his company had missed it, or simply not got around to responding. Mason said no, he could look at the log, there was no fault report prior to the 14th.

'Customers report faults by email as well as telephone, don't they?' Hartley said.

'Some do.'

Hartley's solicitor handed him two sheets of paper which he asked Alison to pass to Mason. Another copy was produced for Jenny.

'Do you see that these are email messages reporting a fault in the camera in the main corridor of the male house unit?'

'Yes, sir.'

'Were they sent to your correct address?'

'They seem to have been.'

'Perhaps you would be so kind as to tell the jury the send dates.'

Mason, troubled, squinted at the documents. 'They say 9 and 14 April, but I'm not sure I believe it. They're not on our log.'

'Are you saying your customer service desk didn't receive those emails?'

'I don't think we did.'

Hartley turned to Jenny. 'Ma'am, could the witness be allowed a few minutes to clarify the situation? It may be that a few phone calls could shed some light.'

Jenny saw Tara Collins catch her eye from the public

gallery, her look saying they both knew what was coming next.

Jenny said, 'See if those emails were received, Mr Mason.'

It was no surprise, when, less than five minutes later, he came back to the box looking baffled with the news that the emails did seem to be on the system after all. He had no explanation for why they weren't logged or actioned. It had never happened before.

Jenny said, 'Could it be that they weren't received then, they just look like they were?'

Mason said, 'I've no idea. I'm not an expert in these matters.'

Hartley interrupted with, 'I don't know quite what you're suggesting, ma'am, but the transmission dates of emails have long been accepted in the criminal courts as thoroughly reliable evidence.'

Jenny said, 'I will decide on the reliability of evidence, Mr Hartley. For the moment I'm keeping an open mind.' Out of the corner of her eye she saw Tara Collins smile.

Darren Hogg looked as if he spent his life in a dark room surrounded by monitors. He had a junk-food complexion and acne scars and stood in the witness box wearing his liveried uniform with the pride you sometimes saw in young policemen. Jenny thought: a career security guard with an unhealthy fantasy life.

She said, 'You were on duty in the camera control room during the early hours of 14 April?'

'I was.'

'What could you see of the male house unit?'

'Only the entrance, ma'am. The camera in the main corridor had been playing up for a week or so.'

'What had been done about that?'

'I'd sent an email to the camera company and so had my colleague.'

'You're sure you sent that email?'

'Yes, ma'am.'

'Why didn't you report the fault by telephone?'

'We weren't meant to use the outside line – cost.'

'Had you told the director's office?'

He hesitated slightly. 'I think my colleague did, yeah. He was on days that week.'

'But you're not sure?'

'No.'

'You'd agree it was an unsatisfactory state of affairs not having that camera working?'

'Of course. But cameras have problems all the time.'

'You're sure that there is no tape covering that corridor for the early hours of the 14th?'

'Absolutely.'

'I want you to think about how serious a question this is before you answer, Mr Hogg . . . Has anyone, at any time, asked you to destroy, alter, lose or otherwise interfere with any images that might be of use to this inquest?'

He thought for a moment and shook his head. 'Nope.'

Jenny glanced at the jury. A couple of the men appeared doubtful.

'Say the camera had been working, what would you expect to have seen?'

'Not a lot. Just the night officer making his checks.'

'How often?'

'Every half-hour.'

'The night officer has to walk up and down that corridor, checking through every window every thirty minutes throughout the night?'

'Yes.'

'From what you've seen, do they sometimes miss a check or two, doze off in the staff room?'

'Not in my experience.'

'Never?'

'No.'

The sceptical jurors both smiled. Others traded glances. Hogg was the kind of guy who'd sell his mother for the chance to wear a uniform and they'd rumbled him.

Jenny said, 'I simply don't believe that's true, Mr Hogg – you've honestly never known a night officer miss a check?'

'Never, ma'am.'

She heard one of the jurors say, 'Yeah, right.'

The final witness of the day was Kevin Stewart, the secure care officer who was on night duty in the male house unit. A wiry, fair-headed man in his forties with a strong note of Glasgow in his accent. His suit jacket hung off his bony shoulders; his shirt collar was too big for his neck. Jenny felt her heartbeat pick up as she watched him reading the oath. This was the one she had to nail. She touched the two tablets floating loose in her pocket and wished she felt calmer. She reached for her glass but stopped herself, noticing a tremor in her hand. Stewart laid down the oath card and turned to face her. She swallowed, forcing the saliva down her dry throat.

They went through the initial formalities. Stewart said he had worked in young offenders' institutions and secure training centres for nearly twenty years, the last two at Portshead Farm. His record was exemplary and no complaints had ever been upheld against him. He normally worked the day shift, but due to several members of staff being off sick he had been working nights for a week when Danny died. He was aware that Danny had been on observation when he first came in and that he had been refusing to leave his room except to eat. He said it was the way with lots of kids, especially ones in for the first time. How staff dealt with it was to let them acclimatize for a week or so. Even the most difficult cases would get bored of sitting in their room by then.

Jenny said, 'Had you spoken to Danny Wills?'

'A couple of times when I came on shift at ten. I got there at a few minutes to, helped round up the stragglers.'

'Did you see him on the night of the 13th?'

'Briefly. He was in his room – he told me his toilet was blocked. I checked it and saw it was emptying slowly. All right for liquids but not for solids, if you know what I mean. I told him I'd get on to maintenance.'

'There were two rooms free in the unit that night, why didn't you move him to one of those?'

'It wasn't a big deal that couldn't wait till morning. It didn't seem worth the paperwork.'

'When did you call maintenance?'

'Straight after lights out. I left a message on the voicemail.'

Jenny made a note. 'Did any of the day staff say anything about him to you?'

'Dave Whiteside, he was on the evening shift, said something about beginning to mix, coming down to the common room in the evening. You'll see it in the comments section on his file.'

Jenny dug out her copy of Danny's trainee progress file and checked the daily log. It confirmed that he had spent the day in his room, gone to the canteen for evening meal and 'socialized in the common room during the evening'. The entry was signed D. Whiteside.

Jenny said, 'What happened at lights out?'

'I make sure everyone's in bed and turn out the lights with the master switch.'

'Were the rooms then in darkness?'

'Not completely. They've got a little night light in the ceiling so we can see in.'

'How many staff were on duty in the male house unit that night?'

'Just me through to wake-up at seven a.m. Sometimes if we had a difficult bunch we'd have two on, but these were quiet. You'd usually find two staff in the female unit – some reason they kick up more at night.'

'What did you do for those ten hours, Mr Stewart?'

'Walked the corridor every thirty minutes, watched some TV, generally kept an eye on things.'

'Any problems?'

'No. It was a quiet night.'

'You know that the pathologist found that Danny died between two and three a.m.'

'So I understand.'

'Even if it was closer to three, that's nine trips up and down the corridor you made without seeing his body hanging from the bars at the window.'

'I explained that at the first inquest, ma'am. I looked in through the window in the door and saw what I thought was him lying under the covers. Turned out he'd stuffed some clothes under there. And I couldn't have seen him hanging anyway, because he was hidden by the wardrobe.'

'I inspected his room last Friday, Mr Stewart. The wardrobe is bolted to the wall next to the window. It doesn't stick far enough out into the room to hide a body, even a small one.'

'Did they not tell you, ma'am? We've only had them fixed to the wall since. It was one thing we learned that night – he was a clever wee lad, tugged it out far enough to hide him. You hear it again and again in my line of work – when someone's going to do it, something gets hold of them. A kid who couldnae do up his shoelaces is suddenly plaiting ropes and tying sheep shanks.'

*

Another pill dulled some of the anxiety which had consumed her. When it was this acute, the physical symptoms were the worst. She had walked back across the city centre to the office having to stop every few hundred yards to catch her breath. Her diaphragm was so tight each intake of air was a conscious effort. At five-minute intervals her entire nervous system stuttered like an electric light flickering in a storm. When it happened she had a sinking sensation as if she had missed her step and had started to fall.

Another half-tablet was pushing it, but it loosened her chest a little and let her breathe more easily again. She sat on the edge of her desk and closed her eyes, trying to relax, to feel her limbs heavy, imagining Dr Travis's deep, reassuring voice.

The day's evidence couldn't have been any worse. Simone's and Ruth Turner's claims that Danny had been suicidal had been painted by Hartley as part of a failed attempt to keep him from the punishment he deserved. Nurse Raven had emerged as a concerned and competent professional who had acted with excessive caution in keeping Danny in an observation cell. UKAM had somehow planted emails on Sectec's computers and Kevin Stewart had denied her the one point which could still have left the door open to a verdict of neglect. Nothing she could throw at Elaine Lewis would be enough to avoid the inevitable verdict of suicide. Her only hope lay with the sixteen-year-old Terry Ryan, the occupant of the next-door cell, but since he'd shown no interest in making a written statement despite numerous calls to his home, she had no idea what he might say.

What angered her most was the fact that she had believed it would be any different. How deluded must she have been? It made her think that somewhere along the line she had lost touch with reality, leaving her stranded in a world of her own making, that David and Ross just did their best to humour her.

She heard the key in the outer door. It opened and shut. Alison took a few steps, then stopped. Jenny sensed her standing, unmoving, in the middle of reception. Neither spoke. The silence seemed to last for more than a minute before Alison moved towards her office door and knocked.

Her nerves spasmed at the sound. 'Yes?'

Alison entered, looking as if she had just heard tragic news. She had been crying and with her make-up washed away her eyes were pale and hollow. The two women looked at each other, neither knowing how to start.

Alison found her voice first. It was quiet and full of regret. 'I have a confession to make, Mrs Cooper . . . I'm afraid I did something I shouldn't have. I let my feelings get the better of me.' She unzipped the briefcase she had had with her at court and brought out a document. 'I found this after Mr Marshall died. It was locked in the drawer where you found the Katy Taylor file . . .' She handed it over.

It was the best part of an inch thick, spiral-bound and marked 'Confidential'. The title read 'Official Tender for a Secure Training Centre to Service Bristol and the South-West Region'. Beneath it, the corporate ident of UKAM Secure Solutions Ltd. Inside, over a hundred and twenty pages, were detailed plans and costings for a juvenile detention facility designed to accommodate up to five hundred inmates. It was to be located on a twenty-five-acre brown-field site to the north-east of the city now owned by the local authority where a cigarette factory had once stood. Jenny flicked to the final summary and saw the build cost: eight million pounds. The annual running cost for each of the first five years was thirty million. The final page was dated 18 January.

She closed the cover and placed the document on the desk, her drum-tight diaphragm holding her lungs in a vice. 'Why didn't you show this to me before?'

'I was afraid he'd been mixed up in some sort of corruption. He was always complaining he didn't make enough money.'

'How did he get hold of this?'

'I've no idea. It's meant to be confidential between the tenderer and the Youth Justice Board. Someone must have leaked it.'

'And he never mentioned it to you?'

She shook her head. 'I've written you a letter of resignation.' She reached into her briefcase and brought out an envelope.

'What good will that do?'

'A young boy died and I've withheld evidence.'

'You want UKAM to finish your career as well?'

'How could you trust me now? I can't even trust myself.'

'You gave me this, didn't you?'

Alison looked at her, disbelieving. 'Don't you want me to go?'

Jenny said, 'I'll make a deal with you. You keep my secrets and I'll keep yours. Everyone else's are fair game.'

The events of the day turned and twisted in her mind. UKAM's dirty tricks and careful coaching of the witnesses had destroyed her every attempt to lay blame at their door. What she hadn't thought through were the lengths to which an aggressive commercial enterprise would go to protect itself. A verdict of neglect wouldn't just result in the rearranging of the furniture as it would in the state prison system, it could threaten tens of millions of pounds' worth of business.

The tender sat in the passenger seat of her car like an unexploded incendiary. Marshall, like her, had read it and realized that the life of a fourteen-year-old criminal was nothing to UKAM compared with the business at stake. He had read it and become enraged, he was going to shake the citadel to its foundations, but instead it shook him. Something happened between him receiving the tender and conducting the sham of an inquest which had destroyed him. Alison was frightened he had been corrupted, but Jenny didn't believe that – UKAM wouldn't have risked him going to the police, they'd have been smarter. Whatever they had come up with, Marshall had been crushed. Simone Wills had been vilified in the press and her house turned over on the eve of the inquest on a malicious tip-off, and Tara Collins, who had tried to make the connection between Danny's death and Katy Taylor's, had found herself on fraud charges that could potentially land her in a US jail.

What was coming her way? she wondered. The tranquillizers she'd ordered illegally on the internet? Her medical history? Threats to her son?

Jenny gripped the steering wheel with hands slippery with sweat and tried to stay alive as she crossed the Severn Bridge, jammed in between the central reservation and an angry row of articulated lorries. With her heart racing and all her old anxiety symptoms raging, she feared she was falling apart.

She rolled up the bottoms of her old jeans and waded barefoot into the stream. The stones were sharp against the soles of her feet but they were soon numbed by the freezing water. Standing in the middle, thigh deep, she looked up into waving leaves of the ash trees and asked the God she'd always tried to believe was there how someone who should feel so free could be so trapped inside herself.

She remained there until she trembled, until her whole body was feeling something more powerful than the grip of intangible fear. When her teeth were chattering so hard she could no longer clamp them together, she struggled back to the edge and sat down at the scrub-top table. In her cold wet clothes, barely able to hold a pen, she started to make notes in a legal pad. She stayed there, shivering, refusing to be beaten, until it was too dark to see.

EIGHTEEN

SHE WOKE FEELING DETACHED, AS if she didn't belong in her body. The face that looked back at her in the bathroom mirror seemed unfamiliar. She had to press her fingers down hard on the wash-hand basin to feel them. Dr Travis had once given this symptom a technical name which she had deliberately chosen to forget. All she knew was that it was part of the syndrome and it frightened her.

As she dressed and breakfasted the sensation began to recede and feeling slowly returned to her fingers, but paranoid, unwanted thoughts slid in to take its place. She didn't like to touch the bread knife; she found herself avoiding treading on the cracks between the flagstones on the kitchen floor. She repeated to herself she had been here before, that these were just symptoms of simple stress that she could weather and overcome if she could force herself through the next few days, but another voice told her that this was it, that she was going down properly this time. For good.

She took control in the only way she could, by planning the day's medication meticulously. A pill now, one just before court, another before the afternoon session. To cover emergencies she repeated the Polo mint trick with four half-tablets, which she placed back in the wrapper. During the drive into the city she rehearsed a selection of the exercises Dr Travis had taught her and managed to force her most bizarre and disturbing thoughts back beneath the surface. She remembered him saying that when she felt like this the important thing was to keep her emotions under control, not become angry or riled. If she could manage to stay level she might just get through the day, and after succeeding once, each subsequent day would be easier. She knew that. She'd climbed this mountain before.

Stepping through the judge's door and once more taking her seat on the throne of justice, she felt almost herself again. Just the right amount of temazepam, twenty minutes of relaxation exercises and no caffeine in her system. She was steady. Coping. The same could not be said for Simone Wills, who looked angry and tearful and was shooting vicious looks in the direction of the huddle of UKAM executives who seemed to be enjoying the break from their usual office routine. Tara Collins was sitting next to her, offering words of reassurance. The woman in the 'Porn Star' T-shirt and most of her other friends hadn't reappeared, leaving gaps on the public benches. The reporters, too, were thinner on the ground, but the two suited officials were in their same places at the back, notebooks out, pens poised. Hartley was reclining in his seat, sharing a joke with his solicitor. The QC's body language said he was feeling supremely confident and expected his day to pass off without a hitch. Resolving to disappoint him, Jenny called her first witness.

Elaine Lewis took several moments to respond to Alison's call. She entered from the lobby and walked at a measured pace to the front of the room, giving every impression of owning the court as absolutely as she did her prison. Dressed in an immaculate trouser suit with only a subtle hint of jewellery, she stepped elegantly into the witness box and read the oath without a flicker of nervousness; her every word and gesture was crafted to assert unwavering, understated confidence. Simone Wills glared murderously at her, but she remained aloof. Regal. Aware of the tension gathering in her own body, Jenny felt a stab of envy.

'Mrs Lewis, in your capacity as director of Portshead Farm, you accept ultimate responsibility for all operational decisions?'

After a beat, Elaine Lewis said, 'Of course.'

'Let's chart Danny's progress through your institution and the decisions that were made about him, shall we? Before he even arrived on your premises your office had been telephoned both by his mother and by the family's social worker warning that he was in a vulnerable mental state.'

'Yes. We have rigorous procedures for assessing trainees on their arrival and these are designed to detect such vulnerabilities. In Danny's case that is exactly what happened.' She spoke in a soft, moderate tone, saying *Danny* as if he were her own nephew.

'Who took those calls?'

'My assistant takes all my calls. I don't have a direct line.'

'Did she convey those messages to you?'

'I am notified of all relevant communications. There was nothing unusual or out of the ordinary about those from Mrs Wills and Mrs Turner. While we try to be responsive to families, Portshead Farm *is* a penal institution.'

'Are you saying you have a policy of not answering calls from concerned family members or professionals?'

'It would be unusual for me to respond personally, yes.'

'Did you do anything with the information in those calls? Contact the medical staff?'

'No. I have every faith in the professional judgement of all our staff, and it was more than justified in this case.'

'So you dismissed the calls as hysterical nonsense?'

'Those aren't words I would ever choose to use. What I would say is that once a trainee is received into Portshead

Farm, he or she is our responsibility. We take that duty extremely seriously.'

Jenny paused to make a note, deliberately dictating the pace. After a long moment, without looking up, she said, 'What effect do you consider dressing a naked, mentally disturbed fourteen-year-old boy in a thick gown that resembles a horse blanket and locking him in a cell for three days might have had on him?'

'I am not a medical professional. I wouldn't like to comment. However, it is an authorized procedure designed to ensure the child doesn't hurt himself.'

'It's designed to ensure the child *can't* physically hurt himself, isn't it? It doesn't address his psychological state at all.'

'Our first priority is to ensure the *physical* well-being of each trainee.'

'He was placed in the cell because it was felt he was at risk of self-harm. That is a psychological disorder, yet he wasn't seen by a psychiatrist. There wasn't one available.'

'You have seen the protocols which by law we are forced to follow. We followed them. In an ideal world Danny would have been seen by a psychiatrist, but due to circumstances beyond our control, none was available during that period.'

'You could have paid for one to come in.'

'If it was considered necessary, of course we would have done that. But Danny had no history of mental illness and was perfectly behaved during his period on observation. He was not in the categories of trainees for whom we would normally have called a psychiatrist.'

'Doesn't it trouble you that he wasn't seen?'

'The entire adult and youth custody system is imperfect. At Portshead Farm we do the very best we can on the budget the government makes available to us. Every aspect of our procedures is strictly controlled and reviewed.'

Elaine Lewis's rehearsed answers were starting to get under her skin, but Jenny told herself to relax, to go at her without emotion, to let the smooth-talking executive hang herself.

'Mrs Lewis, how do you explain the fact that the camera in the male house unit was broken for a week? Aren't cameras subject to your strict controls?'

'That should not have happened. Steps are being taken to make sure that in future all faults are remedied within twenty-four hours.'

'You don't consider it a coincidence that the one camera on site that was broken could have told us whether or not Mr Stewart made the half-hourly checks as he claimed?'

'No, I don't. And Kevin Stewart is one of our most experienced and dependable members of staff.'

Jenny glanced at the jury. Their faces were set and stony. Despite Elaine Lewis's polished performance they weren't warming to her.

'And you don't consider it odd that one of your most experienced members of staff should have failed, not once, but nine times, to spot a body hanging from the window?'

'I am satisfied with his explanation that it wasn't visible, and that unfortunately he was tricked into believing Danny was in bed. It's perfectly possible to have cameras in cells, but I don't think any of us would like that.'

'You don't accept that your systems in any way contributed to Danny's death?'

'No.'

'You accept no responsibility at all?'

'No, I don't.'

There were angry murmurs in the public gallery, Simone Wills's voice rising angrily above the others, and Tara Collins urgently whispering at her to calm down. Jenny gave her a moment to settle, hoping she'd do it without having to make a scene. The officials sitting behind her exchanged glances, surprised at Jenny's failure to intervene. But Simone eventually settled, keeping her cursing under her breath.

Jenny glanced at the Polo mints she had placed on the desk and thought about putting one in her mouth. No, she'd manage this without. She reached between two files and pulled out her copy of the tender, not letting Elaine Lewis see what it was.

'Mrs Lewis, just so the jury fully understands the situation, Portshead Farm, along with many other penal facilities in this country, is owned and run by a private company for a profit, isn't it?'

'Yes, it is.' The first note of defensiveness entered her voice.

Hartley's eyes sharpened and he tilted forward in his seat. The two officials in the public gallery looked up from their notes.

'If you don't run your business to the required standard, you risk losing the franchise. There's a lot of money at stake.'

'Precisely. Which is why we can't afford to make mistakes.'

'Are you aware that trainees are taking drugs inside Portshead Farm and on a regular basis?'

Elaine Lewis's eyes darted to Hartley. Jenny took it as a sign she hadn't been prepped for this.

'Every prison and youth custody facility has problems with drugs. Unless we prevent all physical contact with visitors, it's more or less inevitable.'

'Let me give you an example, Mrs Lewis. There was a girl named Katy Taylor who was a trainee while Danny was there. Unfortunately she died a short while after leaving custody and as part of the post-mortem tests an analysis was carried out on her hair. It proved she had been taking cannabis and crack cocaine more or less daily inside your facility.'

'If that's correct, it's very unfortunate.'

'Most days in a six-week sentence – that's a lot of drugs.'

Hartley rose to his feet, 'Ma'am, far be it from me to dictate the course of your questioning, but do the drugs Miss Taylor may or may not have consumed have any relevance to this case?'

Jenny said, 'It rather takes the shine off the claim that Portshead Farm is beyond reproach if trainees are taking drugs every day.'

'*One* trainee, ma'am.'

Jenny addressed the witness. 'We don't know, do we, Mrs Lewis?'

'We have a testing regime. The problem is dealt with as it would be in state-run prisons.'

Jenny nodded at Hartley to sit back down. He reluctantly did so.

Jenny said, 'Danny was a frequent drug user. Did he take any in Portshead?'

'I'm not in a position to say.'

'So it's possible?'

'Of course. And without being tyrannical, it's not a problem we can completely stamp out.'

Jenny opened the tender to a page she had flagged. 'Do you recognize these words, Mrs Lewis? "The most advanced system of surveillance and testing will be employed, based on those which have proved so successful at Portshead Farm to ensure the facility remains virtually drug-free".'

The director's eyes shot to the UKAM executives, who were already leaning forward over their desks, urgently haranguing Hartley and his solicitor.

'I asked if you recognize those words?'

She refused to answer, waiting for Hartley to rescue her.

Jenny said, 'They come from a tender document written by your employers, who are seeking to win a contract—'

Hartley leapt up. 'Ma'am, my clients inform me that you may be quoting from a highly confidential, commercially sensitive document which is completely irrelevant to the very specific facts of this case.'

'I'll tell you what I'm quoting from, Mr Hartley—'

'Ma'am, please let me address you on an issue of law.'

Jenny felt a surge of adrenalin pass through her, for once the good sort. She was going to face this bastard down. 'No. Please sit down. I want to hear the witness answer.'

The two officials at the back of the court were in animated conversation. The woman nodded in agreement with her colleague and dashed to the door, pulling out her phone.

'Ma'am, I must protest in the strongest terms. This is completely improper. The remit of this inquest is to find out when, where and how this death occurred.'

'That is precisely what I'm doing, Mr Hartley, and you know full well you have no right in this court to tell me what questions to ask.'

'I hope you understand, ma'am, this could have serious legal consequences for you personally. Breach of a commercial confidence—'

Jenny cut in: 'Is not something I will let stand in the way of an inquest into the death of a child.' She turned to the witness. 'Failure to answer my questions is a contempt of court. Do you understand?'

'Yes.'

'Mrs Lewis, do you recognize those words?'

She looked to Hartley, who was urgently flicking through a textbook. He nodded.

'Yes. I do.'

'Portshead Farm can hardly be called drug-free, can it?'

'That's a matter of opinion.'

'Your company, UKAM Secure Solutions Ltd, is bidding for a multi-million-pound contract to build a five-hundred place secure training centre in this city, isn't it? That isn't confidential, only the numbers inside this tender.' She tapped the cover with her finger.

The witness regained her composure. 'Naturally we are. It's a major government contract. We're leaders in the field.'

'I'll put this as delicately as I can . . . The reputation of your company as a safe custodian of young lives is a vital component to winning this contract, isn't it?'

'That is one element of our bid about which I have no anxiety whatsoever.'

Jenny looked at the faces of the jury. The uninterested collection of flotsam which had taken their places yesterday morning were now united in contempt for this corporate creature and her polished evasions. Satisfied she had done enough, Jenny said she had no more questions. Hartley said he had none either.

Jenny excused Elaine Lewis from the witness box and asked for Terry Ryan to be called. As Alison made her way to the door of the court, the male official came to the end of his row and pushed his card at her. Alison looked at it, then glanced back at Jenny, who nodded to her to proceed with calling the witness. The official gave Jenny a stern look, as if she was expected to know who he was. She ignored it.

Alison opened the door of the court and called for Terry Ryan. A skinny sixteen-year-old boy in low-slung jeans and an Ice-T vest top swaggered in. He had chest hair and wanted the world to see it. Alison handed the official's card up to Jenny en route to steering Terry into the witness box. It said: *Simon Moreton, Coroners' Service, Ministry of Justice.* On the back he had scribbled a note: *Could you please adjourn to discuss tender ASAP? Most urgent.* Jenny glanced at the official. He was looking at her expectantly. Jenny placed the card to one side and turned to the witness.

Only twenty-four hours after being released from a week

on remand, Terry appeared unharmed by the experience. He had spent most of the last four years in and out of courts and seemed to thrive on the attention, even more so this time as he wasn't in the dock. Jenny took him back to his time in Portshead Farm. He said he was two weeks off the end of a four-month stretch for domestic burglary when Danny arrived in the next-door cell.

'When was the first time you saw him?' Jenny asked.

'I think they brought him in on the Saturday – he was in his room when we came back from five-a-side in the gym. He never came out that night, though.'

'He was on the unit from Saturday until the following Friday night. Did you talk to him in that time?'

'A bit. Not much. In the showers and that.'

'What was he like?

'Quiet. Didn't say a lot. Wouldn't go to class, went to canteen, that was it.'

'Why wouldn't he go to class?'

'Had a problem with it, I dunno.'

'Did you ask him?'

'Nope.'

'Did you speak to him in the canteen?'

'Once or twice. Asked him what he was in for and that.'

'How did he seem?'

'Pissed off. You're all like that first time in. You can't believe it.'

'Did he have any injuries, look like he'd been in any fights?'

'Not that I noticed.'

'Did he seem upset to you at all?'

Terry shook his head. 'He was no baby, man. Someone said something he'd give them this look, you know, like don't mess with me.'

'Did he talk to anyone else in the canteen?'

Terry shrugged. 'Couple of the girls maybe. He wasn't exactly fitting in, you know.'

'Which girls?'

'I dunno.'

'If you saw him talking to girls, you must remember which ones.'

'I wasn't paying him any notice.'

'Did he ever talk to you about how he was feeling?'

Terry smiled. 'Yeah, right.'

'Did you see him in the evenings, when you came back from class?'

'No. He just sat in his room . . . Apart from the last night. I think he came out and watched TV then.'

'Did he tell you he'd been in an observation cell?'

'No. I didn't know that till it all came out, you know. He never said a thing. Just kept himself to himself.'

'Apart from the girls he spoke to?'

Terry shrugged.

Jenny glanced over at Simone Wills. She looked heartened by what she was hearing, proud that her boy came across as tough.

'Terry, can you tell me about the Friday night, the 13th, the night Danny died. How was he?'

'He came back to the common room after canteen. We were watching TV.'

'Did he talk to anyone?'

'Not really. He was just chilling. We were watching one of those talent shows, having a laugh, rating the girls and that.'

'Was Danny laughing?'

'Yeah. Maybe.'

'What happened then?'

'Telly off half-nine, get washed, into bed.'

'Did you have any contact with Danny in that half-hour?'

'No.'

'So when lights out came, what then?'

'Just lay in my bed. Went to sleep.'

'Did you hear anything from Danny's cell?'

Terry paused, shook his head. 'I'm not sure . . .'

'About what?'

'There was one time, I thought I heard someone go in there, like the door closing, voices maybe.'

Jenny's stomach lurched. V*oices*.

'What time was this?'

'I don't know, late . . . I don't know if I dreamt it or what.'

'What kind of voices did you hear?'

'Just a voice, like someone calling out, something falling over . . . that was it. It went quiet.'

'You said you heard more than one voice.'

'I know . . . I'm not sure . . . I think I must have heard him doing it. It was late, I know that.'

'Can you be sure you heard more than one voice?'

'. . . No. Sorry.'

'Then why did you say it?'

'I don't know.'

Jenny didn't believe him, but flogging the question any more would appear desperate. Playing her last card, she asked, 'Were there a lot of drugs on the house unit?'

'Some.'

'Where did they come from?'

'Stuff gets in.' He pulled back his shoulders, defiant. 'Don't expect me to grass, I'll go back inside first.'

'Do you know if Danny got hold of anything?'

Terry looked at her and nodded, stroking the side of his face, like she'd given him a thought he hadn't had before. He said, 'Yeah. He was definitely chilled, you know. Yeah. Maybe he did.'

That was all she got from Terry. If he knew anything more he wasn't letting on. It was more than his life was worth to tell the world who the dealers were in Portshead. Jenny knew enough about teenage drug culture to know he was serious when he said he'd do more time before he informed. The law of the street, backed up by threats of serious violence, held far more sway than anything the police could impose.

Hartley cross-examined briefly and effectively, neutralizing any damage Terry's vague testimony had done his clients. He repeated again that he couldn't be sure if it was more than one voice he heard, or even if he'd dreamt the whole thing. He admitted that he had no idea whether or not Danny had got hold of drugs that night; in fact, he'd never thought about it until he'd been asked the question.

When he had finished, Hartley turned and smiled to his clients, letting them know that order had been restored. Despite the jury's negative reaction to Elaine Lewis, he knew there was no reason for them to return a verdict other than suicide.

Jenny adjourned for lunch and retreated to her chambers, the energy draining from her limbs as she crashed down from the adrenalin high. She took out the tablet she had reserved for an hour's time, swallowed it and slumped into the chair at her desk. She had a decision to make: whether to press on and begin summing up the case to the jury, or to adjourn and buy herself a couple more days to root around for evidence, maybe try to find the girls Danny spoke to in the canteen, see if one of them was Katy. That one word, *voices*, kept repeating in her mind. If there was another voice, whose was it? She didn't have enough information. If she went the adjournment route she'd have to justify it; going on a fishing trip at this stage in the proceedings risked making her look biased. If she went straight to summing up she'd be heading for a suicide verdict and UKAM would walk away without a stain on their corporate character.

There was a rap at the door. She turned to see the man she recognized as the official from the back of the court enter before she had replied. His expression was stern.

'Mrs Cooper, Simon Moreton. I look after coroners for the Ministry of Justice.'

'I saw your card.' She motioned him to a seat. 'Do you normally barge in without being asked?'

He remained standing and ignored her question. 'There's no tactful way of saying this, so I shan't attempt to. You were warned by the Attorney General's office that your conduct of this inquest was to be sensitive and proportionate, but I'm afraid your behaviour has given us serious cause for concern.'

'Has it? How, exactly?'

'The tender document is, as you know, not only commercially delicate, it is extremely delicate politically also. It is not information in the public arena and it is not your place to put it there. I don't know where you got hold of it, but I'm going to ask you to hand it over now.'

'I thought the coroner was independent of government, Mr Moreton. Isn't that the whole point?'

'Making that document public could jeopardize our prison-building programme. You know how unpalatable the public, led by the media, finds the idea of privately run prisons. It's not even as if a single sentence of that tender is relevant to the death of Danny Wills.'

'I think, as coroner, I'm the best judge of that, don't you?'

'Do I have to be more explicit, Mrs Cooper? If you continue to stray beyond the narrow issue of the when, where and how Danny Wills's death occurred you will have proved yourself unfit for this office. And, quite frankly, your appointment was highly questionable in the first place, particularly given your medical history. Misrepresenting it on your application is a sin easily big enough to see you removed, without a pension and, unfortunately, with no further prospect of employment within the legal or any other profession. Nobody wants a liar with bad references.'

The edges of the room faded. She couldn't find her voice. Moreton reached over and picked the tender document up from the desk, where she had placed it. 'Of course I can't take this without your consent . . .'

She looked at it, then up at his face, unable to focus. He waited and, when she didn't answer, gave a slight nod.

Jenny watched him turn and walk out of the door. As it clicked shut the sensation rushed at her, like unexpected death. She struggled to her feet, clung to the corner of the desk, then slumped to the floor.

'How long did the attack last?'

'About twenty minutes . . . I was palpitating so violently I didn't have the strength to get off the ground. My officer found me.'

'What's happened with your inquest?'

'It's been adjourned until next week. The official word is I've got food poisoning.'

Dr Allen gave her a look of genuine sympathy. He'd driven fifty miles from his clinic in Cardiff to see her after hours in the consulting room at Chepstow. On the positive side she was up, walking and talking; she'd even driven back from Bristol. But she could no longer pretend the problem was under control. She'd had her first full-blown panic attack in months and it was as violent as any she'd had when she'd been at her lowest.

'You've been under a lot of stress?'

'Yes.'

'I did warn you—'

'I know. But I can't stop now. I'm right in the middle of two important cases.'

He gave a patient smile. 'I'm sure you know, but this generalized anxiety disorder from which you suffer falls into roughly three categories. Sometimes it occurs when a person is simply overloaded, and when that load is diminished and with rest, it gradually gets better. But sometimes it's a symptom caused by post-traumatic stress, and sometimes there's no discernible reason for it at all. I've reviewed your notes from Dr Travis thoroughly and I think he and I are of one mind. The immediate cause of these attacks was general unhappiness and overload, but we both feel there is probably an underlying cause. The year-long gap in your childhood memory . . .'

His words triggered a feeling of fast-approaching doom. She tried unsuccessfully to push it away. Dr Allen saw her discomfort.

'If there was a trauma that you were unable to process, it may have oversensitized your fight or flight response. So in situations where a healthy person might feel mild distress, you might be overcome by, quite literally, paralysing fear.'

'I've been through all this with Dr Travis. I can't tell you how many times he tried to regress me.'

'I know how frightened you must be feeling now, Jenny, but sometimes when you're at your rawest, you're at your closest to the root cause of your problem. The pathway between the two is shorter, if you like. If you can get to it, you can deal with it. I really would like to do an exercise with you now . . . What have you got to lose?'

She didn't have the will or the strength to fight. She stretched out on his couch and went through the motions of relaxing her body until she felt as if she were sinking into the floor. It was a routine that had become second nature.

Dr Allen said, 'Good. Now, if you can stand it, I want you to summon up that feeling of fear that comes over you.'

It wasn't difficult.

'I want you to hold on to it and go back to the age of four. You're a young child . . . I want you to tell me what image comes to mind.'

It was always the same one. 'I'm in my bedroom. The walls are yellow. There's an eggshell-blue rug on the floor. I'm sitting on it, playing with a Sindy doll . . . She's got bobbed hair and a black and white checked miniskirt.'

'Are you happy?'

'Yes. Very.'

'What else is going on around you?'

'It's winter. I think it might even be snowing outside, but my room's warm. I feel cosy.'

'Then what?'

'I don't know . . . Maybe some raised voices downstairs. My parents argued a lot.' This was as far as she ever got. She told Dr Allen she remembered the doll, the rug, the gurgle of the radiator, her white ankle socks, the smell of cooking food drifting up the stairs, but never what happened next. If she tried to push it, she simply detached and lost touch.

Dr Allen said, 'Can you hear the voices?'

'My mother, calling down the hall from the kitchen, my father calling back, I think he's in the sitting room, I can hear the TV, then—' She jolted, a brief, violent seizure through her whole body.

'What is it?'

Jenny snatched at her breath, the image gone, back in the consulting room with a dazed feeling like she'd touched a bare wire. She opened her eyes and shook her head. 'A noise . . . like a pounding.'

'On what, a door?'

'I think so.'

'The front door?'

'Could be . . .'

'Can we go back there?'

She shook her head. 'It's like a shutter coming down, I can't get through it.'

'Have you heard this noise before?'

'No.'

Dr Allen smiled, delighted. 'See what I mean? We've got somewhere.' He started excitedly to make notes on his pad. 'This is really something. Maybe your parents could help. Are they still alive?'

'My father is, but he's in a home. He has Alzheimer's. You don't get a lot out of him these days.'

'Any brothers or sisters?'

'No. Just me.'

'Your parents never talked about any incident?'

'They separated when I was seven or eight. My mother married again. I never saw much of my father after that.'

'What was the problem between them?'

'They just weren't right together. He was a down to earth type, ran a garage business. My mother always complained there was no glamour in her life, so she ran off with an estate agent. Figure that one out.'

'At least we've made some progress. If we keep at it I wouldn't be surprised if you unlocked it yourself over the next few weeks.'

'What am I meant to do in the meantime?'

'Ideally you'd take a few weeks off.'

'I can't . . .'

'Then I'll have to prescribe you antidepressants and beta blockers to try to prevent any further attacks, but you'll have to promise me not to mix them with anything else. You won't be able to pop tranquillizers when you feel like it and you'll have no tolerance to alcohol.'

'Will I be able to work?'

'At about eighty-five per cent.'

Jenny thought about it for a moment. 'That'll do.'

She swallowed the first dose in her car outside the late-night chemist in Chepstow High Street. Not having eaten since breakfast, the drugs got into her system fast. It was a sensation she'd almost forgotten. Things flattened out. The anxiety melted away, her diaphragm loosed and she was no longer conscious of her heart beating. It was different from alcohol, a subtler feeling without elation; an absence more than a presence.

Dr Allen said he wasn't going to tell her not to drive, but to be careful. If she even felt the beginnings of an attack she was to pull over. Technically he could take her licence away but he was going to trust her. It was his way of saying they had a deal. He'd cut her some slack if she committed to digging out the trauma.

She didn't want to think about her own past now. As she drove back up the hill towards the edge of town she felt fine behind the wheel. She had three clear working days and the weekend to turn up more evidence.

NINETEEN

THERE WERE TWO MESSAGES ON the machine in her study. The first was from Alison, asking if Jenny would like her to deal with the run of the mill cases for the next couple of days – she could always email her anything that looked out of the ordinary. The court had been reserved for next Monday and everyone notified of the adjournment. There was nothing for her to worry about except getting well. Jenny smiled when she heard that – like all she had was a head cold.

The second was from Tara Collins, sounding concerned. She'd heard Jenny was ill and hoped it wasn't anything sinister. Listening to her questions in court, she'd picked up the connection Jenny was trying to make with Katy Taylor and had been putting the word out that she wanted to speak to Hayley Johnson. A contact had left a message that Hayley had been working the streets in Broadlands the last few nights. Did she want to try and find her?

Jenny dialled Tara's number and got rerouted to her mobile. It sounded like she was in a bar somewhere, a lot of voices and music in the background.

'It's Jenny Cooper. I just picked up your message.'

'How are you? Your officer said you were ill.'

'I'm fine. Nothing serious.'

Tara sounded relieved. 'Buying time, right?'

'Kind of.'

'Thought so. Those bastards thought they had it all sewn up, didn't they? I wouldn't be surprised if they'd even got to Terry Ryan. There's not much a kid like that wouldn't do for a few grams of ice.'

'*Ice?*'

'Crystal meth – the kind you smoke.'

'I'm behind the times.'

'You know what fashion's like now, your trainers are sad before you get 'em home.' Tara was sounding chattier than she'd ever heard her, as if she'd had a few.

'Look, I'd like to talk to Hayley Johnson. Do you think I could find her tonight?'

'It's a bit early yet. She won't hit the street until at least eleven.'

'Any idea where I should start?'

Tara said, 'If you like, I can come with you. She should recognize me.'

'OK. Where do you want to meet?'

'Pick me up at my place. I'm 15B Alexander Road, Bradley Stoke.'

'See you at eleven.'

'Bye, Jenny. Byeee.' She'd definitely had several.

Jenny put the phone down and immediately felt restless. Nearly four hours to kill. She grabbed a sandwich and a cup of herb tea, then tried to settle at her desk and work on a chronology of events to help order her thoughts. She went over all the major dates again but kept coming back to the same point: Marshall began his inquest into Danny's death on Monday 30 April. It was on the previous Thursday or Friday that Simone Wills said his mood had changed. Katy had gone missing from home the Sunday before that and had died or been killed on the Monday or Tuesday. If there was a link to be made, the answer lay in what happened during the last week of April.

She called Alison at home and asked for Mrs Marshall's phone number. Alison was hesitant and hedged around, asking how Jenny was, trying to tease out of her the reason for wanting it. Jenny said she was fine and just wanted to ask Mrs Marshall if she remembered Harry saying anything about either Danny's or Katy's case.

Alison said, 'I told you, he never talked to her about his work. She thought it was morbid.'

'There can't be any harm in asking.'

'You won't say anything to upset her, will you, Mrs Cooper? She and her daughters are still very shocked.'

'What do you think I'm going to do, tell her you and Harry were having a non-affair?'

'*Please.*' She lowered her voice to a whisper. 'My husband's in the other room.'

'If you remember, Alison, we had a deal.'

'I just don't want anything to upset her memory of him. He was such a good man.'

Mary Marshall was a short, timid, grey-haired woman who looked older than Jenny had expected. She could have been a primary school headmistress or a librarian; vanity was certainly not among her sins. She answered the door of her comfortable, detached home in leafy Stoke Bishop on the security chain, a terrier yapping at her heels. Relieved that it wasn't a masked thug on the doorstep, she shooed the dog into the kitchen before returning to let Jenny in.

'Sorry about Sandy. He's been on permanent guard duty since Harry went.'

'He's making a good job of it.'

Mary smiled and led Jenny down a carpeted hallway, passing the open door to a sitting room, where two sensible-looking teenage girls were watching a wildlife documentary.

The house was spotless but hadn't been redecorated since the 1980s.

Jenny declined the offer of a cup of tea or something stronger, so Mary led her straight to the small study which she said had been Harry's, closing the door behind her and turning the key in the lock. Whatever was to be discussed, she didn't want the girls to hear. This was a house, Jenny sensed, where children were to be kept children. She sat in one of two armchairs that looked as if they had been upholstered at evening class. Mary sat in the other. Anxious, and leaning forward with her hands on her knees, she asked how she could help.

'You might have read in the paper that I'm rehearing the last inquest your husband conducted.'

'Yes, I did see that.' She sounded mildly reproachful, as if she took it as a personal slight.

'I got the impression from the notes he left that he cared passionately about this case, but when it came to the hearing he seemed to lose heart.'

'I know he was very unhappy about it. He hated dealing with deaths in custody. He was a long-standing member of Amnesty before his appointment.'

Jenny nodded. 'Did he discuss the case with you at all?'

'Only in passing. He tried not to bring his work home. That's why he became a coroner – so he could devote his evenings and weekends to his family.'

Jenny got the feeling the embargo on shop talk might not have been strictly voluntary. Mary gave the impression she was not to be argued with.

'In the few days before he died he dealt with the case of a fifteen-year-old girl called Katy Taylor – did he ever mention anything about that?'

Mary stiffened. She would have read about the case in the

Post and known that Harry had been found wanting. 'No, he didn't. And I'm sure he was only trying to spare the family. Sometimes going by the book isn't the most compassionate thing. You'll find that out as you become more experienced, I'm sure.'

Jenny gave a neutral smile. Having kept him on a tight leash for years, Mary was giving Harry his posthumous reward: sainthood.

'He left a document in his desk drawer, something he must have been handed by a third party, maybe a whistleblower. It was a tender that the company who ran Portshead Farm had prepared for a major juvenile prison . . .' She paused to consider her words carefully. 'The contract was worth tens of millions. Had your husband's inquest found that the company was somehow to blame for Danny Wills's death it could have put them out of the running . . . I wonder, did he mention any of this to you?'

Defensive, Mary sucked in her cheeks and shook her head. 'No, he didn't.'

'Did you get the impression that anything was weighing on his mind particularly?'

'Nothing more than usual . . . He seemed a bit tired, that's all.'

'I don't really like to broach the subject, Mrs Marshall—'

'I made my views very clear to Alison. Harry would never have taken his own life. Like me, he believed suicide was a sin, all suicide, even euthanasia for the terminally ill.'

'Actually, I was going to ask whether he had ever encountered any sort of corporate corruption before, and if he had, how he dealt with it.'

Mary's face relaxed a little. 'He hated it, of course he did. He was a man of principle. He always had been.'

'How do you think he would have dealt with a sensitive

document like this? The fact is he *didn't* make it public . . . which leads me to think there must have been a very good reason, or, should I say, a very powerful reason.'

Mary sat rigid. 'If you're suggesting he would in any way have allowed himself to be compromised, I can tell you now, it's out of the question.'

'Of course.' Jenny was beginning to think she was wasting her time, but she couldn't believe Marshall's widow was as clueless as she was pretending. In her experience, those who sought refuge in religion were normally more acutely aware of the inherent deviancy in human nature than most. She'd try a different angle before she gave up. 'I understand your husband was a close friend of Frank Grantham.'

'No.' She virtually spat out the denial.

'Oh. Alison said they had quite a lot to do with each other.'

'That's different. Harry had no time for him. He said he was an interfering little fool.'

'But he took notice of him. Grantham certainly gave me the impression he was used to getting his own way with the coroner's office.'

'Harry had a wife and four daughters, he couldn't afford to make enemies.'

'Why was he afraid of Grantham? He doesn't wield any legal power over the coroner.'

'He wasn't afraid of him.'

'Then why did your husband let Grantham push him around?'

Mary closed her eyes for a moment, as if enduring the grip of pain. 'I suppose because Harry did a lot in the community. Frank has a finger in every pie and he's not afraid to speak ill of people. If you want to know the truth, my husband thought he was probably corrupt, but he was decent enough to keep his suspicions to himself.'

'Corrupt in what way?'

'I can't see how any of this could be relevant . . . I hate gossip.'

'Please, Mrs Marshall. It could be important.'

Mary turned her head away while she spoke, as if she were studying titles in the bookcase. 'You only have to see where Frank lives to realize he didn't get it all on his salary. He wouldn't make any more than Harry did.'

'Harry thought he was on the take? What from, property deals?'

'It was just speculation.'

'He didn't mention anything specific?'

'No. He didn't like idle talk either.'

Jenny steeled herself. 'Forgive me for asking, Mrs Marshall, but you understand I have to cover everything . . . Have you noticed any irregularities in your husband's finances since he died, any unusual payments, for example?'

'I think you know the answer to that, Mrs Cooper.' Mary gave her a look conveying that the interview was over. 'It's time I was getting the girls to bed.'

Jenny left the Marshall house with the feeling that if Harry had ever been involved in anything illicit, Mary would have suspected it but buried her suspicions so deep they wouldn't come out until she was senile. She was a woman determined to see the world her way, with God at the top of the tree and everyone else arranged in descending order of virtue according to their frugality and sexlessness. Jenny would be way down the order, just a twig or two above the girl she now hoped to find.

Tara climbed into the passenger seat smelling strongly of wine. She made a brave attempt to pretend she was sober but stumbled over her words and held on to the handle above the window when they went round corners. Jenny was beginning to form a clearer picture of her: a single dyke who lived alone and put her energy into work; there was something self-destructive about her, a sense that she was feeding off the drama of the situation to gain the attention she wasn't getting in a relationship. She wasn't altogether happy with her prefer-ence and probably drank too much quite often, got in the mix down at one of the lesbian bars in town but wasn't hot enough to score regularly, someone you'd move on from. Too intense. Jenny felt a little sorry for her.

They drove into the Broadlands Estate a little before eleven-thirty. Groups of kids hung out on corners and gathered around the benches in a run-down play area. They were drinking, smoking cigarettes, but the atmosphere was relaxed, a lot of laughing going on. You wouldn't want your car to break down here, but you'd lose your wallet not five pints of blood.

When they had been cruising for a few minutes Tara spotted a couple of girls in short skirts standing near the kerb at the edge of the estate. She said to slow down as they passed. Jenny wondered what the girls would make of it, two older women checking them out.

'Maybe we should ask them if they've seen Hayley,' Jenny said.

'No. They'd call her and warn her off.'

Jenny slowed a little, enough for Tara to get a look and shake her head. 'This is where they tend to be, on the edge to catch the passing trade. There's a row of garages behind the shops, that's where they get the punters to park up.'

They swung round and toured the estate a second time. Some kids stepped out in front of them, waving their arms and pulling wild faces, trying to make them stop. Jenny found enough room to drive around them but was anxious for a moment. Tara, playing the streetwise reporter, said, 'They're just having fun.'

They passed the same two girls again and saw that they hadn't done any business. Tara decided it was too early for Hayley to be out, so they stopped off at a filling station and bought coffee, which they drank in the car. It was gone midnight and Tara was heavy-lidded, stuck in a continuous loop talking about the charges against her, claiming that not only had she been set up, her telephones had been tapped and libellous emails about her sent to her boss at the paper. Jenny tried to be sympathetic, but it was hard to know where fact ended and delusion began. When Tara started into the story a fourth time she reached out to switch on the radio, saying she fancied catching the news.

Talking over the radio, Tara said, 'You know there's something I haven't told you, Jenny . . .' She smiled with the smugness of someone enjoying their superior knowledge. 'How I know about your medical history.'

Jenny took a sip of her coffee, feeling her medication fading and beginning to find Tara a little creepy.

'Do you want to know?'

'Not particularly.'

'I hacked them. I've got this sixteen-year-old kid, I won't give you any clues, who I met in a chat room. Claims he can get into anything. I give him a name and he comes up with credit history, medical records, what they've been looking up on the internet lately, it's amazing. *And* he thinks twenty quid's a lot of money.' She gave a wise nod. 'There's no such thing as secrets any more. The only thing between the truth and the person who wants to find it is the effort they're prepared to put in.'

Jenny said, 'What does this kid know about you?'

Tara paused over her cup and gave her a sideways look. 'Sounds like you're fishing.'

'It was just a remark.'

'There's not that much to know . . .' Tara let the statement hang, hoping Jenny would probe further.

She didn't. The atmosphere in the car was thickening and Jenny had a bad feeling that Tara was about to come on to her. She wasn't prejudiced, but she found the idea of another woman having those kinds of feelings towards her uncomfortable. Time to move off.

Several other cars were also driving slowly around the estate, all of them occupied by single men. From what they could make out, there was only a handful of girls to go around, three or four, which left the kerb crawlers in a holding pattern waiting their turn.

It was close to one and Tara was almost asleep. She made a sudden snoring sound and her chin drooped, then fell on to her chest, her head lolling. Great. She had lost her spotter, her anxiety was creeping back and the evening had got her nowhere. She swung the car through a U-turn and headed away from the estate.

The police patrol car came out of nowhere. It shot from a side street, lights flashing, and fired up its siren as it ripped down the road ahead of them.

Tara started awake. 'What was that?'

The police car jammed on its brakes and slewed into the kerb a couple of hundred yards ahead of them, where another police vehicle had cornered an estate car.

Jenny said, 'Looks like someone's getting nicked.'

She slowed to a crawl as they drove past the scene. A fat, balding man was remonstrating with a constable, while a female officer led a young woman in a denim skirt towards one of their vehicles.

Tara said, 'That's Hayley. That's her.'

Jenny fetched out her phone and called Alison.

It was nearly two a.m. when Alison came out of the police station, tired and irritable, and rapped the car window to say she'd talked the custody sergeant into giving them ten minutes in the cells. Jenny had managed to persuade Tara there was no point in her coming along and had dropped her off on the way over from Broadlands.

Alison led her past the clutch of shivering smokers on the steps and through the reception area, where several drunken women were hammering on the glass at the counter. Alison nodded at the beleaguered duty officer, who buzzed them through the security door into the guts of the station.

The cells were at basement level and the custody suite was quietening down for the night; there were only a few sleepy drunks, slumped on a bench and handcuffed to steel rings in the wall, waiting to be processed. The custody sergeant tossed Alison a set of keys and said hello to Jenny, polite but not wanting to get involved. This was strictly a favour for an ex-colleague.

Hayley was curled up on the cot bench holding her bare knees. A pretty girl, she still looked fresh enough not to be automatically marked down as a prostitute. She had long, thick black hair and olive skin. Jenny imagined she could do a lot better than walking the streets in Broadlands. She looked up at them with sleepy eyes, swinging to a sitting position, her skirt only reaching a third of the way to her knees.

'The fuck are you?'

Alison said, 'I'm Mrs Trent, the coroner's officer, and this is Mrs Cooper, the coroner.'

Jenny said, 'This is nothing to do with the offence for which you've been arrested tonight, Miss Johnson, and I'm nothing to do with the police. My job is to find out how people died. I'm investigating the death of a girl called Katy Taylor. I think you might have known her.'

Hayley looked from Jenny to Alison and back again, suspecting a trick. 'Got any cigarettes?'

Alison dipped into her raincoat pocket and brought out a battered packet of Marlboros. She tapped one out and gave Hayley a light with a plastic lighter.

Hayley sucked in sharp and deep, getting her hit of nicotine before she'd speak.

'I saw her once or twice.'

Jenny said, 'We think she was turning tricks in Broadlands.'

'Now and then.'

'The police have got pictures of her getting into a blue Vectra – that's the last time she was seen.'

Hayley shook her head. 'I don't know much about cars.'

Jenny said, 'I don't know if you're any good with dates, Miss Johnson, but Katy got out of Portshead Farm on 17 April, a Tuesday, she'd been inside for six weeks. She went missing from home on Saturday the 21st, and we know the next day she was out on the streets again. She got into the Vectra at eleven p.m. She died, or was killed, sometime shortly afterwards.'

Hayley took another long drag. 'I think I might have seen her on the Saturday night.'

'Where?'

'On the street. She was meant to be on a curfew, right? She was having a laugh about it.'

'What else did she talk about?'

Hayley pulled a face as she tried to recall. 'I think we were talking about where to score some crack. That was her thing. I don't touch that stuff. If you're going take something, make sure it's pure, not mixed up with any crap.'

Alison said, 'What about heroin?'

'No. What was she, fifteen? She was still playing at it.'

Jenny said, 'She didn't say if she was in any trouble at all, no one out to get her?'

'Don't think so.'

'Did she talk about her time in Portshead?'

'She might have mentioned it, about how boring it was . . .'

'What about a boy named Danny Wills who was in there at the same time, did she say anything about him?'

'You got another cigarette?'

Alison handed her the packet. 'Keep them.'

'Thanks.' She tapped one out and lit it from the stub of her first. 'She said there was a kid inside who'd hanged himself who'd been fighting with the screws. Something about him saying he was going to make a knife . . .'

'Is that all? Try to remember, it's important.'

'That's all I know. I remember her saying she thought he was going to stab this screw, but then he hanged himself. She was sad about it. They went to school together or something.'

Alison said, 'Did she say who the screw was?'

'I can't remember . . . but I think she said she'd try to speak to someone about it.'

Jenny said, 'Who? Come on, Hayley. Try.'

Hayley scratched her head and yawned, the effort getting to her. 'Her probation officer?'

'Justin. Justin Bennett. Youth Offending Team.'

'Yeah . . . Maybe.'

It was Alison's idea to doorstep him, catch him when he was least expecting it. They jumped from Jenny's car as he came out through the front door of his flat, the ground floor of a scruffy terrace in Redlands.

Jenny said, 'Good morning, Mr Bennett. Couple of questions for you. How do you fancy a lift to work?'

Alison opened the rear door of the car. Justin took a step backwards and shook his head.

'We can talk out here if you prefer, or back at my office.'

'What do you want?'

Alison said, 'Mrs Cooper's doing the asking. And if I were you, I'd answer.'

Justin agreed on a compromise. He'd come in the car and talk but refused to be driven anywhere. Sitting in the back seat, he was all nerves, unable to keep still. Levelled out on her medication, Jenny noted that she felt detached from his anxiety and wondered fleetingly if this was how policemen or jailers felt, devoid of empathy.

Looking at him in the rear-view mirror, she said, 'Katy Taylor spoke to you after her release from Portshead about Danny Wills. Do you want to tell us about it?'

Justin crossed his hands over his stomach. 'Did she?'

In a voice Jenny had never heard before, Alison said, 'Cut the crap. Tell us what you know or you're getting nicked for perverting the course of justice.'

Justin said, 'She may have mentioned him at our meeting. He died when she was in there, right?'

Alison said, 'She said more than that, we've heard it.'

'I'm trying to remember . . .'

Alison gave Jenny a look. 'She told you that Danny was having trouble with one of the screws and that he was talking about getting a knife to stab him.'

'Yeah, that rings a bell. They tell you so much stuff—'

'Who was the screw?'

'She didn't say.'

'That came out fast.'

'She didn't say a name.'

Alison swivelled round in her seat. 'The truth, Justin.'

'It *is* the truth.'

Jenny said, 'Then why didn't you say any of this before?'

'I did, I told Marshall. I called him the day Katy told me.'

'Which was?'

'The Friday before she disappeared – 20 April.'

Alison said, 'That was over a week before he held Danny's inquest.'

Jenny said, 'Why didn't you tell *me*?'

Justin rubbed the back of his neck with his hand, 'I was frightened, OK? . . . She tells me this and the next thing she's dead. Then I tell the coroner and he dies. It doesn't take a lot of working out.'

TWENTY

HER MEDICATION PLUS A TOP-UP of half a temazepam had given her an energy injection. Despite having had only three hours' sleep, Jenny felt relaxed and purposeful, ready for anything.

Alison came into her office with a typed-up copy of a supplemental statement she had taken from Justin in the back of the car. She sat in the chair across the desk and passed it over. 'What are you going to do with it?'

'When we reconvene I'll call him and Hayley to give evidence,' Jenny said firmly. 'Then I'll recall the staff from Portshead, and if we still don't get anywhere I'll call every child who was in Portshead at the time until we find the officer Danny had a problem with.'

'I can see why you're saying that, Mrs Cooper, but what if we did get a name, they'd just deny everything. We've no forensic evidence of any wrongdoing—'

'I'm talking about a climate of fear. Say Danny was difficult and obstructive and they tried to use force to get him to leave his cell and go to class, some of the other kids might have witnessed it. He was a vulnerable child – if the way staff treated him pushed him over the edge I want the jury to hear about it.'

'Where do you think Katy fits in?'

'She spoke to Justin, who talked to Marshall on Friday

20 April. Marshall sat on it. Her information didn't come up at the inquest and he didn't tell the police, not even when he knew she was dead. What he did do was go to his GP and get himself some pills three days before it started. We can assume he had a copy of the tender by then. He must have been thinking the same way as us – something about Danny's death stinks, but there's too much at stake for UKAM for them to risk a finding against them.'

Alison lowered her head. She looked tired after her disturbed night. 'What's your theory?'

'Something persuaded him to look the other way. He rushed all the evidence through on the Monday, but then came back to the office in the evening to learn that Katy Taylor had been found dead. Her post-mortem was held on the Tuesday, and even though he should have held an inquest he signed her death certificate on the Wednesday. On Thursday night he died . . . You knew him. What do you think?'

Alison looked at her with sad eyes. 'I suppose I was frightened he'd taken someone's money, but Mrs Marshall says there's nothing.'

'He could have hidden it, or the deal could have been that he'd be paid later.'

Alison got out of her chair and started to pace. 'No. He wouldn't have done that. Why would he take money over a child prisoner? He wouldn't have been tempted for a moment.'

'What would money have done for him?'

'The same as for any of us.'

'Don't take this the wrong way, Alison, but do you think he might have thought about leaving his wife?'

Alison stopped and wheeled round. 'Are you asking if we were going to run off together? Don't be ridiculous.'

'I have to ask.'

Red in the face, Alison said, 'There was no sex between us

and there never would have been. I love my husband and Harry was devoted to his family.'

'I'm sorry . . .'

Alison fumed for a moment, then thumped back into her chair, bitter emotions under the surface. She was still angry with him, Jenny realized, furious that he was putting her through this.

'Then maybe there was a threat,' Jenny continued gently. 'Katy met a violent death. Perhaps someone threatened Harry's daughters. Could that have been enough?'

'He wasn't a coward. He would have gone to the police.'

'Whatever he did, it was enough to make him kill himself.'

'We don't know that.'

They exchanged a look, Alison's expression betraying how empty her protest now seemed.

'It would have been a whole lot easier if he'd left a note, but maybe he had his reasons,' Jenny said. 'What he did leave was Katy's file and the tender in the same drawer. He knew you'd be the first person to open it, right?'

'Yes . . .'

'Knowing what I do about Harry Marshall, to me it looks as if they were two signposts to injustice. Injustice he couldn't live with.'

'Don't you think we should bring the police in now?' Alison asked, close to tears.

'Do you really trust them, the way they've handled Katy's case?'

'It's too big to deal with by yourself. You're already in trouble with the Ministry, and look at what's happened to Tara Collins . . .'

'Tara's a loose cannon. I'm far easier to deal with.'

'What do you mean?'

'Let's be honest. I got this job because they thought I'd be someone they could control. If I don't do what I'm expected to and deliver a suicide verdict next week, my medical history will suddenly surface and I'll be out of the door anyway. I've got four days till we sit again. I might as well spend the time finding a bomb to put under the whole thing. Better to go out in a blaze of glory.'

'What are you thinking of?'

'First, I'm going to swing past and have a word with Peterson. I don't believe he's been telling us the whole truth, or anything like it.' Jenny grabbed her briefcase.

'I hate to keep bringing it up, Mrs Cooper – I had another phone call about the accounts.'

'Screw the accounts.'

She made it through the early rush-hour traffic to the hospital only to be told by a mortuary assistant that Peterson had left early for a children's birthday party. It was another forty-minute creep across to Clifton, where Peterson lived in a four-storey Georgian town house in a street that led off from the Downs. He opened the door in jeans and a pink polo shirt with sunglasses balanced on his forehead. There were a lot of excited noises in the background, little girls yelling and frenetic pop music playing.

His face registered surprise, then anger. 'Jesus. What do you want?'

'Ten minutes of your time.'

'This is an afternoon off, for God's sake. It's my daughter's birthday.'

'Believe me, I'm as impatient to be gone as you are. We can talk here if you want.'

'I don't believe this . . .' He stormed back off along the hallway, exchanged some words with his wife, who peered around from the end of the passageway at the intruder, then marched back to the front door and closed it behind him. 'What now?'

'Your post-mortem report on Danny Wills.'

'What about it?'

'I've read a lot of your reports in the last couple of weeks – you've been very good – but Danny's still ranks as one of the shortest, which is surprising, considering the circumstances.'

'There wasn't a lot to say. Otherwise healthy child hanged himself.'

Three excited girls came to the bay window in the front room and made faces through the glass. One of them was dressed in a Princess Barbie outfit and had chocolate smeared across her face. Jenny could see the resemblance to her father.

Jenny said, 'Maybe we should take a walk.'

They turned out of the small, gravelled front garden and headed towards the Downs, Peterson resenting every moment.

She decided to start by keeping things deliberately vague. 'Since you gave evidence I've heard from other witnesses. Apparently Danny had some altercations with one of the officers in Portshead, quite violent altercations.'

'I didn't find any other injuries, if that's what you're asking.'

'I'm afraid that doesn't fill me with confidence, given the quality of your examination of Katy Taylor.'

'If you've a problem with my work why don't you make a complaint? But I think the fact that I run one of the busiest hospital mortuaries in the country single-handedly will weigh quite heavily in my favour.'

'I'm sure it would, but I'm appealing to your conscience.'

'Spare me . . .'

They turned the corner into the main road along the Downs. Peterson strode off ahead of her. Jenny hurried to keep up. 'Evidence in both their cases was suppressed, that much is beyond doubt. Marshall knew that and it's not a great leap of the imagination to think that you did, too.'

'This sounds like the sort of conversation I should be having in the presence of a solicitor.'

'I'm not accusing you of anything, Dr Peterson, in fact I'm prepared to offer you a deal.'

'You really are quite extraordinary.' He shook his head.

'Unfortunately I can't exhume Danny's body to have another look. You're the only one who saw it. The thing is, if this evidence shapes up, more questions might be asked of you than you can comfortably answer, even given your reputation.'

'This is pretty low, Jenny, dragging a man out of his child's birthday party to threaten him.'

'I don't doubt that fundamentally you're a decent man – you put up with all manner of crap in the NHS. I believe Harry Marshall was, as well. But I'm also forced to conclude that someone or something persuaded you not to look as hard as you might have done. That leaves you with a choice – to take a chance on me not getting to the bottom of this thing, or telling me what you know and we can talk about ways of you being able to survive.'

'Danny Wills hanged himself,' Peterson shouted with an unexpected ferocity that made Jenny step backwards. 'It was an open and shut case. Anything of significance I found was in my report. If you don't like it, tough fucking luck, that's all there is.'

'You're very agitated, Dr Peterson.'

'Piss off.' He strode back along the pavement the way they came. 'And don't come to my house again unless you've got a warrant.'

It was a warm enough evening for her to sit at her table on the lawn, which was fast growing back into a meadow, and try to clear some of the backlog of routine cases that had built up. More hospital deaths, a confused old woman who'd been run down by a postal van and a road mender who'd jack-hammered through the mains cable in the street. There were photographs of the dead workman, every inch of his skin burnt charcoal black.

She was nearing the bottom of the pile and wondering whether she could get away with half a glass of red wine when she caught a whiff of smoke on the breeze. She looked up and saw Steve. He was leaning against the corner of the house by the cart track smoking a fat roll-up. Jenny sniffed again – it wasn't just tobacco, there was some weed in there too.

Steve said, 'Busy?'

'Depends what you had in mind.'

He wandered over with a lazy gait and sat opposite, a few days' growth on his face. His face had turned dark tan from working in the sun. He gave her a wicked smile. 'Guess what I found at the end of my garden?'

'I can smell. And one of Her Majesty's Coroners should not be talking to a man who's smoking it.'

'I don't believe in laws. They're made by people who can't trust themselves to be free.'

'You were born thirty years too late, my friend.'

'Don't much believe in time, either. You think that tree cares what decade it is?'

'How much of that stuff have you had?'

'Almost enough. It's my best crop yet.' He offered the joint across the table, the roach end facing towards her.

Jenny was tempted but, managing to resist, said, 'I wondered what had happened to you.'

'I had to wait for the annual harvest to give me the courage to come over.'

'I'm that frightening?'

'It's not you, it's me. I'm out of practice.'

'I wouldn't have noticed, but then so am I.'

'There are worse sins. You ever tried this stuff?'

'My son has . . .'

'It's better for him than alcohol. No chemicals, no hangover. Grown in good honest Welsh soil.'

She watched him take another draw, a serene look on his face, his limbs loose and relaxed, the way she longed to feel. And it smelt so good, taking her back to long-ago parties, the carefree sensation that was close to ecstatic.

He gave her a look, tempting her.

She leaned forward and placed her lips around the joint, but as she touched his fingers with her mouth, she pulled back.

'Scared?'

'I smoked some cigarettes the other night. I remembered how sore they make my lungs.'

Steve gave her a look, seeing straight through her evasion. 'You think I'm a bad influence.'

'I think you're getting a kick out of trying to corrupt a public official.'

'I guess there could be something in that.'

'In my case I don't think it would be much of a conquest.'

He smiled a touch and dropped the joint on to the ground. 'How's it going? I still can't imagine you as a coroner.'

'I can hardly believe it myself.'

'Did you find out what happened to that poor girl?'

'I don't want to talk about it now.' She shuffled her papers into a heap, trying to shut out images of Katy's body on Professor Lloyd's autopsy bench.

Steve reached out a hand and pushed the hair back from her eyes. Then he moved closer and kissed her gently on the cheek.

Later, they lay naked on her bed, laughing like a couple of teenagers, high from the thrill of an unfamiliar touch.

Steve said, 'You know you're the talk of the valley.'

'Oh, yeah?'

'Beautiful woman living on her own, it's the stuff of people's fantasies.'

'I hope they're filthy.'

'Obscene. You should hear what you've been up to with Rhodri Glendower.'

'I'm just grateful for the attention.'

'That makes me feel very special.'

She rolled over and lay on top of him, her elbows either side of his shoulders. 'Don't you dare get needy on me when I'm having such a good time.'

He brought a hand up to the small of her back and stroked it, looking into her eyes. 'I wouldn't dream of it.'

She moved her mouth towards his and kissed him, touching him with every part of her.

Steve was upstairs in the shower and she was in the kitchen wearing just her bathrobe, taking her pills, when the knock at the door came. She glanced at the clock on the stove: it was only just past seven a.m. The caller knocked again, louder, as she hurried through the sitting room to the front door. She tied the robe tight around herself and opened the door a crack.

A stocky middle-aged man in a grey suit and Hush Puppies held up an identification badge. 'Good morning, ma'am, Detective Sergeant Owen Williams from Chepstow. Are you Mrs Cooper?'

'Yes.' She saw two young female constables in uniform standing on the path behind him, two squad cars parked out on the lane. Her first thought was of Ross.

'You wouldn't happen to have a Mr Stephen Painter on the premises, would you?'

'What's the matter?'

Sounding almost apologetic, he said, 'I'm afraid I'm going to have to have a word with him and search the house, ma'am.

I've had information that leads me to believe that arrestable offences have taken place here.'

'Information from where?'

'I'm afraid I'm not at liberty to disclose my source at the present moment. Would you let us in, please?'

'He's in the shower.'

'We'll go up together, then, shall we?'

TWENTY-ONE

THEY KEPT JENNY AND STEVE separate while they searched the house, she in the kitchen, he in the sitting room. Through the door she could hear him saying that she had no idea he'd been smoking some home-grown with his tobacco, it was nothing to do with her. Williams said not to worry, they'd go into all that later, at the station.

They found the dead roaches in the bin and Steve's baggie in his jeans pocket. While the constables wrote out evidence labels and filled in exhibit forms Jenny was allowed to get dressed and make a phone call. She caught Alison before she left home, meaning to tell her the truth, but found herself saying that she had to wait in for an emergency plumber and would come to the office in a while.

She rode in the back of Williams's car to Chepstow. Steve went with the two constables, Williams careful to keep them apart before the interviews, showing the uniforms how a real detective handled suspects: firmly but respectfully. Winding along the valley from Tintern to St Arvans, Jenny was surprised at how relaxed she felt. She couldn't make up her mind if it was the new pills or that the situation was so fantastic she couldn't take it seriously. Williams listened to a Welsh-language radio station: bad pop music and singsong chatter, an English word popping out every now and then. He asked Jenny if she spoke Welsh. She said no, her family were from across the estuary in Somerset, but since she'd moved she'd thought about taking an evening class. Williams said she should, the only downside was that after you'd been speaking Welsh for a while, English sounded as harsh as German, no music in it.

Jenny said she'd never thought of it that way, and, feeling that they were building a rapport, asked, 'Who told you Steve was at my place?'

Williams said, 'You know we can't reveal the identities of our informers, Mrs Cooper.'

'It was that girl who works at the Apple Tree, wasn't it – Annie?'

He glanced at her in the mirror, a wise little smile under his greying moustache.

Jenny and Steve were kept in adjacent interview rooms while Williams went through the laborious process of interview, a female constable at his side for the sake of propriety. Steve was first. Jenny could hear only muffled conversation through the thin walls but the fact he was talking at all made her guess that he was repeating what he had told them at the house. When her turn came she took a chance and said she had no idea what he was smoking; it would never have occurred to her that anyone would smoke drugs in her presence. Williams listened politely, but let her know with his eyes what he thought.

It was past eleven a.m. when he came back into the room and said that the evidence was sufficient for him to be obliged to press charges. Due to the amount of marijuana he had on him, Steve was being charged with possession with intent to supply; Jenny with allowing her premises to be used. He'd bail them both and hand the file to the local CPS. Give it a week or two and there'd be a letter in the post with a court date.

Jenny said, 'How can you prove I *knew or believed* he was smoking marijuana?'

'That's the CPS's problem, Mrs Cooper.'

'Are they going to make these charges public?'

'I've no idea.'

She caught his eye as he shuffled his papers on the table, the morning's business at an end. 'Can I ask you something? Do you really want to do this to me or has someone told you to?'

'I don't know what you mean, ma'am.'

'You've read the papers. I'm in the middle of two inquests which aren't exactly covering our police and prison service in glory.'

He slotted his statements into a file. 'That's news to me.'

'I can tell – you're finding this as weird as I am.'

Williams turned to the constable. 'Show Mrs Cooper out, would you?'

They met on the front step outside the station. Steve held up his hands. 'I'm sorry . . .'

'That might just be the most expensive sex I've ever had.'

'Not the best?'

She gave him a look, not able to laugh, and said, 'Any idea who it was who called them?'

'I guess it was Annie. I was down there briefly before I came round . . .' A guilty look came over his face.

'What?'

'One of the guys down there, Ed, said someone had been in last weekend asking after you.'

'Who?'

'Just a guy. Thirties. He thought he might be a copper, except he was quite fit-looking. Toned.'

'What did he want to know?'

'Whether you came in, who your friends were. Ed thought he must be an ex-boyfriend sniffing around.'

'Did he mention you?'

'I haven't told anyone about us.'

'From what you say, you don't have to.'

He touched her hand, holding her fingers. 'I'm sorry, Jenny.'

'You don't have to keep saying that. It's not your fault.'

'What are you going to do?'

'Get a taxi, and something to eat.'

It was raining again, the tail-end of a heavy summer storm, so they sat at the tiny table in the kitchen. The cramped domestic scene added to the sense of unreality; like watching somebody else's strange day play out. All she had to go in a sandwich were cheese and lettuce. She apologized for her poor supply of groceries and joked that if he wanted a slim girlfriend he couldn't expect to be well fed. She'd said 'girlfriend' without thinking and waited for him to react, but he didn't. Sitting there eating a sandwich, he seemed quite comfortable. Perhaps he was trying to make up for destroying her career.

She asked him again about the man making enquiries about her. Steve said that was all he knew, a man, not young, not old, asking about her habits.

'Who do you think he is?'

She looked at him as she took a sip of her coffee. 'I can trust you, can't I?'

'I guess I've only got you arrested once.'

She put down the cup, feeling annoyed at herself for doubting him, aware of the dark unwanted thoughts creeping in at the edges, getting around the chemical cocktail in her brain. 'No one's asked you anything about me?'

'No. What's this to do with – your work?'

'Why did you come here that first day?'

He stopped eating, a surprised look on his face.

She said, 'The truth.'

It took a moment for him to find the words. 'OK . . . The day you moved in there was a rental van outside. I drove past and saw you lugging this big plastic laundry basket filled with stuff up the front path . . . I thought you looked pretty. It was one of those moments—'

'What moments?'

'When you know something's going to change.'

'You fancied me hauling a laundry basket?'

'If we're being really truthful, it was more than that . . . I knew I had to have you.'

'That would be in the sexual sense?'

'In every sense.'

'And look at us now, we're going to court together.'

Steve looked down at the table. 'I don't know what to say . . . I'll take the blame, it wasn't your fault . . . Maybe I should go now.'

'Swear to me you didn't set me up.'

'I can guess how it happened . . . Annie knows I had grass, I gave her some. And she could have known I was coming here. I passed a couple of guys I know in the lane on my way up. They'd have told her where I was.'

'Are you sleeping with her, too?'

'Not recently.'

'She hates you enough to call the police?'

'It was her who told me about the guy . . . He gave her some money.'

'And you didn't say anything to me?'

'I was going to . . . I got distracted.'

Jenny let out a short laugh, then laughed again, louder, but with tears behind her eyes. She tried to stop them but they caught her by surprise and rinsed her cheeks. Steve got out of his chair and came round the table and hugged her.

Later, when she had control of herself, she told him about Danny Wills and Katy Taylor and what had happened to Harry Marshall and Tara Collins. She told him how she had started out with good intentions, but now she was scared.

Steve asked what he could do to help. Jenny said not to blame himself for what had happened. UKAM would have found a way to get to her one way or another.

From the look on Alison's face Jenny could tell that she knew. She said there had been phone calls from journalists and the story was already up on the *Post*'s website: *Severn Vale Coroner in Dope Bust*. Simon Moreton from the Ministry of Justice had emailed asking Jenny to call him. The list officer at the Law Courts had telephoned to say they'd had a message that the courtroom wouldn't be required on Monday – was that correct? Things were moving fast. She'd also heard that the police inquiry into Katy Taylor's disappearance had been put on hold for a week because officers had been diverted to an investigation into the petrol-bombing of a mosque.

Jenny said, 'If someone came and offered me a bribe now to get clear of this, I don't think it would take much.'

Alison pushed a pile of overnight reports across the desk. 'Do you want to look at these?'

'Might as well.' She picked them up and turned to her office.

'Do you want to tell me what happened?' Alison asked gently.

Beyond caring, Jenny said, 'My new boyfriend was smoking grass. One thing led to another . . . His ex called the police but I think someone from UKAM had got to her first. She's a single mum who works behind a bar.'

'You lead an exciting life.'

'Want to swap?'

Alison gave her a motherly look. 'What shall I tell anyone who asks?'

'You used to be a copper, think of a story.'

*

She sat at her desk knowing there were people she should contact, Simone Wills, Andy and Claire Taylor, but what would she tell them – sorry, but my dope-smoking boyfriend and I were only having some harmless fun? She felt like a fool, humiliated. You couldn't come up with a better set-up – make the victim feel like she's brought it on herself.

The first call was from Moreton. He sounded embarrassed. 'I hear you've got yourself into a drop of hot water, Jenny.'

She said, 'I would explain to you how a wealthy private corrections company skilfully disposed of my predecessor and is now doing the same to me, but I don't think you'd believe me.'

'I'm afraid I have to concern myself with rather more mundane matters, such as what to do with you while these charges are still pending.'

'Am I not innocent until proven guilty?'

'Of course, but we both know that judicial officers can't continue to function while they're the subject of criminal charges.'

'If you spoke to the families of Danny Wills and Katy Taylor I don't think either of them would have a problem with me continuing.'

'The Ministry would have a problem, Jenny, even in these enlightened times. I'm calling to tell you that the decision has been taken to suspend you on full pay pending the resolution of your case.'

The words floated through her.

'What happens to the inquests?'

'They'll be adjourned. Obviously if you're found guilty of an offence another coroner will deal with them in due course.'

'If I'm acquitted?'

'We're rather hoping you might take some time to consider your options while you're away from the office. Should you decide that perhaps the Coroners' Service isn't for you, I'm sure we'd assist with the appropriate references.'

'You make sacking me sound like an act of kindness.'

'I appreciate it must be a very difficult time for you.'

'Actually I feel quite calm, now I know who the bad guys are.'

There was a pause before Moreton responded. 'I'm sending you a confirmatory email with a hard copy in the post. We'd like you to leave the office by six p.m.'

She tried to make progress with the paperwork, her pride telling her to leave a tidy desk behind her, not to give whoever sat here next the pleasure of saying she ran a sloppy office. On the other side of the door she could hear Alison on the phone, speaking in hushed tones to scandalized colleagues in other coroner's offices wanting to know the lurid details. To her credit, she was loyal, saying it was all a fabrication, that a friend of hers might have smoked something but she wouldn't have known. After hearing it a few times, Jenny almost believed it herself.

She worked through the day's reports in a semi-trance, writing out nine death certificates, which she handed to Alison. She made a neat pile of the five current cases requiring inquest, but none of them a full jury hearing, and tidied her files in the Danny Wills and Katy Taylor cases, leaving a brief explanatory note with each. The only thing she hadn't dealt with was the accounts. Alison said not to worry, she'd sort them out somehow.

At six o'clock Jenny packed her briefcase and stepped out of her office to say goodbye, but Alison had already gone, her chair tucked under the desk. She went out of the main door and closed it shut behind her. She turned the key in the lock and posted it back through the letter box. No word of farewell, no note, just a heavy silence and a sense of unresolved sadness which hung in the air like a fog.

David's call came as she was clearing the tolls on the approach to the Severn Bridge. Her hands-free connected to the stereo and his voice barked at her through four speakers. 'Deborah just showed me the paper. Well done. Ross isn't home yet, but I expect he'll have heard the good news. You're not his pusher, are you?'

'Grow up, David.'

'I'm serious. Nothing about you could surprise me.'

'Well, you can relax. I'm not your problem any more.'

'You're still my son's problem.'

'*Your* son.'

'I'm clearly the only one of us capable of taking responsibility.'

'The dope was nothing to do with me.'

'That's fine, then, it's just your hippie boyfriend I've got to worry about.'

'He's a damn sight more intelligent than that pea-brained piece of arse you've got running round your kitchen.'

'I didn't call to trade insults with you, Jenny – there's nothing I could say that would do your behaviour justice – but while he's in my care, I will not have you around my son.'

'Oh, really? Well, in case you hadn't noticed, he's not a child any more. He's nearly sixteen years old and can make his own decisions.'

'He did that some time ago, or are you still too stoned to remember?'

Jenny looked out over water, a pillar of light breaking through a gap in the clouds to the west.

David shouted, 'What I'd really like from you, but I suppose it's too much to ask, is the slightest hint of apology.'

She pushed the red button on the phone, cutting him off, and watched the shaft of sunlight narrow to a sliver and then disappear.

Ross didn't answer his phone and she didn't blame him. It wasn't that she'd been a bad mother; she had tried to be the very best she could. What she was a person who didn't have it in her to be as selfless as everyone wanted her to be. To have got it right she would have had to sacrifice her career and stay at home to keep David's house beautiful, cook him meals, have sex with him when he wanted and find a sporty hobby he would have approved of, like tennis or horseriding. Coming back in her jodhpurs, making love in the shower before putting on a healthy dinner and helping Ross with all the homework from his pushy private school. She tried to imagine it, how she would feel as queen of a perfect home. Suffocated. Desperate. Murderous. The words that came weren't good ones. They proved her point: she had too many emotions of her own to be able to put other people first. The unforgivable thing was that she had known it all along, since before she married. She should have stopped the train then and jumped off, but she had been eager to get romance, marriage and all the rest out of the way so she could proceed with her life. Even on her wedding day she wasn't in the moment, it was always *what next*? How long till I get pregnant? How soon can I get back to work?

Sixteen years on and she was a broken-down, pill-dependent failure of a mother who was about to lose the one thing she hadn't been prepared to sacrifice. It wasn't a spectacular career, but being made a coroner at forty-two was something to be proud of.

She had parked in a lay-by in the thick of the woods a mile or so before Tintern. There was a track to the right which led down to the River Wye. You could easily lose yourself on the way, wander off into the trees where no one could see, crawl into a thicket of holly and briars. Or go down to the water and wait for high tide, take the pills there and slide out to sea. With luck they'd never find you. The last trace a footprint on a muddy bank washed away by the rain.

It had taken three temazepam to achieve the muzzy feeling, not anger or panic, more removed than that. The picture in her mind was of a kite tugging at its string in a strong breeze. There was a strange and unexpected vitality to the sensation, the act of release something to *do*. Her hand found its way into her bag and her fingers closed around the beta blockers. A bottle of those, her heart and lungs would gently relax and she could drift away.

She brought out the container and pressed slowly down on the cap: twist and release. A bottle of sparkling water in the glove box, maybe dissolve them in it first and then drink it, the bubbles helping to make it work faster. No, better to put the pills in your mouth and rinse them down. The choice was frustrating. She wanted the solution to be elegant. Effortless.

A Subaru pulled off the road ahead of her. An outdoorsy couple in their early thirties emerged in matching walking boots, rainproofs tied around their waists. He looked like a professional, a dentist Jenny guessed, from the neat smiles they both had. As they walked past, she holding his hand, he looked in and met Jenny's eyes, holding them for a moment as if he knew. As they turned down the track, he glanced back over his shoulder, sensing something.

Shit. Just the kind who'd get involved.

She shot the woman a smile and turned the key in the ignition. Turning out of the lay-by and heading back to Melin Bach, she thought, what's the hurry, why not have a nice glass of wine first?

TWENTY-TWO

THE TELEPHONE'S PERSISTENT RINGING ENTERED her incoherent dreams and dragged her back to consciousness. She was bunched up on the sofa with a vicious crick in her neck. Light leaked around the closed curtains. On the rug covering the flagstone floor were two empty bottles of red and a wine glass with an inch still in the bottom, next to it two neat rows of pills, their empty containers and an untouched tumbler of water. She stared at them, her eyes slowly coming into focus, dimly recalling the ritual of laying them out late the previous night, remembering how she had done it: imagining herself as a child counting out sweets; then crawling on to the sofa to savour her final glass.

Aching, she swung her feet on to the floor, becoming aware of a dull sensation like waking up to grief or the loss of a lover. Slowly the pieces of the previous day reassembled themselves: her arrest, her suspension, David's call, and the urge to escape, which had seduced her away from anger. Her body was a lead weight, her mind even heavier.

The phone persisted, the caller determined to rouse her. She heaved herself across the room and lifted the cordless receiver, pushing her tangled hair back from her face.

'Hello.' Her voice was thick and croaky.

'Mrs Cooper?'

She cleared her throat. 'Yes.'

'Professor Lloyd, Newport General. I tried calling Mrs Trent but she's not answering her phone.'

Jenny glanced at her watch and saw that it wasn't yet eight.

'Oh—'

Lloyd paused, as if embarrassed. 'I heard about what happened yesterday, but I didn't know who else to call. I've had some more thoughts about Katy Taylor, you see.'

He waited for Jenny to respond, putting the onus on her. She tried to think, her head throbbing now with every heartbeat as the undigested alcohol started to recirculate through her system.

'I've been suspended from my post. I'm not sure there's much point talking to me.'

Another pregnant silence, then: 'But is it justified, Mrs Cooper?'

There was a knowingness in Lloyd's tone. It jolted her like a slap on the face, snapping her reluctant mind back into her complaining body. It was her turn to consider her words carefully.

She said, 'You're a Home Office pathologist, Professor. You know the system better than I do.'

'Quite. Perhaps we could meet and talk, seeing as you've time on your hands.'

'What for?'

'Perhaps that had better wait. What do you say?'

The memory of her dream of dark rooms and ghosts dripped back into her consciousness as she drove up over the hill, taking the winding road to Usk and from there the dual carriageway to Newport. The images were sketchy – dark inchoate figures with a brooding menace in an even darker space – but they stuck like a stubborn stain. She felt the texture of the wheel beneath her fingers, flicked the wipers when a shower scattered the windscreen, but her nose was filled with the smell of damp brick and mouldering plaster, and despite her breakfast-time pills her pulse thumped in anticipation of an unseen predator. The jagged entrance to the secret room of her nightmares had opened a little wider, what lay within tantalizingly close. Part of her wanted to stop everything and journey into it, try to isolate and capture the monster, but still the fear was too great, her instinct to medicate and push it all from view stronger than her need to know.

Once off the country roads with their high, containing hedges and safely surrounded by other vehicles, she allowed herself to recall the events of the previous evening. Her memory of them seemed more remote than her intervening dreams. She saw herself in the lay-by, a pale figure in a nondescript car fingering a bottle of pills, tempted by the prospect of release yet strangely removed from the source of her pain. The unreality of the images told her that this was how it happened: how the suicidal managed to cross the threshold. Sitting cross-legged on the rug, counting out the beta blockers, the thought of leaving had been as comforting as the smell of church incense on a winter's evening. The word death hadn't figured, only *peace*.

She arrived at her destination still locked in a waking dream. She walked from her car towards the Celtic Manor, the large hotel resort set incongruously at the edge of the M4 on the outskirts of Newport, without feeling her feet on the ground. Her voice was someone else's as she asked directions from the reception clerk to the Forum café. She told herself it was a combination of her medication and a deep hangover, but as she passed a happy party of hotel guests on their way to the golf course and saw in their smiles something forbidding, she knew it was more. Many times Dr Travis had told her that the psychotic would project their disturbed emotions on to others

– that madness could be averted only by confronting those feelings before they became fully disassociated from the self and all means of conscious control.

Searching for the health club coffee bar, humming inanely to the muzak, she accepted that at last, after all these years, she was finally entering the end game; the moment she had always dreaded had arrived. She had perhaps a few days to summon the courage to plunge into the dark place inside her. And if she couldn't . . . last night had shown her the route she might take; or which might take her.

Professor Lloyd was seated at a coffee table next to the glass screen overlooking the hotel pool. He smiled brightly as she approached and rose to shake her hand.

'So glad you could make it, Mrs Cooper.' He gestured her to the low-slung chair opposite his, wicker with tartan cushions. There was a pot of tea with two cups waiting. 'This is the closest I've got to a club, I'm afraid, but it does the job. I often steal away here on a rainy afternoon.'

Jenny glanced approvingly at the calming decor. 'Good for you.'

She lowered herself into the chair, which forced the occupant to recline. Professor Lloyd stretched out opposite, maintaining a view of the café entrance, his body relaxed but his eyes alert. She gave a noncommittal smile, happy for him to take the lead. With no badge of office, she was only here for curiosity's sake, after all.

'Well then, Mrs Cooper, I've been reading all about you, and hearing the odd word on the grapevine. Two controversial inquests in your first fortnight . . .'

'I didn't go looking for them.'

'I'm sure you didn't.' He shook his head. 'No, I'm sure. Would you like some tea?'

'Please.'

He carefully lifted the pot and poured her a cup, considering his angle of approach as he stirred in the milk. He hesitated with the wet spoon, then laid it on a paper napkin. 'I hate a drip on my saucer, don't you?'

'Detest it.'

Jenny sipped the tepid liquid. He watched her, as if searching for some clue in her expression. 'I understand both inquests are currently adjourned.'

'Again, not my choice.'

'No, so I gather.' He took a drink from his own cup, buying a final moment before committing himself. 'My thoughts about Katy, you see, were to a certain extent prompted by what I read of your death-in-custody case – Danny Mills?'

'Wills.'

'Yes. The poor boy who hanged himself while Katy was in the same institution.' He gave her a look of innocent enquiry. 'You don't think there's any reason to suppose their deaths were connected in any way?'

Jenny became aware of the feel of the cup in her hands, the smell of chlorine in the air, her drifting spirit returning to her body as Professor Lloyd's words concentrated her attention.

'Why do you think there was a connection?'

He brought his two hands together and rested them on his chin, as if in prayer. 'Before I go any further, Mrs Cooper, perhaps you could tell me what happened to you, or what you *think* happened to you. I hate to give credence to conspiracy theories, but I'm a man not far off his pension, with grown-up children who shouldn't be still sadly dependent on him.'

'Why should I trust you? You could be part of this for all I know.'

'Part of what?'

'The reason my boyfriend and I were arrested the day after I discovered there *was* a connection.'

'Do you know if there was a tip-off?'

'There was more than that, there was a set-up. I have reason to suspect the company that runs Portshead Farm Secure Training Centre has form for this sort of thing. They may hold prisoners but they certainly don't take them.'

Professor Lloyd brought his hands up to cover his nose and eyes. If he wasn't a good actor he was carrying out a serious and painful calculation. After a long moment of reflection, he began to speak quietly, while looking steadily at Jenny. 'Then you'll understand that what I'm telling you is off the record, at least for the time being. This meeting never happened.'

'Whatever you want. There's nothing I can do anyway. Whoever they appoint after me is going to bury both cases so deep they'll never see daylight again.' She shrugged and took another sip of her tea.

Lloyd nodded, coming to a decision. 'What I have to say is rather speculative in any event, but may be of interest.' He glanced towards the door to satisfy himself he had an audience of only one. 'I've done a little reading. The literature on ruptures of the glenohumeral ligament confirms that such injuries usually arise from the arm being forced up behind the back, but it seems this mostly happens in the case of arrest or where C and R methods are used in custodial institutions.'

'C and R?'

'Control and restraint. Prison officers or medical orderlies in secure hospitals are taught techniques to bring their non-cooperating charges to heel. They mostly involve locking the elbow, forcing the subject to the ground, kneeling on the spine and pushing the hand up the back. Once the prisoner is face down on the floor, the officer can contain him or her with one hand, leaving the other free to apply handcuffs or whatever else.'

'Inject something?'

'Of course. Sedatives, usually.'

'You think Katy's killer used C and R?'

'Statistically there's an eighty per cent likelihood, and her chipped front tooth would be consistent with her face being pushed to the floor. The fact the chip was still in her mouth suggests it happened almost immediately before death, perhaps even in the final throes.'

'If she was the passenger in a car? Could the driver have pulled over and done this inside the vehicle?'

'She was only very small, so I don't see why not.'

'What about the clump of hair ripped from the back of her head?'

He raised his eyes to the ceiling, imagining the scene. 'I suppose if her attacker didn't have room to get his knee into her back he could have pushed her wrist up far enough to get a handful of hair to anchor his grip, held her steady with his left, injected her with the right.'

'So the police should be looking for someone trained in these techniques?'

'It would make sense.'

Jenny lapsed into silence for a moment, sorting through the jumbled chronology in her mind. She remembered Katy's body was found on Monday 30 April, day one of Marshall's inquest into Danny's death. Peterson carried out the post-mortem the next day, 1 May, and on the following day Marshall wrote out a death certificate without sight of a written report.

Jenny said, 'What do you know about Peterson?'

'In what sense?'

'You can't believe he didn't spot any of this, but he let a death certificate be written two days after the body was found.'

'I hardly know the man, Mrs Cooper, and I won't speculate, but I've no reason to think he's negligent . . .'

'You're trying to tell me something, why not just say it?'

He sighed, troubled by the implications of professional betrayal, but his expression said his conscience was winning.

'As you probably know, pathologists dictate their notes as they carry out their examinations, though invariably on antiquated equipment. Perhaps if the tape of his original examinations were to be found . . . ?'

'You think he carried out more than one?'

'I was thinking of Danny Wills. As I recall, Dr Peterson's post-mortem report was remarkably brief, at least that was the impression I got from the newspaper. In the absence of physical remains, his tape would be the next best thing.'

She looked at him; deep frown lines creased his forehead.

He said, 'You must think me an unforgivable coward for not mentioning this more publicly. I do apologize.'

'What do you expect me to do with this *speculation*?'

'Having got in this deep, I assumed—'

'That I'd be prepared to drown?'

Professor Lloyd said, 'You give the impression of being a very brave woman, Mrs Cooper.'

Alison sounded shocked to hear her voice over the intercom and hesitated for a moment before buzzing her into the office, telling her that Moreton had left instructions that she wasn't to be allowed on the premises. Jenny said the premises weren't Moreton's to exclude her from, they belonged to the local authority.

She stepped into reception to find Alison hovering anxiously in front of her desk, the accounts file spread out behind her.

'You left without saying anything last night.'

Apologetic, Alison said, 'I didn't know what to say.'

'As it turns out, goodbye might have been a bit premature.'

A look of surprise, then alarm flashed across Alison's face. 'What's happened?'

'Professor Lloyd called me. I've been to see him. He thinks Katy's injuries bear all the hallmarks of control and restraint techniques. I guess you know all about those?'

She nodded. 'What's he telling you this for now?'

'It's all off the record but he wondered if there might not be a connection with Danny's death – he's been following the story.'

'What's he thinking of?'

'He wasn't explicit, and he doesn't know that Katy reported Danny's trouble with a member of staff to Justin Bennett. But what I think he's saying is that Peterson has shown himself to be rather short on detail in both Katy's and Danny's cases. That if anything's been hidden he'll know about it.'

'But there's nothing you can—'

'There's a lot I can do, but I'll need some help. I want to seize Dr Peterson's post-mortem dictation tapes. My legal status while I'm suspended is questionable, but you're still a coroner's officer and can exercise the coroner's delegated powers. There's still no coroner but me in this district so there's a good argument that anything you do at my instruction is legally valid.'

'I've been told not to talk to you, Mrs Cooper.'

'Then why did you let me in?'

Alison looked at her without answering, then slowly lowered herself into her chair, sitting sideways to the desk. 'Mr Moreton says that all new deaths are to be handled by Bristol Central for the time being.'

'What has he said about Danny's and Katy's cases?'

'Nothing.'

'Have you spoken to Simone Wills?'

'What would I tell her?' There was an edge of desperation in Alison's voice, a woman caught between her sense of duty and her conscience.

Jenny said, 'I've made a decision: I'm going to find out how they died. I'd appreciate your help getting hold of Peterson's tapes, but if you feel you can't . . .'

Alison agonized. 'I don't know, Mrs Cooper . . .'

'Wouldn't you like to know what happened to Harry?'

Jenny saw Alison's eyes flick involuntarily leftwards to a document on top of the piles of receipts on the desk – a credit card statement. The jaws of her muscles tensed as she seemed to wrestle with her answer.

Jenny reached out, snatched the statement and stepped away from the desk, anticipating Alison's 'No!' as she started up from her chair.

'Please, Mrs Cooper – it's none of our business.'

Jenny turned away and ran her eyes down the column of payments made on Harry's personal credit card.

Alison tried to step around her and take the statement. 'I opened it by mistake.'

Jenny twisted away again, then spotted it, the second to last entry: 26 *April, Novotel, Bristol*. Too late, Alison grabbed it from her hand.

Jenny looked up into her eyes and saw the depth of her pain. She felt for her. 'What was he doing?'

Alison fingered the crumpled bill and swallowed the hard lump in her throat. 'Sleeping with someone, I assume.'

'Have you checked with the hotel?'

Alison nodded. 'He signed in as Mr and Mrs Marshall . . . I can't believe that, can you?'

Wanting to offer some shred of comfort, Jenny said, 'It could have been due to his depression. And if the two of you weren't—'

'No. It had happened before. I always suspected.' She placed the statement back on the desk. 'I even had to tell lies for him. Not that he realized, but his wife would try to catch him out. He'd tell her he was going to London for the day and would be late home, and she'd call the office to check I wasn't with him.'

'Mary thought you two were having an affair?'

'If she'd tried screwing him instead of Jesus he might have

stayed at home.' She wiped away dry tears. 'I'm having some coffee. Want some?'

'Thanks.'

Alison went over to the kitchenette.

Jenny, watching her, said, 'Did Harry know how you felt about him?'

'Yes . . . He even kissed me once, right where you're standing. Two years ago, completely out of the blue on a Wednesday morning.' And leaden with regret, 'But it wasn't love he was looking for, was it?'

Imagining the moment, Harry, playful, catching her unawares, Jenny wandered over to her desk and glanced over the assorted papers and receipts, guessing that she had been searching among them for further evidence of his infidelity.

Alison came to the kitchenette doorway. 'No, I don't know who she was.'

'Would it help?'

'It might lay a few ghosts to rest.'

Jenny picked up the slender bundles of receipts for April and May and leafed through them. 'He didn't buy her any presents on office expenses?'

'None that I can find.' She turned back to the counter and spooned instant coffee into cups.

Jenny set down the April bundle and picked up May – a month in which Harry had lived only three days. There were three receipts: one dated 1 May for two hundred pounds' worth of office supplies from a mail order firm, one dated 3 May, 10.30 a.m., for a Jiffy bag purchased from WH Smith, and one of the same date timed at 10.52 a.m. for five pounds' worth of postage. Stapled to it was the counterfoil for an item of recorded mail, rubber-stamped but with the space for the sender's details left blank.

'Who was he sending a recorded delivery to the morning before he died?'

Alison emerged with their drinks. 'I don't know. He didn't mention it to me. I usually dealt with all the mail.'

'The ticket's got a track and trace number. Why don't we go online and find out?'

Before Alison could fathom the process she was proposing, Jenny was hitting the keyboard and had brought up the Royal Mail website on the bulky old-style monitor. She clicked through to the track and trace screen. 'This should tell us who the package went to.'

She typed in the thirteen-digit code and hit enter. Alison glanced away as a new screen came up leaving Jenny to read the results alone.

Responding to her surprised silence, Alison said, 'What?'

'It was to Grantham at his council address. It wasn't signed for. It was delivered again the next day and was returned again unsigned. Looks like it's probably still sitting in the sorting office.'

Alison looked relieved. 'I should go and get it.'

'Maybe later. First we're paying a visit to the Vale – that is, if you're on board.'

Alison looked down at her coffee cup and thought for a long moment before lifting her face with a look of philosophical resignation. 'You're right. I do need to know what happened to Harry.'

Jenny said, 'You wish you'd made love with him that time, don't you?'

'It would have been nice. Just the once.'

TWENTY-THREE

THEY MET THE NEXT MORNING, at the Severn Vale District Hospital. Alison knew Peterson's shared PA to be a woman named Kathy Greenway. Her office, on the fifth floor of the main building, could be accessed only by punching in a security code at one of the doors which led off the atrium around the entrance to the lift. Alison was to arrive in a matter-of-fact way and ask for Peterson's dictation tapes for the four weeks from 16 April, treat it as a matter of routine. Jenny would stay out of sight and intervene only if the situation became awkward. If she was challenged, Alison was to say that she had been ordered to collect this evidence before the inquest into Danny's death was adjourned and no one had told her that it was no longer necessary.

For an ex-detective she seemed excessively agitated as they crossed the hospital's main reception. Jenny sensed she was hoping to be let off the hook. As they waited for the lift Jenny said the worst that could happen would be a slap on the wrist – if she stuck to the story no one could disprove that she wasn't just doing her job, trying to tie up loose ends. A professional.

Alison took the lift up alone while Jenny went to wait in the ground-floor canteen, wearing the wireless headset for her phone. A minute later Alison called and said she'd keep the line open and the phone in her jacket pocket so Jenny could hear how she was doing. Jenny bought a cup of weak coffee and found a seat in the quietest corner.

For a while there were only the muffled sounds of the phone jostling in Alison's pocket as she waited to piggyback through the secure door pretending to have dropped her briefcase while typing out the code, then hoping some kind soul would punch it in for her while she gathered up her things.

The opportunity came after only a minute or two. Jenny heard the briefcase hit the floor, Alison's 'Oh dear,' and 'Would you mind?', offers of help from a mild male voice and the click of the door closing behind her. She was in.

It sounded as if Kathy Greenway shared an office with several other PAs. Jenny could hear various concurrent phone conversations and the rattle of numerous keyboards, then Alison's 'Miss Greenway?' and a surprised young voice replying, 'Yes?'

'Alison Trent, coroner's officer – I've often seen your name on the email but never put a face to it.'

The PA responded with a cautious 'Right . . .'

'It's nothing much,' Alison said. 'It's just that the coroner made an order that Dr Peterson's dictation tapes for the month until 7 May of this year be produced. They may contain some evidence relevant to an inquest she's been conducting. I thought they might be up here.'

'Oh. Dr Peterson hasn't said anything to me.'

'It's not really a matter for him. Here's the coroner's order.' Jenny heard Alison unlock her briefcase and hand over the document she had typed out before leaving the office. 'If these tapes are in your possession, custody or control you are required by law to hand them over to me now.'

There was a pause as Kathy Greenway looked at the document. With a note of anxiety she said, 'I'd better get my line manager, Mr Hassan. I don't know anything about this.'

Alison said, 'It's really nothing to do with him. This relates to the person who has possession of the tapes.'

'I still need to speak to Mr Hassan.'

'Miss Greenway, before you call, I need to know if you have those tapes.'

'Not for those dates, no.'

'Well, where would they be?'

'I don't know. They all get recycled.'

'You mean they would have gone back to Dr Peterson?'

'Not necessarily. They all go in that tray over there. Someone takes them away and they get reused.'

'By whom?'

'Any of the typing staff here.'

Another brief hiatus, then Alison said, 'Do you type up all the post-mortem tapes Dr Peterson sends in?'

'Yes.'

'So you'll have copies of all those files on your computer?'

'I'm not going to answer any more questions. I'm calling Mr Hassan now.'

Kathy picked up the phone and informed Hassan that there was someone from the coroner's office here asking to see Dr Peterson's files. Jenny heard the background chatter die down, the other PAs taking an interest. Kathy came off the phone and said Mr Hassan would be along right now, and explained that she wasn't allowed to give out anyone's files under any circumstances.

Alison tried again. 'If you look at the wording of the document, Miss Greenway, it covers transcripts of the tapes. That means if you don't give copies to me now you could be called up in front of the court.'

'If I did that without my boss's permission I'd lose my job, OK?'

Jenny could feel the tension between them as they waited

for Hassan to arrive. The other PAs had stopped talking, only the desultory click of their keyboards filling the silence. They had agreed that Alison would control the phone, but Jenny was impatient to intervene; she could see Hassan calling his boss and so on up the food chain until the chief executive was wheeled in. What was needed was a sharp threat. She pressed the 'end call' button on her phone, waited a moment for the line to disconnect on each side, then dialled Alison's number. It rang only once. She answered with an abrupt hello.

'You need to be tougher. When Hassan comes, tell him he either hands over the files or he and the girl will find themselves in court first thing Monday morning.'

Alison said, 'Yes. It's being dealt with. Goodbye.' She pressed several keys on the phone – probably killing the ring – and stuffed it back in a pocket.

It was at least another five minutes before she heard a cautious, bureaucratic voice say, 'Ali Hassan, and you are?'

'Alison Trent, coroner's officer.'

'OK. This is Alan Yates from our legal department. He's going to handle this request.'

'Mrs Trent.' Yates's voice was that of a young, confident lawyer who spent his life helping the hospital beat off negligence claims. 'Could we step into the corridor, please?'

Alison said, 'I'm here to collect evidence that's been ordered by the coroner. You understand what that means, Mr Yates.'

'If you wouldn't mind, I'd prefer to discuss this privately.'

There were sounds of movement, Alison following him from the room. A door closed behind them, shutting out the office noise.

Dropping all pretence at politeness, Yates said, 'What's going on here? The coroner's been suspended. She's got no legal authority and our staff aren't obliged to give you anything.'

'This order was made before the Danny Wills inquest was adjourned. As far as I'm concerned, it has to be complied with. If it isn't, there will be consequences.'

'We'll take them.'

'You realize you're obstructing a coroner's investigation?'

'Let's cut the crap. I've just spoken to the head of legal at the local authority and you shouldn't even be here. Either you leave now or I'll call security.'

'Mr Grantham has no jurisdiction over the coroner's office.'

Yates said, 'Nice try. Come back with an arrest warrant and we might take you seriously.'

There was a moment of silence, then a click as Alison reached into her pocket and ended the call.

She found Jenny at the corner table swallowing her lunchtime pills, no longer making any effort to conceal them.

'How much of that did you hear?'

'Pretty much everything. Sounds like he called your bluff.'

'What was I meant to do – lie? He'd spoken to Grantham. He knew you'd sent me on a fishing trip. Face it, Mrs Cooper, we're not going to get anything out of them.'

'I'm not your boss any more. You can call me Jenny.'

'I'd prefer not to.'

Alison sat stiffly on the edge of her chair, avoiding Jenny's gaze, annoyed with herself and embarrassed at her failure. She said, 'I suppose that's it, then. We're not going to get any further here.'

'Not by asking politely we're not.'

'We've got no authority, Mrs Cooper. It'll have to wait until you're back in post.'

'I appreciate your optimism, but I think we both know what'll happen to those files in the meantime.'

Indignant, Alison said, 'You make it sound as if it was my fault. I don't see what else I could have done.'

'You couldn't, they were wise to us. If they won't let us through the front door we'll just have to go through the back.'

Jenny pulled out her phone and address book and looked up a number. 'You don't have to be involved with this. In fact, you probably don't want to be anywhere near it.'

'Who are you calling?'

'Tara Collins. She claims to have a young hacker friend.'

Alison said, 'I'd better be getting back to the office.' She stepped away from the table. 'I'll find myself a taxi.'

Jenny waited until she was out of earshot.

Tara answered her land line with a cautious 'Who is it?'

'Jenny Cooper.'

'Hi. I was going to call you – I saw the *Post*. Tell me they fitted you up.'

'Something like that.'

'*Allowing your premises to be used?* I don't like to pull rank, but it could be worse.'

'I'm working on it.'

'I've had Simone on the phone wanting to know what the hell's going on. I used to think she was flaky enough to survive this but I'm not so sure.'

'I don't know how safe it is to talk to you on this thing—'

'What the hell. For all I know they've got a bug up my backside.'

Jenny thought of suggesting they meet somewhere but it was nearly one. If Peterson's files were still intact by the close of business she'd be amazed.

'I've had some information. I need to get hold of certain computer files on the Vale District Hospital server – transcripts of Peterson's post-mortem notes. You mentioned you knew a kid—'

'I do.' A note of excitement entered her voice.

'Do you think he'd be able to help? It's urgent.'

'I can call him, but there's a problem.'

'OK . . .'

'As I recall, the Vale's on an intranet. There's no outside access and no wi-fi. He'd have to work off one of the terminals in the building, or at least get a lead plugged into the system.'

'I'm here now. Any ideas?'

'Have a look around, I'll call you back in a minute.' She rang off.

Jenny pocketed her phone and went in search of a spare computer terminal. The admin floors were out of bounds, limiting her to the clinical areas of the building. She scouted along corridors, glancing into offices and reception areas of obs and gynae, paediatrics and gastroenterology, but each area of the building felt as if it was already holding twice as many people as it was designed for. Playing lost, she wandered through two adjacent geriatric wards on the first floor; the handful of terminals were all behind glass in the nurses' stations, positioned to keep patients and public well away from them. She nudged at the doors of a housemen's common room, but it, too, was overcrowded, young doctors queuing up to get at the handful of grubby machines. An under-resourced hospital was a tough place to get screen time.

She was coming back down the stairs to reception, wondering what secret corners the intranet cables passed through and whether, like in a movie she'd seen, it could be spliced into, when Tara Collins called back. She said that Tony had agreed to help, but wanted a hundred to cover the risk. Jenny said fine, but they'd need to move fast. How soon could they get here?

'Be there in half an hour. Found a terminal yet?'

'You've got to be joking. I was thinking about hacking into the cable.'

'Not a chance. They'll all be in armoured conduits running between the floors. Keep looking.'

*

Jenny was there to meet Tara and Tony as they climbed out of her battered Fiat. Tony was a pale, skinny kid wearing a baseball cap and a fluorescent waistcoat, IT TEAM, printed across the front and back. He had a laptop bag over his shoulder and a jumble of leads stuffed in his waistcoat pockets.

He looked at her with grey, unblinking eyes and in a flat drawl said, 'Hi, I'm Tony. Tara said you were cool about the money.'

'Sure. I'll give it to you as soon as I get to a cashpoint.'

He shrugged, happy with that.

Tara said, 'How are we doing? Have you found a terminal?'

'Not a chance. Every one I've found is being used or has got a queue for it. I was hoping you'd have some ideas.'

Tony said, 'I'd usually go into someone's office, say I'm fixing a problem.'

Jenny and Tara exchanged a look. Tara said, 'He's done it before.'

Jenny said, 'How long do you need?'

'We're probably talking about a six-digit password made up of letters and numbers. Could take maybe half an hour with my software, or quicker if I can get a link out and get some remote machines working on it.'

Tara said, 'Password hacking takes computing power. You basically have an electronic dictionary containing every permutation, millions of them. Tony's part of a network that shares the load – hundreds of machines around the world get working on it at once.'

Tony, faintly bored, picked at a spot on his chin.

Jenny thought about trying to get him into one of the offices she'd passed and couldn't see how. More than likely people who worked at the same computer all day would smell a rat. She was thinking about the geriatric ward, maybe finding a way to distract the skeleton staff of nurses, when she realized they were standing thirty yards away from the hospital mortuary.

On the two occasions she'd been inside there'd been only Peterson and a couple of technicians in the building. She fetched out her phone and scrolled through its address book, looking for his number.

Tara said, 'What are you thinking?'

'Give me a moment.'

Peterson's phone rang five times before the answer machine clicked in. She glanced at her watch – it was just gone two.

She rang off. 'Right. I've got an idea. We'll go straight to Peterson's office – he's not in there now and there's a good chance he'll be in the autopsy room for the rest of the afternoon. I'll go in with Tony and cover for him, pretend I'm there to speak to Peterson personally if anyone asks questions.'

Tara said, 'Wouldn't it less risky if he went in by himself?'

Jenny said, 'I'm taking full responsibility. And besides, I'd like to have a root around.'

Tara moved her car to a space close to the mortuary entrance, facing out so she could keep watch while Jenny and Tony went to the door. Tony pressed the intercom but there was no answer. Jenny guessed it meant Peterson and his technicians were busy. They waited a while before buzzing again – still no response. Tony wondered about trying some of the windows around the back. Jenny said no, too risky, but when they'd been standing there ten minutes she started to flirt with the idea. Tony was all set with a thin plastic blade he said could slip most window catches and Yale locks when Jenny saw the Filipina cleaner she'd met on her first visit, pushing a steel janitor's trolley across the car park.

She hurried over and, in a mixture of sign language and pidgin, indicated that she needed to get through the door. The woman took a moment to place her, but when she had she gave her a tired but friendly smile and took a detour with her trolley, pulling a heavy bunch of keys out of her overalls. She unlocked the door and Jenny gave her a warm thank-you.

She walked a few paces ahead of Tony, telling him to act as if they were here on separate business, at least until they got into Peterson's office. The entrance hall was empty, as was the small lobby and the two offices which led off it. Jenny noticed they were signed 'Technicians' and 'Reception'. She glanced through the safety glass and saw that reception had become an ad hoc storeroom housing boxes of files. The technician's office looked more like a common room; there was a computer terminal inside but the door was locked. She gestured Tony to follow her to the slap doors, warning him that he might see some dead bodies.

Tony was unimpressed. 'You should see rotten.com.'

She nudged through the doors into the main corridor. Corpses stretched along the wall in an unbroken line, parked two deep at one point: the result of her no report no release policy. The shrill whine of a buzz saw came from the autopsy room and up around the corner, out of sight, she could hear a gurney clattering and a drawer being slid out of the fridge. She moved quickly and quietly over to Peterson's office, Tony following, and pushed down the door handle. She walked straight in, ready with her lines in case he was in there, but he wasn't. She motioned Tony to follow and took a breath. Despite an extra beta blocker her heart was pounding; her shirt was sticking to her back.

Tony got straight to work. Having checked that Peterson hadn't left his machine on and logged in – no such luck – he started to unplug leads and reroute them through his laptop. He set up an external modem and stuck an array of flash drives into both Peterson's machine and his own box of tricks. Pulling up a chair, he said, 'Ever heard of Crack 5 or John the Ripper?'

'No. Should I have?'

'Password-cracking programs, meant to be the best, but the one I've got, they wouldn't see it for dust.' He started tapping on the laptop, his eyes flicking between it and the desktop's screen. 'Does this look suspicious?'

'I'd have to say so, even with the waistcoat.'

'Then you'd better try doing something with the door and open the window.'

Fighting a sensation of panic which was rising despite the heavy wall of medication, Jenny tried to keep her breathing even and shallow as she dragged over the spare chair and wedged it tightly under the door handle. The window was more of a problem: it had a simple pull-down catch and a side hinge but wouldn't open more than a few inches.

Tony said, 'There's a lock on the bottom. There'll be a key around here somewhere.'

She scoured the windowsills and shelves but couldn't find it.

Tony said, 'Guess there's only one way out.'

She flapped the front of her blouse. 'How long's this going to take?'

'A while.'

He was crouched over the laptop, the peak of his cap pulled down over his face. Jenny didn't know what he was doing or how he was doing it, she just wanted it to happen fast, before her nerves gave way.

She tried to distract herself by nosing around Peterson's things. She got the impression his office was somewhere he didn't spend much time. He had five shelves of textbooks and journals, mostly covered in a thick layer of dust, and the same again of box files filled with copy post-mortem reports, but they seemed to peter out two years ago: probably when the hospital intranet went in. His desktop printer was only a small inkjet which wouldn't have coped with more than a few pages.

She guessed the system was designed to keep things paperless and centralized.

On the wall behind his desk was a noticeboard with all the usual corporate regs and a dull calendar from a medical supply company. A couple of snapshots of his daughter's birthday party had been added since her last visit. The way he'd tacked up the birthday photos, at the bottom of the board, felt uncomfortable, like he didn't know if his children's images should share the same space as a lot of dead people. She repeated the thought to herself, dead *people* . . .

Tony glanced up from his keyboard. 'There's eighty-five machines working on the password. I'd like more but America's only just waking up.'

'No clue how long it's going to take?'

They both froze at the sound of footsteps on the tiles outside the door. The door handle rattled, then rattled again. A voice that wasn't Peterson's said, 'He-llo?'

Jenny shot Tony an urgent glance. He twitched his shoulders, passing the problem back to her. She stepped over to the door, tiptoeing on the carpet, and held the chair steady as the handle jiggled a third time. 'Dr Peterson?' It was a local accent, maybe one of the technicians. Jenny felt the sweat drip down her back, gather at her waistband and trickle round towards her stomach. Whoever it was grunted, sounding puzzled, and moved off to the right towards the autopsy room.

Jenny said, 'How long?'

Tony said, 'Ask the machine.'

She scanned the room and started searching – what for, she didn't know. She rifled through each of the drawers in the filing cabinet, checked the two drawers in Peterson's desk, then started on the box files she hadn't already checked. There were invoices from undertakers, supplies contracts, receipts and service agreements for technical equipment and bulletins from the Royal College of Pathologists. Many of the files weren't marked and it looked as if Peterson had stuffed them away without any thought to finding the contents again. A busy man with no assistant to do his legwork.

The door handle rattled again. This time the voice was firmer. 'Hello? Anybody in there?'

Jenny stood still but a file on the end of the row chose that moment to tumble sideways and spill its contents on the floor.

'Open the door. You've got no permission to be in there.'

The rattling became more determined. Jenny rammed the chair harder up against the handle. The man on the other side said, 'I'm calling security.' Jenny heard him hurry across the corridor to the internal phone, shouting through to the autopsy room, 'There's someone in there.'

'Can't you hurry up?'

Tony hit some more keys. 'I think we're getting somewhere.'

Jenny pulled down another two files and tipped the contents on the floor. More invoices, minutes of meetings. She reached up to the shelf again and in the line of dust saw a small Allen key. She picked it up and took it to the window. It opened the lock, the window swung open.

'*Yes.* Got it.'

Jenny spun round. 'What?'

Tony's fingers were flying over the laptop. 'Angel2. Romantic.'

'I want all his documents created in April and May this year.'

Tony hit some more keys and scanned the screen. 'Everything's in the one file.'

'Take it all.'

He yanked out a couple of flash drives, stuck another into the laptop.

More footsteps approached the door, several sets. It was Peterson's voice this time. 'Who's in there? Open up.'

Tony said, 'I've got it,' and started pulling out leads and stuffing them in his pocket. 'Get my machine in the bag.'

Peterson was alternately wrenching at the handle and pounding on the door, the chair legs starting to slip.

Jenny shoved the laptop into its case as Tony grabbed the last of the trailing leads.

'Now what?'

'Out the window.'

Peterson bellowed through, 'OK, this door's coming in.'

Jenny got a foot up on to the sill as the plywood door buckled with the force of a determined shove. Tony stuck a hand against her rear and pushed her. She clattered out on to the tarmac and ran towards Tara's waiting car, Tony chasing after her. Tara pulled out of the space and pushed open the passenger door. Jenny dived in. They were already moving when Tony sprawled into the back seat. Tara moved off at a steady pace, no dramatics.

Jenny glanced in the side mirror and saw Peterson arrive at the window, stick out his head, look left and right, and home in on a black guy unlocking his car opposite.

Lying across the back seat, Tony said, 'I think we'd better call it one-fifty.'

They dropped Jenny off around the corner, where she picked up her Golf, arranging to rendezvous in Patchway McDonald's – Tony's choice. She stopped off at a petrol station to draw out some cash and drove over to their meeting place, the restaurant part of the giant sprawl of American style malls on the north-west fringe of the city.

Alison called as she drew up outside.

'Mrs Cooper?' She sounded worried.

'How are you?'

'Not too good. We've had a visit.'

'The police?'

'No, the local authority. Someone from the legal department called, telling me I'd have to leave the building. They sent two men down to see me out and change the locks. I managed to get a few files into the car but I had to sign a document saying I had no official papers in my possession. I get the feeling I might be out of a job.'

Trying to lift the mood, Jenny said, 'It nearly killed me, but we've got Peterson's files.'

'What do they say?'

'Just about to find out. I'm with Tara and the hacker over at Patchway. Why don't you join us?'

Alison thought about it, then said, 'It's not like I've got anything to lose.'

'What about the package?'

'I called the sorting office – Harry didn't fill out a sender's address, so it's still there. I'll pick it up on the way over.'

Sitting on a plastic chair bolted to the floor, Tony counted out the money, all one hundred and fifty pounds, and said, 'Sweet.'

Tara, sucking milkshake through a straw, smiled across at Jenny, both of them letting him believe he'd hit the big time.

He flipped up the screen on his laptop and stuck in the flash drive containing Peterson's files. They were all stored in the standard 'My Documents' folder and started two years ago. Each file name followed an identical format 'NJP/' for Peterson, then the initials of the deceased, the day, month and year. Jenny took over the mouse and scrolled down to April.

Tara said, 'What exactly are we looking for?'

Jenny found NJP/DW on 16 April and clicked it open. 'Evidence of what Peterson saw when he first looked at Danny's and Katy's bodies. Professor Lloyd thinks he hasn't been telling us the whole truth.'

She was looking at the original of Danny's post-mortem report. It was identical to the one in Marshall's file: a simple finding of asphyxiation due to strangulation consistent with suicide. She closed it and searched on, her eyes running ahead to a file headed NJP/KT dated 1 May. It was Katy's post-mortem report, again, identical to the report she had on file: death by heroin overdose.

'Damn. It's what I've already seen.'

Tony leaned over and pointed halfway down the screen. 'What's NJP/DWAmend?'

Jenny looked at the date: 23 April. She clicked it open.

'Oh, my God . . .'

Tara said, 'What does it say?'

Jenny sat back and turned the screen around so they could both read:

Re-examination of Wills D (14 years)
At the instruction of the Severn Vale Coroner I am today
re-examining the body of a fourteen-year-old boy who was
found hanging by a bed sheet from his cell window in
Portshead Farm Secure Training Centre. On the post-
mortem on 16th of this month I determined the cause of
death as asphyxiation as a result of suicide. The coroner
has requested further examination for evidence of violence
or assault occurring at the time of or prior to death.

On close examination of the subject's torso I note minor
bruising and oedema to the front, mid-section of the chest.
There is further minor bruising and scratching to the
subject's left wrist. On the upper lumbar section of the
subject's back there is evidence of further localized bruising.
Dissection of the area confirms some considerable degree of
force was applied. A further, possibly insignificant finding,
was a small bare patch approximately half an inch across
the rear left side of the subject's scalp.

349

While not remarkable in themselves, taken together,
these injuries may suggest that the subject was placed in
face-down physical restraint at some point prior to death.
Reported cases (such as Reay et al. 1988; O'Halloran and
Lewman 1993) suggest that such restraint techniques, when
applied for a period of several minutes or more, may cause
death by asphyxiation. In my opinion, from the pattern and
bruising and oedema in the subject's face and neck, death
was caused by hanging strangulation. However, in the
absence of flailing injuries – scratches on the neck area
indicating attempts to loosen the ligature etc. – it is
clinically possible that the subject was only partially
conscious, or indeed unconscious, at the time of
asphyxiation.

Jenny sat back in her chair and looked at Tara. 'He had the same injuries as Katy. We're looking for the same killer.'

Tara said, 'Jesus Christ.'

Tony nodded across the restaurant. 'Who's the granny?'

Jenny turned and saw Alison approaching. She looked whiter than death.

Alison wouldn't show Jenny the contents of the package in front of Tony and Tara, so they went into the Ladies. She turned away, avoiding her reflection in the mirror, as Jenny opened the Jiffy bag and pulled out a bunch of A5 stills. Some of the images were blurred at the edges, as if they'd been captured from poor-quality video. They had been taken from a camera mounted in the ceiling of what looked like an average hotel room and were date-coded: 25 April. The first shot showed an overweight middle-aged man lying naked, face up on the bed. Straddling him, also naked, was a beautiful young blonde with short hair and a slender, tapered waist. Only when she reached the shots where the lovers had switched positions did Jenny realize what had seemed strange: the heavenly young creature screwing Harry Marshall's brains out was male.

Attached to the final picture was one of Harry's compliment slips. He had written: *Dear Frank, Your friend. H.*

TWENTY-FOUR

JENNY PUT THE PHOTOGRAPHS AND slip back in the Jiffy bag, trying to find the right words. She settled on, 'I guess you didn't know?'

Alison shook her head, turning back to face her now the pictures were out of sight.

'It makes a few things clearer.'

'He had four daughters.'

'He did well holding it together as long as he did . . . Or perhaps he was confused.'

Alison said, 'I don't want to talk about it now.' She reached for the package.

'Why don't I keep hold of these?'

'What for?'

'Because I can see what you might do with them. They could be useful.'

'I don't see how.'

'They're evidence.'

'I'm not allowing those pictures to be seen.'

'They can't hurt him now. He's dead.'

'What about his family? Why do you think he killed himself?'

'Maybe they'd have preferred him alive and gay? His daughters anyway.'

Alison's expression hardened. 'I want your word that his family won't ever find out about these, Mrs Cooper.'

'I can't—'

The older woman stepped towards her. 'Give them to me.'

Jenny clutched the Jiffy bag tight to her chest. 'You don't even know what I've found ... We've got all Peterson's computer files from the hospital server. On 23 April, he says at Marshall's request he examined Danny Wills's body a second time and found injuries which looked to him like they'd been caused by forced restraint. He says he could even have been strung up before he was dead. Marshall had already known for three days from Justin Bennett that Katy had said Danny was having trouble with one of the staff. The pictures explain what happened next . . .'

Alison eased back, putting the pieces together.

'Harry had two days, the 24th and 25th, the Tuesday and Wednesday before Danny's inquest, when he must have been acting on that information. I'm assuming he didn't tell the police, otherwise you'd have known about it. My guess is he made some more enquiries at Portshead, tried to find out which staff had contact with Danny. Maybe he even told Elaine Lewis what Peterson had found. So, what does she do?'

Alison's eyes dipped towards the envelope in Jenny's hands.

'Right. UKAM go into overdrive. They already know about Harry's tastes – say they've followed him in his car or hacked into his web trails – and set something up for him. A boy he's been with before phones up and says he's short of cash, can they meet in the Novotel, whatever.'

Alison shuddered.

'The next date we've got is the Friday, the 27th. That's when Harry went to his doctor and got himself some pills. I think we can make a solid guess that's just after the pictures arrived. On the Monday he held the inquest: Peterson gave evidence and didn't even mention the second examination.' She paused for breath. 'However we deal with this, Alison, these pictures are going to have to be part of it.'

She looked up and met Jenny's eyes with an expression of wounded resignation. 'You might be right, Mrs Cooper, but don't expect me to say well done. Right now I wish you'd never started down this road.' She turned to go.

'I'd rather you were part of what happens next—'

Alison said, 'I'm not sure you and I could ever understand each other,' and went out of the door.

When Jenny returned to the table, Tara, her eyes lit up with excitement, said, 'So what's the big secret?'

'It seems Marshall had a penchant for young men. He managed to get himself caught on camera two days after Peterson's second report.'

'You're kidding me. You've got pictures?'

Jenny nodded towards Tony. 'I'd rather not.'

'Are you serious?' Tara said. 'There's not a sex act ever performed kids like Tony haven't seen on the internet.'

Tony sucked on his Pepsi, not appearing to mind either way.

Jenny said, 'Not while he's eating.'

Tara rolled her eyes, giving Tony a look. She turned to Jenny. 'We've got a suppressed post-mortem report and some dirty pictures featuring the coroner.' She smiled. 'All you need now is a good journalist. This could be huge. The only question is, how big do you want it to go?'

Jenny thought about it. Having the whole story told across the centre pages had its attractions, but she didn't share Tara's faith in the press. Sure, they'd let her write some righteous investigative copy, but it'd be subbed out of sight. They'd lead on the pictures of Marshall and make it a story about a coroner (they'd call him a 'judge') who buried the truth because he'd been caught having sex with a boy. Danny Wills would barely get a mention, Katy none at all because of the on-going police investigation. Mrs Marshall, bless her, would never be able to show her face again.

Jenny said, 'I'm not going to the press with this.'

'*What?*'

She turned to Tony. 'Can I have a copy of those files?'

He plugged a flash drive into his laptop and hit some keys.

'What other option do you have? You're on a drugs charge, you're suspended from office—'

'I need to think it through.'

Trying to strike a reasonable tone, Tara said, 'Why don't I come over to your place this afternoon? We'll go through what we've got together.' Now she sounded needy: 'I have been on this since the beginning.'

Jenny said, 'I'll call you in the morning. Thanks for your help.'

She took the flash drive and Jiffy bag and left the restaurant. Behind her, she heard Tara, disbelieving, say, 'Jenny? . . . What's your problem? Don't you trust me? I'm the one who's looking at a prison sentence, for Christ's sake.'

She experienced a dulling of the senses that felt like grief, even though she hadn't known Harry. There was something about degraded sex so close to death which disturbed her in a way she could only describe to herself as mental nausea. The way Tara had lit up when she heard about the photographs, almost as if she were aroused, had made her want to run away and find some clear space, somewhere uncontaminated, to breathe.

Leaving the English side of the bridge and heading out towards Wales, she wound down all four windows. The earlier rain had passed over, it was a clear late afternoon and the air rushing through her hair was warm. She willed what she was feeling to blow away and sweep off out to sea, but it stuck fast.

As she passed Chepstow racecourse the sun retreated behind the clouds and the valley closed in. The woods on either side of the road were dense and forbidding, the trigger for a sensation of dread which started as a pinpoint in her solar plexus and spread outwards, seizing her chest and torso, blasting through the barricade of pills. She tried the steady controlled breath, *my right arm is heavy*, but it merely held her on the brink of a panic attack. Somewhere she heard Dr Allen's voice reminding her to pull over if she felt this way, but as she rounded the tight hairpin a mile after St Arvans she realized the only spot was the lay-by she stopped at before. It lay half a mile ahead and became the focus of her fear: the intense kind she'd tried to describe to her uncomprehending ex-husband as like facing not certain death, but nothingness; an empty space in which there was no possibility for life or hope or joy or any sensation at all.

Her fingernails digging deep into the steering wheel, she tried another way: face the fear and let the tide wash through. *Come on, you bastard, give me what you've got.* She touched the brakes, dropping her speed, and let it come. The ring around her diaphragm tightened, her vision narrowed to a blurred tunnel and her ears filled with a static buzz as the electrical pulses shot up her spine and through her skull. She clung to the threads of consciousness – *Come on, come on and take me, you evil bastard* – then felt the plunge, like falling off a cliff, and slewed across the road into the opposite carriage-way. Snatching a breath, she jerked the wheel left, staring down the tunnel, seeing a whirl of trees. A cold rush over the top of her head and down her back as she approached the lay-by, fighting an invisible hand stronger than hers trying to pull the car over and into the woods. She fought it, jamming her foot on the throttle, and cleared the next bend . . .

And she'd done it, taken all the adrenalin and cortisol her body could spew out. She was drained, exhausted and shaking, but still driving, still alive.

The relief was short-lived. Making the turn to Melin Bach and starting up the lane, her fear shifted from what might lie in the darkness of the woods to being alone in her home with the old disgruntled ghost. It was a child's fear, no different from the terror of a dark basement or a malevolent stranger, and all the pleading of her rational adult mind wouldn't dissolve it. When she arrived outside, too afraid to turn off the engine, her eye was drawn to the bedroom window, where she felt sure she'd seen a lined and disapproving face swiftly retreating.

She was too frustrated with herself to cry, too conflicted between self-loathing and self-pity to find such easy relief. She *knew* from countless expensive hours on the couch that this was something that had to be faced, that her mind was suffering a chain reaction: past hidden trauma fuelled by current anxieties sending her nervous system into neurotic seizures. If she could only force herself inside she could check each room and prove to herself there was no ghost, but after yesterday she was, she realized, equally frightened of herself. A glass of wine to dull the anxiety and she might lose grip again, find herself lining up her stash of temazepam.

At least she was sane enough to see her situation as it was: pressed hard up against the membrane between life and death, she could see glimpses of the other side and, in knowing it, felt its tug.

She had friends, only a handful who knew what she'd been through, but none she could ask to come running. She picked her handbag up from the passenger seat and reached for her many bottles of pills. She settled on a beta blocker. As she unscrewed the lid, she asked herself why she needed drugs to see her boyfriend. The answer came as she swallowed: she was scared she was falling for him. Another person in her life to let down.

She pulled up in his yard next to the Land Rover. The canvas was off the back, which was stacked with fresh bales of hay.

Alfie lay in the sun in the dust by the gate, keeping an eye on a hen scratching with a new brood of chicks. Recognizing her, the sheepdog thumped his tail, barely lifting his head. Over in one of the sheds was a beaten-up old Peugeot with the bonnet up, tools lying nearby.

She rang the brass ship's bell that hung at the side of the already half-open front door. There was a sound of movement from somewhere inside. She stepped over the threshold into the kitchen: old quarry tiles and pale oak cupboards. Beyond it, the layout was semi-open plan to a wooden spiral staircase and living room.

'Steve? It's Jenny.'

The noises came from upstairs, a woman's voice in whispered protest, then a guilty silence. She glanced at the table and saw two cups, an empty packet of cigarettes across from his tobacco, next to a set of car keys dangling a bunch of plastic charms.

'Fuck you. Fuck you, Steve.' Her shouts echoed around the bare walls and up the stairs.

She hurled the table on to its side and slammed out.

Spinning her tyres in the rough gravel, Jenny caught sight of the figure in the upstairs window: Annie, annoyed, pulling on her bra.

Her anger propelled her inside. She screamed at the ghost to go to hell and unscrewed a litre of cheap Italian red, taking her first pull straight from the bottle. There. A few good mouthfuls on an empty stomach and she was battle-ready, not afraid of anything. Screw Steve, screw his lies and his dead-end girlfriend. Screw everything. From now on it was going to be Jenny first and last. She'd sort out her cases, blow UKAM apart and get her life back, all on her terms.

She tipped out her handbag and found the beta blockers and antidepressants, emptied them into the sink and ran the hot tap until they were small enough to push down the plughole. She didn't need pills; it was other people's junk, not her own, that had brought her down. What she needed was to fight back, let the world know who she was. She'd hold on to a few tranquillizers, just to keep her anger from boiling over so she didn't kill anyone, but that was the only reason. She was too wild, too close to the truth, for people to handle her, that was her problem. Poor, weak people, too frightened to face the truth.

She took the wine and a glass through to the study. It was obvious now what had to be done: she'd write a formal, scholarly report that would set out in devastating detail the cover-up over Danny's death. Marshall's suicide would have to be part of it, but she didn't feel so sorry for him now. He'd paid the price for being weak and his family would have to live with it. She'd send a copy to the Ministry of Justice, one to the local authority, one to the Severn Vale District Hospital Trust and another to Simone Wills, and lodge one with a solicitor. If a new inquest wasn't held which brought the full truth to light she'd deal with the newspapers personally, and tie them up in a contract so tight they couldn't change a word of her copy.

She sat at her laptop for four hours without looking up from the screen, drafting and editing until her report read like a House of Lords judgement. She'd worked through the wine and needed a little something extra before proofreading. In the back of a kitchen cupboard was a half-bottle of brandy that was meant to be used for cooking. She poured two inches into a tumbler and had a taste. It was good, warm all the way down. She topped up her glass and brought it through.

She must have been staring at the screen harder than she thought, because the words merged when she tried to read a printed copy. She rummaged around for the glasses she always resisted wearing and tried again. Better, but not much. She must be tired. One read through and hit the sack, set the alarm for five a.m., make sure her pristine report was on all relevant desks at start of business. Then sit back and wait for the phone calls, maybe do some work around the garden to pass the time.

She was shutting down her computer when her landline rang. It was nearly eleven. She pictured Steve, huddled in a phone box, full of beer and remorse, wanting to come up and spill his heart out, tell her that he was in love. She let it continue and when it fell silent picked up the receiver to check the caller's number. It wasn't Steve, it was Ross's mobile. She remembered she hadn't called him all week. *How could she have forgotten?* She punched in his number.

'Ross?'

'Mum. How are you?'

'Good. What about you?'

'OK. A few more days to freedom.'

'Of course. Hey, sorry I haven't called—'

'It's OK. I know what happened.'

Jenny stalled, not sure how to explain herself, where to begin.

Ross said, 'Allowing your place to be used, that's not a crime, is it?'

'Apparently so. Not a very serious one.'

'I bet you didn't even know what he was smoking.'

'No . . .' She cringed at her lie.

'I guess you'll get off, then. It's not like you've got a record.' He gave an ironic laugh. 'You should've heard Dad. He thinks you've turned me into a delinquent.'

'I'll tell you what really happened in a day or two. I've been working on a couple of cases.'

He was quiet for a moment. 'Are you OK, Mum? Dad says . . .'

'What? . . . What does he say?'

'It doesn't matter.'

Jenny sighed, a familiar guilt welling up. 'I'm sorry to put you through this. It'll work out . . . Give it a couple of weeks. I just want you to get through your exams without worrying about me.'

'What about next term, do you still want me to come over and stay?'

'Of course.'

He fell into another silence.

'Ross? What's the matter? . . . What's your father been saying? Tell me.'

'I'm fine. You know what he's like.'

'I need to know . . . I promise I'm not going to pick a fight with him.'

'He thinks . . . he thinks you're not very well. He keeps saying you need help but you're too stubborn to get it.'

'Oh, really? Does he say what for?' Her words came out sounding sharper than she intended. 'Sorry . . .'

'Just forget I said it. I was just worried, that's all.'

'Well, don't be. I'm fine.'

'But you don't sound it.'

'Honestly.' Through the gap in the curtains she noticed headlights pulling up outside. She tugged them back and saw the outline of an expensive saloon, like nothing Steve would drive. Two male figures climbed out.

'After my exams, can I come and stay? . . . I could help with your place.' He sounded concerned.

'That'd be great . . .' She heard footsteps on the path, two solid strikes of the knocker. 'Ross, can I call you right back? There's someone at the door.'

'This late?'

'I think it'll be something to do with work.'

'Yeah, right. Check what he's smoking this time.'

'Ross—' He rang off. Hearing the dial tone made her want to cry.

The knocker sounded again, louder this time. Who the hell could it be at this time of night? Detectives? A process server? She grabbed the flash drive from her laptop and scanned the room for a place to hide it. Another two knocks. She went out to the hall, reached up and tucked it in the narrow gap between the top of the door frame and the plaster where she kept a spare key.

She called through the closed door, 'Who is it?'

'Open up, Mrs Cooper.' The voice was hard and abrupt, like a policeman's.

'Tell me who you are and I might think about it.'

The sound of smashing glass came from the kitchen. Jenny spun round and pulled the living-room door shut, but there was no key in the hallway side of the lock.

Another crash of glass in the study. She jerked round to see a gloved hand reach in and pull back the catch on the sash. She dived for the stairs, but stumbled on the first tread and cracked her knee hard. *Shit.* She groped for the banister as the two men appeared behind her at once. The shorter one was squat, fortyish, muscular, in a waist-length jacket, greying hair cropped short. He grabbed her arm and yanked her upright on to the hall floor, her shoulder feeling like it had popped from its socket. The taller of the two, dark, craggy-featured, sank a heavy fist into her stomach, taking the wind out of her. She dropped, choking, to her knees; the shorter one back-fisted her hard across the face. She felt her head crack against the flags and tasted the blood pouring from her nose. She lay with her legs twisted under her but with no strength to move.

The shorter one, fading in and out of focus, leaned over her, his hands on his thighs. 'If you want to live, Jenny, you know what to do.'

She sucked in a breath, blood clogging her throat. He straightened and kicked her sharply between the legs, a pain that split her pelvis.

'You'll fucking leave it alone.'

She didn't feel the boot hit her chin, only her neck snapping back like a whip as the lights went out.

Steve said he found her face down on the living-room floor, a cushion under her head. He'd driven over just after midnight and seen the window smashed, computer leads and pieces of paper strewn across the front garden. He rode with her in the ambulance, holding her hand while she tried to tell him through a jaw she could barely move what had happened. He said not to worry, the police were already at the house and could see it was a robbery.

They took her to Newport General and loaded her with painkillers. She drifted in and out of consciousness as several pairs of hands lifted her this way and that under the X-ray machine. As they wheeled her back along the corridor, she saw Steve smile down at her with tired red eyes and say it looked like good news, nothing broken, just knocked about. She heard a doctor tell him he couldn't stay, there were people asleep on the ward where they were taking her. She heard him ask where in the building he could wait out the night. A woman's voice said the only place was the waiting room in A&E.

Jenny squeezed his hand. All she could manage was a whisper. 'I want to speak to Williams.'

TWENTY-FIVE

THE HOSPITAL SHOWER SMELT OF disinfectant but the water was hot and got into her aching muscles. Everything she moved hurt: her legs, her torso, her left shoulder and her jaw. The right side of her face was bruised like a boxer's and she had a swollen lump the size of half an orange on her pubic bone. She tried to cross her wrists on the wall and lean her head against them but she couldn't raise her arm up. All she could do was stand upright under the jet, leaning slightly to make the water change its course.

In a strange way she felt grateful for the physical pain, it seemed to bring her mental turmoil to the surface, like a boil rising to a head. Whatever chemicals her body churned out to create sensations of panic seemed to be fully occupied combating her more immediate trauma. She was in physical agony, but her mind felt almost peaceful, happy at the uncomplicated simplicity of her current struggle.

Steve was waiting at her bedside when she limped slowly back into the ward. He looked at her as if she was a terminal case. 'How are you?'

'Alive.'

'I spoke to Williams. He's going to come in shortly.'

'Thanks. I might have to go and see him first.' She eased into a sitting position on the bed. 'They don't waste any sympathy here, said I can go.'

'That's crazy.'

'Hang around too long in these places you catch something. Believe me, hospitals are fatal.' She tried to reach for her clothes, folded in the nightstand. 'I might need a hand.'

He glanced up and down the ward for a nurse. 'I'll go and find someone.'

'Just pull the curtain. It's nothing you haven't seen before.'

He tried not to look as he helped her into clean knickers and jeans and clipped up her bra. She felt his anxiety and guilt but was happy to let him stew in it for a while. He didn't ask any questions and nor did she, not till she was dressed and brushing her hair with her good arm.

'Does Annie know you're here?'

'What happened yesterday was a mistake. There was a problem with her car. I didn't even know she was coming over.'

'It's your life, Steve, you can do what you like. Just don't expect me to stand in line.'

'If it makes any difference, I didn't even—'

She cut him off with a look.

He said, 'I'm going to sort it with her, tell her it's all over. For good, Jenny.'

'I was going to ask you to come back to my place last night.' Jesus. She couldn't believe she could be so manipulative. What was she *doing*?

She was looking for a reaction, that's what. She watched him agonize, regret and shame on his face.

'I'm sorry.' He touched her hand. 'I mean it.'

She pulled away. 'I need to get to a phone. I want to call that detective.'

They rode back to her house in a taxi in uneasy silence, neither of them knowing how to take the next step, no sexual charge to break the ice. When they arrived she expected him to make his excuses and go, but he surprised her. He helped her from the cab into the house, made her comfortable on the sofa and fetched her breakfast while she waited for Williams to arrive. She had to admit he knew how to behave when he had to. There was hope.

The intruders had taken her computer and several boxes of papers, none of which had anything to do with Danny's or Katy's case, but they hadn't found the flash drive, which Steve fetched from its hiding place in the door frame, nor had they picked up the photographs of Marshall that still lay on the passenger seat of her Golf, which was parked at the side of the house. When Williams arrived with a young male detective in tow, he was able to fetch his police-issue paving slab of a laptop from his car and look at Peterson's files. With Steve hovering at the kitchen door, she talked through the events of the previous fortnight, telling them her theory that once Harry Marshall had Peterson's second report, UKAM had gone for him, and possibly Peterson, too. The fact that Peterson hadn't even produced a written report on Katy's post-mortem until weeks later suggested he'd found himself in a quandary: he hadn't wanted to commit a misleading report to paper. If further proof were needed, the two people who had come anywhere close to the truth, her and Tara Collins, had both found themselves facing criminal charges. All right, Steve was smoking dope, but a man meeting the description of one of her attackers had been at the local pub gathering information in the days beforehand. She'd lay money on him being Williams's informer.

The Welsh detective listened impassively, taking careful notes and asking few questions. When he looked at the photographs of Harry and the boy, he lowered his eyes and shook his head, genuinely appalled.

'I take it Mr Marshall's wife doesn't know about these?'

'No.'

'We'll do our best to keep it that way, shall we?'

Jenny found herself nodding, infected by his moral certainty.

He read back through his notes, getting the sequence cemented in his mind. He turned and spoke to his young colleague in whispered Welsh, conferring with him for some time before turning back to her.

'Obviously what you've told us, Mrs Cooper, could mean a very serious and involved criminal investigation. You're alleging a far-reaching conspiracy – a many-headed hydra, you could say.'

'It all goes back to the same source.'

He nodded, rubbing a finger along his carefully trimmed moustache. 'You see, what concerns me is the jurisdictional issue. Obviously, for some reason best known to themselves, our colleagues in England haven't chosen to investigate the death of Miss Taylor with what you might call appropriate rigour—'

'I'd guess that was a political rather than a police issue. We're talking millions of pounds' worth of prison-building contracts.'

'Very few of them in Wales, I'm sure.' He smiled, inviting her trust. 'What I'm thinking is that if for the time being you were to make a statement relating purely to the assault and break-in you suffered last night, we can start our wider inquiry under the radar, if you like.'

'I'm not sure I follow.'

Williams tilted his head, patient. 'Which police force investigates what crime can be a thorny issue. If what you're telling me is true, I'm sure both of us would like to avoid the situation where the Bristol police are charged with investigating all these matters. Not that I'm in any way a racist, you understand, but I wouldn't trust those English bastards further than I could pee.'

'You want to go after UKAM alone?'

He smiled with his eyes. 'It's been a slow couple of years to tell you the truth, Mrs Cooper. I could do with the excitement.'

'Mr Williams, I could do with having my job back.'

The detective nodded, as if he'd already given this some thought. 'My colleagues in the CPS might be persuaded.' Then, turning to Steve, his face reddening, 'But I'll tell you this, Mr Painter – another whiff of that filth on my patch and I'll have your bloody head.'

Steve, catching Jenny's eye, said, 'Point taken.'

After the detectives had gone, Steve came and sat on the arm of the chair opposite, his movements edgy, as if he wasn't sure that he was still welcome. Jenny, focused on a sharp new pain that was piercing her shoulder, ignored him while she clumsily popped another dose of painkillers out of the foil strip the hospital had given her.

Trying to make conversation, he said, 'Did you see how angry he got there, in like half a second? I've only seen the Welsh do that . . . and maybe Italians.'

Jenny said, 'That's probably where it comes from. There's lots of Italians in Wales. They came in the nineteenth century, when the place was booming.'

'Yeah? I didn't know that.'

He watched her swallow her pills with the cold dregs of her tea.

She coughed and, between swearing at the pain it caused her, said, 'Don't feel you have to hang around. I can move enough to take care of my bodily functions.'

'I don't think you should be alone.'

'You want to sit here all day?'

'Look, I meant what I said about what happened yesterday . . .'

'Why not admit that when she came looking you couldn't say no?'

'I'm going to. From now on. That's what I want you to know.'

'Good for you.' She lifted her legs up on to the cushions, trying to get comfortable.

'Won't you give me a chance?'

She glanced over him, unimpressed. 'At what?'

'Whatever you want . . .'

She shrugged. 'I don't want anything.' Whether she meant it or not, it felt like the right thing to say. 'I'll be honest with you, I'm not interested in love, commitment or talking about the future. It's all bullshit.'

'You turned my kitchen over because I was upstairs with another woman.'

'I'm neurotic. I've been seeing a psychiatrist for two years.'

'You're really doing a good sell.'

'What I'm saying, Steve, is I'm not interested in your self-control problems or any other kind, I've got enough of my own.'

He nodded, hurt. 'So what's the deal, are we still sleeping with each other?'

'Have you seen where I got kicked?'

He got up from the chair and reached down for her dirty teacup. 'Why don't you try to get some rest?'

He woke her from a restless doze and offered her the phone – Williams was asking to speak to her. She groaned, as every joint and muscle had stiffened during her fitful sleep. Steve told her not to move and held the phone to her ear.

Williams said, 'I've had a word with the local CPS and they've reviewed the situation.'

'What does that mean?'

'They've decided not to proceed against you as the case isn't the strongest, but they're rather expecting a guilty plea from Mr Painter for possession.'

She glanced at Steve. 'I'm sure that'll be fine.'

'Excellent. I'll pass it on.'

'Could you ask them to put it in writing? I need to get a copy to the Ministry of Justice. I've got an inquest due to restart Monday morning.'

'Certainly. And if there's anything I can do to assist . . .?'

'I'll be in touch.'

Steve said, 'Well?'

She smiled and handed him the phone. 'You've got a chance to show me what you're really made of. What's the time?'

'Two o'clock. How?'

'I'll tell you while you're driving me to the station. First help me put some decent clothes on.'

'Where are you going?'

'London.'

'In your state?'

'I'll survive.'

She called Simon Moreton's office from the car and was answered by a PA, who said he was in a meeting until the end of the day, could she try again on Monday? Jenny said there was an urgent letter on his fax machine that she needed to discuss with him this afternoon; it concerned a high-profile inquest that was due to resume on Monday. When the PA said she doubted if he'd have time to read a letter, let alone arrange an unscheduled meeting, Jenny said, 'If you'd be kind enough to tell him that Jenny Cooper, the Severn Vale District Coroner, will be in his office by five p.m., I'm sure he'll find a moment.'

Selborne House was one of the strip of identically soulless glass and concrete offices that lined Victoria Street on the approach to Parliament Square. It was the kind of building that would normally have made her claustrophobic, but the single temazepam she'd taken during the journey was keeping panic at bay. Her nerves weren't as steady as they had been on antidepressants and beta blockers, but she was at least feeling emotions she could distinguish. The PA, a tight-lipped woman in her late fifties, met her in reception and walked briskly to the lift with the minimum of chat, passing no comment on Jenny's bruised face or the painful awkwardness with which she limped behind her. Ascending to the fifth floor in impatient silence, Jenny sensed her acute disapproval, leaving her in no doubt that her arrival was being treated as a rogue and eccentric event.

She had been waiting nearly twenty minutes when Moreton arrived, a fresh copy of the letter from the Newport branch of the Crown Prosecution Service in his hand. He looked tired at the end of a long week, and seemed equally troubled and embarrassed by her presence. Like his PA, no mention of her battered face.

'I see you've had some good news, Mrs Cooper.' He dithered over where to sit at the large conference table, settling on the chairman's seat at its head. 'Do you have any notion what prompted it?'

'I think they must have believed I told them the truth. I didn't know what my guest was smoking in his cigarettes.'

Moreton gave an amused smile. 'Even I know what marijuana smells like.'

'Smoking it seems to be a requirement for high government office these days – seven cabinet ministers at the last count.'

'Politicians come and go, Mrs Cooper. A coroner is a permanent fixture.'

Staying calm, surprising herself, Jenny said, 'A coroner can only be removed from office for misbehaviour in the discharge of her duty. I am facing no criminal charges and I have not misbehaved in my professional capacity.'

'A moot point.'

'Could you be specific?'

'You were about to make public a commercially sensitive tender document. You would have jeopardized our entire prison-building programme. At the very least, tenders would have had to be resubmitted and the public would have borne the cost.'

Jenny felt like telling him what she thought of his building programme, but contained her anger enough to reply, 'I sincerely apologize for that error of judgement, Mr Moreton, and would ask you to put that down to overzealousness at the start of my tenure. I can assure you that I won't be making any such mistakes in future.'

'I'd like to accept that reassurance, Mrs Cooper, but when a coroner makes such a grave miscalculation . . .'

'I have given over fifteen years' public service working for a provincial local authority in childcare law when I could have made three times my salary in private practice. No one could accuse me of not having a sense of duty.'

'Of course not.'

'I admit, I may have been swayed by emotion, but if I've learned one thing from this experience it's that being a coroner requires a level of detachment that I haven't been used to. I will endeavour to exercise that in future.' She held his gaze, aware of his eyes dipping to the inch of cleavage she was showing, and gave him the subtle look which said she didn't mind.

'We are aware—' He faltered slightly, his face pinking. 'Your records show that you had some "personal" difficulties towards the end of your time in your previous position.'

'I had had a serially unfaithful husband who sued me for custody of our son. It was a miracle I could work at all.' She kept her eyes on him.

'I see.'

'I'm not simply asking to be reinstated; I'd welcome your help and encouragement over the coming months. A coroner can feel very isolated with no immediate colleague to support her.'

Moreton nodded slowly. Jenny could tell he was already picturing day trips to Bristol, lunch on expenses, touching her legs under the table. He said, 'What happened to your face, if you don't mind my asking?'

'I had an encounter with burglars. So much for retreating to the country.'

'How dreadful.'

'Nothing broken. It could have been worse.'

'Yes . . .' He glanced at his watch. 'You must be in a need of a drink. I don't have to be on my way for half an hour.'

'Maybe just one.'

He took her to a wine bar across the road and bought a thirty-pound bottle of Pouilly Fumé which came in an ice bucket. Out of the office he wasn't bad company, pointing out the different cliques who occupied separate corners of the bar: the civil servants in cheap suits and no ties, the TV people in designer glasses and goatees who weren't allowed to dress a day over thirty no matter how old they were, and the handful of politicians and their snaky advisers who were always either on the phone or looking over their companions' shoulders for more important ears to bend.

It wasn't what she had expected of high public office, showing off her assets to a repressed civil servant, leading him on, but it did the trick. Moreton put in a call to the Lord Chancellor's office and, as he poured out the last of the bottle, got a call back saying there was no objection to her reinstatement.

Looking at him over her glass, Jenny said, 'You won't stop me concluding the Danny Wills inquest next week? I feel it's the least we do for his mother to bring it all to an end.'

'I'm sure you'll handle it expertly, Jenny.'

She felt the warmth of his knee hovering an inch or two away from hers. She moved slightly, allowing them to touch for a moment.

TWENTY-SIX

ALISON'S HUSBAND ANSWERED THE PHONE and said she wasn't well, not feeling herself at all. He was delighted to hear that things were returning to normal but he wasn't sure she'd make it in for a few days, they'd have to see how she was. He was kindly and apologetic but Jenny detected a trace of exasperation, his ambiguous use of words giving away the story: Alison sunk in a depression he couldn't understand or penetrate, telling him just to leave her alone when he came to the bedroom door with his latest theories on what was ailing her.

Without her help it would take the whole weekend to organize a reconvened inquest for Monday, but if she left it any later the element of surprise would be gone and the witnesses she wanted back would have time to get their stories straight. She wanted the jury to see them on the back foot, to watch them stumble and then confess as she ripped the truth out of them, getting the job done before anything else could derail her.

During the train journey back to Bristol she tried to raise someone from Grantham's department with authority to let her back in her office. Getting only a succession of answer machines, she finally reached an architect from the office upstairs at his home. Amazing herself at the ease with which she could lie, she explained that she'd had her bag stolen in a burglary and needed to get through the front door to have the locks changed before the thieves struck again. It worked. She collected a copy of the front door key from him at his mews house in Clifton village, then jumped back into a cab to meet with an emergency locksmith at the office. By ten p.m. she was inside and back in charge.

It was gone midnight when she hobbled into the house with a holdall full of files, aching all over and feeling anxious again. She hadn't taken any pills for over eight hours. During the taxi ride back she'd found herself hoping Steve would be there waiting for her, but there was only the lingering smell of his cigarette smoke and a scribbled note: *Hope it's good news. You know where to find me. S x*. She studied the *x*, looking for clues as to whether he'd written it without thinking or it really meant something. She was tempted to drive over now but thought it might look too eager, build up his ego when he should be feeling ashamed. She'd wait for him to come past tomorrow, and when he did she'd set another condition for sharing her bed – he'd have to get a telephone.

She was eating a late breakfast at the table on the lawn and leaving a message for Ross with the good news when a police squad car pulled up on the cart track. Williams climbed out of the passenger door. The female constable who had been one of the search team earlier in the week waited in the driver's seat. Williams apologized for disturbing her but thought she'd want to know that he had a lead on her intruders: a black Mercedes 320 had been clocked on a speed camera further up the valley a few minutes after she'd said the break-in happened. There were two men in the front seat and the car had been hired from a firm in Bristol. It was paid for by a company credit card: the firm was called TRK Ltd. It was a shell with no official turnover, but its sole director was a one-time employee of a private security company wholly owned by UKAM. Williams had a couple of men out looking for him now.

Jenny said, 'You'd think they'd have covered their tracks more carefully.'

'They were banking on you not making a fuss, but to be on the safe side you might want to spend the next couple of nights in a hotel, at least until we catch up with them. It might be an idea to tell your son to keep a lookout, too.'

She nodded, a wave of anxiety passing through her as she realized the enormity of what she was taking on. 'I'm planning on trying to resume my inquest on Monday. It's going to ruffle a lot of feathers. I'm summoning the director of Portshead Farm, some of the staff, Frank Grantham, Dr Peterson . . .'

'I've been thinking about that, Mrs Cooper. I was wondering if you might consider a change of venue?'

'I'm not even sure what the venue is yet. I lost my courtroom when I was suspended.'

'Would it be fair to say that you're anticipating a certain lack of cooperation?'

'What did you have in mind?'

'Let's imagine you held it on this side of the water, in Chepstow, say. My boys could make sure your witnesses turn up, and if any of them drag their heels it gives us the chance to go and get them. And once we're lawfully on a premises —'

'You can look around all you like.'

Williams smiled.

She packed a suitcase with enough clothes for several days and loaded them, along with her files and textbooks, into the boot of her Golf. She braced herself to call David and tried to explain the situation as calmly as possible. He replied coldly that he'd never realized the job of coroner could be so eventful, implying that only she, the ultimate drama queen, could have contrived to make it so. She would have pointed that out to him if she hadn't also detected a note of jealousy: if his screwy ex-wife was presiding over important and dangerous cases it meant she was in danger of eclipsing him. Which one of them would have their son's respect then?

Steve wasn't in when she drove by on her way out, so she left him a note: *Success. Working all weekend and staying in town. Call me. J* – she hesitated, then added an *x*.

She spent the morning in Chepstow securing a courtroom. At Williams's suggestion she hired a church hall set back from the high street and tracked down a retired usher from the County Court, Arvel Hughes, a precise, ex-military man and stalwart of many local committees, who agreed to stand in as coroner's officer. The afternoon was taken up with drafting summonses in the office, each one of which had to contain sufficient 'conduct money', in cash, to get the witness to court. The list for day one included Justin Bennett, the CCTV operator Darren Hogg, Kevin Stewart, Elaine Lewis, Dr Peterson and Frank Grantham.

Her next task was to locate a firm of process servers who could be persuaded to turn out on a Saturday night for anything less than a four-figure fee. After working through most of the firms in the *Yellow Pages*, she finally succeeded with a one-man outfit in St Pauls who agreed to do it for five hundred cash. She was one of Her Majesty's Coroners, an official with powers on a par with a High Court judge, but late in the evening she found herself counting out tenners for the greaseball who'd pulled up outside her office and tooted her, too lazy to climb out of his car. Her early days in court injuncting drunk and violent fathers had been more glamorous. Once the summonses were dispatched, she had to phone every juror and give them painstaking directions to the new and obscure venue, telling them yes, they would be getting lunch. Her last call, one she'd been putting off, was to Simone Wills.

The phone was answered by a boy of about ten or eleven who said his mum was upstairs. There were younger kids screaming in the background, competing with the TV. Jenny said would he mind going to fetch her, it was important. The boy said he couldn't at the moment, she was with Kenny.

'I can wait a minute.'

The boy said OK and set the phone down on a hard surface. He shouted up the stairs that there was someone on the phone but didn't get an answer. Over the yelling toddlers and cartoons, Jenny heard a woman's moans and a thump-thump going in time with them. She decided to leave it until the morning. Simone obviously had other things on her mind.

She had never felt as alone as she did sitting in the office at the back of the hall decorated with pictures of Noah and his ark. She'd spent two nights away from home in this small Welsh town and had had only one message from Steve, to say congratulations on getting her job back. He would have come over and seen her only he'd picked up a few days' forestry work and needed the money. She had detected an edge in his voice: she had things to do, so had he. Alison hadn't called and nor had Moreton. The only person who had was Williams, and he was beginning to worry her: he was so eager to stick it to the English, she'd had to tell him to calm down and make sure not to be too heavy-handed. Her isolation had, however, allowed her to realize something about her own motives. It was no longer just about getting justice for Danny Wills or Katy Taylor; she wanted to do it properly, she wanted to be Jenny Cooper, the coroner, and be successful at it. Respected.

She had taken a single temazepam and had a tube of primed mints in her pocket. Short of sleep and scared, the medication was barely touching her. Her heartbeat was up, her palms were clammy and her tongue felt too big for her mouth. She should have found a doctor over the weekend and replaced the pills she had thrown down the sink, but she'd convinced herself she'd be so fired up she wouldn't need them. It had made perfect sense in a hotel room, but about to hold court she couldn't see how she'd get through.

Arvel's funereal footsteps approached on the other side of the door. He knocked twice.

'Come in.' The words stuck in her throat.

The seventy-year-old entered and stood to attention, wearing a regimental blazer and tie beneath his usher's gown, grey hair slicked down, shoes gleaming. 'We're ready for you now, ma'am.'

She stepped into the roomy, high-ceilinged hall, which had been built in Victorian times as a school room and still conveyed a sense of grim purpose. Her table, draped with green baize, was positioned by itself, a good twelve feet away from a row of desks spanning nearly the entire width of the hall at which sat a row of aggressive, indignant-looking lawyers. Hartley held pole position in the centre.

To her right, occupying two rows of four chairs, sat the jury. The rest of the hall was crammed with hungry journalists. Simone Wills and two friends, women Jenny remembered from the adjourned hearing, were squeezed on to the end of a row, shooting angry looks at the reporters invading their space. There was no sign of any UKAM executives and the only one of the summoned witnesses she could see was Justin Bennett, wedged in by the door. Jenny took her seat with a growing sense of unreality. A hundred pairs of eyes fixed on her.

Keeping it brief to hide the tremor in her voice, she thanked everyone for their patience during the adjournment and said she hoped their business could now be concluded swiftly. She could see Hartley trying to catch her eye, eager to take the stage, but made him wait, turning to Arvel, who had tucked himself at a desk with a tape recorder to her left, between her and the lawyers.

'Mr Hughes, have each of the witnesses answered their summons?'

He stood up and bowed in a studied display of deference. 'No, ma'am.' He read from his clipboard through reading glasses. 'Mr Justin Bennett is present; witnesses Mrs Elaine Lewis, Dr Nicholas Peterson, Mr Frank Grantham, Mr Darren Hogg and Mr Kevin Stewart have failed to attend.'

'Thank you.' Jenny turned to the lawyers. She counted two counsel apart from Hartley and four instructing solicitors. 'I take it some of these parties are represented here this morning.'

Hartley, their nominated leader, got to his feet. 'Ma'am, as you know, I represent UKAM Secure Solutions Ltd and by agreement Mrs Elaine Lewis—'

'Not Mr Hogg or Mr Stewart?'

'No, ma'am. I have received no instructions to do so. Indeed, I had no idea they had been summoned until this morning. I think it's fair to say that, given recent events, this resumed hearing came as rather a surprise to most of us in this room.'

Ignoring his attempt to embarrass her, Jenny said, 'Perhaps you could ask your instructing solicitors to find out where they are? I have certificates from the process server confirming that documents and conduct monies were delivered to their home addresses on Saturday evening. As their employers, your clients have to let them comply with this court's request even if it means missing work.'

'I can assure you my clients are perfectly aware of their obligations—'

'Then where is Mrs Lewis?' Jenny heard herself snap like a schoolmistress, her tension spilling over into irritation.

'Mrs Lewis is in Washington, DC, ma'am, on an extended business trip expected to last several weeks.'

'She received her summons in person thirty-six hours ago. If you're telling me she has left the country since, then I'll have to treat it as contempt.'

Hartley said, 'Firstly, I would like to extend my client's sincere apologies for not being able to defer her trip, and secondly, I would ask you to consider a less drastic course of action, namely taking evidence from her, should it be necessary, via a video link. The use of such technology has been encouraged by the Lord Chief Justice in recent practice directions.'

Several of the other lawyers smiled at Hartley's subtle jibe at the primitive facilities in the make-do courtroom.

Jenny held her temper. 'You will provide me with details of her current whereabouts and I will apply to the High Court for a warrant for her arrest.'

She knew that a UK coroner had no power to issue a warrant with effect beyond the borders of the UK, a fact which UKAM's lawyers had doubtless confirmed to their anxious clients some time late on Saturday night. To repatriate Elaine Lewis would involve a lengthy and costly procedure which a team of highly paid lawyers in the US courts could postpone indefinitely.

Assured of his client's safety, Hartley said, 'I will gladly furnish those details to your officer,' and resumed his seat, omitting to bow.

Next on his feet was a foppish young barrister in a hand-stitched pinstripe suit who attempted an imitation of Hartley's attitude of mild disdain. He announced himself as Henry Golding representing Dr Peterson, who, he said, was seeking a clarification of the issues on which he was being asked to give evidence. Having already testified, Golding argued that his client was entitled to know exactly why he was being called back. And if the answer to that raised any controversial issues he was instructed to seek an adjournment on the grounds that Peterson's computer files had recently been hacked into and disturbed. It would be impossible for him to refer to any of them, Golding assured her, until their integrity had been established beyond all shadow of doubt.

Confident she was on firm ground, Jenny said, 'Mr Golding, you have given no lawful excuse for your client's failure to answer his summons and the questions I wish to ask him are about a body he examined only a few weeks ago.'

With a smile he clearly considered endearing, Golding said that, with respect, Dr Peterson was carrying out up to half a dozen post-mortems per day. He couldn't be expected to recall details of a case he dealt with nearly two months ago.

'Thank you, Mr Golding,' Jenny said. 'I have noted your submissions.'

Thrown by her response, he mouthed emptily for a moment, then, with a theatrical shrug, said, 'And your decision is, ma'am?'

'I'll hear from remaining counsel first.'

Golding sat down with a bemused expression and looked to Hartley for confirmation that he was right to be confused. The older lawyer gave him an insincere smile, glad the young man was no threat.

The third barrister, Pamela Sharpe, a woman of a similar age to Jenny whom she vaguely recognized from the family courts, rose slowly to her feet, pretending to be engrossed in far more important matters in her file. Drawing herself away with apparent reluctance, she said that she had been instructed to inform the court that Mr Grantham was also seeking clarification and an adjournment, firstly, on the grounds that no senior manager in a vital public service could be expected to answer a summons at such short notice, and secondly, on the grounds that he had no material evidence to give, never having had anything to do with Danny Wills or his case. Before Jenny could answer she sat down, as if there was no conceivable argument to the contrary.

'Do you want me to respond to that, Miss Sharpe?'

The barrister rose wearily to her feet, her look to the jury saying this had better be worth the effort.

'You and your client both appear to have similar attitudes towards the authority of this court,' Jenny said. There were smirks among the instructing solicitors. 'The most perfunctory reading of the law would have informed you that I alone determine which witnesses it is necessary and in the interests of justice to call, and that refusal to attend when lawfully summoned is an offence.'

'It is customary to ask a witness to an inquest to provide a statement in advance, ma'am.'

Pamela Sharpe's unyielding defiance sent a bolt of anxiety through her. It was always the way: people who refused to connect emotionally while inviting conflict caused her to panic.

'Miss Sharpe,' Jenny said, her heart crashing against her ribs, 'I am issuing warrants for the arrest of your client, Dr Peterson, Mr Hogg and Mr Stewart.'

'Surely a brief adjournment—'

'No.'

Golding shot to his feet in protest. 'Ma'am, I'm sure my client will come to court without having to be arrested.'

Erupting, Jenny said, 'Do I have to spell it out, Mr Golding? Each of your clients has ignored a summons. That's a criminal offence.' She aimed her last word at Hartley: 'And fleeing the jurisdiction is particularly serious. Mrs Lewis can expect the consequences to be severe.'

Hartley, untroubled, traded a look of mutual condescension with Pamela Sharpe, assuming their victory in Jenny's loss of cool. Just wait, their expressions seemed to say, she'll do our job for us.

Jenny nodded to Arvel, who brought over a sheaf of pre-prepared warrants. She signed each of them and asked him to telephone Williams with instructions to execute them immediately. While he retreated to a side room to make the call, she ordered Justin Bennett forward to the witness chair.

It took her a while to register the full change in Bennett's appearance. He still wore a short ponytail, but the dreadlocks had vanished, as had all but one of the earrings and studs. He was dressed in a brand-new charcoal suit with a shirt and tie. He read the oath card in a quiet, obedient voice, giving every impression of wanting to assist the court. Jenny felt her anxiety subside a little.

The three barristers listened intently, taking verbatim notes as Justin explained that he had dealt with and met Danny on numerous occasions before his reception into Portshead Farm. He confirmed that he was a difficult boy from an unstable family and it was no surprise to him that the family's social worker, Ruth Turner, had called him a fortnight before his sentencing hearing to say he was in a fragile mental state. Jenny asked him if he acted on Ruth Turner's phone call in any way. He glanced guiltily over at Simone Wills and said no, apart from mentioning in the pre-sentence report that Danny was deeply disturbed at the prospect of custody.

'Mr Bennett,' Jenny said, 'with hindsight, would you have done anything differently?'

'I could have tried for a psychiatric referral. But I'm not saying I would have got one. Every young person I see could do with some help of that kind. That's just the way it is.'

Simone's overweight friend – the trainee porn star – put an arm around her as she started to sob. Looking at her, Jenny felt oddly dispassionate, thinking about Simone on Saturday night, noisily humping her new boyfriend with five kids downstairs.

'After he went into custody, did you have any further contact with Danny?'

Justin shook his head. 'No.'

'But you did hear about him?'

'Yes . . .' The lawyers all looked up at once. 'I was dealing with another client, Katy Taylor, a fifteen-year-old girl who came out of Portshead Farm at the end of her sentence on 17 April. I saw her on the 18th at my office and again on the Friday, the 20th. That's when she spoke about Danny.'

'What did she say?'

Justin aimed his answer at the floor, his voice hardly carrying across the room. 'We'd been talking about whether her time in custody had changed her. She told me she thought it had, but only because she was frightened to go back . . . I asked her why that was and she wouldn't really say . . . It's the way we're trained, not to push kids to answer, to let things come out in their own time . . . It was right near the end of our session and she was getting up to go when she asked if I remembered Danny. I said of course, she knew I did. She kind of went quiet for a moment – unusual for her – then said she'd been worried about him at Portshead. She'd bumped into him a couple of times in the canteen before he hanged himself. He'd seemed in a bad way, quiet and depressed. The last time she saw him, the evening before he died, she went over and asked him what was the matter, and he told her he was having trouble with one of the staff, didn't say who. I think she said why didn't he do something about it. Danny told her he was going to, he was going to get hold of a knife to defend himself . . . That was it, all the conversation they had.'

'Did she have anything else to say about him?'

'Only that it seemed strange he was thinking about defending himself just before he committed suicide.'

'Did she mention having any problems of her own with the staff?'

'No, not specifically, but—'

'But what, Mr Bennett?'

'I got a feeling from her that there might have been something, but, like I said, I didn't push it. I was expecting to see her again in a few days.'

Jenny turned to the jury. 'The reason Mr Bennett didn't see Katy Taylor again was that she went missing two days later and was found dead on the outskirts of the city, eight days after that. You may have read about her case in the press. The police are currently investigating.'

She braced herself for Hartley's objection, but none came. He'd turned to his solicitor and was in whispered conversation. The expressions on the jurors' faces were suddenly deadly serious, as if a dark cloud had settled over the courtroom. Simone had stopped sobbing but looked ashen.

Jenny said, 'How well did Katy and Danny know each other?'

'They weren't exactly close,' Bennett replied, 'but they'd been on the same drugs awareness course last December, and I think they'd been at the same primary school.'

'What was your reaction to this information?'

'I was very worried by it. I'd known Danny a long time. I was shocked when I heard he was dead.'

'Did you tell anyone what Katy had said?'

'Yes. I'd already had a call from the coroner, Mr Marshall, a few days before, asking if I knew anything relevant. He left me his number, so I called him that same evening and passed on what she had told me.'

'What did he say?'

'He thanked me very much and said he'd like to talk to her himself.

'I said, maybe it would be best if he left it a few days and let me speak to her first, see if she came out with anything more. I didn't think Katy would have opened up to a complete stranger like that. But he insisted, so I gave him her mobile number.'

'So, as of the evening of Friday 20 April, Mr Marshall, the then coroner, knew that Danny had told Katy Taylor he was having trouble with a member of staff and that he was seeking a knife to defend himself?'

'Yes. He did.'

'And did he call Katy?'

'I've no idea.'

'Thank you, Mr Bennett. If you'd like to wait there. You may be asked some more questions.'

Hartley had a hurried word with his two fellow counsel and rose to represent all of them. 'Mr Bennett, Miss Taylor gave you no information about the circumstances of Danny Wills's death, did she?'

'No.'

'She had a lengthy criminal record and was a frequent drug user, was she not?'

'Yes.'

'And despite her tender years she was also suspected of prostitution.'

'Yes . . .' A note of annoyance entered Justin's voice. 'But there was a lot more to her than that.'

'I'm sure there was, and I'm sure we're all extremely sorry for her tragic death.' He paused in a moment of unconvincing sympathy. 'Now, if you could please tell me whether Danny Wills had previous convictions for crimes of violence?'

'He did. Several.'

'Then would it be fair to say that if he was having trouble with a member of staff, whatever that might mean, he was the kind of young man who might well have thought in terms of a violent response?'

Jenny watched Justin, his gaze fixed on his feet, blink several times as if suppressing an uncharacteristic violent urge of his own and then round on his questioner. 'He was the kind of kid we try to help but usually fail. I don't know what happened to him any more than you do, but I do know that if he hadn't been sent away he wouldn't be dead. Custody doesn't work – if it did, I'd be out of a job and so would you.'

'Your passion is admirable, Mr Bennett. I don't think anyone in this room feels anything other than deeply sad that a young life was lost. And in my long experience it's always so much more perplexing when it happens for no apparent reason.'

Jenny was about to call an adjournment when there was a disturbance at the back of the hall. Journalists who'd finally got a clear view of the action were forced to shuffle aside as two uniformed police officers arrived with Grantham and Peterson. Grantham was puce with rage; Peterson had the grey pallor of a man facing the gallows. DS Williams stepped in behind them with a look of profound satisfaction. Bennett's evidence had taken less than forty minutes, which meant his officers must have been already waiting for the two men, ready to pounce.

Williams nodded to Arvel, who got to his feet. 'Witnesses Mr Frank Grantham and Dr Nicholas Peterson are now present, ma'am.'

A murmur of anticipation spread through the gallery. Jenny called for quiet and asked Grantham to come forward. She felt an unhealthy burst of adrenalin, and while a constable followed him all the way to the witness chair, she picked a mint out of the packet on her desk and sucked out the half-pill.

She then thanked the police officer and released him, affording Grantham the dignity of being able to face the court without looking like a criminal. But he nevertheless glared at her with a degree of venom she had only experienced in the bitterest of marital rows. She fought the tightness in her throat and offered a brief, silent prayer. She was in charge and had to act as if she meant it.

Affecting the look of only partial interest that Pamela Sharpe had used so effectively to intimidate her, she glanced down at her notes at her notes. 'Are you Mr Frank Grantham of 18 Belvedere Park, Bristol?'

'Yes.' His answer was terse, given with no attempt to disguise his anger.

'You failed to answer your summons this morning, why was that?'

'I should imagine my counsel made that perfectly clear.'

Pamela Sharpe rose to her feet. 'Ma'am, if I might—'

'Not at the moment, Miss Sharpe. I'll deal with the issues of contempt later.' She turned to Arvel. 'We'll have the witness sworn, please.'

Grantham looked to Pamela Sharpe, but all she could offer was a slight shrug, as if to say that if he didn't know anything, he'd have nothing to fear.

Looking at his swollen, indignant face as he boomed out the oath, Jenny was surprised at how much loathing she felt for him. She checked herself. In the quiet of her hotel room she had planned this moment, and it was to be sober and low-key. She wanted only one piece of information from him and she wanted it extracted without exposing herself to even the slightest risk of criticism.

'Mr Grantham, you are head of the legal department of the Severn Vale Local Authority?'

'Yes. I've held the position for twelve years.'

'And your department advises the council on a whole range of legal issues which confront it?'

'It does.'

'Without giving away any commercially sensitive information, can you confirm that at the time of Danny Wills's death UKAM Secure Solutions Ltd was a bidder for a multi-million-pound contract to build and operate a new secure training centre in the Severn Vale Local Authority's area?'

Grantham looked straight at the jury. 'No. I have no knowledge of that.'

'Your department wasn't asked to advise on any planning issues the tender may have raised – I understand the proposed site would have been substantial, thus raising numerous issues.'

'No. I have no knowledge of any such tender.'

Jenny made a note, more to steady herself for the next phase than to record his answer. She continued with a change of tack: 'The former coroner, Mr Marshall, was a close friend and colleague of yours, was he not?'

'We'd certainly known each other a long time.'

'Personally as well as professionally?'

Grantham cast an uneasy glance at Pamela Sharpe. 'We socialized on occasions, certainly. I was technically his employer, however. My department pays the coroner's salary, as you know, ma'am.'

Reacting to several puzzled looks in the jury box, Jenny said, 'A historical anomaly, members of the jury: the coroner's office is paid for by the local authority, but the coroner is in no way answerable to or a servant of local government. He or she answers directly to the Lord Chancellor . . .' She couldn't resist adding, 'No matter what Mr Grantham may say.'

Those who understood smiled. The rest were losing interest. Jenny nodded to Arvel, certain she'd soon have their attention again. 'Would you please hand the envelope to Mr Grantham.'

As Arvel carried the Jiffy bag across to the witness chair, Jenny said, 'Do you recall the date Mr Marshall suffered his fatal coronary?'

Not liking the turn her questions were taking, Grantham twisted his neck in his collar, as if it were too tight. 'Not the exact date, no.'

Jenny double-checked her notes. 'He died in the early hours of Friday 4 May. On Thursday the 3rd he posted an item of recorded mail to you. I have the receipt if you wish to see it later.'

He looked suspiciously at the envelope that had been handed to him.

'Do you recognize the handwriting on the address label as Mr Marshall's?'

Grantham peered at the distinctive, looping script. 'It resembles his.'

'The envelope was addressed to you at your office but you didn't sign for it. Why was that?'

'The post goes to our mail room. I'd never be there to sign for anything personally.'

A fact Marshall must have known, surely. Jenny wondered if he ever meant for it to arrive, or if he had seen as far as the situation they were now in, his sins and Grantham's dragged simultaneously into the public gaze.

Jenny said, 'For reasons of confidentiality I don't intend the contents of that envelope to be made public, but would you please look at them.'

Arvel stood in front of Grantham, screening him from the rest of the courtroom, affording the jury only a sideways view. With clumsy fingers, Grantham reached into the envelope and brought out the photographs with Harry's handwritten note attached: *Dear Frank, Your friend. H.* She watched his expression turn from apprehensive to horrified as he glanced at the first photograph, then the second and third.

'Hand them back to the usher when you've seen enough.'

He fumbled the photographs back into the envelope, which Arvel took and carried to his desk. A room full of reporters saw the undisguised shock on Grantham's face. Williams, standing against the wall at the back of the room, gave Jenny a look of approval, admiring the elegant way she'd handled him.

With no trace of admonishment, she said, 'I appreciate you oversee a department that must be dealing with literally hundreds of issues at any one time, but I would ask you to cast your mind back and think again. Are you sure you know nothing about a tender?'

Pamela Sharpe and Hartley both rose at once with the same objection. Miss Sharpe got the first word in. 'Ma'am, can the witness please be informed of his right against self-incrimination?'

'Certainly. Mr Grantham, you do not have to say anything which may incriminate you.' She turned to the jury. 'In other words, a witness does not have to answer a question the answer to which may lay him open to criminal charges.'

The lawyers resumed their seats, leaving Grantham on the horns of a dilemma. Jenny watched him look out at the rows of eager press, calculating how much they would dig out in any event, and weighing it against what would be made of his silence if he refused to answer. With admirable nerve, he turned to the jury and said, 'Obviously we deal with thousands of planning applications. Now that I'm thinking about it, I do recall an enquiry relating to some sort of juvenile prison.'

Jenny said, 'Do you know if the plan was to build the prison on local-authority-owned land?'

The flare of alarm in his eyes gave her the answer, but Pamela Sharpe's look stopped him from giving it. Jenny wanted to push him, to get the fact admitted so she could legitimately go after the details until the whole rotten core of the deal and the reason for UKAM's cover-up had been exposed, but she sensed he had gone as far as he would. His expression now became one of entrenched stubbornness. He had calculated that he could distance himself from the photographs of Harry Marshall, leaving him only one problem to deal with, on ground he controlled.

She probed one last time. 'You must know if your authority was doing a land deal with UKAM Secure Solutions Ltd on a multi-million-pound contract.'

Calling her bluff, Grantham said, 'I would have to consult with those who handle such matters and come back to you.'

What worried her was the fact that, given time, he could bury the trail, spend the night in the office feeding the shredders, but any more questions would meet with the same resistance. She agreed on a compromise. 'I'll stand you down while I take evidence from the next witness. You can make the necessary enquiries by telephone. Please don't go any further than a hundred yards from this building. I expect an answer by the end of the morning.'

He hurried from the witness chair and marched outside, pursued by his twitching solicitor. From the back of the hall Williams gave her a nod, as if to say she'd done what he needed, enough to get him through Grantham's office door.

Moving straight on, she called Dr Peterson forward. She had expected the lawyers to rise as one to demand a private audience in chambers, where they would demand to know what it was in the envelope and what exactly Grantham was accused of being involved in. But as Peterson threaded his way to the front, the three counsel were locked in secret discussion: Hartley and Golding seemed to be in cahoots and Pamela Sharpe appeared to be hearing something shocking for the first time.

Peterson's face was lined with fatigue; it wouldn't have surprised her to learn that he hadn't slept since receiving his summons. While she had no sympathy for Grantham, there was a part of her which felt for the overworked pathologist. There could be no way back for a member of his profession who had wilfully covered up evidence which might have proved an unlawful killing.

'Dr Peterson, you examined Danny Wills's body on Monday 16 April and concluded that his death was a simple case of suicide – that he asphyxiated by hanging himself from the bars of his cell window with a strip of bed sheet.'

'That's right.'

'And that is what you told the inquest Mr Marshall held on 1 May, isn't it?'

'Yes.'

He couldn't have sounded more contrite, but Jenny noticed Golding was showing no obvious signs of concern. The lawyers' attitude was disconcerting.

'Could you confirm, please, that you conducted a second examination of Danny's body on Monday 23 April.'

There was an excited rustle of paper as the journalists who had followed the story scented a revelation.

Peterson said, 'Yes. On the Monday morning Mr Marshall asked me to examine the body again.'

The fact that he had answered at all was surprising. She had expected him to claim his right against self-incrimination. What it meant, she didn't have time to think through. She had to plough on.

'Can you tell me why you carried out that second examination?'

'Mr Marshall telephoned me on that Monday morning and asked me to. He said that he had received information that Danny might have been involved in violence of some sort prior to his death and requested that I check for any signs of injury.'

'Did he say that this information had come from a fellow inmate at Portshead Farm, Katy Taylor?'

'No. He didn't tell me where it came from.'

Jenny tried to read him. He was flat, solemn, but not shocked like Grantham had been. He was *resigned*. She glanced again at Golding and it dawned on her that he and Hartley already knew the worst, perhaps even about the photographs of Marshall, and were somehow prepared with a tactical response. She took another mint from her packet.

'What did you find when you examined him again?'

Peterson reached into his pocket and pulled out a document. 'Would you like me to read you my report?'

Jenny said yes, if he wouldn't mind. While she struggled to make sense of what was happening, he read out his report concluding that Danny had suffered restraint injuries at a time proximate to his death, and could have been partially conscious or even unconscious when he was hanged from the sheet.

'Does that mean, Dr Peterson, that it's possible in your opinion that he didn't hang himself, but was hanged by someone else?'

Simone Wills held on to her friend's hand, too shocked for tears.

'All I can say is that it's possible. I see lots of hangings where there are signs that the victim has tried to loosen the ligature and a number where there aren't any. I couldn't possibly say either way.'

'But he did have injuries consistent with forced restraint, to the extent that a patch of his hair had been pulled out.'

'Yes.'

'And you gave this second report to Mr Marshall?'

'Yes, I did.'

Jurors exchanged looks. Journalists whispered to each other, but the lawyers barely reacted. The lump in Jenny's throat swelled, a rock sitting in her oesophagus. She took a gulp of water.

'The question then remains why you didn't mention this second examination at the inquest into Danny's death held by Mr Marshall?'

'On the Friday beforehand, 27 April, he telephoned me to say that he had received evidence that Danny had been involved in altercations with staff which explained the injuries. He said could I please not mention them in open court because it would lead the family to believe he had been murdered when clearly he hadn't been: all the evidence, including CCTV, he said, proved that Danny was alone in his cell at the time of his death.'

'He asked you to suppress evidence to stop his family jumping to conclusions?'

Peterson glanced apologetically towards Simone. 'I'll put it in context. For the entire fourteen years I've been in my job, Harry Marshall was the coroner. From time to time we dealt with distressing deaths, usually suicides, where he was very keen to deliver a clear verdict. He said to me on many occasions that if families didn't come away knowing exactly how their loved one had died, it could destroy not just one but many lives. I didn't always agree with him, and on this occasion I'm not afraid to say I was wrong not to make these findings public. Since that inquest I had resolved to make them known, and I am grateful now for the opportunity to do so. I would add, however, that I would not alter my original finding of suicide. I firmly believe that Danny Wills died by his own hand.'

TWENTY-SEVEN

HER LUNCH LAY UNEATEN ON her desk, her stomach so tight with tension she could barely swallow her own saliva. Every calculation she had made was wrong. Not asking Grantham to explain the photographs in public, and not having forced him to an answer on the tender, had allowed him to slip through her fingers. He had come back to the box before the recess with a vague formulation about the local authority having been approached by UKAM over a possible purchase of land, but flatly denied any personal involvement. She could have pushed him harder, asked him to deny outright any contact with UKAM, but she'd succumbed to her desire not to appear oppressive. She'd let her own weakness get in the way of exposing the ultimate motive for UKAM's cover-up. Maybe Williams would find evidence of his corruption eventually, but it would be too late to have any impact on her inquest.

The revelation of Peterson's second examination had also misfired. She had expected him to deny it, or at least to have refused to answer, creating a cloud of suspicion that would have left the jury in no doubt there was a reason for his previous silence which amounted to deliberate deception. Instead, he had expertly shifted the blame to Harry Marshall and at the same time neutralized the evidence of Danny's injuries. How he had found the courage to take such an audacious risk, she didn't know. Perhaps he had so much dirt on so many surgeons at the Vale he had frightened his bosses into letting him keep his job in exchange for his silence on their negligence and misdemeanours. However he had arrived at his decision, it was clearly one the lawyers knew about. Their expressions during his testimony had confirmed to her beyond doubt that they were playing to a plan. And so far it was going their way.

She reached for her temazepam and shook out another dose. It would dull her, but she had to make a calculated risk of her own: to find the strength to beat something out of the two remaining witnesses Williams's men had rounded up and hauled to court just before the lunch break: Kevin Stewart and Darren Hogg. If she didn't make headway with one of them, the jury would still be left with no alternative but to return a verdict of suicide. She would have failed, with only herself to blame.

She looked at the single tablet in her hand and wondered what it said about her, the fragility of life and the elusiveness of truth that any hope of justice depended on her swallowing it.

Darren Hogg, the Portshead Farm CCTV operator, claimed a drunk housemate had answered the door to the process server on Saturday night and had forgotten to hand him the papers. It raised a laugh from the jury. Unsmiling, Jenny pushed him to recall any incidents he may have seen in the days leading up to Danny's death where forcible restraint was used on him. Hogg said he hadn't seen any and reminded her that the camera covering the corridor in the male house unit was down. She asked whether he had seen any incidents where restraint was used on any of the inmates in any part of Portshead Farm in the days leading up to Danny's death. Again, she met with denial. If restraint was used, he insisted, he hadn't seen it.

Losing patience, she said, 'Tell me about an occasion, *any* occasion, when you've seen members of staff forcibly restrain an inmate.'

Hogg, dressed in his brown uniform, his thin tie done up tight to his collar, didn't appear fazed. 'It happens now and again, someone kicks off, they've got to be brought under control.'

'Tell me what you have seen, a typical incident.'

Hogg scratched his acne-scarred neck, which was red with shaving burn. 'They just keep the kid up against the wall or whatever, wait till he calms down.'

'Have you seen inmates pushed to the floor, officers kneeling on their backs, hands forced up to their necks?'

He gave a noncommittal shake of his head. 'Can't say that I have, ma'am.'

'Never?'

'No.'

Jenny, at boiling point, paused for a moment to calm down. 'Mr Hogg, I'll accept that for a man who spends his life looking at CCTV monitors you are extremely unobservant, but surely you can tell me the name of one officer you have seen using a forcible restraint technique on a trainee.'

'Sorry.'

'How long have you worked at Portshead Farm?'

'Three years.'

'And you can't give me the name of one single officer?'

'Not so that I could be sure, no.'

Her patience gave way. 'You're lying to this court, aren't you?'

'No, ma'am.'

'What you're asking us to believe is so incredible it simply cannot be true.'

'No.'

'And if you've lied about one thing, nothing else you have

told us can be trusted either, can it? We can't believe you when you say the camera was down in the male house unit.'

'It was.'

'Or that Kevin Stewart made regular thirty-minute checks on all occupants of the unit throughout the night.'

'He did.'

Hartley rose to his feet. 'Ma'am, merely in a spirit of assistance to the court, I would remind you of the coroner's obligation to avoid any appearance of bias.'

'Mr Hartley, I would like to remind this witness that he has sworn to tell the whole truth, something I am quite satisfied he has failed utterly to do.'

Hartley exchanged a surprised glance with his fellow counsel and sat back in his seat to add another heading to his swelling grounds of appeal.

Jenny turned to the witness. 'I have no further interest in you, Mr Hogg, other than to order you to pay a fine of five hundred pounds for contempt in failing to attend court this morning.'

'*Five hundred?* I can't afford that.'

'Then you'll go to prison for five days.' She turned to the constable who had brought him to court. 'Make sure Mr Hogg doesn't go anywhere. I'll deal with him at the end of the day.'

It was Golding's turn to interrupt in the spirit of assistance. 'Ma'am, shouldn't Mr Hogg at least have been given the opportunity to seek legal representation before being sentenced to imprisonment?'

'Are you offering, Mr Golding?'

He looked over at the security guard. 'Well, I—'

'I can assure you, I intend to be even-handed. All the witnesses who failed to answer their summons will receive the same punishment.' She turned to Hartley. 'Except Mrs Lewis, of course.'

Golding sat back down and conferred with Pamela Sharpe,

who picked up a textbook, flicking urgently to the relevant law. Their solicitors rushed to the back of the hall to reassure Grantham and Peterson they wouldn't be going to prison. The constable stepped forward and led Hogg, complaining loudly, to the side of the room.

Ignoring his protests and fired up by her show of strength, Jenny ordered Kevin Stewart to the witness chair.

The Scot was even more intransigent than Hogg. His explanation for not answering his summons was that he assumed there had been a mistake – he had said everything he had to say last week. He denied being involved in any use of forcible restraint on Danny and had no knowledge of any occasion on which he had been brought physically to heel.

'Are you telling me that in the six days Danny was in the house unit, you don't recall him having been physically restrained once?'

'Not on my shifts.'

'So it could have happened during the day when you weren't there?'

'I wouldn't know.'

'No record is kept if there is a violent altercation with a trainee?'

'Not unless it's something serious.'

'Danny had major bruising and a patch of his hair ripped out.'

'No one said anything to me. And he never gave me any trouble.'

'Mr Stewart, we have evidence from the pathologist that at some time shortly before his death, Danny was involved in a violent struggle which bore all the hallmarks of him being subjected to control and restraint procedures. Are you asking me to believe you have no knowledge of that?'

'Yes, I am.'

'There was no gossip in the house unit, no talk about it?'

'None that I heard.'

'Your colleagues on the earlier shift didn't tell you to keep an eye out for him because they'd had trouble?'

'No, ma'am.'

Jenny glanced at the jury and sensed they were with her, suspicious of Stewart's evasiveness, asking themselves what he was hiding.

'How often do you have to use forcible restraint?'

'Every week or so. Not that often.'

'And would you force a trainee face down on the floor and push his arms up his back?'

'Very rarely.'

'But it happens.'

'If there's no other way, you have to.'

'If it's that rare, it's all the more surprising that no one mentioned it to you. It's just the kind of thing you'd talk about with colleagues, isn't it?'

Stewart looked straight at the jury and answered with the same emotionless matter-of-factness he'd shown in the witness box the week before. 'I don't know how Danny got those injuries. Perhaps he'd had a run in with staff I didn't know about, perhaps it was with some of the other boys. All I know is that he was fine at lights out, and as far as I was aware nothing untoward happened after that time.'

Jenny said, 'Dr Peterson says that it's possible Danny was unconscious or only partially conscious when the sheet went around his neck.'

'He's wrong.'

'And we're not to read anything suspicious into the fact that the camera wasn't working in the corridor?'

'You can read into it what you like. It was nothing to do with me.'

'Don't be insolent, Mr Stewart, we are dealing with a child's death.'

He folded his hands on the table in front of him, not offering any apology. More so than for the halfwit Hogg, she felt contempt for this man. He was not obstructive out of stupidity, but out of calculated self-interest. She could have balled up her fists and hit him hard in the face until he bled; she could have thrashed him senseless and dug her nails into his eyeballs until he spilled his dirty secrets.

Instead she forced herself to keep her voice level. 'Do you feel any remorse at all for what happened to Danny Wills?'

'I'm sorry he hanged himself, of course.'

'Then why haven't you offered a single word of assistance? Why haven't you offered any suggestion of who might have inflicted those injuries?'

'I don't know who.'

'Mr Stewart, you work in that institution. You knew all the staff and all the male trainees at the time of Danny's death. Either you have made a personal decision deliberately to withhold information from this inquest or you have been instructed by your employers to do so. Which is it?'

Hartley objected. 'Ma'am, I resent the implication of that question. No evidence whatsoever has been offered that suggests my clients have sought to suppress relevant information.'

'What other conclusion can I draw, Mr Hartley? This witness clearly isn't being completely honest and nor was Mr Hogg. And Mrs Lewis was so intent on avoiding this inquiry she left the country. It doesn't take a highly educated legal mind to realize that your clients are terrified of anything approximating the truth being heard in this court.'

'Are you sure you meant to express yourself in quite that way, ma'am?'

Kevin Stewart laughed, only a short derisory burst, but enough to snap her last strands of self-control. She railed at Hartley. 'I am sick of hearing your sneering, sarcastic tone. I have no doubt that you were personally involved in the decision to allow Mrs Lewis to flee the court's jurisdiction and I will be asking the police to investigate. I will also be asking them to look into who instructed Mr Hogg and Mr Stewart not to cooperate with this inquest. Your clients may think that enough money spent on organized obfuscation can get them the outcome they want, but I will not, I *shall* not allow that to happen.'

Her outburst rang around the courtroom. In the silence that followed, Hartley tapped the tips of his fingers together, then closed his notebook and replaced the cap on his fountain pen. He looked up with a pained, regretful expression.

'I'm afraid, ma'am, that your remarks leave me with no option other than to go to a higher court to seek an order quashing whatever verdict this inquest may arrive at, if indeed it proceeds that far. The erratic nature of your conduct of this case, your clear indications of bias, not to mention the bizarre events of last week, leave me with no other option.'

He picked up his file and, followed by his solicitor, made his way through the astonished public gallery towards the door. Golding and Pamela Sharpe exchanged a look. Pamela rose uncertainly to her feet. 'Mr Golding and I also share my learned friend Mr Hartley's sentiments, but will remain in the interests of our clients.'

Jenny gazed out over the sea of stunned faces. She had given the journalists their moment of drama and the evening headlines had already been written: *Lawyers Walk Out on Drugs Shame Coroner*. Moreton would pick up the first stories on his email this evening and read another slew in the morning. The call would come before she sat at ten a.m. She'd had her chance and she'd blown it. She wanted to apologize to Simone Wills, who was looking across at her with a perplexed expression: she'd like to say she'd tried her best, but deep down she knew she hadn't.

She turned to the witness Kevin Stewart, who was picking

idly at his nails, but words wouldn't come. The edges of her vision started to cloud and pressure mounted on her temples; the low babble of chatter in the room was drowned out by the rushing of blood in her ears. She plunged her hand into her pocket, searching for the mints, but her fingers refused to close around the tube. She saw Arvel moving swiftly from her left and guessed he was coming to catch her as she fell, but he strode past and up between the rows of seats and went to a woman, a blonde older woman, and exchanged urgent, whispered words. It was *Alison*. And as Arvel turned Jenny saw Tara at her shoulder and between them a slender, straw-haired youth with a seraphic face. The boy.

Arvel hurried back to Jenny's desk, almost at a jog. 'A Mrs Alison Trent, your officer. Apparently, she has a witness for you, Mr Mark Clayton.'

As quickly as the wave of panic rose, it subsided again. Jenny felt her feet on solid ground and the band around her diaphragm loosen. She reached for water, forced a mouthful down and found her voice.

'Stand down, Mr Stewart. But don't leave the room.'

He pushed up from the chair and strolled to the back with a dismissive shake of the head.

'I call Mr Mark Clayton.'

The blond boy, no more than eighteen or nineteen, turned to Alison, who urged him forward, a hand in the small of his back like a protective mother. Tara stood behind them, her face dancing with excitement.

Clayton came nervously to the front, Arvel steering him to the witness chair and standing close by as he stumbled through the oath, his eyes wide and frightened.

Jenny said, 'You are Mark Clayton?'

'I am.'

He gave his age – eighteen – and his address in the south of the city with a soft accent, more Somerset than Bristol. She could tell he'd never stood in a witness box before: he had none of the swagger of the seasoned delinquent.

With no notes to question him from, no rehearsed plan, no idea what it was he had to say, she had only Alison's stoical frown to reassure her that whatever it might be was for the best.

'Could you please tell us what connection, if any, you have with the deceased, Danny Wills?'

Clayton glanced at Alison, as if taking her cue from her, and turned self-consciously to the jury. 'I was . . . I was a friend of the coroner, Mr Harry Marshall.'

Jenny said, 'When you say *friend*?'

'Yeah . . . Well, actually it was more than that, you know . . . I met him about three months ago, saw him every couple of weeks.'

There was a surge of energy through the room. The journalists looked up in unison, the most cynical eyes agog.

She trod carefully. 'Was this a romantic friendship?'

'Kind of . . . I met him online.' Another glance to Alison. 'He'd pay me.'

'Harry Marshall, the coroner who was investigating Danny Wills's death, paid you once a fortnight to have sex with him?'

'Yes.'

She caught sight of Williams lowering his head in sadness for what would now greet Mary Marshall and her daughters, but there could be no going back. She asked Arvel to bring the envelope to the witness chair and invited Clayton to open it. He pulled out the photographs.

'Can you tell us please what those are?'

Clayton seemed surprised, disgusted even, at what he saw. 'They're pictures of me and Harry in a hotel room.'

'Is there a date on them?'

'Yes – 25 April.'

'Where were you?'

'In the Novotel in Bristol. It's where we always went.'

'Were you aware that photographs were being taken?'

'No . . . Neither of us was.'

'There's a note attached to the photographs. Can you read what it says?'

Jenny glanced over at where Frank Grantham had been sitting, but he was no longer there.

'It says, *Dear Frank, Your friend. H.*'

'Is there a date?'

'Yes – 3 May.'

Jenny turned to the jury. 'You'll remember that Mr Marshall mailed those photographs to Mr Grantham on the morning of the 3rd and died later that day.' She addressed Clayton again. 'What do you know about them?'

'Harry called me on my mobile, I think on the Friday before and said he was sorry, but there was a chance some pictures of us together might appear in the press. He said someone had sent copies to his office. He didn't know how it had happened.'

'How did he sound?'

'Upset . . . very.'

'Did he mention anything to you about his work?'

'Not that time. It was only a short call . . . I was angry.'

'About the pictures?'

'What else? Yeah.'

'You said, *Not that time—*'

'He called me once more, the next week, the Thursday. To be honest I didn't want to know, but he kept calling, wouldn't leave it, so I picked up . . .'

'What time?'

'I don't know exactly. Late in the evening, may even have been past midnight.'

Jenny glanced over at Alison, thinking of the call she had received from Harry, the call that might have stopped him had she found the courage to ring back.

'What did he say?'

'He sounded quiet, not upset, just sort of sad . . . He said he wasn't well. And that if anything happened to him, I was to tell his office that the man he was looking for was called Sean Loughlin and he was a nurse at Portshead Farm. He said, *Sean Loughlin killed Danny Wills and I wasn't brave enough to prove it*. That was it.'

'Why didn't you call his office, Mr Clayton?'

'I didn't want to have anything more to do with him. It was just business, you know. And when his wife started calling me, that was all I needed.'

Williams had sent a note suggesting an adjournment when she'd finished with Clayton, but didn't say why. Later he would tell her how in that half-hour, with the news crews whipping themselves into a frenzy outside on the pavement, the real story was happening in the alley at the back of the hall, where he had his constables bring Stewart and Hogg. With the same look in his eye that appeared when he talked about outdoing the English, he told her how he'd offered a deal to the first one who talked. Hogg turned out to be quicker than he looked, sticking his hand up like a schoolboy. Stewart swung a punch at him, then tried to bolt, but ended up cuffed in the van parked at the other end of the alley, where they already had Frank Grantham. Williams told her Grantham was the worst, kept saying, 'Do you know who I am?' He had given him an answer, but it wasn't repeatable in polite company.

The Welsh country detective, whose workload consisted mostly of shed break-ins and, if he was lucky, the odd domestic, was enjoying himself.

Hartley and the UKAM solicitors were back in the hall when Jenny reconvened in the middle of the afternoon, but were gathered in a corner of the public gallery, trapped between their need to stay in with the action and too proud to lose face by retaking their seats at the front. Several rows ahead of them, Alison and Tara Collins were sitting with Simone Wills and her friends, Tara having taken the place of the trainee porn star, holding Simone's hand.

Jenny called Hogg to the front and reminded him that he was still on oath. There was no trace of shame or embarrassment in his demeanour. He had all the arrogant confidence of a man who believed he had got away with it.

'Mr Hogg, I believe that since you gave evidence earlier this afternoon you have had some further thoughts and now wish to clarify certain matters.'

Hogg glanced across at Williams, double-checking he was fireproof. Williams responded with a nod. Hogg said, 'Yes, ma'am.'

'Mr Hogg, could you tell us what you saw on the night of 13–14 April, the night Danny Wills died.'

'I saw someone, a member of staff, going into his room.'

'You saw this from where?'

'On one of my monitors.'

'You're telling the court the camera covering the corridor in the male house unit was working?'

'Yes, ma'am. It was.'

Jenny resisted looking at the jury. She could hear their quiet gasps, but didn't want to respond to their emotion, her heart was hammering hard enough. Nor did she dare look at Hartley or his team. She had to remain focused; all that mattered was getting the undiluted truth out of Hogg.

'It hadn't been broken?'

'No.' Still no hint of regret. He was shameless.

'Then why did you say it had been?'

'I was instructed to say so and to report it broken early the next morning before the end of my shift.'

'Who by?'

'The director, Mrs Lewis.'

Jenny heard the stirring from the UKAM lawyers, knowing that they would already be planning their tactics to smear and discredit the witness.

'You didn't report the camera broken until the morning of the 14th, after Danny was dead?'

'That's right.'

She took a steadying breath. 'Tell me what you saw on the camera, Mr Hogg.'

'During the evening I saw Mr Stewart making his checks, but he came to the outside of the door of one room several times – it was Danny's. I couldn't see what was going on inside, but Mr Stewart seemed to be shouting. It looked like the prisoner was causing a disturbance. I'd noticed it on the previous nights, too.'

'What had you noticed?'

'Mr Stewart was having problems with Danny. He wouldn't settle. He'd have to keep going to his door, then eventually he'd call Loughlin.'

'Who was Loughlin?'

'One of the nurses in the reception unit.'

Jenny said, 'Why haven't I seen his name on any of the staff rosters?'

'I didn't see him again after the 14th . . .' For the first time, Hogg dipped his head. 'We were told that as far as we were concerned he'd been off for the last two weeks . . . That if the police or coroner asked any questions that's what we were to say.'

'Mrs Lewis told you this?'

He nodded.

'And if you disobeyed?'

'We'd lose our jobs and never get another one . . . And no one would have wanted to get on the wrong side of Loughlin . . . The kids called him the Butcher.'

'Any particular reason?'

'I don't know if it's true or not . . .' Hogg was starting to sweat. He rubbed a cuff over his waxy forehead. 'It was just the rumour I'd heard – he'd get them drugs but treat them like meat.'

'Meaning?'

Hogg reached for his tie knot, loosening it a touch. 'They'd pay for them with sex, I guess. But I never saw it happen. All I know is he was on a lot at nights. The duty nurse'd get called out when someone needed quietening down. Mostly that was him.'

'At what time did Loughlin come to Danny's room?'

'About two-ish.'

'Did Mr Stewart go in with him?'

'No. He went in alone. He was in there maybe ten, fifteen minutes. I couldn't see what had happened inside obviously, but when he came out I remember he looked up at the camera, just a little look, you know . . .'

'What happened after that?'

'It was all quiet . . . Mr Stewart didn't go up and down again till about six. That's when he saw Danny.' Before Jenny intervened, he said, 'It wasn't unusual. He didn't really bother when the kids were asleep.'

Jenny said, 'Mr Hogg, tell me how often you saw trainees being forcibly restrained by staff at Portshead Farm.'

'Every day. They have to. Some of them are like wild animals. How else are they going to control them?'

She eased back in her chair and allowed herself a moment to take in the full sweep of the courtroom: Alison pulling tissues from her sleeve to hand to Simone; Hartley and his crew in a desperate huddle; Williams, quietly smiling; Peterson, pensive, staring into space; Sharpe and Golding, their clients momentarily forgotten, as gripped and horrified by what they were hearing as the jury.

Jenny turned to Hogg for one last question. 'Tell me, do you recall what kind of car Sean Loughlin drove?'

Hogg pushed up his chin in a strange contortion as he tried to picture it. 'Yeah . . . I think it was a Vectra. A blue one.'

It was during the brief adjournment Jenny called for both herself and the jury to absorb the full impact of the afternoon's evidence that Alison knocked on her office door and came in with the news that she had used Williams's laptop to go online and check the itemized office phone bill for the months of April and May. She handed her a streaky printout which showed Marshall had gone into the office on the morning of Saturday 21 April and made numerous calls to Portshead Farm and to numbers which tallied with those on the staff roster he'd been working through. Jenny noticed that Loughlin's name did not appear on this document. Between these calls Harry had tried unsuccessfully to get through to Katy Taylor's mobile, but at 12.52 he had connected with her number for three and a half minutes. What was said, they would never know, and the jury could not be allowed to speculate, but if she had mentioned Loughlin, Marshall had left no record of it among his papers. It was a detail Harry had taken with him, but Jenny could imagine him, frantic, after first receiving the photographs, then hearing of Katy's death, weeding Danny's file for anything which could later incriminate him; but as he tipped into despair, succumbing to an overwhelming conscience and locking Katy's file in the drawer in the desperate hope of posthumous redemption. She could tell from Alison's fixed, though pained expression that her policeman's mind was playing through a similar scenario, but this was not the occasion for such conjecture: grief was enough to cope with for now. There would be plenty of time for her to deal with Harry's shame.

*

She summed up the evidence to the jury until past five o'clock, then carefully explained the range of potential verdicts open to them. To return a verdict of suicide or unlawful killing, they had to be satisfied to the criminal standard of proof: beyond reasonable doubt. For all other potential verdicts – accidental death, misadventure, neglect or an open verdict – the civil standard – the balance of probabilities – applied. And although they had no eyewitness account of what happened at the precise moment of Danny Wills's death, they were entitled to form an opinion from the patchwork of circumstantial evidence. How credible they found each of the witnesses and what weight they chose to give their testimony were matters for them to decide, applying common sense. Lastly, she told them to be as precise as possible in their findings: a coroner's jury had to determine in as much detail as the evidence would justify the exact time, cause and circumstances of death.

The jury retired to the only available room – the one Jenny had used as an office – leaving her to hover alone in the only other private space: a small, windowless kitchen that smelt of ageing lino. Arvel had thoughtfully erected a folding table and chair but it was a long way from what she'd pictured when she'd thought of a coroner's chambers. Yet its cosy, communal domesticity somehow seemed to fit the intimacy of her task. Her job was not to judge and condemn a criminal, but to discover, in so far as was possible, what had caused a young, vulnerable and confused soul to make an unhappy and untimely departure from his earthly body.

The jury took less than forty minutes to reach a verdict. There was a respectful silence as they filed back into the hall and resumed their seats.

Jenny said, 'Could the foreman please stand?'

A confident young woman in the back row stood up, holding the completed form of inquisition.

'Madam Foreman, have you reached a unanimous decision to all the questions on the form of inquisition and have you put your signatures to the same?'

'We have.'

'So that those answers may be heard, could you please state aloud the name of the deceased.'

'Daniel Wills.'

'Injury or disease causing his death.'

'Asphyxiation due to strangulation.'

'Time and place in which injury was sustained.'

'Daniel Wills died shortly after two a.m. on 14 April in his cell at Portshead Farm Secure Training Centre.'

'Conclusion of the jury as to the cause of death.'

'Daniel Wills was unlawfully killed by Sean Loughlin, a nurse at Portshead Farm. Loughlin placed him in forced restraint, causing him injuries which rendered him unconscious. Believing he was dead, Loughlin hanged his body by a sheet from the bars of his cell window to give the appearance of suicide.'

Over the sound of Simone Wills's tears Jenny thanked the jury for their efforts and informed them that she would be handing her file immediately to the police, recommending that Sean Loughlin be investigated for murder. Without missing a beat, she ordered Grantham and Peterson to the front of the court and sentenced them both to five days' imprisonment for contempt. Their lawyers would scurry to a High Court judge to appeal, but at least they'd taste a night in prison. Williams had told her he'd have a car outside ready to drive them to Swansea, a jail that never liked to let an Englishman go.

Amid the ensuing uproar she met Alison's steady gaze and mouthed a heartfelt thank you.

TWENTY-EIGHT

IT WAS LATE AFTERNOON. She pulled up on the newly mown cart track and came around the back of the house to find Steve in flip-flops and cut-offs, his shirt soaked through with sweat, admiring the wide stripes he'd made on the lawn with an old iron roller. Alfie was lying, stretched out on his side, in the shade by the back door.

Jenny said, 'What have you done? It looks like the suburbs.'

'It appeals to my sense of order.'

'Since when did you have one of those?'

'Six years of architecture can't have been for nothing.'

She dumped her briefcase on the scrub-top table and took off her suit jacket. After a rainy June, July had at last brought out the sun.

'You never told me what stopped you finishing, apart from the crazy girlfriend.'

'Fear of becoming a man in a suit, I suppose. Wife, kids, mortgage, all that.'

'There are worse things.'

He turned to look at her, his eyes drifting over her blouse, the two buttons undone at the top. 'I know.' He started to push the roller back to the mill. 'You had a call from Alison a while ago. Said she'd been trying to reach you for the last two hours.'

'I've been busy. What did she want?'

'She got the DNA results – the hairs they found in Lough-lin's car turned out to be Katy Taylor's. I think she said they're charging him with murder.' He disappeared into the tumble-down building. Jenny heard him moving sheets of corrugated iron and pieces of timber.

'That's all you've got to say? . . . How about a well done for single-handedly finding a double killer?'

'Single-handed, huh?'

She started after him, her heels sinking into the grass. 'What's that supposed to mean?'

'It was Alison and that journalist who found the Clayton boy.'

'I'd have got to him. It was me who unearthed the photo-graphs.'

'And who got hold of the pathologist's files?'

She came to the open space where the doorway once was. 'I was there.'

'With the kid.'

He pushed the roller under the makeshift shelter he'd erected against the side wall.

'What is this, your attempt to diminish me because I've got status and you haven't?'

Steve looked at his filthy, rust-stained hands and strolled back towards her. 'You know your problem, Jenny? All you seem to want to be is alone.'

'That's *not* true.'

'Except when you're so successful at it you scare yourself.'

'You don't even know me.'

'Sometimes strangers see more clearly.'

'Really.'

'Look at you, Jenny. You're a beautiful woman dressed like an undertaker.' He planted his dirty hands around her middle.

'What the hell are you doing?'

'It's hot. You bought a house by a stream. Aren't you ever going to swim in it?'

'Get *off* me.'

He let her go. 'Whatever you want.' He pulled off his shirt and waded out into a spot where it almost reached his waist and plunged in head first. He came up laughing, shook his head and rolled over, kicking his bare feet in the air. 'This could be you, Jenny . . . This could be you.'

She watched him for a moment, paralysed – realizing she had always been frightened of water – then slowly kicked off her shoes and unhooked the catch on her waistband. Maybe it was time to get over it.

'Listen for it again. Tell me what kind of sound.'

'It's the door . . . fists on a door. Violent, pounding—'

'And then?'

'. . . A voice . . . an angry voice. Shouting . . . Louder than shouting.'

'Yes?'

'I don't know . . . I can't—'

'Try, Jenny. Stay with it. Your father's voice?'

'No, it's not him . . . Oh, God . . .'

'Whose voice? . . . It's all right, you can let the tears come . . . Just stay there.'

'. . . My grandfather . . . He's screaming . . . I can't. I can't.'

She opened her streaming eyes and took another Kleenex from the packet Dr Allen held out for her. 'I'm sorry . . . I can't get any further.'

'You've taken another big step – your grandfather's voice. Do you have any idea what the shouting was about?'

She shook her head. 'No.'

'Maybe it'll come to you. I think we're going to get there very soon.' Making a note in his pad, he said, 'Tell me what it made you feel when you heard your grandfather.'

Another river of salt water ran down her face. 'I don't know where this is coming from—'

'Try to think of a word, a feeling.'

'I can't.'

'Just try. The first thing that comes to you.'

'. . . Death.'

'Good.' He wrote it down. 'Did someone you know die around that time?'

'No.'

'Try looking back over some old photographs, letters, anything. I've a feeling we're really close.' He looked up from his notes. 'Now tell me, how are you coping with this high-pressure job of yours?'

She dried her eyes. 'The new drugs are just about getting me through.'

'From what I've read in the papers you've managed a good deal more than that.'

'I've made a lot of mistakes, too.'

'No more self-destructive thoughts?'

'Nothing serious . . . They're always there, lurking in the shadows, but as long as they stay there, it's fine.'

'Panic attacks?'

'Not in the last week or so. I feel pretty steady.'

'You sound almost disappointed.'

'You don't feel as much medicated . . . I'm not complaining.'

'You're mending. Think of the drugs as a sticking plaster. You'll only need them while the wound's healing underneath.'

'I suppose . . .' She eased back into a sitting position, wiping away the last of her tears.

'Tell me, how are things with your son?'

'Fine. He's coming to stay with me next week for the summer, maybe longer.'

'His cannabis problem?'

'I'm hoping he'll get into girls instead.'

'And you won't have a problem with that?'

'Of course I will, I'm his mother, but at least I can scare the bad ones away.'

Dr Allen smiled. 'You know, whatever's happened between you, you'll never fix the past, but if you get the present right, you can at least come to terms with it.'

Jenny said, 'I'm a coroner. I spend my life laying things to rest.'

EPILOGUE

DETECTIVE SERGEANT WILLIAMS AND HIS team successfully brought Sean Loughlin to justice. At Newport Crown Court, he pleaded guilty to the manslaughter of Danny Wills and not guilty to the murder of Katy Taylor. At his subsequent trial, evidence was heard that on the day of Katy's disappearance he had lawfully purchased an air pistol in the style of a Glock handgun which, it was alleged, he used to persuade her into his vehicle. Loughlin declined to give evidence and was convicted. He was sentenced to mandatory life imprisonment with a recommendation that he serve at least twenty-five years.

Kevin Stewart was tried for perjury and, following evidence from Jan Smirski given via video link from Poland, pleaded guilty to a single count of perverting the course of justice. He was sentenced to four years. Williams attempted to bring similar charges against a number of other staff at Portshead Farm but the Crown Prosecution Service decided not to proceed to trial for lack of evidence. Darren Hogg continues to work as a CCTV operator, though shortly after the Danny Wills inquest he was transferred by his employer to an adult jail. Elaine Lewis remains in the USA and attempts to extradite her to the UK have so far proved unsuccessful. Giles Hartley and his instructing solicitors were formally investigated but no criminal charges arose.

Despite a lengthy investigation, no documentary evidence was discovered implicating Frank Grantham in a corrupt deal to sell local authority-owned land to UKAM Secure Solutions Ltd. The company, meanwhile, completed the purchase and is currently building a secure training centre with capacity for five hundred trainees. The identity of the whistleblower who handed the tender document to Marshall was never discovered.

Andy and Claire Taylor made an official complaint about the initial handling of the investigation into their daughter's death. While the Independent Police Complaints Commission found several shortcomings in the CID's response, these were attributed to lack of resources; elements of the investigation were found to be regrettable, but no individual officer could be said to be at fault.

By remortgaging her home, Tara Collins engaged a firm of forensic data retrieval experts who traced the alleged fraudulent transactions made on her laptop to a wi-fi connection in a Starbucks coffee shop in Burtonsville, Maryland. No link with UKAM or its associated companies was proved, but the judge at her trial at Bristol Crown Court accepted there was no case to answer and ordered the jury to return a not guilty verdict.

Nick Peterson left the Severn Vale District Hospital to take up a position at a community hospital in Johannesburg, South Africa.

An inquest into the death of Harry Marshall held by the Bristol Central Coroner reached an open verdict. Neither Mrs Marshall nor any of her daughters attended. However, at a short chapel service held following Katy Taylor's reinterment, she read the lesson, her late husband's favourite passage from the King James Bible: Isaiah 61:

THE CORONER

The Spirit of the Lord God is upon me; because the Lord hath anointed me to preach good tidings unto the meek; he hath sent me to bind up the brokenhearted, to proclaim liberty to the captives, and the opening of the prison to them that are bound.

If you enjoyed THE CORONER you'll love

The Disappeared

**The next thrilling novel in the
Coroner Jenny Cooper series**

Two young British students, Nazim Jamal and Rafi Hassan, vanish without a trace. The police tell their parents that the boys had been under surveillance, that it was likely they left the country to pursue their dangerous new ideals. Seven years later, Nazim's grief-stricken mother is still unconvinced. Unable to understand why the police failed to investigate the suspicious circumstances surrounding the boys' disappearance, or the mysterious involvement of the Security Services, she has exhausted every avenue in her search for the truth. Jenny Cooper is her last hope . . .

The Disappeared is out now

The first two chapters follow here . . .

ONE

DURING HER SIX MONTHS AS coroner for the Severn Vale District, Jenny Cooper had known only a handful of corpses remain unidentified for more than a day or two. Jane Doe, or JD0110, had been wrapped in her white plastic shroud in the refrigerator's bottom drawer at the Vale hospital's mortuary for a little over a week. Owing to the large backlog of bodies awaiting post-mortem, she remained unopened and unexamined.

She had been washed up on the English side of the Severn estuary at the mouth of the Avon; sucked in with the tide and deposited naked on a mudbank a little downstream from where the M5 motorway thundered across the river. She was blonde, five feet eight inches tall, had no body hair and had been partially eaten by gulls. There was little left of the soft tissue of her abdomen and breasts, and in common with all corpses left open to the elements for any length of time there were empty sockets where her eyes had once been. For the purposes of identification Jenny had insisted that glass ones be fitted. An unnatural blue, they gave her face a dumb, doll-like quality.

Alison Trent, the coroner's officer, had arranged for a number of potential identifiers to attend the mortuary late on a Friday afternoon, but at the last minute she had been called to a supermarket depot, where the bodies of three young

African men had been discovered in a refrigerated trailer amongst a cargo of beef carcasses imported from France. Rather than leave the families in suspense, Jenny reluctantly left the office early to preside at the mortuary herself.

It was the final week of January; freezing sleet slanted from a gunmetal sky. It was not yet four o'clock and daylight had all but bled away. Jenny arrived to find a group of a dozen or so waiting in the unmanned reception area of the mortuary building at the rear of the hospital. The antique radiators were either not switched on or were broken. As the couples amongst them whispered to one another their breath emerged in wispy clouds. Most were middle-aged parents who wore expressions of dread masking deeper feelings of guilt and shame. *How did it come to this?* their grim, lined faces seemed to say.

Since there was no assistant available to help conduct the viewings, Jenny was forced to address the group in the manner of a schoolteacher, instructing them to take it in turns to pass through the slap doors and along the corridor to the refrigerator at the far end. She warned them that the body might not be instantly recognizable and provided the details of a private laboratory which would take their DNA samples and compare them with that of the Jane Doe: it entailed a modest expense but not one her meagre budget would extend to. They dutifully noted down the company's email address and phone number, but one of them, Jenny noticed, did not. Nor did he enter his details onto the list of those wishing to be informed in the event that other unidentified bodies surfaced. Instead, the tall, lean man, somewhere in his mid-fifties, stood away from the huddle, his slender sun-weathered face expressionless, his only sign of anxiety the occasional raising of his hand to smooth his short black hair streaked with grey. Jenny noticed his arresting green eyes and hoped he wasn't the one whose tears would spill onto the tiled floor.

There were always tears.

The building was arranged to maximize the visitors' trauma. Their twenty-yard journey through the mortuary required them to pass an extended row of gurneys, each bearing a corpse wrapped in an envelope of shiny white polythene. The stale air was heavy with the smell of decay, disinfectant and an illicit hint of cigarette smoke. One after another, three separate couples made the walk along the corridor and steeled themselves to look down on the bare head and shoulders of the Jane Doe, her skin now starting to yellow and take on a papery texture. And one after another they shook their heads, their expressions of relief mixed with uncertainty and the fear of similar ordeals to follow.

The man with green eyes did not carry himself like the others. His footsteps approached briskly, his manner was abrupt and businesslike, yet somehow seemed to cover a sadness or uncertainty that Jenny read as regret. Without flinching, he looked down at the Jane Doe's face, studied her for a moment, then shook his head decisively. Curious, Jenny asked him who he was looking for. In a cultured transatlantic accent he explained briefly that his stepdaughter had been travelling in the UK and had failed to make contact for several weeks. Her last email was sent from an internet cafe in Bristol. The police had told him about the body. Before Jenny could find a pretext to extend the conversation, he turned and left as quickly as he had come.

Mr and Mrs Crosby arrived after the main group. He was in his late fifties and dressed in the business suit that befitted a high-level professional or businessman; she was several years younger and had the well-preserved features and softer manner of a woman who had not been ground down by life in the workplace. With them came a young man in his late twenties, also dressed formally in a suit and tie. Mr Crosby introduced him stiffly as Michael Stevens, his daughter's boyfriend. The term seemed to embarrass him: a father not yet ready to surrender the affections of his grown-up daughter. Jenny offered a sympathetic smile and watched them gaze down at the body, take in the contours of the staring, lifeless face, exchange glances and shake their heads.

'No, it's not Anna Rose,' Mrs Crosby said with a trace of doubt. 'Her hair isn't that long.'

The statement seemed to satisfy her husband, but the young man was stealing another glance, wise enough to know, Jenny could tell, that the dead can look deceptively different from the living.

'The eyes are glass,' she said, 'so the colour could be different. There are no distinguishing marks and the body was completely depilated.'

Mr Crosby's eyes flitted questioningly towards her.

'She has no body hair,' his wife explained.

He gave a dismissive grunt.

'It's not her,' Michael Stevens said finally. 'No, it's definitely not her.'

'If you're at all unsure I'd advise you to take a DNA test,' Jenny said to the parents.

'We adopted Anna Rose,' Mrs Crosby said, 'but I expect we can find something of hers. A hairbrush would do, wouldn't it?'

'A hair sample would be fine.'

Mr Crosby offered a terse thank you and placed a hand in the small of his wife's back, but as he made to lead her away she turned to Jenny.

'Anna Rose has been missing for ten days. She's a physics graduate – she works at Maybury with Mike. She didn't have any problems, she seemed perfectly happy with life.' Mrs

Crosby paused briefly to collect herself. 'Do you ever come across that?'

Mr Crosby, embarrassed at his wife's naivety, lowered his eyes to the floor. Mike Stevens glanced uncertainly between his missing girlfriend's parents. There was alarm in his eyes. He was out of his depth.

'No. Not often,' Jenny said. 'In my experience, suicide – if that is what's in your mind – is invariably preceded by depression. If you were close to the person, I think you would know.'

'Thank you,' Mrs Crosby said. 'Thank you.'

Her husband steered her away.

Mike Stevens glanced briefly at Jenny in such a way that she assumed he had a question of his own, but whether from shyness or family protocol, he kept it to himself and followed the Crosbys out.

As they disappeared from view, Jenny vaguely recalled an item she had heard on the radio about a young woman who had gone missing from her home in Bristol – a trainee at Maybury, the decommissioned nuclear power station that sat three miles east of the Severn Bridge. Maybury and the other three retired stations on the estuary had been much discussed in the local media lately: a new generation of scientists was being recruited to decommission the fifty-year-old reactors and build the new ones that had been given the go-ahead by the government. Listening to the heated phone-in debates, Jenny had felt a stirring of her teenage idealism, evoking memories of weekend trips with fellow students to peace camps outside American airbases. It seemed strange to her that a generation later a young woman would embark on a career in an industry which she had spent her formative years believing represented all that was corrupt and dangerous in the world.

Jenny slipped on a latex glove, pulled the fold of plastic over the Jane Doe's face and pushed the heavy drawer shut.

After five months of the mortuary being staffed exclusively by a string of unreliable locums, a new full-time pathologist was arriving on Monday. Jenny looked forward to prompt post-mortem reports and not having to waste her afternoons with tasks that his staff should have been assigned to. Professional dignity had been hard to maintain in a cash-strapped coroner's office and, though she had now seen many hundreds of corpses in every conceivable state of dismemberment and decay, being close to dead bodies still terrified her.

She disposed of the spent glove and hurried as quickly as she could on her narrow heels out into the sharp air. She had an appointment to keep.

Death, and her uneasy relationship with it, occupied most of the time she had spent with Dr Allen in the consulting room at Chepstow hospital during their fortnightly early evening meetings. Progress had been slow and insights limited, but Jenny had managed to keep to the regime of anti-depressants and beta blockers, and had largely respected his injunction forbidding alcohol and tranquillizers. Though by no means cured, her generalized anxiety disorder had, for the previous five months, been chemically contained.

The fresh-faced Dr Allen, as punctilious as ever, reached for the thick black notebook he reserved exclusively for her sessions. He turned to the previous entry and carefully read it through. Jenny waited patiently, prepared with polite replies to the questions about her son, Ross, with which he usually opened. After a short while she began to sense that something was different today. Dr Allen seemed engrossed, distracted.

'Dreams . . .' he said. 'I don't often put a lot of store by them. They're usually just reprocessed garbage from the day, but I confess I've been doing some reading on the subject.' His eyes remained firmly on the book.

'Really?'

'Yes. I dabbled in Jungian analysis when I was at college, but it wasn't really encouraged; something of a cul-de-sac, I remember my professor saying. Never known a patient who'd been cured by understanding the meaning of his dreams.'

'Does this mean I've driven you to despair?'

'Not at all.' He flicked back through his notes, searching for an earlier entry. 'It's just I remember that before the medication you used to have some quite vivid ones. Yes . . .' He found what he was looking for. 'An ominous crack opening in the wall of your childhood bedroom to a dark forbidding space beyond. A terrifying presence lurking in there that you could never see or even fully visualize . . . an unspeakable horror of some description.'

Jenny felt the vessels of her heart enlarge, a pulse of heat cross her face, a flutter of anxiety in her solar plexus. She tried to keep her voice steady. *Act calm, stay calm*, she repeated silently to herself.

'You're right. I used to have those dreams.'

'How old were you when you first had them?' He turned back to a blank page, ready and alert.

'I was in my early thirties, I suppose.'

'A time of stress, juggling work and motherhood?'

'Yes.'

'And how old are you, as the dreamer, in your dream?'

'I'm a child.'

'You're certain about that?'

'I don't ever *see* myself . . . I suppose I just assume.'

'And as a child you feel helpless? Terrified of a threat you have no power to control?'

She nodded. 'And I think I know what you're going to say next.'

'What's that?'

'That it's nothing to do with childhood. That the dream merely reflects my state of fear and paralysis.'

'That's one interpretation.' His face fell slightly at having his theory anticipated so easily.

'I agree. But I still have no memory between the ages of four and five. And don't tell me I've imagined that.' She fixed him with a look that gave him pause.

'There is one school of thought which says that a memory gap is a subconscious defence mechanism,' he said, 'a buffer if you like, a void into which the conscious mind can project a credible reason, a logical explanation for its distress. An intelligent, rational mind like yours – so the theory goes – would head for the answer most likely to satisfy it: hence while the pain persists, your mind has to satisfy itself with the notion that the cause remains undiscovered—'

She interrupted. 'It does.'

'But what if we're looking for the wrong cause? What if the cause is utterly simple and straightforward – mere stress, for example?'

Jenny allowed herself to consider the possibility, though she remained aware that he might merely be attempting to blind-side her, to distract her with one novel thought before firing the penetrating question while she was off guard. She waited for his follow-up, but it didn't come.

'So what do you think?' he said, his eyes alight with the ingenious simplicity of his diagnosis.

'You'll be telling me to take a long holiday next, or to change my job.'

A sterner note entered his voice. 'To be fair, you have stubbornly resisted trying either of those tried and tested methods.'

Jenny smoothed out the creases in her skirt as a way of

hiding her despondency. 'Is this a polite way of telling me we've exhausted what you can usefully do for me?'

'I'm only trying to rule out the obvious.'

'And having done so?'

'An extended holiday, at least—'

'I'll tell you what happens to me on holidays: everything comes flooding back. The anxiety, the unwanted thoughts, irrational fears, dreams . . .' she paused, her tongue feeling thick in her mouth – a recent addition to her ever-increasing palette of symptoms.

'What, Jenny?'

She saw the tears land in her lap even before she felt them flood her eyes.

'What's making you cry?'

There was no immediate reason, just a vague, familiar sense of dread that was slowly tightening its grip, like vast, suffocating hands around her mind. 'I don't know—'

'The last word you said was *dreams*.'

Another river of tears and the inchoate fear became sharper; a shudder passed through her body and left her hands trembling as she reached for the ever-ready box of tissues.

'Tell me about your dreams.'

She began to shake her head – the medication had blocked, or saved, her from dreams – but then the image flashed behind her eyes, a single frame that connected with her fear, causing a further tremor, like a dull electric shock, to pass through her.

'You've had a dream?'

'I had one . . . the same one—' Her words stuttered out between stifled sobs.

'When?'

'Years ago . . . I was nineteen, twenty . . .'

'Tell me.'

'It's a garden.' The image held fast in her mind. 'There are lots of children, young girls in skirts and pigtails . . . They're following each other in groups of three, holding each others' hands and skipping, it's joyful. And then . . .' She pressed the soggy Kleenex to her eyes. 'They stop. And in their groups of three two girls hold a skipping rope and the third jumps . . . and as the ropes pass over their heads, they *vanish*.'

'Who vanishes?'

'The girls in the middle.'

Dr Allen wrote in his notebook. 'Where do they go?'

'Where? I don't . . . I don't know . . . It's just *nothingness*.'

'And the girls left behind?'

'They don't seem to notice.'

'And that's it?'

'Yes.' Jenny sucked in a breath, the tide of fear slowly washing out, leaving her beached and numb. She stared out of the window at the sodium light catching the thin rain falling on the barren patch of garden.

'How old were you when you had this dream?'

'I was at university . . . It kept coming. I remember it lingering on throughout days that should have been carefree.'

'What does it represent to you?'

She shook her head, pretending to herself that she didn't know, but words were forming by themselves and spilled out almost against her conscious will. 'For every something there is a nothing. For every object an absence . . . It's not death I'm afraid of, it's *emptiness*.'

'You fear being disappeared?'

'No . . .' She struggled to bring her mental state into words. 'It's of being where there is nothing . . . and of not being where there is everything.'

Dr Allen's face registered his struggle to understand. 'Like being trapped on the wrong side of the looking glass? Out of time, out of place, out of context.'

'I suppose.'

There was silence as the doctor scanned his notes, then rubbed his eyes, straining with a thought his expression said he found troublesome but necessary to express. He looked up and studied her face for a moment before deciding to voice it. 'Are you a woman of faith, Mrs Cooper?' His use of her surname confirmed his unease.

'Why do you ask?'

'The trinity is a powerful Christian symbol. Father, son and holy ghost . . .'

'Lots of things come in threes: mother, father, child. Good, bad, indifferent. Heaven, earth, hell.'

'An apt example. You were brought up in faith, as I remember. The concepts are vivid to you.'

'We were sort of Anglican, I suppose. And there was Sunday school.'

Dr Allen looked thoughtful. 'You know, I think you're right. There is a piece missing – the girl, the space beyond the room. Whether it is emotional, or physical, or spiritual I couldn't yet say. But sometimes what we fear most is what we need. The most powerful stories are often those about strange saviours, demons who become an inspiration . . . like St Paul, or—'

'Darth Vader?'

He smiled. 'Why not?'

'This is sounding like a good old-fashioned diagnosis of suppression. Believe me, I've tried letting it all hang out; it wasn't a happy experience.'

'Would you do one thing for me?' He was suddenly earnest. 'I really would like to have one big push to crack this open.'

'Fire away.'

'For the next fortnight, keep a journal. Write down your feelings, your impulses, your extremes, no matter how bizarre or irrational.'

'In the hope of finding what, exactly?'

'We'll know when we see it.'

'You can be honest. Is this a last throw of the dice?'

He shook his head and smiled gently. 'I wouldn't still be here if I didn't think I could help you.'

Jenny pretended to be comforted, but couldn't help feeling that psychiatry was a slow road to nowhere. She had a small grain of faith that somehow, some day she would look up into a clear sky and feel nothing but undiluted happiness, but how that would come to pass was something she couldn't yet begin to answer. Perhaps her discussions with Dr Allen were worthwhile; at the very least he stirred her up from time to time, made her look into the corners she would otherwise avoid.

Later, as she drove home through the starless night, a single phrase of his kept repeating itself: *strange saviours*. It was a new idea to her. She liked it.

TWO

JENNY HAD BECOME USED TO living with the noise of a sixteen-year-old in the house, and part of her missed it when Ross spent the weekend with his father in Bristol. She would have phoned Steve, the infuriatingly free spirit she described as her 'occasional boyfriend', but he hadn't called her for nearly a fortnight, even though he had been forced to acquire a phone by the architects' practice he was articled to during his final year of study. She had encouraged him to break out from his self-imposed exile on the small farm above Tintern, where, for ten years, he had tried to live out a self-sufficient fantasy. Now that he went to work in the city and spent his nights at a draughtsman's desk, they scarcely saw each other.

She didn't like to admit to loneliness – escaping from a suffocating marriage to live in the country was meant to be a liberation – but driving south along the twisting Wye valley early on Monday morning through the dense, leafless woods, she was glad that she'd shortly be relieved of her own company. A workaday week awaited: hospital and road deaths, industrial accidents and suicides. She drew a certain comfort from dealing with others' unimaginable traumas with professional detachment. Being a coroner had given her an illusion of control and immortality. While Jenny Cooper the forty-two-year-old woman was still struggling to stay sane and sober, Jenny Cooper the coroner had come to enjoy her job.

*

With a take-out coffee in one hand and her briefcase in the other, Jenny shouldered open the door to the reception area of her two-room suite on the ground floor of the eighteenth-century terrace off Whiteladies Road. While her small domain had been made over, the common parts of the building remained tatty and the boards in the hallway still creaked under the threadbare carpet. The landlord's refusal to pay for so much as a coat of paint irked her each time she crossed the threshold. Alison, her officer, was pleased with the compromise, however. Having spent most of her adult life in the police force, she was comfortable in down-to-earth surroundings and suspicious of outward show. She liked things simple and homely. The stylish kidney-shaped desk at which she now sat, sorting through the pile of documents that had arrived in the overnight DX, was home to a selection of pot plants, and her state-of-the-art computer monitor was decorated with inspirational message cards bought at the church bookshop: *Shine as a Light in the World*, encircled with childlike angels.

'Hi, Alison.'

'Good morning, Mrs Cooper. Fifteen death reports over the weekend, I'm afraid.' She pushed a heap of papers across the desk. 'And there's a lady coming in to see you in about five minutes. I told her she'd have to make an appointment, but—'

'Who?' Jenny interrupted, running through a mental list of the several persistent obsessives she'd had to fend off lately.

Alison checked her message pad. 'Mrs Amira Jamal.'

'Never heard of her.' Jenny reached for a spiral-bound folder of police photographs sitting in her mail tray and flicked through several pictures of the frozen corpses in the supermarket lorry. 'What did she want?'

'I couldn't quite make it out – she was gabbling.'

'Great.' Scooping up the reports, Jenny noticed that Alison was wearing a gold cross outside her chunky polo neck. Not yet fifty-five, she wasn't unattractive – she had curves and kept her thick bob of hair dyed a natural shade of blonde – but a hint of staidness had recently crept into her appearance. Ever since she'd become involved with an evangelical church.

'It was a baptism present,' Alison said, a challenging edge to her voice as she scrolled through her emails.

'Right . . .' Jenny wasn't sure how to respond. 'Was this a recent event?'

'Yesterday.'

'Oh. Congratulations.'

'You don't have a problem with me wearing it at work?' Alison said.

'Feel free.' Jenny gave a neutral smile and pushed through the heavy oak door into her office, wondering if she'd go the same way at Alison's age. Organized religion and late-onset lesbianism seemed to be what hit most frequently. She couldn't decide which she'd opt for given the choice. Maybe she'd try both.

*

Amira Jamal was a small, round woman barely more than five feet tall and somewhere in her fifties. She wore a smart black suit with a large, elaborate silk scarf, which she lowered from her head and draped around her shoulders as she took her seat. From a small pull-along suitcase she produced a box file containing a mass of notes, documents, statements and newspaper articles. She was clearly an educated woman, but emotional and overwrought: she spoke in short excited bursts about a missing son, as if assuming Jenny was already familiar with her case.

'Seven years it's taken,' Mrs Jamal said, '*Seven years*. I went to the High Court in London last week, the Family

Court, I can't tell you how hard it was to get there. I had to sack the solicitor, and three others before him – none of them would believe me. They're all fools. But I knew the judge would listen. I don't care what anyone says, I have always believed in British justice. Look at these papers . . .' She reached for the box.

'Hold on a moment, Mrs Jamal,' Jenny said patiently, feeling anything but. 'I'm afraid we'll have to rewind for a moment.'

'What's the matter?' Mrs Jamal flashed uncomprehending deep brown eyes at her, her lashes thick with mascara and her lids heavily pencilled.

'This is the first I've heard of your case. We'll need to take it a step at a time.'

'But the judge said to come to you,' Mrs Jamal said with a note of panic.

'Yes, but the coroner is an independent officer. When I look into a case I have to start afresh. So, please, perhaps you could explain briefly what's happened.'

Mrs Jamal rifled through her disorganized documents and thrust a photocopy of a court order at her. 'Here.'

Jenny saw that it was dated the previous Friday: 23 January. Mrs Justice Haines of the High Court Family Division had made a declaration that Nazim Jamal, born 5 May 1982, and having been registered as a missing person on 1 July 2002, and having remained missing for seven years, was presumed to be dead.

'Nazim Jamal is your son?'

'My only son. My only child . . . All I had.' She wrung her hands and rocked to and fro in a way which Jenny could see would eventually have caused her lawyers to feel more irritation than sympathy. But she had spent enough years in the company of distressed mothers – fifteen years as a family lawyer employed by the legal department of a hard-pressed local authority – to tell melodrama from the real thing, and it was genuine torment she saw in the woman's eyes. Against all her better instincts she decided to hear Mrs Jamal's story.

'Perhaps you could tell me what happened, from the beginning?'

Mrs Jamal looked at her as if she had briefly forgotten why she was there.

'Can we get you some tea?' Jenny said.

Armed with a cup of Alison's strong, thick builder's tea, Mrs Jamal started falteringly into the story she had told countless times to sceptical police officers and lawyers. She appeared mistrustful at first, but once she saw that Jenny was listening carefully and taking detailed chronological notes, she slowly relaxed and became more fluent, pausing only to wipe away tears and apologize for her displays of emotion. She was a highly strung but proud woman, Jenny realized; a woman who given different chances in life might have been sitting on her side of the desk.

And the more Jenny heard, the more troubled she became.

Amira Jamal and her husband Zachariah had both been brought to Britain as children in the 1960s. Their marriage was arranged by their families when they were in their early twenties, but fortunately for them they fell in love. Zachariah trained as a dentist and they moved from London to Bristol for him to join his uncle's practice in early 1980. They had been married for three years before Amira fell pregnant. It came as a huge relief: she was becoming frightened that her husband's very conservative family might put pressure on him to divorce her, or even to take another wife. It was a moment of great joy when she gave birth to a healthy boy.

With all the love and attention his doting parents lavished on him, Nazim sailed through primary school and won a scholarship to the exclusive Clifton College. And as their son became absorbed into mainstream British culture, so Amira and Zachariah adapted themselves to their new social milieu of private school parents. Nazim went from strength to strength, scoring highly in exams and playing tennis and badminton for the school.

The family's first major convulsion occurred when Nazim was seventeen, at the start of his final year. Having spent so much time mixing with other mothers, Amira had come to appreciate what she had been missing cooped up at home. Against Zachariah's wishes she insisted on going out to work. The only position she could find was that of a sales assistant in a respectable women's outfitters, but it was still too much for her husband's pride to stand. He made her choose between him and the job. She called his bluff and chose the job. That evening she came home to find her two brothers-in-law waiting with the news that he was divorcing her and that she was to leave the house immediately.

Nazim gave in to irresistible family pressure and continued to live with his father, who shortly afterwards took a younger wife, with whom he was to have a further three children. Amira was forced out to a rented flat. Nazim loyally visited her several evenings each week, and rather than leave her isolated refused an offer from Imperial College London, and instead took up a place at the University of Bristol to study physics.

He started at university in the autumn of 2001 in the weeks when the world was still reeling and the word 'Muslim' had become synonymous with atrocity. Uninterested in politics, Nazim barely mentioned events in America and went off happily to college; and in his first act of rebellion against his father he decided to live on campus.

'I didn't see much of him that year,' Mrs Jamal said with a touch of sadness tinged with pride. 'He got so busy with his work and playing tennis – he was trying to get on the university team. When I did see him he looked so well, so happy. He wasn't a boy any more, I saw him change into a man.' A trace of emotion re-entered her voice and she paused for a moment. 'It was in the second term, after the Christmas holidays, that he became more distant. I only saw him three or four times. The thing I noticed was that he'd grown a beard and sometimes he wore the prayer cap, the taqiyah. I was shocked. Even my husband wore Western dress. One time he came to my flat wearing full traditional dress: a white robe and sirwal like the Arabs. When I asked him why, he said a lot of his Muslim friends dressed that way.'

'He was becoming religious?'

'We were always a religious family, but peaceful. My husband and I followed Sheikh Abd al-Latif: our religion was between us and God. No politics. That's how Nazim was brought up, to respect his fellow man, no matter who.' A look of incomprehension settled on her face. 'Later they said he'd been going to the Al Rahma mosque, and to meetings . . .'

'What sort of meetings?'

'With radicals, Hizb ut-Tahrir, the police said. They told me he went to a halaqah.'

'*Halaqah*?'

'A small group. A cell, they called it.'

'Let's stop there. When did he start going to these meetings?'

'I don't know exactly. Some time after Christmas.'

'OK . . .' Jenny made a note to the effect that whatever had happened to Nazim was linked to people he met in the winter of 2001–2. 'You noticed a change in your son in early 2002. What then?'

'He was much the same in the Easter vacation. His father didn't speak to me so I didn't know how he behaved at his house, but I was worried.'

'Why?'

'Nazim didn't talk about religion in my presence, but I'd

heard things. We all had. These Hizb, followers of that criminal Omar Bakri, it's all politics with them: telling our young men they have to fight for their people, for a khalifah – an Islamic state. It's poison for young minds.'

'Do you know for certain your son was involved with radicals?'

'I knew nothing. I still don't, only what the police tell me.' She motioned towards the file of papers. 'They say they saw him going in and out of a house in St Pauls every Wednesday night for halaqah. Him and Rafi Hassan, a friend from university.'

'Tell me about Rafi.'

'He was in Nazim's year. He studied law. They had rooms in the same building, Manor Hall. His family comes from Birmingham.'

'Did you meet him?'

'No. Nazim hardly mentioned him. I got all this from the police . . . afterwards.' She pulled a fresh handkerchief from her pocket and dabbed her eyes, rocking back and forth in her chair.

'After what?' Jenny said, tentatively.

'I saw Nazim only once in May. He came on a Saturday, my birthday. His aunties were there and cousins. It was a wonderful day, he was himself again . . . And then once more in June, the 22nd, another Saturday.' All the dates were etched on her memory. 'He arrived in the morning looking pale. He told me he wasn't feeling well, a fever and headache. He lay in the spare bed and slept all afternoon and evening. He ate a little soup but said he was still too tired to go back to college, so he stayed the night. I woke at dawn and heard him praying: with perfect tajwid – reciting from the Koran like he'd learned as a boy.' She took a shaky breath and closed her eyes. 'I must have fallen asleep again. When I got up to make breakfast he'd gone. He left me a note. *Thanks,*

Mum. Bye. Naz. It's there in the papers . . . I never saw him again.' Tears ran down her cheeks. She pressed her mascara-stained handkerchief to them and tried to steady herself. 'The police said . . . they said they saw him come out of the halaqah at ten-thirty on the night of Friday, 28 June 2002. That was in Marlowes Road in St Pauls. He walked to the bus stop with Rafi Hassan and that was it. He didn't go to tennis the next morning and neither of them was at class on Monday. The police spoke to all the students in the hall, but no one saw them over the weekend, or ever again.'

For the first time in their interview Mrs Jamal was overcome. Jenny let her weep uninterrupted. She had learned that the best response to grieving relatives was to observe a respectful silence, to offer a sympathetic smile but to say as little as possible. However well meant, words seldom eased the pain of grief.

When her tears eventually subsided, Mrs Jamal described how the college authorities had telephoned first her husband, who then called her when Nazim failed to attend his tutorial the following Wednesday. He had been due to hand in an important dissertation. Zachariah and several of his nephews scoured the campus, but no one had seen Nazim or Rafi since the previous week, and neither boy seemed to have any close friends apart from one another. Even the students who lived in adjoining rooms could claim only a nodding acquaintance.

Initially the police responded with their usual indifference to reports of missing persons. A liaison officer even went so far as to suggest that the two young men might have fallen into a sexual relationship and run away together. Mrs Jamal knew her son well enough to know this wasn't likely. Then it emerged that both boys' laptop computers and mobile phones were missing. The police sergeant who had searched their rooms found evidence that their doors had been forced with a similar implement, probably a wide screwdriver. And then, nearly a week later, a girl who had a room in a neighbouring building, Dani James, came forward to tell police that she'd seen a man in a puffy anorak with a baseball cap pulled down over his face walking quickly out of Manor Hall at around midnight on the night of 28 June. She thought he had a large rucksack or a holdall over his shoulder.

Despite protests from both families, the police remained reluctant to investigate. Mrs Jamal was writing to her local councillor and MP, desperate for help, when she had a visit at home from two young men, one white, one Asian, who said they worked for the Security Services. They said they suspected that Nazim and Rafi had become involved with Hizb ut-Tahrir and that they had been observed by the police attending a radical halaqah.

'It was the first I'd heard of it, although I'd suspected something like this,' Mrs Jamal said, 'but I didn't want it to be true. I put those thoughts out of my mind. They kept asking me questions. They wouldn't believe I didn't know about what he got up to college. They virtually accused me of lying to protect him.'

'What did they think had happened to him?'

'They kept asking whether he'd mentioned going to Afghanistan, whether he'd talked about al-Qaeda. I told them he'd never said anything like that. Never, never.'

'They thought he and Rafi might have gone abroad to train with extremists?'

'That's what they said. But his passport was still at his father's house.'

'And Rafi's?'

'He didn't even have one. And they went through all their bank records – there was nothing suspicious.'

'Did either of them use their bank accounts or credit cards after the 28th?'

'No. They just vanished. Disappeared.'

Jenny felt a jolt of anxiety pass through her, the feeling of mental constriction that was the first stage of panic. She took a breath, relaxed her limbs, trying to let the sensation drain away. 'Did you ever find out anything more?'

'Two weeks later, a man named Simon Donovan gave a statement to the police saying that he was on a train to London on the morning of the 29th and saw two young Asian men who met their description. Both with beards and traditional dress, he said. His statement's in the file. This made the police think they had gone abroad, so they spoke again to all the students at the hall. A girl called Sarah Levin claimed she'd once heard Rafi say something in the canteen about "brothers" who were going to Afghanistan.' Mrs Jamal shook her head adamantly. 'He wouldn't have done that, Mrs Cooper. I know my own son. He wouldn't have done that.'

Jenny thought of Ross, of having to fetch him from school last summer when he was high on cannabis; of his unpredictable moods and occasional outbursts of staggering hurtfulness. She thought she knew the sensitive boy underneath, but sometimes she wondered; sometimes it occurred to her that we can't truly know even those closest to us.

'What did the police do with this information?' Jenny said.

'They looked for evidence, but the didn't find any. They said they would have left the country on false papers, gone to Pakistan.'

'Did they check passenger lists? It's not easy to get through an airport unnoticed.'

'They told us they checked everything. They even said they could have gone through another European country, or Africa or the Middle East . . . I don't know.' The energy had drained from her. She seemed a smaller, more fragile figure than before.

'How did it end?'

'We had a letter in December 2002. The police said they had done everything they could and that the most likely explanation was that they had gone abroad with an Islamist group. That was all. Nothing more. Nothing.'

'What about the mosque and the halaqah?'

'The police told us that the mosque had closed in August that year and the halaqah as well. They said that the Security Services had been following their activities, but nothing else had been learned about Nazim or Rafi. They promised us they would tell us if anything became known.'

'Did these people from the Security Services ever contact you again?'

Mrs Jamal shook her head.

'You mentioned lawyers . . .'

'Yes. I tried to get them to ask questions, to speak to the Security Services and police, but all they did was take my money. It was left to me. I found out for myself that after seven years a missing person can be declared dead.' She met Jenny's gaze. 'And I also read that the coroner must find out how a person died. His father's address, Nazim's official residence at the time, is in your district, so that is why I am here.'

From the moment she had seen the judge's declaration Jenny had assumed that Mrs Jamal had come seeking an inquest, but the prospect threw up a raft of problems, not least the fact that there was no body and only a presumption of death. In such circumstances Section 15 of the Coroner's Act required her to get the Home Secretary's permission to hold one. That would only be granted where holding an inquest was judged to be in the public interest, which was as much a political as a legal decision. And even if that hurdle were cleared, it would be no easy task so many years after the event to cajole reluctant police officers and government officials to dust down their files and release whatever information wasn't deemed a threat to national security. Broad as they were, the coroner's powers would, in this instance, struggle against the powerful machinery of the state.

'Mrs Jamal,' Jenny said, with what she hoped was an appropriate balance of caution and concern, 'I will gladly look into your son's case, but all I can do is write a report to the Home Secretary requesting—'

'I know that. The judge told me.'

'Then you'll know that the chance of getting as far as holding an inquest is slim, probably non-existent. It's extremely unusual in cases where is there no actual proof of death.'

Mrs Jamal shook her head, her expression hardening with disappointment. 'What are you telling me – that I should give up after all this struggle?'

If she were being completely honest, Jenny would have told her that in the absence of a body, and after the passage of seven years, the best thing she could do would be to treat the court order as final proof that Nazim was dead, allow herself to grieve, and then move on. She would have told her that the main obstacle to her happiness was her obsession with her son's fate, and that an inquest was unlikely to satisfy or cure it.

'It would be wrong of me to hold out any hope of finding out what happened to your son,' Jenny said. 'I think perhaps you should ask yourself what purpose you think an inquest might serve. It won't bring him back.'

Mrs Jamal started to gather to gather her jumble of papers. 'I'm sorry I wasted your time.'

'I'm not refusing to investigate—'

'You're obviously not a mother, Mrs Cooper, otherwise you would understand I have no choice. My life is nothing compared with my son's. I would rather die trying to find out what happened to him than live in ignorance.'

Mrs Jamal stood up from her chair as if ready to march out without another word, but seemed suddenly to lose energy and falter. She slowly placed the file back on the desk and folded her hands across her middle, her head dipping forwards as if she hadn't the strength to hold it up. 'I apologize, Mrs Cooper. I expected too much of you. I don't hope for miracles . . . I know that Nazim is dead. When he came to my flat that afternoon with a fever, I had a feeling. Yes . . . when I think of waking and hearing him reciting the tajwid the next morning, I still can't be sure if it was him or his ghost.' She looked up with dry, desolate eyes. 'Maybe you are right. Too much time has passed.'

Jenny had recoiled in the face of what she had perceived as Mrs Jamal's all-encompassing self-pity, but not for the first time in their meeting she saw beyond to the deep and profound grief of a mother in search of her lost child. The last thing she needed was another fraught and time-consuming case, but her emotions were already churning, the faces of the missing boys were already vivid, their spectres already haunting her.

'Leave the file with me,' Jenny said. 'I'll look through it this afternoon and get back to you.'

'Thank you, Mrs Cooper,' Mrs Jamal replied quietly. She reached for the scarf lying across her shoulders and raised it over her hair.

'What about Rafi Hassan – are his family seeking a declaration?' Jenny asked.

'We don't speak. They were very hostile to me. They chose to believe that Nazim was responsible for what happened to their son.'

'And your husband?'

'He gave up long ago.'

*

Jenny detected a frostiness in Alison's demeanour as she showed Mrs Jamal out. During six months of working together she had learned to read every slight shift in her officer's mood. Alison was one of those women with an uncanny ability to let you know precisely what she was feeling without ever saying a word. What Jenny read in her reaction to Mrs Jamal was suspicion bordering on outright disapproval. When, several minutes later, she returned to the doorway to report that the police were agitating to see the post-mortem reports on the bodies in the refrigerated trailer, Jenny remarked that she seemed irritated by Mrs Jamal.

Alison crossed her arms. 'I remember her son's case. I was in CID at the time. Everyone knew he and the other lad had gone off to fight abroad.'

Another trait that Jenny had noticed: Alison's stubborn adherence to the consensus amongst her former police colleagues.

Jenny said, '*Everyone* being . . . ?'

'The squad who were on the obbo for five months. The extremists were operating freely back then.'

Jenny felt a twinge of annoyance. 'His mother still has the right to know what happened to him, insofar as that's possible.'

'If I was her, I'm not sure I'd want to know. We can't exactly call witnesses from Afghanistan.'

'No. You don't happen to remember who was in charge of the observation?'

'I can probably find out. Just don't expect to get very far – the spooks are all over this sort of thing.' Alison changed the subject: 'What about these bodies in the lorry – do you want me to have a look? I expect the police will want that one for themselves as well.'

'It might be as well for you to make your own report,' Jenny said, and couldn't resist adding, 'we know how our friends in blue can see one thing and write down another.'

'I'm only telling you what I heard at the time, Mrs

Cooper,' Alison retorted. 'And back then we still gave Muslims the benefit of the doubt.'

Jenny held her tongue, sensing in Alison's reaction that Mrs Jamal had stirred complicated emotions. Six months on, Jenny knew that Alison was still privately grieving for the man she'd been in love with: the late Harry Marshall, her predecessor as coroner. They had been close. The messy circumstances of his sudden and unexpected passing had left a mess of unresolved feelings which she was attempting to clear up with a dose of full-strength Christianity. When insecure, Alison cleaved to institutions – the police, the church – and resisted anything that threatened them. It was irrational, but who was Jenny to pass judgement? Without her medication she was beset by irrational fears too.

'Her son's been declared dead.' Jenny said. 'She's entitled to an investigation, however limited. I doubt very much it'll amount to anything.'

Alison's hostility hung in the air like an unwelcome presence long after she'd left the office. Jenny felt almost guilty as she arranged Mrs Jamal's papers into a semblance of order. She hadn't felt like this again since the first case she and Alison had worked on together – that of the fourteen-year-old Danny Wills, who'd been found dead in his cell at a privately run prison. Perhaps, as an ex-policewoman, Alison sensed trouble more keenly than she did.

Although numerous, Mrs Jamal's documents cast little light. There were lists of students who lived in the halls of residence at the time; statements from members of both families; statements from police officers who had searched the campus; copies of ineffective correspondence with various councillors and politicians. There was a copy of the original identification statement given by Simon Donovan, in which he described the two young men on the train, and statements from students Dani James and Sarah Levin, describing the mysterious intruder and Rafi's overheard remark about Muslim brothers heading for Afghanistan. There was a sketchy photocopy of Nazim's UK passport, confirmation from the Passport Office that Rafi Hassan had never possessed or applied for one, and a dry letter written by a DC Sarah Owens, Family Liaison Officer, explaining in patronizing tones that the police had decided to suspend their investigation until such time as further evidence came to light. The final document was a 'missing' poster put together on a home computer displaying various head shots of the young men. Jenny was struck by how handsome they both were: keen-eyed and slender featured. She stared at them for a long moment, then felt an unexpected wave of almost unbearable sadness: they weren't even dead. It was worse than that; they had simply *disappeared*.

She pushed the file aside, fighting against the irrational connections her mind was already making with her discussions with Dr Allen. People vanished without trace all the time. It was purely coincidental that this case had arrived on her desk when it had. Technically it could also have been handled by the Bristol coroner as Jamal was last seen in his jurisdiction. Jenny needn't take it at all . . . but yet she knew she had no choice.

The telephone rang in the empty outer office and was automatically diverted to the phone on her desk. She answered in her most businesslike voice. 'Severn Vale Coroner's office. Jenny Cooper speaking.'

'Good morning. Andrew Kerr. New pathologist at the Vale.' He sounded chatty and energetic. 'I've just had a look at this Jane Doe of yours. I think perhaps we ought to meet.'

Jenny Cooper investigates . . .

Also by M. R. HALL

The Redeemed

Book 3 in the Jenny Cooper series

A mystery from the past. A deadly secret in the present.

Jenny's lone quest for justice will take her to the dark heart of an
establishment who wish to silence her, and on an inner journey to
confront ghosts that have haunted her for a lifetime.

'Breathlessly enjoyable' *The Times*

The Flight

Book 4 in the Jenny Cooper series

A tragic accident or a terrible crime?

Under pressure from a grieving mother, and opposed by those at the
very highest levels of government, Jenny must race against time to seek
the truth behind a terrible disaster, before it can happen again . . .

'Wonderful stuff, chillingly plausible' *Independent on Sunday*

The Chosen Dead

Book 5 in the Jenny Cooper series

An unlikely suicide or a deadly conspiracy?

In an investigation which will take her into the sinister realms of
unbridled human ambition and corrupt scientific endeavour, Jenny
is forced to risk the love and lives of those closest to her,
as a deadly race to uncover the truth begins . . .

'Hall's Gold Dagger-nominated books, quite simply, get
better each time' *Independent on Sunday*